The Case of Richard Meynell

"'My dear fellow! No woman ought to marry under
nineteen or twenty'"

THE CASE OF
RICHARD MEYNELL

BY

MRS. HUMPHRY WARD

ILLUSTRATIONS BY
CHARLES E. BROCK

WILDSIDE PRESS

THE COUNTRY LIFE PRESS, GARDEN CITY, N. Y.

TO

THE MEMORY

OF A BELOVED CHILD

A FOREWORD

MAY I ask those of my American readers who are not intimately acquainted with the conditions of English rural and religious life to remember that the dominant factor in it—the factor on which the story of Richard Meynell depends—is the existence of the State Church, of the great ecclesiastical corporation, the direct heir of the pre-Reformation Church, which owns the cathedrals and the parish churches, which by right of law speaks for the nation on all national occasions, which crowns and marries and buries the Kings of England, and, through her bishops in the House of Lords, exercises a constant and important influence on the lawmaking of the country? This Church possesses half the elementary schools, and is the legal religion of the great public schools which shape the ruling upper class. She is surrounded with the prestige of centuries, and it is probable that in many directions she was never so active or so well served by her members as she is at present.

At the same time, tnere are great forces of change ahead. Outside the Anglican Church stands quite half the nation, gathered in the various non-conformist bodies — Wesleyan, Congregational, Baptist, Presbyterian, and so on. Between them and the Church exists a perpetual warfare, partly of opinion, partly of social difference and jealousy. In every village and small town this warfare exists. The non-conformist desires to deprive the

vii

Church of her worldly and political privileges; the churchman talks of the sin of schism, or draws up schemes of
reunion which drop still-born. Meanwhile, alike in the
Church, in non-conformity, and in the neutral world
which owes formal allegiance to neither, vast movements
of thought have developed in the last hundred years,
years as pregnant with the germs of new life as the wonderful hundred years that followed the birth of Christ.
Whether the old bottles can be adjusted to the new wine,
whether further division or a new Christian unity is to
emerge from the strife of tongues, whether the ideas of
modernism, rife in all forms of Christianity, can be ac-
commodated to the ancient practices and given a share in
the great material possessions of a State Church; how in-
dividual lives are affected in the passionate struggle of
spiritual faiths and practical interests involved in such an
attempt; how conscience may be enriched by its success
or sterilized by its failure; how the fight itself, ably waged,
may strengthen the spiritual elements, the power of living and suffering in men and women — it is with such
themes that this story attempts to deal. Twenty-two
years ago I tried a similar subject in "Robert Elsmere."
Since then the movement of ideas in religion and philosophy has been increasingly rapid and fruitful. I am deeply
conscious how little I may be able to express it. But those
who twenty years ago welcomed the earlier book — and
how can I ever forget its reception in America! — may
perhaps be drawn once again to some of the old themes
in their new dress.

MARY A. WARD

ILLUSTRATIONS

BOOK I

MEYNELL

"Truth fails not; but her outward forms that bear
The longest date do melt like frosty rime,
That in the morning whitened hill and plain
And is no more; drop like the tower sublime
Of yesterday, which royally did wear
His crown of weeds, but could not even sustain
Some casual shout that broke the silent air,
Or the unimaginable touch of Time."

CHAPTER I

"HULLO, Preston! don't trouble to go in."

The postman, just guiding his bicycle into the Rectory drive, turned at the summons and dismounted. The Rector approached him from the road, and the postman, diving into his letter-bag and into the box of his bicycle, brought out a variety of letters and packages, which he placed in the Rector's hands.

The recipient smiled.

"My word, what a post! I say, Preston, I add to your burdens pretty considerably."

"It don't matter, sir, I'm sure," said the postman civilly. "There's not a deal of letters delivered in this village."

"No, we don't trouble pen and ink much in Upcote," said the Rector; "and it's my belief that half the boys and girls that do learn to read and write at school make a point of forgetting it as soon as they can — for all practical purposes, anyway."

"Well, there's a deal of newspapers read now, sir, compared to what there was."

"Newspapers? Yes, I do see a *Reynolds'* or a *People* or two about on Sunday. Do you think anybody reads much else than the betting and the police news, eh, Preston?"

Preston looked a little vacant. His expression seemed to say, "And why should they?" The Rector, with his arms full of the post, smiled again and turned away, looking back, however, to say:

"Wife all right again?"

"Pretty near, sir; but she's had an awful bad time, and the doctor — he makes her go careful."

"Quite right. Has Miss Puttenham been looking after her?"

"She's been most kind, sir, most attentive, she have," said the postman warmly, his long hatchet face breaking into animation. ,

"Lucky for you!" said the Rector, walking away. "When she cuts in, she's worth a regiment of doctors. Good-day!"

The speaker passed on through the gate of the Rectory, pausing as he did so with a rueful look at the iron gate itself, which was off its hinges and sorely in want of a coat of new paint.

"Disgraceful!" he said to himself; "must have a go at it to-morrow. And at the garden, too," he added, looking round him. "Never saw such a wilderness!"

He was advancing toward a small gabled house of an Early Victorian type, built about 1840 by the Ecclesiastical Commissioners on the site of an old clergy house, of which all traces had been ruthlessly effaced. The front garden lying before it was a tangle of old and for the most part ugly trees; elms from which heavy, decayed branches had recently fallen; acacias choked by

The Rectory

the ivy which had overgrown them; and a crowded thicket of thorns and hazels, mingled with three or four large and vigorous though very ancient yews, which seemed to have drunk up for themselves all that life from the soil which should have gone to maintain the ragged or sickly shrubbery. The trees also had gradually encroached upon the house, and darkened all the windows on the porch side. On a summer afternoon, the deep shade they made was welcome enough; but on a rainy day the Rector's front-garden, with its coarse grass, its few straggling rose-bushes, and its pushing throng of half-dead or funereal trees, shed a dank and dripping gloom upon the visitor approaching his front door. Of this, however, the Rector himself was rarely conscious; and to-day, as he with difficulty gathered all the letters and packets taken from the postman into one hand, while he opened his front door with the other, his face showed that the state of his garden had already ceased to trouble him.

He had no sooner turned the handle of the door than a joyous uproar of dogs arose within, and before he had well stepped over the threshold a leaping trio were upon him — two Irish terriers and a graceful young collie, whose rough caresses nearly made him drop his letters.

"Down, Jack! Be quiet, you rascals! I say — Anne!"

A woman's voice answered his call.

"I'm just bringing the tea, sir."

"Any letter for me this afternoon?"

"There's a note on the hall-table, sir."

The Rector hurried into the sitting-room to the right of the hall, deposited the letters and packets which he held on a small, tumble-down sofa already littered with books and papers, and returned to the hall-table for the letter. He tore it open, read it with slightly frowning brows and a mouth that worked unconsciously, then thrust it into his pocket and returned to his sitting-room.

"All right!" he said to himself. "He's got an odd list of 'aggrieved parishioners!' "

The tidings, however, which the letter contained did not seem to distress him. On the contrary, his aspect expressed a singular and cheerful energy, as he sat a few moments on the sofa, softly whistling to himself and staring at the floor. That he was a person extravagantly beloved by his dogs was clearly shown meanwhile by the exuberant attentions and caresses with which they were now loading him.

He shook them off at last with a friendly kick or two, that he might turn to his letters, which he sorted and turned over, much as an epicure studies his *menu* at the Ritz, and with an equally keen sense of pleasure to come.

A letter from Jena, and another from Berlin, addressed in small German handwriting and signed by names familiar to students throughout the world; two or three German reviews, copies of the *Revue Critique* and the *Revue Chrétienne*, a book by Solomon Reinach, and three or four French letters, one of them shown by the cross preceding the signature to be the letter of a bishop; a long letter from Oxford, enclosing the proof of an article in a theological review; and, finally, a letter sealed with red wax and signed "F. Marcoburg" in a corner of the envelope, which the Rector twirled in his hands a moment without opening.

"After tea," he said at last, with the sudden breaking of a smile. And he put it on the sofa beside him.

As he spoke the door opened to admit his housekeeper with the tray, to the accompaniment of another orgie of barks. A stout woman in a sun-bonnet, with a broad face and no features to speak of, entered.

"I'll be bound you've had no dinner," she said sulkily, as she placed the tea before him on a chair cleared with difficulty from some of the student's litter that filled the room.

"All the more reason for tea," said Meynell, seizing thirstily on the teapot. "And you're quite mistaken, Anne. I had a magnificent bath-bun at the station."

"Much good you'll get out of that!" was the scornful reply. "You know what Doctor Shaw told you about that sort o' goin' on."

"Never you mind, Anne. What about that painter chap?"

"Gone home for the week-end." Mrs. Wellin retreated a foot or two and crossed her arms, bare to the elbow, in front of her.

The Rector stared.

"I thought I had taken him on by the week to paint my house," he said at last.

"So you did. But he said he must see his missus and hear how his little girl had done in her music exam."

Mrs. Wellin delivered this piece of news very fast and with evident gusto. It might have been thought she enjoyed inflicting it on her master.

The Rector laughed out.

"And this was a man sent me a week ago by the Birmingham Distress Committee — nine weeks out of work — family in the workhouse — everything up the spout. Goodness gracious, Anne, how did he get the money? Return fare, Birmingham, three-and-ten."

"Don't ask me, sir," said the woman in the sun-bonnet. "I don't go pryin' into such trash!"

"Is he coming back? Is my house to be painted?" asked the Rector helplessly.

"Thought he might," said Anne, briefly.

"How kind of him! Music exam.! Lord save us! And three-and-ten thrown into the gutter on a week-end ticket — with seven children to keep — and all your possessions gone to 'my uncle.' And it isn't as though you'd been starving him, Anne!"

"I wish I hadn't dinnered him as I have been doin'!" the woman broke out. "But he'll know the difference next week! And now, sir, I suppose you'll be goin' to that place again to-night?"

Anne jerked her thumb behind her over her left shoulder.

"Suppose so, Anne. Can't afford a night-nurse, and the wife won't look after him."

"Why don't some one make her?" said Anne, frowning.

The Rector's face changed.

"Better not talk about it, Anne. When a woman's been in hell for years, you needn't expect her to come out an angel. She won't forgive him, and she won't nurse him — that's flat."

"No reason why she should shovel him off on other people as wants their night's rest. It's takin' advantage — that's what it is."

"I say, Anne, I must read my letters. And just light me a bit of fire, there's a good woman. July! — ugh! — it might be February!"

In a few minutes a bit of fire was blazing in the grate, though the windows were still wide open, and the Rector, who had had a long journey that day to take a funeral for a friend, lay back in sybaritic ease, now sipping his tea and now cutting open letters and parcels. The letter signed "F. Marcoburg" in the corner had been placed, still unopened, on the mantelpiece now facing him.

The Rector looked at it from time to time; it might have been said by a close observer that he never forgot it; but, all the same, he went on dipping into books and reviews, or puzzling — with muttered imprecations on the German tongue — over some of his letters.

"By Jove! this apocalyptic Messianic business is getting interesting. Soon we shall know where all the

Pauline ideas came from — every single one of them! And what matter? Who's the worse? Is it any less wonderful when we do know? The new wine found its bottles ready — that's all."

As he sat there he had the aspect of a man enjoying apparently the comfort of his own fireside. Yet, now that the face was at rest, certain cavernous hollows under the eyes, and certain lines on the forehead and at the corners of the mouth, as though graven by some long fatigue, showed themselves disfiguringly. The personality, however, on which this fatigue had stamped itself was clearly one of remarkable vigour, physical and mental. A massive head covered with strong black hair, curly at the brows; eyes grayish-blue, small, with some shade of expression in them which made them arresting, commanding, even; a large nose and irregular mouth, the lips flexible and kind, the chin firm — one might have made some such catalogue of Meynell's characteristics; adding to them the strength of a broad-chested, loose-limbed frame, made rather, one would have thought, for country labours than for the vigils of the scholar. But the hands were those of a man of letters — bony and long-fingered, but refined, touching things with care and gentleness, like one accustomed to the small tools of the writer.

At last the Rector threw himself back in his chair, while some of the litter on his lap fell to the floor, temporarily dislodging one of the terriers, who sat up and looked at him with reproach.

"Now then!" he said, and reached out for the letter on the mantelpiece. He turned it over a moment in his hand and opened it.

It was long, and the reader gave it a close attention. When he had finished it he put it down and thought a while, then stretched out his hand for it again and reread the last paragraph:

"You will, I am sure, realize from all I have said, my dear Meynell, that the last thing I personally wish to do is to interfere with the parochial work of a man for whom I have so warm a respect as I have for you. I have given you all the latitude I could, but my duty is now plain. Let me have your assurance that you will refrain from such sermons as that to which I have drawn your attention, and that you will stop at once the extraordinary innovations in the services of which the parishioners have complained, and I shall know how to answer Mr. Barron and to compose this whole difficult matter. Do not, I entreat you, jeopardize the noble work you are doing for the sake of opinions and views which you hold to-day, but which you may have abandoned to-morrow. Can you possibly put what you call 'the results of criticism' — and, remember, these results differ for you, for me, and for a dozen others I could name — in comparison with that work for souls God has given you to do, and in which He has so clearly blessed you? A Christian pastor is not his own master, and cannot act with the freedom of other men. He belongs by his own act to the Church and to the flock of Christ; he must always have in view the 'little ones' whom he dare not offend. Take time for thought, my dear Meynell —

and time, above all, for prayer — and then let me hear from you. You will realize how much and how anxiously I think of you.

'Yours always sincerely in Christ,

"F. Marcoburg."

"Good man — true bishop!" said the Rector to himself, as he again put down the letter; but even as he spoke the softness in his face passed into resolution. He sank once more into reverie.

The stillness, however, was soon broken up. A step was heard outside, and the dogs sprang up in excitement. Amid a pandemonium of noise, the Rector put his head out of window.

"Is that you, Barron? Come in, old fellow; come in!"

A slender figure in a long coat passed the window, the front door opened, and a young man entered the study. He was dressed in orthodox clerical garb, and carried a couple of books under his arm.

"I came to return these," he said, placing them beside the Rector; "and also — can you give me twenty minutes?"

"Forty, if you want them. Sit down."

The newcomer turned out various French and German books from a dilapidated armchair, and obeyed. He was a fresh-coloured, handsome youth, some fifteen years younger than Meynell, the typical public-school boy in appearance. But his expression was scarcely less harassed than the Rector's.

"I expect you have heard from my father." he said abruptly.

"I found a .etter waiting for me," said Meynell, holding up the note he had taken from the hall-table on coming in. But he pursued the subject no further.

The young man fidgeted a moment.

"All one can say is" — he broke out at last — "that if it had not been my father, it would have been some one else — the Archdeacon probably. The fight was bound to come."

"Of course it was!" The Rector sprang to his feet, and, with his hands under his coat-tails and his back to the fire, faced his visitor. "That's what we're all driving at. Don't be miserable about it, dear fellow. I bear your father no grudge whatever. He is under orders, as I am. The parleying time is done. It has lasted two generations. And now comes war — honourable, necessary war!"

The speaker threw back his head with emphasis, even with passion. But almost immediately the smile, which was the only positive beauty of the face, obliterated the passion.

"And don't look so tragic over it! If your father wins — and as the law stands he can scarcely fail to win — I shall be driven out of Upcote. But there will always be a corner somewhere for me and my books, and a pulpit of some sort to prate from."

"Yes, but what about *us?*" said the newcomer, slowly.

"Ah!" The Rector's voice took a dry intonation.

"Yes — well! — you Liberals will have to take your part, and fire your shot some day, of course — fathers or no fathers."

"I didn't mean that. I shall fire my shot, of course. But aren't you exposing yourself prematurely — unnecessarily?" said the young man, with vivacity. "It is not a general's part to do that."

"You're wrong, Stephen. When my father was going out to the campaign in which he was killed, my mother said to him, as though she were half asking a question, half pleading — I can hear her now, poor darling! — 'John, it's *right* for a general to keep out of danger?' and he smiled and said, 'Yes, when it isn't right for him to go into it, head over ears.' However, that's nonsense. It doesn't apply to me. I'm no general. And I'm not going to be killed!"

Young Barron was silent, while the Rector prepared a pipe, and began upon it; but his face showed his dissatisfaction.

"I've not said much to father yet about my own position," he resumed; "but, of course, he guesses. It will be a blow to him," he added, reluctantly.

The Rector nodded, but without showing any particular concern, though his eyes rested kindly on his companion.

"We have come to the fighting," he repeated, "and fighting means blows. Moreover, the fight is beginning to be equal. Twenty years ago — in Elsmere's time — a man who held his views or mine could only go. Voysey, of course, had to go; Jowett, I am inclined to think, ought to have gone.   But the distribution of the forces, the lie of the field, is now altogether changed.   *I* am not going till I am turned out; and there will be others with me.   The world wants a heresy trial, and it is going to get one this time."

A laugh — a laugh of excitement and discomfort — escaped the younger man.

"You talk as though the prospect was a pleasant one!"

"No — but it is inevitable."

"It will be a hateful business," Baron went on, impetuously.   "My father has a horribly strong will. And he will think every means legitimate."

"I know.   In the Roman Church, what the Curia could not do by argument they have done again and again — well, no use to inquire how!   One must be prepared.   All I can say is, I know of no skeletons in the cupboard at present.   Anybody may have my keys!"

He laughed as he spoke, spreading his hands to the blaze, and looking round at his companion.   Barron's face in response was a face of hero-worship, undisguised. Here plainly were leader and disciple; pioneering will and docile faith.   But it might have been observed that Meynell did nothing to emphasize the personal relation; that, on the contrary, he shrank from it, and often tried to put it aside.

After a few more words, indeed, he resolutely closed the personal discussion.   They fell into talk about certain recent developments of philosophy in England

and France — talk which showed them as familiar comrades in the intellectual field, in spite of their difference of age. Barron, a Fellow of King's, had but lately left Cambridge for a small College living. Meynell — an old Balliol scholar — bore the marks of Jowett and Caird still deep upon him, except, perhaps, for a certain deliberate throwing over, here and there, of the typical Oxford tradition — its measure and reticence, its scholarly balancing of this against that. A tone as of one driven to extremities — a deep yet never personal exasperation — the poised quiet of a man turning to look a hostile host in the face — again and again these made themselves felt through his chat about new influences in the world of thought — Bergson or James, Eucken or Tyrell.

And to this under-note, inflections or phrases in the talk of the other seemed to respond. It was as though behind the spoken conversation they carried on another unheard.

And the unheard presently broke in upon the heard.

"You mentioned Elsmere just now," said Barron, in a moment's pause, and with apparent irrelevance. "Did you know that his widow is now staying within a mile of this place? Some people called Flaxman have taken Maudeley End, and Mrs. Flaxman is a sister of Mrs. Elsmere. Mrs. Elsmere and her daughter are going to settle for the summer in the cottage near Forkéd Pond. Mrs. Elsmere seems to have been ill for the first time in her life, and has had to give up some of her work."

"Mrs. Elsmere!" said Meynell, raising his eyebrows. "I saw her once twenty years ago at the New Brotherhood, and have never forgotten the vision of her face. She must be almost an old woman."

"Miss Puttenham says she is quite beautiful still, in a wonderful, severe way. I think she never shared Elsmere's opinions?"

"Never."

The two fell silent, both minds occupied with the same story and the same secret comparisons. Robert Elsmere, the Rector of Murewell, in Surrey, had made a scandal in the Church, when Meynell was still a lad, by throwing up his orders under the pressure of New Testament criticism, and founding a religious brotherhood among London workingmen for the promotion of a simple and commemorative form of Christianity.

Elsmere, a man of delicate physique, had died prematurely, worn out by the struggle to find new foothold for himself and others; but something in his personality, and in the nature of his effort — some brilliant, tender note — had kept his memory alive in many hearts. There were many now, however, who thrilled to it, who could never speak of him without emotion, who yet felt very little positive agreement with him. What he had done or tried to do made a kind of landmark in the past; but in the course of time it had begun to seem irrelevant to the present.

"To-day — would he have thrown up? — or would he have held on?" Meynell presently said, in a tone of reverie, amid the cloud of smoke that enveloped him. Then, in another voice, "What do you hear of the daughter? I remember her as a little reddish-haired thing at her mother's side."

"Miss Puttenham has taken a great fancy to her. Hester Fox-Wilton told me she had seen her there. She liked her."

"H'm!" said the Rector. "Well, if she pleased Hester — critical little minx!"

"You may be sure she'll please *me!*" said Barron suddenly, flushing deeply.

The Rector looked up, startled.

"I say?"

Barron cleared his throat.

"I'd better tell you at once, Rector. I got Hester's leave yesterday to tell you, when an opportunity occurred — you know how fond she is of you? Well, I'm in love with her — head over ears in love with her — I believe I have been since she was a little girl in the schoolroom. And yesterday — she said — she'd marry me some day."

The young voice betrayed a natural tremor. Meanwhile, a strange look — a close observer would have called it a look of consternation — had rushed into Meynell's face. He stared at Barron, made one or two attempts to speak, and, a last, said abruptly:

"That'll never do, Stephen — that'll never do! You shouldn't have spoken."

Barron's face showed the wound.

"But, Rector —— "

"She's too young," said Meynell, with increased harshness, "much too young! Hester is only seventeen. No girl ought to be pledged so early. She ought to have more time — time to look round her. Promise me, my dear boy, that there shall be nothing irrevocable — no engagement! I should strongly oppose it."

The eyes of the two men met. Barron was evidently dumb with surprise; but the vivacity and urgency of Meynell's expression drove him into speech.

"We thought you would have sympathized," he stammered. "After all, what is there so much against it? Hester is, you know, not very happy at home. I have my living, and some income of my own, independent of my father. Supposing he should object —— "

"He would object," said Meynell quickly. "And Lady Fox-Wilton would certainly object. And so should I. And, as you know, I am co-guardian of the children with her."

Then, as the lover quivered under these barbs, Meynell suddenly recovered himself.

"My dear fellow! No woman ought to marry under twenty-one. And every girl ought to have time to look round her. It's not right; it's not just — it isn't, indeed! Put this thing by for a while. You'll lose nothing by it. We'll talk of it again in two years."

And, drawing his chair nearer to his companion, Meynell fell into a strain of earnest and affectionate entreaty, which presently had a marked effect on the younger man. His chivalry was appealed to — his consideration for the girl he loved; and his aspect began to show the force of the attack. At last he said gravely:

"I'll tell Hester what you say — of course I'll tell her. Naturally we can't marry without your consent and her mother's. But if Hester persists in wishing we should be engaged?"

"Long engagements are the deuce!" said the Rector hotly. "You would be engaged for three years. Madness! — with such a temperament as Hester's. My dear Stephen, be advised — for her and yourself. There is no one who wishes your good more earnestly than I. But don't let there be any talk of an engagement for at least two years to come. Leave her free — even if you consider yourself bound. It is folly to suppose that a girl of such marked character knows her own mind at seventeen. She has all her development to come."

Barron had dropped his head on his hands.

"I couldn't see anybody else courting her — without ——"

"Without cutting in. I daresay not," said Meynell, with a rather forced laugh. "I'd forgive you that. But now, look here."

The two heads drew together again, and Meynell resumed conversation, talking rapidly, in a kind, persuasive voice, putting the common sense of the situation — holding out distant hopes. The young man's face gradually cleared. He was of a docile, open temper, and deeply attached to his mentor.

At last the Rector sprang up, consulting his watch.

"I must send you off, and go to sleep. But we'll talk of this again."

"Sleep!" exclaimed Barron, astonished. "It's just seven o'clock. What are you up to now?"

"There's a drunken fellow in the village — dying — and his wife won't look after him. So I have to put in an appearance to-night. Be off with you!"

"I shouldn't wonder if the Flaxmans were of some use to you in the village," said Stephen, taking up his hat. "They're rich, and, they say, very generous."

"Well, if they'll give me a parish nurse, I'll crawl to them," said the Rector, settling himself in his chair and putting an old shawl over his knees. "And as you go out, just tell Anne, will you, to keep herself to herself for an hour and not to disturb me?"

Stephen Barron moved to the door, and as he opened it he turned back a moment to look at the man in the chair, and the room in which he sat. It was as though he asked himself by what manner of man he had been thus gripped and coerced, in a matter so intimate, and, to himself, so vital.

Meynell's eyes were already shut. The dogs had gathered round him, the collie's nose laid against his knee, the other two guarding his feet. All round, the walls were laden with books, so were the floor and the furniture. A carpenter's bench filled the further end of the room. Carving tools were scattered on it, and a large piece of wood-carving, half finished, was standing propped against it. It was part of some choir decoration that Meynell and a class of village boys were making for the church, where the Rector had already carved with his own hand many of the available surfaces, whether of stone or wood. The carving, which was elaborate and rich, was technically faulty, as an Italian primitive is faulty, but *mutatis mutandis* it had much of the same charm that belongs to Italian primitive work: the same joyous sincerity, the same passionate love of natural things, leaves and flowers and birds.

For the rest, the furniture of the room was shabby and ugly. The pictures on the walls were mostly faded Oxford photographs, or outlines by Overbeck and Retsch, which had belonged to Meynell's parents and were tenderly cherished by him. There were none of the pretty, artistic trifles, the signs of travel and easy culture, which many a small country vicarage possesses in abundance. Meynell, in spite of his scholar's mastery of half-a-dozen languages, had never crossed the Channel. Barron, lingering at the door, with his eyes on the form by the fire, knew why. The Rector had always been too poor. He had been left an orphan while still at Balliol, and had to bring up his two younger brothers. He had done it. They were both in Canada now and prospering. But the signs of the struggle were on this shabby house, and on this shabby, frugal, powerfully built man. Yet now he might have been more at ease; the living, though small, was by no means among the worst in the diocese. Ah, well! Anne, the housekeeper

and only servant, knew how the money went — and didn't
go, and she had passed on some of her grievances to
Barron. They two knew — though Barron would never
have dared to show his knowledge — what a wrestle
it meant to get the Rector to spend what was decently
necessary on his own food and clothes; and Anne spent
hours of the night in indignantly guessing at what he
spent on the clothes and food of other people — mostly,
in her opinion, "varmints."

These things flitted vaguely through the young man's
sore mind. Then in a flash they were absorbed in a
perception of a wholly different kind. The room seemed
to him transfigured; a kind of temple. He thought
of the intellectual life which had been lived there; the
passion for truth which had burnt in it; the sermons
and books that had been written on those crowded tables;
the personality and influence that had been gradually
built up within it, so that to him, as to many others,
the dingy study was a place of pilgrimage, breathing
inspiration; and his heart went out, first in discipleship,
and then in a pain that was not for himself. For over
his friend's head he saw the gathering of clouds not now
to be scattered or dispersed; and who could foretell the
course of the storm?

The young man gently closed the door and went his
way. He need not have left the house so quietly. The
Rector got no sleep that evening.

CHAPTER II

THE church clock of Upcote Minor was just striking nine o'clock as Richard Meynell, a few hours later than the conversation just recorded, shut the Rectory gate behind him, and took his way up the village.

The night was cold and gusty. The summer this year had forgotten to be balmy, and Meynell, who was an ardent sun-lover, shivered as he walked along, buttoning a much-worn parson's coat against the sharp air. Before him lay the long, straggling street, with its cottages and small shops, its post-office, and public-houses, and its occasional gentlefolks' dwellings, now with a Georgian front plumb on the street, and now hidden behind walls and trees. It was evidently a large village, almost a country town, with a considerable variety of life. At this hour of the evening most of the houses were dark, for the labourers had gone to bed. But behind the drawn blinds of the little shops there were still lights here and there, and in the houses of the gentility.

The Rector passed the fine perpendicular church standing back from the road, with its churchyard about it; and just beyond it, he turned, his pace involuntarily slackening, to look at a small gabled house, surrounded

24

by a garden, and overhung by a splendid lime tree. Suddenly, as he approached it, the night burst into fragrance, for a gust of wind shook the lime-blossom, and flung the scent in Meynell's face; while at the same time the dim masses of roses in the garden sent out their sweetness to the passers-by.

A feeling of pleasure, quick, involuntary, passed through his mind; pleasure in the thought of what these flowers meant to the owner of them. He had a vision of a tall and slender woman, no longer young, with a delicate and plaintive face, moving among the rose-beds she loved, her light dress trailing on the grass. The recollection stirred in him affection, and an impulse of sympathy, stronger than the mere thought of the flowers, and the woman's tending of them, could explain. It passed indeed immediately into something else — a touch of new and sharp anxiety.

"And she's been very peaceful of late," he said to himself ruefully, "as far at least as Hester ever lets her be. Preston's wife was a godsend. Perhaps now she'll come out of her shell and go more among the people. It would help her. Anyway, we can't have everything rooted up again just yet — before the time."

He walked on, and as the farther corner of the house came into view, he saw a thinly curtained window with a light inside it, and it seemed to him that he distinguished a figure within.

"Reading? — or embroidering? Probably, at her work. She had that commission to finish. Busy woman!"

He fell to imagining the little room, the embroidery frame, the books, and the brindled cat on the rug, of no particular race or beauty; for use not for show; but sensitive and gentle like its mistress, and like her, not to be readily made friends with.

"How wise of her," he thought, "not to accept her sister's offer since Ralph's death — to insist on keeping her little house and her independence. Imagine her! — prisoned in that house, with that family. Except for Hester — except for Hester!"

He smiled sadly to himself, threw a last troubled look at the little house, and left it behind him. Before him, the village street, with its green and its pond, widened under the scudding sky. Far ahead, about a quarter of a mile away, among surrounding trees, certain outlines were visible through the July twilight. The accustomed eye knew them for the chimneys of the Fox-Wiltons' house, owned now, since the recent death of its master, Sir Ralph Fox-Wilton, by his widow, the sister of the lady with the cat and the embroidery, and mother of many children, for the most part an unattractive brood, peevish and slow-minded like their father. Hester was the bright, particular star in that house, as Stephen Barron had now found out.

Alack! — alack! The Rector's face resumed for a moment the expression of painful or brooding perplexity it had worn during his conversation of the afternoon with young Barron, on the subject of Hester Fox-Wilton.

Another light in a window — and a sound of shouting and singing. The "Cowroast," a "public" mostly frequented by the miners who inhabited the northern end of the village, was evidently doing trade. The Rector did not look up as he passed it; but in general he turned an indulgent eye upon it. Before entering upon the living, he had himself worked for a month as an ordinary miner, in the colliery whose tall chimneys could be seen to the east above the village roofs. His body still vividly retained the physical memory of those days — of the aching muscles, and the gargantuan thirsts.

At last the rows of new-built cottages attached to the colliery came in view on the left; to the right, a steep hillside heavily wooded, and at the top of it, in the distance, the glimmering of a large white house — stately and separate — dominating the village, the church, the collieries, and the Fox-Wiltons' plantations.

The Rector threw a glance at it. It was from that house had come the letter he had found on his hall-table that afternoon; a letter in a handwriting large and impressive like the dim house on the hill. The handwriting of a man accustomed to command, whether his own ancestral estate, or the collieries which had been carved out of its fringe, or the village spreading humbly at his feet, or the church into which he walked on Sunday with heavy tread, and upright carriage, conscious of his threefold dignity — as squire, magistrate, and churchwarden.

"It's my business to fight him!" Meynell thought, looking at the house, and squaring his broad shoulders unconsciously. "It's not my business to hate him — not at all — rather to respect and sympathize with him. I provoke the fight — and I may be thankful to have lit on a strong antagonist. What's Stephen afraid of? What can they do? Let 'em try!"

A smile — contemptuous and good-humoured — crossed the Rector's face. Any angry bigot determined to rid his parish of a heretical parson might no doubt bə tempted to use other than legal and theological weapons, if he could get them. A heretic with unpaid bills and some hidden vice is scarcely in a position to make much of his heresy. But the Rector's smile showed him humorously conscious of an almost excessive innocence of private life. The thought of how little an enemy could find to lay hold on in his history or present existence seemed almost to bring with it a kind of shamefacedness — as for experience irrevocably foregone, warm, tumultuous, human experience, among the sinners and sufferers of the world. For there are odd, mingled moments in the lives of most scholars and saints — like Renan in his queer envy of Théophile Gautier — when such men inevitably ask themselves whether they have not missed something irreplaceable, the student, by his learning — the saint even, by his goodness.

Here now was "Miners' Row." As the Rector approached the cottage of which he was in search the clouds lightened in the east, and a pale moonshine, suffusing the dusk, showed in the far distance beyond the village, the hills of Fitton Chase, rounded, heathy hills, crowned by giant firs. Meynell looked at them with longing, and a sudden realization of his own weariness. A day or two, perhaps a week or two, among the fells, with their winds and scents about him, and their streams in his ears — he must allow himself that, before the fight began.

No. 8. A dim light showed in the upper window. The Rector knocked at the door. A woman opened — a young and sweet-looking nurse in her bonnet and long cloak.

"You look pretty done!" exclaimed the Rector. "Has he been giving trouble?"

"Oh, no, sir, not more than usual. It's the two of them."

"She won't go to her sister's?"

"She won't stir a foot, sir."

"Where is she?" The nurse pointed to the living-room on her left.

"She scarcely eats anything — a sup of tea sometimes. And I doubt whether she sleeps at all."

"And she won't go to him?"

"If he were dying, and she alone with him in the house, I don't believe she'd go near him."

The Rector stepped in and asked a few questions as to arrangements for the night. The patient, it seemed, was asleep, in consequence of a morphia injection, and likely to remain so for an hour or two. He was dying of an internal injury inflicted by a fall of rock in the mine some ten days before. Surgery had done what it could, but signs of blood-poisoning had appeared, and the man's days were numbered.

The doctor had left written instructions, which the nurse handed over to Meynell. If certain symptoms appeared, the doctor was to be summoned. But in all probability the man's fine constitution, injured though it had been by drink, would enable him to hold out another day or two. And the hideous pain of the first week had now ceased; mortification had almost certainly set in, and all that could be done was to wait the slow and sure failure of the heart.

The nurse took leave. Meynell was hanging up his hat in the little passageway, when the door of the front parlour opened, after being unlocked.

Meynell looked round.

"Good evening, Mrs. Bateson. You are coming up-stairs, I hope, with me?"

He spoke gently, but with a quiet authority.

The woman in the doorway shook her head. She was thin and narrow-chested. Her hair was already gray, though she could not have been more than thirty-five, and youth and comeliness had been long since battered from her face, partly by misery of mind, partly by direct ill usage of which there were evident traces. She looked steadily at the Rector.

"I'm not going," she said. "He's nowt to me. But I'd like to know what the doctor was thinkin' of him."

"The doctor thinks he may live through to-night and to-morrow night — not much more. He is your husband, Mrs. Bateson, and whatever you have against him, you'll be very sorry afterward if you don't give him help and comfort in his death. Come up now, I beg of you, and watch with me. He might die at any moment."

And Meynell put out his hand kindly toward the woman standing in the shadow, as though to lead her.

But she stepped backward.

"I know what I'm about," she said, breathing quick. "He made a fule o' me wi' that wanton Lizzie Short, and he near killt me the last morning afore he went. And I'd been a good wife to him for fifteen year, and never a word between us till that huzzy came along. And she's got a child by him, and he must go and throw it in my face that I'd never given him one. And he struck and cursed me that last morning — he wished me dead, he said. And I sat and prayed God to punish him. An' He did. The roof came down on him. And now he mun die. I've done wi' him — and she's done wi' him. He's made his bed, and he mun lig on it."

The Rector put up his hand sternly.

"Don't! Mrs. Bateson. Those are words you'll repent when you yourself come to die. He has sinned toward you — but remember! — he's a young man still — in the prime of life. He has suffered horribly — and he has only a few hours or days to live. He has asked for you already to-day, he is sure to ask for you to-night. Forgive him! — ask God to help him to die in peace!"

While he spoke she stood motionless, impassive.

Meynell's voice had beautiful inflections, and he spoke with strong feeling. Few persons whom he so addressed could have remained unmoved. But Mrs. Bateson only retreated farther into the dreary little parlour, with its wool mats and antimacassars, and a tray of untasted tea on the table. She passed her tongue round her dry lips to moisten them before she spoke, quite calmly:

"Thank you, sir. Thank you. You mean well. But we must all judge for ourselves. If there's anything you want I can get for you, you knock twice on the floor — I shall hear you. But I'm not comin' up."

Meynell turned away discouraged, and went upstairs.

In the room above lay the dying man — breathing quickly and shallowly under the influence of the drug that had been given him. The nurse had raised him on his pillows, and the window near him was open. His powerful chest was uncovered, and he seemed even in his sleep to be fighting for air. In the twelve hours that had elapsed since Meynell had last seen him he had travelled with terrible rapidity toward the end. He looked years older than in the morning; it was as though some sinister hand had been at work on the face, expanding here, contracting there, substituting chaos and nothingness for the living man.

The Rector sat down beside him. The room was small and bare — a little strip of carpet on the boards, a few chairs, and a little table with food and nourishment beside the bed. On the mantelpiece was a large printed card containing the football fixtures of the winter before.

Bateson had once been a fine player. Of late years, however, his interest had been confined to betting heavily on the various local and county matches, and it was to his ill-luck as a gambler no less than to the influence of the flimsy little woman who had led him astray that his moral break-up might be traced.

A common tale! — yet more tragic than usual. For the bedroom contained other testimonies to the habits of a ruined man. There was a hanging bookcase on the wall, and the Rector sitting by the bed could just make out the titles of the books in the dim light.

Mill, Huxley, a reprint of Tom Paine, various books by Blatchford, the sixpenny editions of "Literature and Dogma," and Renan's "Life of Christ," some popular science volumes of Browning and Ruskin, and a group of well-thumbed books on the birds of Mercia — the little collection, hardly earned, and, to judge from its appearance, diligently read, showed that its owner had been a man of intelligence. The Rector looked from it to the figure in the bed with a pang at his heart.

All was still in the little cottage. Through the open window the Rector could see fold after fold of the Chase stretching north and west above the village. The moorland ridges shone clear under the moon, now bare, or scantily plumed by gaunt trees, and now clothed in a dense blackness of wood. Meynell, who knew every yard of the great heath and loved it well, felt himself lifted there in spirit as he looked. The "bunchberries" must just be ripening on the high ground — nestling scarlet and white amid their glossy leaves. And among them and beside them, the taller, slender bilberries, golden green; the exquisite grasses of the heath, pale pink, and silver, and purple, swaying in the winds, clothing acre after acre with a beauty beyond the looms of men; the purple heather and the ling flushing toward its bloom: and the free-limbed scattered birch trees, strongly scrawled against the sky. The scurry of the clouds over the purple sweeps of moor, the beat of the wind, and then suddenly, pools of fragrant air sun-steeped — he drew in the thought of it all, as he might have drunk the moorland breeze itself, with a thrill of pleasure, which passed at once into a movement of soul.

"*My God — my God!*"

No other words imagined or needed. Only a leap of the heart, natural, habitual, instinctive, from the imagined beauty of the heath, to the "Eternal Fountain" of all beauty.

The hand of the dying man made a faint rustling with the sheet. Meynell, checked, rebuked almost, by the slight sound, bent his eyes again on the sleeper, and leaning forward tried to meditate and pray. But to-night he found it hard. He realized anew his physical and mental fatigue, and a certain confused clamour of thought, strangely persistent behind the more external experience alike of body and mind; like the murmur of a distant sea heard from far inland, as the bond and background of all lesser sounds.

The phrases of the letter he had found on the hall-table recurred to him whether he would or no. They were mainly legal and technical, intimating that an application had been made to the Bishop of Markborough to issue a Commission of Inquiry into certain charges made by parishioners of Upcote Minor against the Rector of the parish. The writer of the letter was one of the applicants, and gave notice of his intention to prosecute the charges named, with the utmost vigour through all the stages prescribed by ecclesiastical law.

But it was, rather, some earlier letters from the same hand — letters more familiar, intimate, and discursive — that ultimately held the Rector's thoughts as he kept his watch. For in those letters were contained almost all the objections that a sensitive mind and heart had had to grapple with before determining on the course to which the Rector of Upcote was now committed. They were the voice of the "adversary," the "accuser." Crude or conventional, as the form of the argument might be, it yet represented the "powers and principalities" to be reckoned with. If the Rector's conscience could not sustain him against it, he was henceforth a dishonest and unhappy man; and when his lawyers had failed to protect him against its practical result — as they must no doubt fail — he would be a dispossessed priest:

"What discipline in life or what comfort in death can such a faith as yours bring to any human soul? Do, I beg of you, ask yourself this question. If the great miracles of the Creed are not true, what have you to give the wretched and the sinful? Ought you not in common human charity to make way for one who can offer the consolations, utter the warnings, or hold out the heavenly hopes from which you are debarred?"

The Rector fixed his gaze upon the sick man. It was as though the question of the letter were put to him through those parched lips. And as he looked, Bateson opened his eyes.

"Be that you, Rector?" he said, in a clear voice.

"I've been sitting up with you, Bateson. Can you take a little brandy and milk, do you think?"

The patient submitted, and the Rector, with a tender and skilful touch, made him comfortable on his pillows and smoothed the bedclothes.

"Where's my wife?" he said presently, looking round the room.

"She's sleeping downstairs."

"I want her to come up."

"Better not ask her. She seems ill and tired."

The sick man smiled — a slight and scornful smile.

"She'll ha' time enough presently to be tired. You goa an' ask her."

"I'd rather not leave you, Bateson. You're very ill."

"Then take that stick then, an' rap on the floor. She'll hear tha fast enough."

The Rector hesitated, but only for a moment. He took the stick and rapped.

Almost immediately the sound of a turning key was heard through the small thinly built cottage. The door below opened and footsteps came up the stairs. But before they reached the landing the sound ceased. The two men listened in vain.

"You goa an' tell her as I'm sorry I knocked her aboot," said Bateson, eagerly. "An' she can see for hersen as I can't aggravate her no more wi' the other woman." He raised himself on his elbow, staring into the Rector's face. "I'm done for — tell her that."

"Shall I tell her also   hat you love her? — and you want her love?"

"Aye," said Bateson, nodding, with the same bright stare into Meynell's eyes. "Aye!"

Meynell made him drink a little more brandy, and then he wen⁺ out to the person standing motionless on the stairs.

"What did you want, sir?" said Mrs. Bateson, under her breath.

"Mrs. Bateson — he begs you to come to him! He's sorry for his conduct — he says you can see for yourself that he can't wrong you any more. Come — and be merciful!"

The woman paused. The Rector could see the shiver of her thin shoulders under her print dress. Then she turned and quietly descended the cottage stairway. Half way down she looked up.

"Tell him I should do him nowt but harm. I" — her voice trembled for the first time — "I doan't bear him malice; I hope he'll not suffer. But I'm not comin'."

"Wait a moment, Mrs. Bateson! I was to tell you that in spite of all, he loved you — and he wanted your love."

She shook her head.

"It's no good talkin' that way. It'll mebbe use up his strength. Tell him I'd have got Lizzie Short to come an' nurse 'im, if I could. It's her place. But he knows as she an' her man flitted a fortnight sen, an' theer's no address."

And she disappeared. But at the foot of the stairs — standing unseen — she said in her usual tone:

"If there was a cup o' tea, I could bring you, sir — or anythin'?"

Meynell, distressed and indignant, did not answer. He returned to the sick-room. Bateson looked up as the Rector bent once more over the bed.

"She'll not coom?" he said, in a faint voice of surprise. "Well, that's a queer thing. She wasn't used to be a tough 'un. I could most make her do what I wanted. Well, never mind, Rector, never mind. Sit tha down — mebbe you'd be wanting to say a prayer. You're welcome. I reckon it'll do me no harm."

His lips parted in a smile — a smile of satire. But his brows frowned, and his eyes were still alive and bright, only now, as the watcher thought, with anger.

Meynell hesitated.

"I will say the church prayers, if you wish it, Bateson. Of course I will say them."

"But I doan't believe in 'em," said the sick man, smiling again, "an' you doan't believe in 'em, noather, if folk say true! Don't tha be vexed — I'm not saying it to cheek tha. But Mr. Barron, ee says ee'll make tha give up. Ee's been goin' roun' the village, talkin' to folk. I doan't care about that — an' I've never been one o' your men — not pious enough, be a long way — but I'd like to hear — now as I can't do tha no harm, Rector, now as I'm goin', an' you cawn't deny me — what tha does really believe. Will tha tell me?"

He turned, open-eyed, impulsive, intelligent, as he had always been in life.

The Rector started. The inward challenge had taken voice.

"Certainly I will tell you, if it will help you — if you're strong enough."

Bateson waved his hand contemptuously.

"I feel as strong as onything. That sup o' brandy has put some grit in me. Give me some more. Thank tha. . . . Does tha believe in God, Rector?"

His whimsical, half-teasing, yet, at bottom, anxious look touched Meynell strangely.

"With all my life — and with all my strength!"

Meynell's gaze was fixed intently on his questioner. The night-light in the basin on the farther side of the room threw the strong features into shadowy relief, illumining the yearning kindliness of the eyes.

"What made tha believe in Him?"

"My own life — my own struggles — and sins —

and sufferings," said Meynell, stooping toward the sick man, and speaking each word with an intensity behind which lay much that could never be known to his questioner. "A good man, Bateson, put it once in this way, 'There is something in me that asks something of me.' That's easy to understand, isn't it? If a man wants to be filthy, or drunken, or cruel, there is always a voice within — it may be weak or it may be strong — that asks of him to be — instead — pure and sober and kind. And perhaps he denies the Voice, refuses it — talks it down — again and again. Then the joy in his life dies out bit by bit, and the world turns to dust and ashes. Every time that he says No to the Voice he is less happy — he has less power of being happy. And the voice itself dies away — and death comes. But now, suppose he turns to the Voice and says 'Lead me — I follow!' And suppose he obeys, like a child stumbling. Then every time he stretches and bends his poor weak will so as to give *It* what it asks, his heart is happy; and strength comes — the strength to do more and do better. *It* asks him to love — to love men and women, not with lust, but with pure love; and as he obeys, as he loves — he *knows* — he knows that it is God asking, and that God has come to him and abides with him. So when death overtakes him he trusts himself to God as he would to his best friend."

"Tha'rt talkin' riddles, Rector!"

"No. Ask yourself. When you fell into sin with that woman, did nothing speak to you, nothing try to stop you?"

The bright half-mocking eyes below Meynell's wandered
a little — wavered in expression.

"It was the hot blood in me — aye, an' in her too.
Yo cawn't help them things."

"Can't you? When your wife suffered, didn't that
touch you? Wouldn't you undo it now if you could?"

"Aye — because I'm goin' — doctor' says I'm done
for."

"No — well or ill — wouldn't you undo it — wouldn't
you undo the blows you gave your wife — the misery
you caused her?"

"Mebbe. But I cawn't."

"No — not in my sense or yours. But in God's sense
you can. Turn your heart — ask Him to give you love
— love to Him, who has been pleading with you all your
life — love to your wife, and your fellow men — love —
and repentance — and faith."

Meynell's voice shook. He was in an anguish at
what seemed to him the weakness, the ineffectiveness,
of his pleading.

A silence. Then the voice rose again from the bed.

"Dost tha believe in Jesus Christ, Rector? Mr.
Barron, he calls tha an infidel. But he hasn't read the
books you an' I have read, I'll uphold yer!"

The dying man raised his hand to the bookshelves
beside him with a proud gesture.

The Rector slowly raised himself. An expression
as of some passion within, trying at once to check and
to utter itself, became visible on his face in the half light.

"It's not books that settle it, Jim. I'll try and put it to you — just as I see it myself — just in the way it comes to me."

He paused a moment, frowning under the effort of simplification. The hidden need of the dying man seemed to be mysteriously conveyed to him — the pang of lonely anguish that death brings with it; the craving for comfort beneath the apparent scorn of faith; the human cry expressed in this strange catechism.

"Stop me if I tire you," he said at last. "I don't know if I can make it plain — but to me, Bateson, there are two worlds that every man is concerned with. There is this world of everyday life — work and business, sleeping and talking, eating and drinking — that you and I have been living in; and there is another world, within it, and alongside of it, that we know when we are quiet — when we listen to our own hearts, and follow that voice I spoke of just now. Jesus Christ called that other world the Kingdom of God — and those who dwell in it, the children of God. Love is the king of that world, and the law of it — Love, which *is* God. But different men — different races of men — give different names to that Love — see it under different shapes. To us — to you and to me — it speaks under the name and form of Jesus Christ. And so I come to say — so all Christians come to say —'*I believe — in Jesus Christ our Lord.*' For it is His life and His death that still to-day — as they have done for hundreds of years — draw men and women into the Kingdom — the Kingdom of Love —

and so to God. He draws us to love — and so to God.
And in God alone is the soul of man satisfied; *satisfied
— and at rest.*"

The last words were but just breathed — yet they
carried with them the whole force of a man.

"That's all very well, Rector. But tha's given up
th' Athanasian Creed, and there's mony as says tha
doesn't hold by tother Creeds. Wilt tha tell *me*, as
Jesus were born of a virgin? — or that a got up out o'
the grave on the third day?"

The Rector's face, through all its harass, softened
tenderly.

"If you were a well man, Bateson, we'd talk of that.
But there's only one thing that matters to you now —
it's to feel God with you — to be giving your soul to
God."

The two men gazed at each other.

"What are tha nursin' me for, Rector?" said Bateson,
abruptly — "I'm nowt to you."

"For the love of Christ," said Meynell, steadily,
taking his hand — "and of you, in Christ. But you
mustn't talk. Rest a while."

There was a silence. The July night was beginning
to pale into dawn. Outside, beyond the nearer fields,
the wheels and sheds and the two great chimneys of the
colliery were becoming plain; the tints and substance of
the hills were changing. Dim forms of cattle moved
in the newly shorn grass; the sound of their chewing
could be faintly heard.

Suddenly the dying man raised himself in bed.

"I want my wife!" he said imperiously. "I tell tha, I want my wife!"

It was as though the last energy of being had thrown itself into the cry — indignant, passionate, protesting.

Meynell rose.

"I will bring her."

Bateson gripped his hand.

"Tell her to mind that cottage at Morden End — and the night we came home there first — as married folk. Tell her I'm goin' — goin' fast."

He fell back, panting. Meynell gave him food and medicine. Then he went quickly downstairs, and knocked at the parlour door. After an interval of evident hesitation on the part of the occupant of the room, it was reluctantly unlocked. Meynell pushed it open wide.

"Mrs. Bateson — come to your husband — he is dying!"

The woman, deadly white, threw back her head proudly. But Meynell laid a peremptory hand on her arm.

"I command you — in God's name. Come!"

A struggle shook her. She yielded suddenly — and began to cry. Meynell patted her on the shoulder as he might have patted a child, said kind, soothing things, gave her her husband's message, and finally drew her from the room.

She went upstairs, Meynell following, anxious about

the physical result of the meeting, and ready to go for
the doctor at a moment's notice.

The door at the top of the stairs was open. The dying
man lay on his side, gazing toward it, and gauntly illumined by the rising light.

The woman went slowly forward, drawn by the eyes
directed upon her.

"I thowt tha'd come!" said Bateson, with a smile.

She sat down upon the bed, crouching, emaciated;
at first motionless and voiceless; a spectacle little less
piteous, little less deathlike, than the man on the pillows.
He still smiled at her, in a kind of triumph; also silent,
but his lips trembled. Then, groping, she put out her
hand — her disfigured, toil-worn hand — and took his,
raising it to her lips. The touch of his flesh seemed to
loosen in her the fountains of the great deep. She slid
to her knees and kissed him — enfolding him with her
arms, the two murmuring together.

Meynell went out into the dawn. His mystical
sense had beheld the Lord in that small upper room;
had seen as it were the sacred hands breaking to those
two poor creatures the sacrament of love. His own
mind was for the time being tranquillized. It was as
though he said to himself, "I know that trouble will
come back — I know that doubts and fears will pursue me again; but this hour — this blessing — is from
God!" . . .

The sun was high in a dewy world, already busy with
its first labours of field and mine, when Meynell left

the cottage. The church clock was on the stroke of eight.

He passed down the village street, and reached again the little gabled house which he had passed the night before. As he approached, there was a movement in the garden. A lady, who was walking among the roses, holding up her gray dress from the dew, turned and hastened toward the gate.

"Please come in! You must be tired out. The gardener told me he'd seen you about. We've got some coffee ready for you."

Meynell looked at the speaker in smiling astonishment.

"What are you up for at this hour?"

"Why shouldn't I be up? Look how lovely it is! I have a friend with me, and I want to introduce you."

Miss Puttenham opened her garden gate and drew in the Rector. Behind her among the roses Meynell perceived another lady — a girl, with bright reddish hair.

"Mary!" said Miss Puttenham.

The girl approached. Meynell had an impression of mingled charm and reticence as she gave him her hand. The eyes were sweet and shy. But the unconscious dignity of bearing showed that the shyness was the shyness of strong character, rather than of mere youth and innocence.

"This is my new friend, Mary Elsmere. You've heard they're at Forkéd Pond?" Alice Puttenham said, smiling, as she slipped her arm round the girl. "I captured her for the night, while Mrs. Elsmere went to town. I want you to know each other."

"Elsmere's daughter!" thought Meynell, with a thrill, as he followed the two ladies through the open French window into the little dining-room, where the coffee was ready. And he could not take his eyes from the young face.

CHAPTER III

I AM in love with the house — I adore the Chase —
I like heretics — and I don't think I'm ever going
home again!"

Mrs. Flaxman as she spoke handed a cup of tea to a
tall gentleman, Louis Manvers by name, the possessor
of a long, tanned countenance; of thin iron-gray hair,
descending toward the shoulders; of a drooping moustache, and eyes that mostly studied the carpet or the
knees of their owner. A shy, laconic person at first sight,
with the manner of one to whom conversation, of the
drawing-room kind, was little more than a series of
doubtful experiments, that seldom or never came off.

Mrs. Flaxman, on the other hand, was a pretty woman
of forty, still young and slender, in spite of two boys at
Eton, one of them seventeen, and in the Eleven; and her
talk was as rash and rapid as that of her companion was
the reverse. Which perhaps might be one of the reasons
why they were excellent friends, and always happy in
each other's society.

Mr. Manvers overlooked a certain challenge that Mrs.
Flaxman had thrown out, took the tea provided, and
merely inquired how long the rebuilding of the Flaxmans'
own house would take. For it appeared that they were

only tenants of Maudeley House — furnished — for a year.

Mrs. Flaxman replied that only the British workman knew. But she looked upon herself as homeless for two years, and found the prospect as pleasant as her husband found it annoying.

"As if life was long enough to spend it in one county, and one house and park! I have shaken all my duties from me like old rags. No more school-treats, no more bean-feasts, no more hospital committees, for two whole years! Think of it! Hugh, poor wretch, is still Chairman of the County Council. That's why we took this place — it is within fifty miles. He has to motor over occasionally. But I shall make him resign that, next year. Then we are going for six months to Berlin — that's for music — *my* show! Then we take a friend's house in British East Africa, where you can see a lion kill from the front windows, and zebras stub up your kitchen garden. That's Hugh's show. Then of course there'll be Japan — and by that time there'll be airships to the North Pole, and we can take it on our way home!"

"Souvent femme varie!" Mr. Manvers raised a pair of surprisingly shrewd eyes from the carpet. "I remember the years when I used to try and dig you and Hugh out of Bagley, and drive you abroad — without the smallest success."

"Those were the years when one was moral and well-behaved! But everybody who is worth anything goes a little mad at forty. I was forty last week" — Rose

Flaxman gave an involuntary sigh —"I can't get over it."

"Ah, well, it's quite time you were a little nipped by the years," said Manvers dryly. "Why should you be so much younger than anybody else in the world? When you grow old there'll be no more youth!"

Mrs. Flaxman's eyes, of a bright greenish-gray, shone gayly into his; then their owner made a displeased mouth. "You may pay me compliments as much as you like. They will not prevent me from telling you that you are one of the most slow-minded people I have ever met!"

"H'm?" said Mr. Manvers, with mild interrogation.

Rose Flaxman repeated her remark, emphasizing with a little tattoo of her teaspoon on the Chippendale tea-tray before her. Manvers studied her, smiling.

"I am entirely ignorant of the grounds of this attack."

"Oh, what hypocrisy!" cried his companion hotly. "I throw out the most tempting of all possible flies, and you absolutely refuse to rise to it."

Manvers considered.

"You expected me to rise to the word 'heretic?'"

"Of course I did! On the same principle as 'sweets to the sweet.' Who — I should like to know — should be interested in heretics if not you?"

"It entirely depends on the species," said her companion cautiously.

"There couldn't be a more exciting species," declared Mrs. Flaxman. "Here you have a Rector of a parish simply setting up another Church of England — services, doctrines and all — off his own bat, so to speak — without a 'with your leave or by your leave'; his parishioners backing him up; his Bishop in a frightful taking and not the least knowing what to do; the fagots all gathering to make a bonfire of him, and a great black six-foot-two Inquisitor ready to apply the match — and yet — I can't get you to take the smallest interest in it! I assure you, Hugh is *thrilled*."

Manvers laid the finger-tips of two long brown hands lightly against each other.

"Very sorry — but it leaves me quite cold. Heresy in the Church of England comes to nothing. Our heretics are never violent enough. They forget the excellent text about the Kingdom of Heaven! Now the heretics in the Church of Rome are violent. That is what makes them so far more interesting."

"This man seems to be drastic enough!"

"Oh, no!" said the other, gently but firmly incredulous. "Believe me — he will resign, or apologize — they always do."

"Believe *me!* — you don't — excuse me! — know anything about it. In the first place, Mr. Meynell has got his parishioners—all except a handful—behind him——"

"So had Voysey," interjected Manvers, softly.

Mrs. Flaxman took no notice.

"— And he has hundreds of other supporters — thousands perhaps — and some of them parsons — in this diocese, and outside it. And they are all convinced that they must fight — fight to the death — and *not* give in. That, you see, is what makes the difference! My brother-in-law"— the voice speaking changed and softened —"died twenty years ago. I remember how sad it was. He seemed to be walking alone in a world that hardly troubled to consider him — so far as the Church was concerned, I mean. There seemed to be nothing else to do but to give up his living. But the strain of doing it killed him."

"The strain of giving up your living may be severe — but, I assure you, your man will find the strain of keeping it a good deal worse."

"It all depends upon his backing. How do you know there isn't a world behind him?" Mrs. Flaxman persisted, as the man beside her slowly shook his head. "Well, now, listen! Hugh and I went to church here last Sunday. I never was so bewildered. First, it was crowded from end to end, and there were scores of people from other villages and towns — a kind of demonstration. Then, as to the service — neither of us could find our way about. Instead of saying the Lord's Prayer four times, we said it once; we left out half the psalms for the day, the Rector explaining from the chancel steps that they were not fit to be read in a Christian church; we altered this prayer and that prayer; we listened to an extempore prayer for the widows and orphans of some poor fellows who have been killed in a mine ten miles from here, which made me cry like baby; and, most amazing of all, when it came to the Creeds ——"

Manvers suddenly threw back his head, his face for

the first time sharpening into attention. "Ah! Well
— what about the Creeds?"

Mrs. Flaxman bent forward, triumphing in the capture
of her companion.

"We had both the Creeds. The Rector read them —
turning to the congregation — and with just a word of
preface — 'Here follows the Creed, commonly called the
Apostles' Creed,'— or 'Here follows the Nicene Creed.'
And we all stood and listened — and nobody said a
word. It was the strangest moment! You know —
I'm not a serious person — but I just held my breath."

"As though you heard behind the veil the awful
Voices —'*Let us depart hence?*'" said Manvers, after a
pause. His expression had gradually changed. Those
who knew him best might have seen in it a slight and
passing trace of conflicts long since silenced and resolutely
forgotten.

"If you mean by that that the church was irreverent
— or disrespectful — or hostile — well, you are quite
wrong!" cried Mrs. Flaxman impetuously. "It was
like a moment of new birth — I can't describe it — as
though a Spirit entered in. And when the Rector finished — there was a kind of breath through the church
— like the rustling of new leaves — and I thought of
the wind blowing where it listed. . . . And then the
Rector preached on the Creeds — how they grew up and
why. Fascinating!— why aren't the clergy always telling us such things? And he brought it all round to
impressing upon us that some day *we* might be worthy of

another Christian creed — by being faithful — that it would flower again out of our lives and souls — as the old had done. . . . I wonder what it all meant!" 'she said abruptly, her light voice dropping.

Manvers smiled. His emotion had quite passed away.

"Ah! but I forgot" — she resumed hurriedly — "we left out several of the Commandments — and we chanted the Beatitudes — and then I found there was a little service paper in the seat, and everybody in the church but Hugh and me knew all about it beforehand!"

"A queer performance," said Manvers, "and of course childishly illegal. Your man will be soon got rid of. I expect you might have applied to him the remark of the Bishop of Cork on the Dean of Cork — 'Excellent sermon! — eloquent, clever, argumentative! — and not enough gospel in it to save a tom-tit!'"

Mrs. Flaxman looked at him oddly.

"Well, but — the extraordinary thing was that Hugh made me stay for the second service, and it was as Ritualistic as you like!"

Manvers fell back in his chair, the vivacity on his face relaxing.

"Ah! — is that all?"

"Oh! but you don't understand," said his companion, eagerly. "Of course Ritualistic is the wrong word. Should I have said 'sacramental'? I only meant that it was full of symbolism. There were lights — and flowers, and music, but there was nothing priestly — or super-stitious" — she frowned in her effort to explain. "It was all poetic — and mystical — and yet practical. There were a good many things changed in the Service, — but I hardly noticed — I was so absorbed in watching the people. Almost every one stayed for the second service. It was quite short — so was the first service. And a great many communicated. But the spirit of it was the wonderful thing. It had all that — that magic — that mystery — that one gets out of Catholicism, even simple Catholicism, in a village church — say at Benediction; and yet one had a sense of having come out into fresh air; of saying things that were true — true at least to you, and to the people that were saying them; things that you did believe, or could believe, instead of things that you only pretended to believe, or couldn't possibly believe! I haven't got over it yet, and as for Hugh, I have never seen him so moved since — since Robert died."

Manvers was aware of Mrs. Flaxman's affection for her brother-in-law's memory; and it seemed to him natural and womanly that she should be touched — artist and wordling though she was — by this fresh effort in a similar direction. For himself, he was touched in another way: with pity, or a kindly scorn. He did not believe in patching up the Christian tradition. Either accept it — or put it aside. Newman had disposed of "neo-Christianity" once for all.

"Well, of course all this means a row," he said at length, with a smile. "What is the Bishop doing?"

"Oh, the Bishop will have to prosecute, Hugh says; of

course he must! And if he didn't, Mr. Barron would
do it for him."

"The gentleman who lives in the White House?"

"Precisely. Ah!" cried Mrs. Flaxman, suddenly,
rising to her feet and looking through the open window
beside her. "What do you think we've done? We
have evoked him! *Parlez du diable*, etc. How stupid
of us! But there's his carriage trotting up the drive —
I know the horses. And that's his deaf daughter —
poor, downtrodden thing! — sitting beside him. Now
then — shall we be at home? Quick!"

Mrs. Flaxman flew to the bell, but retreated with a
little grimace.

"We must! It's inevitable. But Hugh says I
can't be rude to new people. Why can't I? It's so
simple."

She sat down, however, though rebellion and a little
malice quickened the colour in her fair skin. Manvers
looked longingly at the door leading to the garden.

"Shall I disappear?— or must I support you?"

"It all depends on what value you set on my good
opinion," said Mrs. Flaxman, laughing.

Manvers resettled himself in his chair.

"I stay — but first, a little information. The gentleman owns land here?"

"Acres and acres. But he only came into it about
three years ago. He is on the same railway board where
Hugh is Chairman. He doesn't like Hugh, and he
certainly won't like me. But you see he's bound to be

civil to us. Hugh says he's always making quarrels on the board — in a kind of magnificent, superior way. He never loses his temper — whereas the others would often like to flay him alive. Now then"— Mrs. Flaxman laid a finger on her mouth —"'Papa, potatoes, prunes, and prism'!"

Steps were heard in the hall, and the butler announced "Mr. and Miss Barron."

A tall man, with an iron-gray moustache and a determined carriage, entered the room, followed by a timid and stooping lady of uncertain age.

Mrs. Flaxman, transformed at once into the courteous hostess, greeted the newcomers with her sweetest smiles, set the deaf daughter down on the hearing side of Mr. Manvers, ordered tea, and herself took charge of Mr. Barron.

The task was not apparently a heavy one. Mrs. Flaxman saw beside her a portly man of fifty-five, with a penetrating look, and a composed manner; well dressed, yet with no undue display. Louis Manvers, struggling with an habitual plague of shyness, and all but silenced by the discovery that his neighbour was even deafer than himself, watched the "six-foot-two Inquistor" with curiosity, but could find nothing lurid nor torturous in his aspect. There was indeed something about him which displeased a rationalist scholar and ascetic. But his information and ability, his apparent adequacy to any company, were immediately evident. It seemed to Manvers that he had very quickly disarmed Mrs. Flaxman's vague prejudice against him. At any rate she was soon picking his brains diligently on the subject of the neighbourhood and the neighbours, and apparently enjoying the result, to judge from her smiles and her questions.

Mr. Barron indeed had everything that could be expected of him to say on the subject of the district and its population. He descanted on the beauty of the three or four famous parks, which in the eighteenth century had been carved out of the wild heath lands; he showed an intimate knowledge of the persons who owned the parks, and of their families, "though I myself am only a newcomer here, being by rights a Devonshire man"; he talked of the local superstitions with indulgence, and a proper sense of the picturesque; and of the colliers who believed the superstitions he spoke in a tone of general good humour, tempered by regret that "agitators" should so often lead them into folly. The architecture of the district came in, of course, for proper notice. There were certain fine old houses near that Mrs. Flaxman ought to visit; everything of course would be open to her and her husband.

"Oh, tell me," said Mrs. Flaxman, suddenly interrupting him, "how far is Sandford Abbey from here?"

Her visitor paused a moment before replying.

"Sandford Abbey is about five miles from you — across the park. The two estates meet. Do you know — Sir Philip Meryon?"

Rose Flaxman shrugged her shoulders.

"We know something of him — at least Hugh does. His mother was a very old friend of Hugh's family."

Mr. Barron was silent.

"Is he such a scamp?" said Mrs. Flaxman, raising her fine eyes, with a laugh in them. "You make me quite anxious to see him!"

Mr. Barron echoed the laugh, stiffly.

"I doubt whether your husband will wish to bring him here. He gathers some strange company at the Abbey. He is there now for the fishing."

Manvers inquired who this gentleman might be; and Mrs. Flaxman gave him a lightly touched account. A young man of wealth and family, it seemed, but spoilt from his earliest days, and left fatherless at nineteen, with only an adoring but quite ineffectual mother to take account of. Some notorious love affairs at home and abroad; a wild practical joke or two, played on prominent people, and largely advertised in the newspapers; an audacious novel, and a censored play — he had achieved all these things by the age of thirty, and was now almost penniless, and still unmarried.

"Hugh says that the Abbey is falling into ruin — and that the young man has about a hundred a year left out of his fortune. On this he keeps apparently an army of servants and a couple of hunters! The strange thing is — Hugh discovered it when he went to call on the. Rector the other day — that this preposterous young man is a first cousin of Mr. Meynell's. His mother, Lady Meryon, and the Rector's mother were sisters. The Rector, however, seems to have dropped him long ago."

Mr. Barron still sat silent.

"Is he really too bad to talk about?" cried Mrs. Flaxman, impatiently.

"I think I had rather not discuss him," said her visitor, with decision; and she, protesting that Philip Meryon was now endowed with all the charms, both of villainy and mystery, let the subject drop.

Mr. Barron returned, as though with relief, to architecture, talked agreeably of the glories of a famous Tudor house on the west side, and an equally famous Queen Anne house on the east side of the Chase. But the churches of the district, according to him, were on the whole disappointing — inferior to those of other districts within reach. Here, indeed, he showed himself an expert; and a far too minute discourse on the relative merits of the church architecture of two or three of the midland counties flowed on and on through Mrs. Flaxman's tea-making, while the deaf daughter became entirely speechless; and Manvers — disillusioned — gradually assumed an aspect of profound melancholy, which merely meant that his wits were wool gathering.

"Well, I thought Upcote Minor church a very pretty church," said Rose Flaxman at last, with a touch of revolt. "The old screen is beautiful — and who on earth has done all that carving of the pulpit — and the reredos?"

Mr. Barron's expression changed. He bent toward

his hostess, striking one hand sharply and deliberately with the glove which he held in the other.

"You were at church last Sunday?"

"I was." Mrs. Flaxman's eyes as she turned them upon him had recovered their animation.

"You were present then," said Mr. Barron with passionate energy, "at a scandalous performance! I feel that I ought to apologize to you and Mr. Flaxman in the name of our village and parish."

The speaker's aspect glowed with what was clearly a genuine fire. The slight pomposity of look and manner had disappeared.

Mrs. Flaxman hesitated. Then she said gravely: "It was certainly very astonishing. I never saw anything like it. But my husband and I liked Mr. Meynell. We thought he was absolutely sincere."

"He may be. But so long as he remains clergyman of this parish it is impossible for him to be honest!"

Mrs. Flaxman slowly poured out another cup of tea for Mr. Manvers, who was standing before her in a drooping attitude, like some long crumpled fly, apparently deaf and blind to what was going on, his hair falling forward over his eyes. At last she said evasively:

"There are a good many people in the parish who seem to agree with him. Except yourself — and a gaunt woman in black who was pointed out to me — everybody in the church appeared to us to be enjoying what the Rector was doing — to be entering into it heart and soul."

Mr. Barron flushed.

"We do not deny that he has got a hold upon the people. That makes it all the worse. When I came here three years ago he had not yet done any of these things — publicly; these perfectly monstrous things. Up to last Sunday, indeed, he kept within certain bounds as to the services; though frequent complaints of his teaching had been made to the Bishop, and proceedings even had been begun — it might have been difficult to touch him. But last Sunday!——" He stopped with a little sad gesture of the hand as though the recollection were too painful to pursue. "I saw, however, within six months of my coming here — he and I were great friends at first — what his teaching was, and whither it was tending. He has taught the people systematic infidelity for years. Now we have the results!"

"He also seems to have looked after their bodies," said Mrs. Flaxman, in a skirmishing tone that simply meant she was not to be brought to close quarters. I am told that it was he brought the water-supply here; and that he has forced the owners to rebuild some of the worst cottages."

Mr. Barron looked attentively at his hostess. It was as though he were for the first time really occupied with her — endeavouring to place her, and himself with regard to her. His face stiffened.

"That's all very well — excellent, of course. Only, let me remind you, he was not asked to take vows about the water-supply! But he did promise and vow at his ordination to hold the Faith — to 'banish and drive away strange doctrines'!"

"What are 'strange doctrines' nowadays?" said a mild, falsetto voice in the distance.

Barron turned to the speaker — the long-haired dishevelled person whose name he had not caught distinctly as Mrs. Flaxman introduced him. His manner unconsciously assumed a note of patronage.

"No need to define them, I think — for a Christian. The Church has her Creeds."

"Of course. But while this gentleman shelves them — no doubt a revolutionary proceeding — are there not excesses on the other side? May there not be too much — as well as too little?"

And with an astonishing command of ecclesiastical detail Manvers gave an account — gently ironic here and there — of some neo-Catholic functions of which he had lately been a witness.

Barron fidgeted.

"Deplorable, I admit — quite deplorable! I would put that kind of thing down, just as firmly as the other."

Manvers smiled.

"But who are 'you'? if I may ask it philosophically and without offence? The man here does not agree with you — the people I have been describing would scout you. Where's your authority? What is the authority in the English Church?"

"Well, of course we have our answer to that question," said Barron, after a moment.

Manvers gave a pleasant little laugh. "Have you?"

Barron hesitated again, then evidently found the controversial temptation too strong. He plunged head-long into a great gulf of cloudy argument, with the big word "authority" for theme. But he could find no foot-hold in the maze. Manvers drove him delicately from point to point, involving him in his own contradictions, rolling him in his own ambiguities, till — suddenly — vague recollections began to stir in the victim's mind. *Manvers?* Was that the name? It began to recall to him certain articles in the reviews, the Church papers. Was there not a well-known writer — a Dublin man — a man who had once been a clergyman, and had resigned his orders?

He drew himself together with dignity, and retreated in as good order as he could. Turning to Mrs. Flaxman, who was endeavouring to make a few commonplaces audible to Miss Barron, while throwing occasional sly glances toward the field of battle, he somewhat curtly asked for his carriage.

Mrs. Flaxman's hand was on the bell, when the draw-ing-room door opened to admit a gentleman.

"Mr. Meynell!" said the butler.

And at the same moment a young girl slipped in through the open French window, and with a smiling nod to Mrs. Flaxman and Mr. Manvers went up to the tea-table and began to replenish the teapot and relight the kettle.

Mr. Barron made an involuntary movement of annoyance as the Rector entered. But a few minutes of waiting before the appearance of his carriage was inevitable. He stood motionless therefore in his place, a handsome, impressive figure, while Meynell paid his respects to Mrs. Flaxman, whose quick colour betrayed a moment's nervousness.

"How are you, Barron?" said the Rector from a distance with a friendly nod. Then, as he turned to Manvers, his face lit up.

"I *am* glad to make your acquaintance!" he said cordially.

Manvers took the outstretched hand with a few mumbled words, but an evident look of pleasure.

"I have just read your Bishop Butler article in the *Quarterly*," said Meynell eagerly. "Splendid! Have you seen it?" He turned to his hostess, with one of the rapid movements that expressed the constant energy of the man.

Mrs. Flaxman shook her head.

"I am an ignoramus — except about music. I make Mr. Manvers talk to me."

"Oh, but you must read it! I hope you won't mind my quoting a long bit from it?" The speaker turned to Manvers again. "There is a clerical conference at Markborough next week, at which I am reading a paper. I want to make 'em all read you! What? Tea? I should think so!" Then, to his hostess : "Will you mind if I drink a good deal? I have just been down a pit — and the dust was pretty bad."

"Not an accident, I hope?" said Mrs. Flaxman, as she handed him his cup.

"No.   But a man had a stroke in the pit while he was at work.   They thought he was going to die — he was a great friend of mine — and they sent for me. We got him up with difficulty.   He has a bedridden wife — daughters all away, married.   Nobody to nurse him as usual.   I say!"— he bent forward, looking into his hostess's face with his small, vivacious eyes —"how long are you going to be here — at Maudeley?"

"We have taken the house for a year," said Rose, surprised.

"Will you give me a parish nurse for that time?   It won't cost much, and it will do a lot of good," said the Rector earnestly.   "The people here are awfully good to each other — but they don't know anything — poor souls — and I can't get the sick folk properly looked after.   Will you?"

Mrs. Flaxman's manner showed embarrassment.   Within a few feet of her sat the squire of the parish, silent and impassive.   Common report made Henry Barron a wealthy man.   He could, no doubt, have provided half a dozen nurses for Upcote Minor if he had so chosen. Yet here was she, the newcomer of a few weeks, appealed to instead!   It seemed to her that the Rector was not exactly showing tact.

"Won't Mr. Barron help?"   She threw a smiling appeal toward him.

Barron, conscious of an irritation and discomfort he had

some difficulty in controlling, endeavoured nevertheless to strike the same easy note as the rest. He gave
his reasons for thinking that a parish nurse was not
really required in Upcote, the women in the village being
in his opinion quite capable of nursing their husbands
and sons.

But all the time that he was speaking he was chafing
for his carriage. His conversation with Mrs. Flaxman
was still hot in his ears. It was all very well for Meynell
to show this levity, this callous indifference to the situation. But he, Barron, could not forget it. That
very week, the first steps had been taken which were to
drive this heretical and audacious priest from the office
and benefice he had no right to hold, and had so criminally
misused. If he submitted and went quietly, well and
good. But of course he would do nothing of the kind.
There was a lamentable amount of disloyalty and infidelity in the diocese, and he would be supported. An
ugly struggle was inevitable — a struggle for the honour
of Christ and his Church. It would go down to the roots
of things and was not to be settled or smoothed over
by a false and superficial courtesy. The days of friendship, of ordinary social intercourse, were over. Barron
did not intend to receive the Rector again within his
own doors, intimate as they had been at one time; and
it was awkward and undesirable that they should be
meeting in other people's drawing-rooms.

All these feelings were running through his mind while
aloud he was laboriously giving Mrs. Flaxman his reasons

for thinking a parish nurse unnecessary in Upcote Minor. When he came to the end of them, Meynell looked at him with amused exasperation.

"Well, all I know is that in the last case of typhoid we had here — a poor lad on Reynolds's farm — his mother got him up every day while she made his bed, and fed him — whatever we could say — on suet dumpling and cheese. He died, of course — what could he do? And as for the pneumonia patients, I believe they mostly eat their poultices — I can't make out what else they do with them — unless I stay and see them put on. Ah, well, never mind. I shall have to get Mrs. Flaxman alone, and see what can be done. Now tell me" — he turned again with alacrity to Manvers — "what's that new German book you quote about Butler? Some uncommonly fine things in it! That bit about the Sermons — admirable!"

He bent forward, his hands on his knees, staring at Manvers. Yet the eyes for all their intensity looked out from a face furrowed and pale — overshadowed by physical and mental strain. The girl sitting at the tea-table could scarcely take her eyes from it. It appealed at once to her heart and her intelligence. And yet there were other feelings in her which resisted the appeal. Once or twice she looked wistfully at Barron. She would gladly have found in him a more attractive champion of a majestic cause.

"What can my coachman be about?" said Barron impatiently. "Might I trouble you, Mrs. Flaxman, to

ring again? I really ought to go home." Mrs. Flaxman
rang obediently. The butler appeared. Mr. Barron's
servants, it seemed, were having tea.

"Send them round, please, at once," said their master,
frowning. "At once!"

But the minutes passed on, and while trying to keep
up a desultory conversation with his hostess, and with
the young lady at the tea-table, to whom he was not
introduced, Mr. Barron was all the while angrily conscious
of the conversation going on between the Rector and
Manvers. There seemed to be something personally
offensive and humiliating to himself in the knowledge
displayed by these two men — men who had deserted
or were now betraying the Church — of the literature of
Anglican apologetics, and of the thought of the great
Anglican bishop. Why this parade of useless learning
and hypocritical enthusiasm? What was Bishop Butler
to them? He could hardy sit patiently through it, and
it was with most evident relief that he rose to his feet
when his carriage was announced.

"How pretty Mrs. Flaxman is!" said his daughter as
they drove away. "Yet I'm sure she's forty, papa."

Her face still reflected the innocent pleasure that Rose
Flaxman's kindness had given her. It was not often
that the world troubled itself much about her. Her
father, however, took no notice. He sat absent and pondering, and soon he stretched out a peremptory hand and
lowered the window which his daughter had raised against

an east wind to protect a delicate ear and throat which had been the torment of her life. It was done with no conscious unkindness; far from it. He was merely absorbed in the planning of his campaign. The next all-important point was the selection of the Commission of Inquiry. No effort must be spared by the Church party to obtain the right men.

Meanwhile, in the drawing-room which he had left, there was silence for a moment after his departure. Then Meynell said:

"I am afraid I frightened him away. I beg your pardon, Mrs. Flaxman."

Rose laughed, and glanced at the girl sitting hidden behind the tea-table.

"Oh, I had had quite enough of Mr. Barron. Mr. Meynell, have I ever introduced you to my niece?"

"Oh, but we know each other!" said Meynell, eagerly. "We met first at Miss Puttenham's, a week ago — and since then — Miss Elsmere has been visiting a woman I know."

"Indeed?"

"A woman who lost her husband some days since — a terrible case. We are all so grateful to Miss Elsmere."

He looked toward her with a smile and a sigh; then as he saw the shy discomfort in the girl's face, he changed the subject at once.

The conversation became general. Some feeling that she could not explain to herself led Mrs. Flaxman into a closer observation of her niece Mary than usual. There was much affection between the aunt and the niece, but on Mrs. Flaxman's side, at least, not much understanding. She thought of Mary as an interesting creature, with some striking gifts — amongst them her mother's gift for goodness. But it seemed to the aunt that she was far too grave and reserved for her age; that she had been too strenuously brought up, and in a too narrow world. Rose Flaxman had often impatiently tried to enliven the girl's existence, to give her nice clothes, to take her to balls and to the opera. But Mary's adoration for her mother stood in the way.

"And really if she would only take a hand for herself" — thought Mrs. Flaxman — "she might be quite pretty! She is pretty!"

And she looked again at the girl beside her, wondering a little, as though a veil were lifted from something familiar. Mary was talking — softly, and with a delicate and rather old-fashioned choice of words, but certainly with no lack of animation. And it was quite evident to an inquisitive aunt with a notorious gift for match making that the tired heretic with the patches of coal dust on his coat found her very attractive.

But as the clock struck six Meynell sprang up.

"I must go. Miss Elsmere" — he looked toward her —"has kindly promised to take me on to see your sister at the Cottage — and after to-day I may not have another opportunity." He hesitated, considering his hostess — then burst out: "You were at church last Sunday — I know — I saw you. I want to tell you — that you have a church quite as near to you as the parish church, where everything is quite orthodox — the church at Haddon End. I wish I could have warned you. I — I did ask Miss Elsmere to warn her mother."

Rose looked at the carpet.

"You needn't pity us," she said, demurely. "Hugh wants to talk to you dreadfully. But — I am afraid I am a Gallio."

"Of course — you don't need to be told — it was all a deliberate defiance of the law — in order to raise vital questions. We have never done anything half so bad before. We determined on it at a public meeting last week, and we gave Barron and his friends full warning."

"In short, it is revolution," said Manvers, rubbing his hands gently, "and you don't pretend that it isn't."

"It is revolution!" said Meynell, nodding. "Or a forlorn hope! The laymen in the Church want a real franchise — a citizenship they can exercise — and a law of their own making!"

There was silence a moment. Mary Elsmere took up her hat, and kissed her aunt; Meynell made his farewells, and followed the girl's lead into the garden.

Mrs. Flaxman and Manvers watched them open the gate of the park and disappear behind a rising ground. Then the two spectators turned to each other by a common impulse, smiling at the same thought. Mrs.

Flaxman's smile, however, was almost immediately drowned in a real concern. She clasped her hands, excitedly.

"Oh! my poor Catharine! What would she — what *would* she say?"

CHAPTER IV

MEYNELL and his companion had taken a footpath winding gently down hill and in a north-
west direction across one of the most beautiful
parks in England. It lay on the fringe of the Chase and
contained, within its slopes and glades, now tracts of primitive woodland whence the charcoal burners seemed to
have but just departed; now purple wastes of heather, wild
as the Chase itself; or again, dense thickets of bracken and
fir, hiding primeval and impenetrable glooms. Maudeley
House, behind them, a seemly Georgian pile, with a colum-
nar front, had the good fortune to belong to a man not
rich enough to live in or rebuild it, but sufficiently attached to it to spend upon its decent maintenance the
money he got by letting it. So the delicately faded
beauty of the house had survived unspoilt; while there
had never been any money to spend upon the park,
where the woods and fences looked after themselves year
by year, and colliers from the neighbouring villages
poached freely.

The two people walking through the ferny paths leading
to the cottage of Forkéd Pond were not, however, paying
much attention to the landscape round them. Meynell
showed himself at first preoccupied and silent. A load

of anxiety depressed his vitality; and on this particular day long hours of literary work and correspondence, beginning almost with the dawn and broken only by the colliery scene of which he had spoken to Mrs. Flaxman, had left deep marks upon him. Yet the girl's voice and manner, and the fragments of talk that passed between them, seemed gradually to create a soothing and liberating atmosphere in which it was possible to speak with frankness, though without effort or excitement.

The Rector indeed had so far very little precise knowledge of what his companion's feeling might be toward his own critical plight. He would have liked to get at it; for there was something in this winning, reserved girl that made him desire her good opinion. And yet he shrank from any discussion with her.

He knew of course that the outlines of what had happened must be known to her. During the ten days since their first meeting both the local and London newspapers had given much space to the affairs of Upcote Minor. An important public meeting in which certain decisions had been taken with only three dissentients had led up to the startling proceedings in the village church which Mrs. Flaxman had described to Louis Manvers. The Bishop had written another letter, this time of a more hurried and peremptory kind. An account of the service had appeared in the *Times*, and columns had been devoted to it in various Mercian newspapers. After years of silence, during which his heart had burned within him; after a shorter period of

growing propaganda and expanding utterance, Meynell
realized fully that he had now let loose the floodgates.
All round him was rising that wide response from human
minds and hearts — whether in sympathy or in hostility
— which tests and sifts the man who aspires to be a
leader of men — in religion or economics. Every trade
union leader lifted on the wave of a great strike, representing the urgent physical need of his fellows, knows
what the concentration of human passion can be —
in matters concerned with the daily bread and the
homes of men. Religion can gather and bring to bear
forces as strong. Meynell knew it well; and he was like
a man stepping down into a rushing stream from which
there is no escape. It must be crossed — that is all
the wayfarer knows; but as he feels the water on his
body he realizes that the moment is perhaps for life or
death.

Such crises in life bring with them, in the case of the
nobler personalities, a great sensitiveness; and Meynell
seemed to be living in a world where not only his own
inner feelings and motives but those of others were
magnified and writ large. As he walked beside Mary
Elsmere his mind played round what he knew of her
history and position; and it troubled him to think that,
both for her and her mother, contact with him at this
particular moment might be the reviving of old sorrows.

As they paused on the top of a rising ground looking
westward he looked at her with sudden and kindly
decision.

"Miss Elsmere, are you sure your mother would like to see me? It was very good of you to request that I should accompany you to-night — but — are you sure?"

Mary coloured deeply and hesitated a moment.

"Don't you think I'd better turn back?" he asked her, gently. "Your path is clear before you." He pointed to it winding through the fern. "And you know, I hope, that anything I could do for you and your mother during your stay here I should be only too enchanted to do. The one thing I shrink from doing is to interfere in any way with her rest here. And I am afraid just now I might be a disturbing element."

"No, no! please come!" said Mary, earnestly. Then as she turned her head away, she added: "Of course — there is nothing new — to her ——"

"Except that my fight is waged from inside the Church — and your father's from outside. But that might make all the difference to her."

"I don't think so. It is" — she faltered — "the change itself. It is all so terrible to her."

"Any break with the old things? But doesn't it ever present itself to her — force itself upon her — as the upwelling of a new life?" he asked, sadly.

"Ah! — if it didn't in my father's case ——"

The girl's eyes filled with tears.

But she quickly checked herself, and they moved on in silence. Meynell, with his pastoral instinct and training, longed to probe and soothe the trouble he divined in her. A great natural dignity in the girl — delicacy of feeling in the man — prevented it.

None the less her betrayal of emotion had altered their relation; or rather had carried it farther. For he had already seen her in contact with tragic and touching things. A day or two after that early morning when he had told the outlines of the Batesons' story to the two ladies who had entertained him at breakfast he had found her in Bateson's cottage with his wife. Bateson was dead, and his wife in that dumb, automaton state of grief when the human spirit grows poisonous to itself. The young girl who came and went with so few words and such friendly timid ways had stirred, as it were, the dark air of the house with a breath of tenderness. She would sit beside the widow, sewing at a black dress, or helping her to choose the text to be printed on the funeral card; or she would come with her hands full of wild flowers, and coax Mrs. Bateson to go in the dusk to the churchyard with them. She had shown, indeed, wonderful inventiveness in filling the first week of loss and anguish with such small incident as might satisfy feeling, and yet take a woman out of herself.

The level sun shone full upon her as she walked beside him, and her face, her simple dress, her attitude stole gradually like a spell on the mind of her companion. It was a remarkable face; the lower lip a little prominent, and the chin firmly rounded. But the smile, though rare, was youth and sweetness itself, and the dark eyes beneath the full mass of richly coloured hair were finely

conscious and attentive — disinterested also; so that
they won the spectator instead of embarrassing him.
She was very lightly and slenderly made, yet so as to
convey an impression of strength and physical health.
Meynell said to himself that there was something cloistered in her look, like one brought up in a grave atmosphere — an atmosphere of "recollection." At the same
time nothing could be merrier — more childish even —
than her laugh.

Their talk flowed on, from subject to subject, yet always
tending, whether they would or no, toward the matter
which was inevitably in both their minds. Insensibly
the barrier between them and it broke away. Neither,
indeed, forgot the interposing shadow of Catharine
Elsmere. But the conversation touched on ideas; and
ideas, like fire in stubble, spread far afield. Oxford: the
influences which had worked on Elsmere, before Meynell's own youth felt them; men, books, controversies,
interwoven for Mary with her father's history, for Meynell with his own; these topics, in spite of misgivings
on both sides, could not but reveal them to each other.
The growing delight of their conversation was presently
beyond Meynell's resisting. And in Mary, the freedom
of it, no less than the sense of personal conflict and tragic
possibilities that lay behind it, awakened the subtlest
and deepest feelings. Poignant, concrete images rushed
through her mind — a dying face to which her own had
been lifted, as a tiny child; the hall of the New Brotherhood, where she sat sometimes beside her veiled mother;

the sad nobility of that mother's life; a score of trifling, heartpiercing things, that, to think of, brought the sob to her throat. Silent revolts of her own too, scattered along the course of her youth, revolts dumb, yet violent; longings for an "ampler ether" — for the great tumultuous clash of thought and doubt, of faith and denial, in a living and daring world. And yet again, times of passionate remorse, in which all movement of revolt had died away; when her only wish had been to smooth the path of her mother, and to soften a misery she but dimly understood.

So that presently she was swept away — as by some released long-thwarted force. And under the pressure of her quick, searching sympathy his talk became insensibly more personal, more autobiographical. He was but little given to confession, but she compelled it. It was as though through his story she sought to understand her father's — to unveil many things yet dark to her.

Thus gradually, through ways direct and indirect, the intellectual story of the man revealed itself to the pure and sensitive mind of the girl. She divined his home and upbringing — his father an Evangelical soldier of the old school, a home imbued with the Puritan and Biblical ideas. She understood something of the struggle provoked — after his ordination, in a somewhat late maturity — by the uprising of the typical modern problems, historical, critical, scientific. She pieced together much that only came out incidentally as to the counsellors within the Church to whom he had gone in his first urgent distress — the Bishop whom he reverenced — his old teachers at Oxford — the new lights at Cambridge.

And the card houses, the frail resting-places, thus built, it seemed, along the route, had lasted long; till at last a couple of small French books by a French priest and the sudden uprush of new life in the Roman Church had brought to the remote English clergyman at once the crystallization of doubt and the passion of a freed faith. "Modernism" — the attempt of the modern spirit, acting religiously, to refashion Christianity, not outside, but *inside*, the warm limits of the ancient churches — was born; and Richard Meynell became one of the first converts in England.

"Ah, if your father had but lived!" he said at last, turning upon her with emotion. "He died his noble death twenty years ago — think of the difference between then and now! Then the Broad Church movement was at an end. All that seemed so hopeful, so full of new life in the seventies, had apparently died down. Stanley, John Richard Green, Hugh Pearson were dead, Jowett was an old man of seventy; Liberalism within the Church hardly seemed to breathe; the judgment in the Voysey case — as much a defiance of modern knowledge as any Papal encyclical — though people had nearly forgotten it, had yet in truth brought the whole movement to a stand. All *within* the gates seemed lost. Your father went out into the wilderness, and there, amid everything that was poor and mean and new, he laid down his life. But we! — we are no longer alone,

or helpless. The tide has come up to the stranded ship —
the launching of it depends now only on the faithfulness
of those within it."

Mary was moved and silenced. The man's power, his
transparent purity of heart, affected her, as they had
already affected thousands. She was drawn to him also,
unconsciously, by that something in personality which
determines the relations of men and women. Yet
there were deep instincts in her that protested. Girl
as she was, she felt herself for the moment more alive
than he to the dead weight of the World, fighting the tug
of those who would fain move it from its ancient bases.

He seemed to guess at her thought; for he passed on
to describe the events by which, amid his own dumb or
hidden struggle, he had become aware of the same forces
working all round him; among the more intelligent and
quick-witted miners, hungry for history and science,
reading voraciously a Socialist and anti-Christian literature, yet all the while cherishing deep at heart certain
primitive superstitions, and falling periodically into hot
abysses of Revivalism, under the influence of Welsh
preachers; or among the young men of the small middle
class, in whom a better education was beginning to awaken
a number of new intellectual and religious wants; among
women, too, sensitive, intelligent women —

"Ah! but," said Mary, quickly interrupting him,
"don't imagine there are many women like Miss Puttenham! There are very, very few!"

He turned upon her with surprise.

"I was not thinking of Miss Puttenham, I assure you. She has taken very little part in this particular movement. I never know whether she is really with us. She stands outside the old things, but I can never make myself happy by the hope that I have been able to win her to the new!"

Mary looked puzzled — interrogative. But she checked her question, and drew him back instead to his narrative — to the small incidents and signs which had gradually revealed to him, among even his brother clergy, years before that date, the working of ideas and thoughts like his own. And now ——

He broke off abruptly.

"You have heard of our meeting last week?"

"Of course!"

"There were men there from all parts of the diocese — and some from other counties. It made me think of what a French Catholic Modernist said to me two years ago — 'Pius X may write encyclicals as he pleases — I could show him whole dioceses in France that are practically Modernist, where the Seminaries are Modernist, and two thirds of the clergy. The Bishop knows it quite well, and is helpless. Over the border perhaps you get an Ultramontane diocese, and an Ultramontane bishop. But the process goes on. Life and time are for *us!*'" He paused and laughed. "Ah, of course I don't pretend things are so here — yet. Our reforms in England — in Church and State — broaden slowly down. In France, reform, when it moves at all, tends to be catastrophic. But in the Markborough diocese alone we have won over perhaps a fifth of the clergy, and the dioceses all round are moving. As to the rapidity of the movement in the last few months it has been nothing short of amazing!"

"And what is the end to be? Not only — oh! not only — *to destroy!*" said Mary. The soft intensity of the voice, the beauty of the look, touched him strangely.

He smiled, and there was a silence for a minute, as they wandered downward through a purple stretch of heather to a little stream, sun-smitten, that lay across their path. Once or twice she looked at him timidly, afraid lest she might have wounded him.

But at last he said:

"Shall I answer you in the words of a beloved poet?

"'What though there still need effort, strife?
  Though much be still unwon?
Yet warm it mounts, the hour of life!
  Death's frozen hour is done!

"'The world's great order dawns in sheen
  After long darkness rude,
Divinelier imaged, clearer seen,
  With happier zeal pursued.

"'What still of strength is left, employ,
  This end to help attain —
*One common wave of thought and joy
  Lifting mankind again!*'

"There" — his voice was low and rapid — "*there* is the goal! a new *happiness:* to be reached through a new comradeship — a freer and yet intenser fellowship. We want to say to our fellowmen: 'Cease from groping

among ruins! — from making life and faith depend upon
whether Christ was born at Bethlehem or at Nazareth,
whether He rose or did not rise, whether Luke or some
one else wrote the Third Gospel, whether the Fourth Gospel is history or poetry. The life-giving force is *here*, and
now! It is burning in your life and mine — as it burnt
in the life of Christ. Give all you have to the flame of
it — let it consume the chaff and purify the gold. Take
the cup of cold water to the thirsty, heal the sick, tend
the dying, and feel it thrill within you — the ineffable,
the immortal life! Let the false miracle go! — the true
has grown out of it, up from it, as the flower from the
sheath.' Ah! but then" — he drew himself up unconsciously; his tone hardened — "we turn to the sons of
tradition, and we say: 'We too must have our rights in
what the past has built up, the past has bequeathed —
as well as you! Not for you alone, the institutions, the
buildings, the arts, the traditions, that the Christ-life
has so far fashioned for itself. They who made them are
our fathers no less than yours — give us our share in
them! — we claim it! Give us our share in the cathedrals and churches of our country — our share in the
beauty and majesty of our ancestral Christianity.' The
men who led the rebellion against Rome in the sixteenth
century claimed the *plant* of English Catholicism. 'We
are our fathers' sons, and these things are *ours!*' they
said, as they looked at Salisbury and Winchester. We
say the same — with a difference. 'Give us the rights
and the citizenship that belong to us! But do not

imagine that we want to attack yours. In God's name, follow your own forms of faith — but allow us ours also — within the common shelter of the common Church. We are children of the same God — followers of the same Master. Who made you judges and dividers over us? You shall not drive us into the desert any more. A new movement of revolt has come — an hour of upheaval — and the men, with it!'"

Both stood motionless, gazing over the wide stretch of country — wood beyond wood, distance beyond distance, that lay between them and the Welsh border. Suddenly, as a shaft of light from the descending sun fled ghostlike across the plain, touching trees and fields and farms in its path, two noble towers emerged among the shadows — characters, as it were, that gave a meaning to the scroll of nature. They were the towers of Markborough Cathedral. Meynell pointed to them as he turned to his companion, his face still quivering under the strain of feeling.

"Take the omen! It is for *them*, in a sense — a spiritual sense — we are fighting. They belong not to any body of men that may chance to-day to call itself the English Church. They belong to *England* — in her aspect of faith — and to the English people!"

There was a silence. His look came back to her face, and the prophetic glow died from his own. "I should be very, very sorry" — he said anxiously — "if anything I have said had given you pain."

Mary shook her head.

"No — not to me. I — I have my own thoughts. But one must think — of others." Her voice trembled. The words seemed to suggest everything that in her own personal history had stamped her with this sweet, shrinking look. Meynell was deeply touched. But he did not answer her, or pursue the conversation any farther. He gathered a great bunch of harebells for her, from the sun-warmed dells in the heather; and was soon making her laugh by his stories of colliery life and speech, *à propos* of the colliery villages fringing the plain at their feet.

The stream, as they neared it, proved to be the boundary between the heath land and the pastures of the lower ground. It ran fresh and brimming between its rushy banks, shadowed here and there by a few light ashes and alders, but in general open to the sky, of which it was the mirror. It shone now golden and blue under the deepening light of the afternoon; and two or three hundred yards away Mary Elsmere distinguished two figures walking beside it — a young man apparently, and a girl. Meynell looked at them absently.

"That's one of the most famous trout-streams in the Midlands. There should be a capital rise to-night. If that man has the sense to put on a sedge-fly, he'll get a creel-full."

"And what is that house among the trees?" asked his companion presently, pointing to a gray pile of building about a quarter of a mile away, on the other side of the stream. "What a wonderful old place!"

For the house that revealed itself stood with an impressive dignity among its stern and blackish woods. The long, plain front suggested a monastic origin; and there was indeed what looked like a ruined chapel at one end. Its whole aspect was dilapidated and forlorn; and yet it seemed to have grown into the landscape, and to be so deeply rooted in it that one could not imagine it away.

Meynell glanced at it.

"That is Sandford Abbey. It belongs, I regret to say, to a neer-do-weel cousin of mine who has spent all his time since he came into it in neglecting his duties to it. Provided the owner of it is safely away, I should advise you and Mrs. Elsmere to walk over and see it one day. Otherwise it is better viewed at a distance. At least those are my own sentiments!"

Mary followed the house with her eyes as they walked along the bank of the stream toward the two figures on the opposite bank.

A sudden exclamation from her companion caught her ear — and a light musical laugh. Startled by something familiar in it, Mary looked across the stream. She saw on the farther bank a few yards ahead a young man fishing, and a young girl in white sitting beside him.

"Hester! — Miss Fox-Wilton!" — the tone showed her surprise; "and who is that with her?"

Meynell, without replying, walked rapidly along the stream to a point immediately opposite the pair.

"Good afternoon, Philip. I did not know you were

here. Hester, I am going round by Forkéd Pond, and then home. I shall be glad to escort you."

"Oh! thank you — thank you *so* much. But it's very nice here. You can't think what a rise there is. I have caught two myself. Sir Philip has been teaching me."

"She frames magnificently!" said the young man. "How d'ye do, Meynell? A long time since we've met."

"A long time," said Meynell briefly. "Hester, will you meet Miss Elsmere and me at the bridge? We sha'n't take you much out of your way."

He pointed to a tiny wooden bridge across the stream, a hundred yards farther down.

A look of mischievous defiance was flung at Meynell across the stream. "I'm all right, I assure you. Don't bother about me. How do you do, Mary? We don't 'miss' each other, do we? Isn't it a lovely evening? Such good luck I wouldn't go with mother to dine at the White House! Don't you hate dinner parties? I told Mr. Barron that spiders were so much more refined than humans — they did at least eat their flies by themselves! He was quite angry — and I am afraid Stephen was too!"

She laughed again, and so did the man beside her. He was a dark, slim fellow, finely made, dressed in blue serge, and a felt hat, which seemed at the moment to be slipping over the back of his handsome head. From a little distance he produced an impression of Apollo-like strength and good looks. As the spectator came closer, this impression was a good deal modified by certain loose and common lines in the face. But from Mary Elsmere's position only Sir Philip Meryon's good points were visible, and he appeared to her a dazzling creature.

And in point of looks his companion was more than his match. They made indeed a brilliant pair, framed amid the light green of the river bank. Hester Fox-Wilton was sitting on a log with her straw hat on her lap. In pushing along the overgrown stream, the coils of her hair had been disarranged and its combs loosened. The hair was of a warm brown shade, and it made a cloud about her head and face, from which her eyes and smile shone out triumphantly. Exceptionally tall, with clear-cut aquiline features, with the movements and the grace of a wood nymph, the girl carried her beautiful brows and her full throat with a provocative and self-conscious arrogance. One might have guessed that fear was unknown to her; perhaps tenderness also. She looked much older than seventeen, until she moved or spoke; then the spectator soon realized that in spite of her height and her precocious beauty she was a child, capable still of a child's mischief.

And on mischief she was apparently bent this afternoon. Mary Elsmere, shyly amused, held aloof, while Meynell and Miss Fox-Wilton talked across the stream. Meynell's peremptory voice reached her now and then, and she could not help hearing a sharp final demand that the truant should transfer herself at once to his escort.

The girl threw him an odd look; she sprang to her feet, flushed, laughed, and refused.

"Very well!" said Meynell. "Then perhaps, as you won't join us, you will allow me to join you. Miss Elsmere, I am very sorry, but I am afraid I must put off my visit to your mother. Will you give her my regrets?"

The fury in Hester's look deepened. She lost her smile.

"I won't be watched and coerced! Why shouldn't I amuse myself as I please!"

Meanwhile Sir Philip Meryon had laid aside his rod and was apparently enjoying the encounter between his companion and the Rector.

"Perhaps you have forgotten — this is *my* side of the river, Meynell!" he shouted across it.

"I am quite aware of it," said the Rector, as he shook hands with the embarrassed Mary. She was just moving away with a shy good-bye to the angry young goddess on the farther bank, when the goddess said:

"Don't go, Mary! Here, Sir Philip — take the fly-book!" She flung it toward him. "Good night."

And turning her back upon him without any further ceremony, she walked quickly along the stream toward the little bridge which Meynell had pointed out.

"Congratulations!" said Meryon, with a mocking wave of the hand to the Rector, who made no reply. He ran to catch up Mary, and the two joined the girl in white at the bridge. The owner of Sandford Abbey stood meanwhile with his hand on his hip watching the receding figures. There was a smile on his handsome mouth, but it was an angry one; and his muttered remark as he turned away belied the unconcern he had affected.

"That comes, you see, of not letting me be engaged to Stephen!" said Hester in a white heat, as the three walked on together.

Mary looked at her in astonishment.

"I see no connection," was the Rector's quiet reply. "You know very well that your mother does not approve of Sir Philip Meryon, and does not wish you to be in his company."

"Precisely. But as I am not to be allowed to marry Stephen, I must of course amuse myself with some one else. If I can't be engaged to Stephen, I won't be anything at all to him. But, then, I don't admit that I'm bound."

"At present all you're asked" — said Meynell dryly — "is not to disobey your mother. But don't you think it's rather rude to Miss Elsmere to be discussing private affairs she doesn't understand?"

"Why shouldn't she understand them? Mary, my guardian here and my mother say that I mustn't be engaged to Stephen Barron — that I'm too young — or some nonsense of that kind. And Stephen — oh, well, Stephen's too good for this world! If he really loved me, he'd do something desperate, wouldn't he? — instead of giving in. I don't much mind, myself — I don't really care so much about marrying Stephen — only if I'm not to marry him, and somebody else wants to please me, why shouldn't I let him?"

She turned her beautiful wild eyes upon Mary Elsmere. And as she did so Mary was suddenly seized with a strong sense of likeness in the speaker — her gesture — her attitude — to something already familiar. She could not identify the something, but her gaze fastened itself on the face before her.

Meynell meanwhile answered Hester's tirade.

"I'm quite ready to talk this over with you, Hester, on our way home. But don't you see that you are making Miss Elsmere uncomfortable?"

"Oh, no, I'm not," said Hester coolly. "You've been talking to her of all sorts of grave, stupid things — and she wants amusing — waking up. I know the look of her. Don't you?" She slipped her arm inside Mary's. "You know, if you'd only do your hair a little differently — fluff it out more — you'd be so pretty! Let me do it for you. And you shouldn't wear that hat — no, you really shouldn't. It's a brute! I could trim you another in half an hour. Shall I? You know — I really like you. *He* sha'n't make us quarrel!"

She looked with a young malice at Meynell. But her brow had smoothed, and it was evident that her temper was passing away.

"I don't agree with you at all about my hat," said Mary with spirit. "I trimmed it myself, and I'm extremely proud of it."

Hester laughed out — a laugh that rang through the trees.

"How foolish you are! — isn't she, Rector? No! —
I suppose that's just what you like. I wonder what you
have been talking to her about? I shall make her tell
me. Where are you going to?"

She paused, as Mary and the Rector, at a point where
two paths converged, turned away from the path which
led back to Upcote Minor. Mary explained again that
Mr. Meynell and she were on the way to the Forkéd
Pond cottage, where the Rector wished to call upon her
mother.

Hester looked at her gravely.

"All right! — but your mother won't want to see me.
No! — really it's no good your saying she will. I saw
her in the village yesterday. I'm not her sort. Let
me go home by myself."

Mary half laughed, half coaxed her into coming with
them. But she went very unwillingly; fell completely
silent, and seemed to be in a dream all the way to the
cottage. Meynell took no notice of her; though once or
twice she stole a furtive look toward him.

The tiny house in which Catharine Elsmere and her
daughter had settled themselves for the summer stood
on a narrow isthmus of land belonging to the Maudeley
estate, between the Sandford trout-stream and a large
rushy pond of two or three acres. It was a very lonely
and a very beautiful place, though the neighbourhood
generally pronounced it damp and rheumatic. The
cottage, sheltered under a grove of firs, looked straight

out on the water, and over a bed of water-lilies. All
round was a summer murmur of woods, the call of water-
fowl, and the hum of bees; for, at the edges of the water,
flowers and grasses pushed thickly out into the sunlight
from the shadow of the woods.

By the waterside, with a book on her knee, sat a lady
who rose as they came in sight.

Meynell approached her, hat in hand, his strong
irregular face, which had always in it a touch of *naiveté*,
of the child, expressing both timidity and pleasure.
The memory of her husband was enshrined deep in the
minds of all religious liberals; and it was known to many
that while the husband and wife had differed widely
in opinion, and the wife had suffered profoundly from
the husband's action, yet the love between them had been,
from first to last, a perfect and a sacred thing.

He saw a tall woman, very thin, in a black dress. Her
brown hair, very lightly touched with gray and arranged
with the utmost simplicity, framed a face in which
the passage of years had emphasized and sharpened all
the main features, replacing also the delicate smoothness
of youth by a subtle network of small lines and shadows,
which had turned the original whiteness of the skin
into a brownish ivory, full of charm. The eyes looked
steadily out from their deep hollows; the mouth, austere
and finely cut, the characteristic hands, and the unconscious dignity of movement — these personal traits made
of Elsmere's wife, even in late middle age, a striking
and impressive figure.

Yet Meynell realized at once, as she just touched his offered hand, that the sympathy and the homage he would so gladly have brought her would be unwelcome; and that it was a trial to her to see him.

He sat down beside her, while Mary and Hester — who, on her introduction to Mrs. Elsmere, had dropped a little curtsey learnt at a German school, and full of grace — wandered off a little way along the water-side. Meynell, struggling with depression, tried to make conversation — on anything and everything that was not Upcote Minor, its parish, or its church. Mrs. Elsmere's gentle courtesy never failed; yet behind it he was conscious of a steely withdrawal of her real self from any contact with his. He talked of Oxford, of the great college where he had learnt from the same men who had been Elsmere's teachers; of current books, of the wild flowers and birds of the Chase; he did his best; but never once was there any living response in her quiet replies, even when she smiled.

He said to himself that she had judged him, and that the judgments of such a personality once formed were probably irrevocable. Would she discourage any acquaintance with her daughter? It startled him to feel how much the unspoken question hurt.

Meanwhile the eyes of his hostess pursued the two girls, and she presently called to them, greeting their reappearance with an evident change and relaxation of manner. She made Hester sit near her, and it was not long before the child, throwing off her momentary

awe, was chattering fast and freely, yet, as Mary perceived, with a tact, conscious or unconscious, that kept
the chatter within bounds.

Mrs. Elsmere watched the girl's beauty with evident
delight, and when Meynell rose to go, and Hester with
him, she timidly drew the radiant creature to her and
kissed her. Hester opened her big eyes with surprise.

Catharine Elsmere sat silent a moment watching the
two departing figures; then as Mary found a place in the
grass beside her, she said, with some constraint:

"You walked with him from Maudeley?"

"Mr. Meynell? Yes, I found him there at tea. He
was very anxious to pay his respects to you; so I brought
him."

"I can't imagine why he should have thought it
necessary."

Mary colored brightly and suddenly, under the vivacity
of the tone. Then she slipped her hand into her mother's.

"You didn't mind, dearest? Aunt Rose likes him
very much, and — and I wanted him to know you!" She
smiled into her mother's eyes. "But we needn't see
him any more if ——"

Mrs. Elsmere interrupted her.

"I don't wish to be rude to any friend of Aunt Rose's,"
she said, rather stiffly. "But there is no need we should
see him, is there?"

"No," said Mary; her cheek dropped against her
mother's knee, her eyes on the water. "No — not that

I know of." After a moment she added with apparent inconsequence, "You mean because of his opinons?"

Catharine gave a rather hard little laugh.

"Well, of course he and I shouldn't agree; I only meant we needn't go out of our way ——"

"Certainly not. Only I can't help meeting him sometimes!"

Mary sat up, smiling, with her hands round her knees. "Of course."

A pause. It was broken by the mother — as though reluctantly.

"Uncle Hugh was here while you were away. He told me about the service last Sunday. Your father would never — never — have done such a thing!"

The repressed passion with which the last words were spoken startled Mary. She made no reply, but her face, now once more turned toward the sunlit pond, had visibly saddened. Inwardly she found herself asking — "If father had lived? — if father were here now?"

Her reverie was broken by her mother's voice — softened — breathing a kind of compunction.

"I daresay he's a good sort of man."

"I think he is," said Mary, simply.

They talked no more on the subject, and presentlv Catharine Elsmere rose, and went into the house.

Mary sat on by the water-side thinking. Meynell's aspect, Meynell's words, were in her mind — little traits too and incidents of his parochial life that she had come across in the village. A man might preach and preach, and be a villain! But for a man — a hasty, preoccupied, student man — so to live, through twenty years, among these vigorous, quick-tempered, sharp-brained miners, as to hold the place among them Richard Meynell held, was not to be done by any mere pretender, any spiritual charlatan. How well his voice pleased her! — his tenderness to children — his impatience — his laugh.

The thoughts, too, he had expressed to her on their walk ran kindling through her mind. There were in her many half-recognized thirsts and desires of the spirit that seemed to have become suddenly strong and urgent under the spur of his companionship.

She sat dreaming; then her mother called her to the evening meal, and she went in. They passed the evening together, in the free and tender intimacy which was their habitual relation. But in the mind of each there were hidden movements of depression or misgiving not known to the other.

Meanwhile the Rector had walked home with his ward. A stormy business! For much as he disliked scolding any young creature, least of all, Hester, the situation simply could not be met without a scolding — by Hester's guardian. Disobedience to her mother's wishes; disloyalty toward those who loved her, including himself; deceit, open and unabashed, if the paradox may be allowed — all these had to be brought home to her. He talked, now tenderly, now severely, dreading to hurt her, yet hoping to make his blows smart enough to be remembered. She was not to make friends with

Sir Philip Meryon. She was not to see him or walk with him. He was not a fit person for her to know; and she must trust her elders in the matter.

"You are not going to make us all anxious and miserable, dear Hester!" he said at last, hoping devoutly that he was nearly through with his task. "Promise me not to meet this man any more!" He looked at her appealingly.

"Oh, dear, no, I couldn't do that," said Hester cheerfully.

"Hester!"

"I couldn't. I never know what I shall want to do. Why should I promise?"

"Because you are asked to do so by those who love you, and you ought to trust them."

Hester shook her head.

"It's no good promising. You'll have to prevent me."

Meynell was silent a moment. Then he said, not without sternness:

"We shall of course prevent you, Hester, if necessary. But it would be far better if you took yourself in hand."

"Why did you stop my being engaged to Stephen?" she cried, raising her head defiantly.

He saw the bright tears in her eyes, and melted at once.

"Because you are too young to bind yourself, my child. Wait a while, and if in two years you are of the same mind, nobody will stand in your way."

"I sha'n't care a rap about him in two years," said Hester vehemently. "I don't care about him now. But

I should have cared about him if I had been engaged to
him. Well, now, you and mamma have meddled — and
you'll see!"

They were nearing the opening of the lane which led
from the main road to North Leigh, Lady Fox-Wilton's house. As she perceived it Hester suddenly took
to flight, and her light form was soon lost to view in the
summer dusk.

The Rector did not attempt to pursue her. He turned
back toward the Rectory, perturbed and self-question-
ing. But it was not possible, after all, to set a tragic
value on the love affair of a young lady who, within
a week of its breaking off, had already consoled herself
with another swain. Anything less indicative of a broken
heart than Hester's behaviour during that week the
Rector could not imagine. Personally he believed that
she spoke the simple truth when she said she no longer
cared for Stephen. He did not believe she ever had
cared for him.

Still he was troubled, and on his way toward the
Rectory he turned aside. He knew that on his table
he should find letters waiting that would take him half
the night. But they must lie there a bit longer. At
Miss Puttenham's gate he paused, hesitated a moment,
then went straight into the twilight garden, where he
imagined that he should find its mistress.

He found her, in a far corner, among close-growing
trees and with her usual occupations, her books and her
embroidery, beside her. But she was neither reading

nor sewing. She sprang up to greet him, and for an hour of summer twilight they held a rapid, low-voiced conversation.

When he pressed her hand at parting they looked at each other, still overshadowed by the doubt and perplexity which had marked the opening of their interview. But he tried to reassure her.

"Put from you all idea of immediate difficulty," he said earnestly. "There really is none — none at all. Stephen is perfectly reasonable, and as for the escapade to-day ——"

The woman before him shook her head.

"She means to marry at the earliest possible moment — simply to escape from Edith — and that house. We sha'n't delay it long. And who knows what may happen if we thwart her too much?"

"We *must* delay it a year or two, if we possibly can — for her sake — and for yours," said Meynell firmly. "Good night, my dear friend. Try and sleep — put the anxiety away. When the moment comes — and of course I admit it must come — you will reap the harvest of the love you have sown. She does love you! — I am certain of that."

He heard a low sound — was it a sobbing breath? — as Alice Puttenham disappeared in the darkness which had overtaken the garden.

CHAPTER V

BREAKFAST at the White House, Upcote Minor, was an affair of somewhat minute regulation.

About a fortnight after Mr. Barron's call on the new tenants of Maudeley Hall, his deaf daughter Theresa entered the dining-room as usual on the stroke of half-past eight. She glanced round her to see that all was in order, the breakfast table ready, and the chairs placed for prayers. Then she went up to a side-table on which was placed a large Bible and prayer-book and a pile of hymn-books. She looked at the lessons and psalms for the day and placed markers in the proper places. Then she chose a hymn, and laid six open hymn-books one upon another. After which she stood for a moment looking at the first verse of the psalm for the day: "I will lift up mine eyes unto the hills, from whence cometh my help." The verse was one of her favourites, and she smiled vaguely, like one who recognizes in the distance a familiar musical phrase.

Theresa Barron was nearly thirty. She had a long face with rather high cheek-bones, and timid gray eyes. Her complexion was sallow, her figure awkward. Her only beauty indeed lay in a certain shy and fleeting charm of expression, which very few people noticed. She passed

generally for a dull and plain woman, ill-dressed, with a
stoop that was almost a deformity, and a deafness that
made her socially useless.   But the young servants whom
she trained, and the few poor people on her father's estate
to whom she was allowed to minister, were very fond of
"Miss Theresa."   But for her, the owner of Upcote
Minor Park would have been even more unpopular than
he was, indoors and out.   The wounds made by his
brusque or haughty manner to his inferiors were to a
certain extent healed by the gentleness and the good
heart of his daughter.   And a kind of glory was reflected
on him by her unreasoning devotion to him.   She suffered under his hardness or his self-will, but she adored
him all the time; nor was her ingenuity ever at a loss for
excuses for him.   He always treated her carelessly, sometimes contemptuously; but he would not have known how
to get through life without her, and she was aware of it.

On this August morning, having rung the bell for the
butler, she placed the Bible and prayer-book beside her
father's chair, and opening the door between the library
and the dining-room, she called, "Papa!"

Through the farther door into the hall there appeared
a long procession of servants, headed by the butler,
majestically carrying the tea-urn.   Something in this
daily procession, and its urn-bearer, had once sent
Stephen Barron, the eldest son — then an Eton boy just
home from school — into an uncontrollable fit of laughter,
which had cost him his father's good graces for a week.
But the procession had been in no way affected, and

at this later date Stephen on his visits home took it as
gravely as anybody else.

The tea-urn, pleasantly hissing, was deposited on the
white cloth; the servants settled themselves on their
chairs, while Theresa distributed the open hymn-books
amongst them; and when they were all seated, the master
of the house, like a chief actor for whom the stage waits,
appeared from the library.

He read a whole chapter from the Bible. It told the
story of Gehazi, and he read it with an emphasis which
the footman opposite to him secretly though vaguely
resented; then Theresa at the piano played the hymn,
in which the butler and the scullery-maid supported the
deep bass of Mr. Barron and the uncertain treble of his
daughter. The other servants remained stolidly silent,
the Scotch cook in particular looking straight before her
with dark-spectacled eyes and a sulky expression. She
was making up her mind that either she must be excused
from prayers in future, or Mr. Barron must be content
with less cooking for breakfast.

After the hymn, the prayer lasted about ten minutes.
Stephen, a fervently religious mind, had often fidgeted
under the minute and detailed petitions of it, which
seemed to lay down the Almighty's precise course of
action toward mankind in general for the ensuing day.
But Theresa, who was no less spiritual, under other forms,
took it all simply and devoutly, and would have been
uncomfortable if any item in the long catalogue had been
omitted. When the Amen came, the footman, who never

knew what to do with his legs during the time of kneeling, sprang up with particular alacrity.

As soon as the father and daughter were seated at breakfast — close together, for the benefit of Theresa's deafness — Mr. Barron opened the post-bag and took out the letters. They arrived half an hour before breakfast, but were not accessible to any one till the master of the house had distributed them.

Theresa looked up from hers with an exclamation.

"Stephen hopes to get over for dinner to-night!"

"Unfortunate — as I may very probably not see him," said her father, sharply. "I am going to Markborough, and may have to stay the night!"

"You are going to see the Bishop?" asked his daughter, timidly. Her father nodded, adding after a minute, as he began upon his egg:

"However, I must have some conversation with Stephen before long. He knows that I have not felt able to stay my hand to meet his wishes; and perhaps now he will let me understand a little more plainly than I do, what his own position is."

The speaker's tone betrayed bitterness of feeling. Theresa looked pained.

"Father, I am sure ——"

"Don't be sure of anything, my dear, with regard to Stephen! He has fallen more and more under Meynell's influence of late, and I more than suspect that when the time comes he will take sides openly with him. It will be a bitter blow to me, but that he doesn't consider. I

don't expect consideration from him, either as to that —
or other things. Has he been hanging round the Fox-
Wiltons lately as usual?"

Theresa looked troubled.

"He told me something the other night, father, I
ought to have told you. Only ——"

"Only what? I am always kept in the dark between
you."

"Oh, no, father! but it seems to annoy you, when —
when I talk about Stephen, so I waited. But the Rector
and Lady Fox-Wilton have quite forbidden any engagement between Stephen and Hester. Stephen *did* propose
— and they said — not for two years at least."

"You mean to say that Stephen actually was such a
fool?" said her father violently, staring at her.

Theresa nodded.

"A girl of the most headstrong and frivolous character!
— a trouble to everybody about her. Lady Fox-Wilton
has often complained to me that she is perfectly unman-
ageable with her temper and her vanity! The worst
conceivable wife for a clergyman! Really, Stephen ——"

The master of the house pushed his plate away from
him in speechless disgust.

"And both Lady Fox-Wilton and the Rector have
always taken such trouble about her — much more than
about the other children!" murmured Theresa, helplessly.

"What sort of a bringing up do you think Meynell
can give anybody?" said her father, turning upon her.

Theresa only looked at him silently, with her large

mild eyes. She knew it was of no use to argue. Besides, on the subject of the Rector she very much agreed with her father. Her deafness and her isolation had entirely protected her from Meynell's personal influence.

"A man with no religious principles — making a god of his own intellect — steeped in pride and unbelief — what can he do to train a girl like Hester? What can he do to train himself?" thundered Barron, bringing his hand down on the table-cloth.

"Every one says he is a good man," said Theresa, timidly.

"In outward appearance. What's that? A man like Meynell, who has thrown over the Christian faith, may fall into sin at any moment. His unbelief is the result of sin. He can neither help himself — nor other people — and you need never be surprised to find that his supposed goodness is a mere sham and delusion. I don't say it is always so, of course," he added.

Theresa made no reply, and the subject dropped. Barron returned to his letters, and presently Theresa saw his brow darken afresh over one of them.

"Anything wrong, father?"

"There's always something wrong on this estate. Crawley [Crawley was the head keeper] has caught those boys of John Broad again trespassing and stealing wood in the west plantation! Perfectly abominable! It's the second or third time. I shall give Broad notice at once, and we must put somebody into that cottage who will behave decently!"

"Poor Broad!" said Theresa, with her gentle, scared look. "You know, father, there isn't a cottage to be had in the village — and those boys have no mother — and John works very hard."

"Let him find another cottage all the same," said Barron briefly. "I shall go round, if I do get back from Markborough, and have a talk with him this evening."

There was silence for a little. Theresa was evidently sad. "Perhaps Lady Fox-Wilton would find him something," she said anxiously at last. "His mother was her maid long ago. First she was their schoolroom maid — then she went back to them, when her husband died and John married, and was a kind of maid housekeeper. Nobody knew why Lady Fox-Wilton kept her so long. They tell you in the village she had a shocking temper, and wasn't at all a good servant. Afterward I believe she went to America and I think she died. But she was with them a long while. I daresay they'd do something for John."

Barron made no reply. He had not been listening, and was already deep in other correspondence.

One letter still remained unopened. Theresa knew very well that it was from her brother Maurice, in London. And presently she pushed it toward Barron.

"Won't you open it? I do want to know if it's all right."

Barron opened it, rather unwillingly. His face cleared, however, as he read it.

"Not a bad report. He seems to like the work, and

says they treat him kindly.   He would like to come down for the Sunday — but he wants some money."

"He oughtn't to!" cried Theresa, flushing.   "You gave him plenty."

"He makes out an account," said her father, glancing at the letter; "I shall send him a small cheque.   I must say, Theresa, you are always rather inclined to a censorious temper toward your brother."

He looked at her with an unusual vivacity in his hard, handsome face.   Theresa hastily excused herself, and the incident dropped.   But when breakfast was over and her father had left the room, Theresa remained sitting idly by the table, her eyes fixed on the envelope of Maurice's letter, which had fallen to the floor.   Maurice's behaviour was simply disgraceful!   He had lost employment after employment by lazy self-indulgence, trusting always to his father's boundless affection for him, and abusing it time after time.   Theresa was vaguely certain that he was besmirched by all sorts of dreadful things — drinking, and betting — if not worse.   Her woman's instinct told her much more than his father had ever discovered about him.   Though at the same time she had the good sense to remind herself that her own small knowledge of the world might lead her to exaggerate Maurice's misdoings.   And for herself and Stephen, no less than for her father, Maurice was still the darling and Benjamin of the family, commended to them by a precious mother whose death had left the whole moral structure of their common life insecure.

She was still absorbed in uneasy thoughts about her brother, when the library door opened violently and her father came in with the Markborough *Post* in his hand.

His face was discomposed; his hand shook. Theresa sprang up.

"What is the matter, father?"

He pointed to the first page of the paper, and to the heading — "Extraordinary meeting at Markborough. Proceedings against the Rector of Upcote. Other clergy and congregations rally to his support."

She read the account with stupefaction. It described a meeting summoned by the "Reformers' Club" of Markborough to consider the announcement that a Commission of Inquiry had been issued by the Bishop of Markborough in the case of the Rector of Upcote Minor, and that legal proceedings against him for heretical teaching and unauthorized services would be immediately begun by certain promoters, as soon as the Bishop's formal consent had been given.

The meeting, it seemed, had been so crowded and tumultuous that adjournment had been necessary from the rooms of the Reformers' Club to the Town Hall. And there, in spite of a strong orthodox opposition, a resolution in support of the Rector of Upcote had been passed, amid scenes of astonishing enthusiasm. Three or four well-known local clergy had made the most outspoken speeches, declaring that there must be room made within the church for the liberal wing, as well as for the

Ritualist wing; that both had a right to the shelter of the common and ancestral fold; and that the time had come when the two forms of Christianity now prevailing in Christendom should be given full and equal rights within the Church of the nation.

Meynell himself had spoken, urging on the meeting the profound responsibility resting on the Reformers — the need for gentleness no less than for courage; bidding them remember the sacredness of the ground they were treading, the tenacity and depth of the roots they might be thought to be disturbing.

"Yet at the same time we must *fight!* — and we must fight with all our strength.   For over whole classes of this nation, Christianity is either dying or dead; and it is only we — and the ideas we represent — that can save it."

The speech had been received with deep emotion rather than applause; and the meeting had there and then proceeded to the formation of a "Reformers' League" to extend throughout the diocese.   "It is already rumoured," said the *Post*, "that at least sixteen or eighteen beneficed clergy, with their congregations, have either joined, or are about to join, the Reformers. The next move now lies with the Bishop, and with the orthodox majority of the diocese.   If we are not mistaken, Mr. Meynell and his companions in heresy will very soon find out that the Church has still power enough to put down such scandalous rebellions against her power and authority as that of the Rector of Upcote, and to purge her borders of disloyal and revolutionary priests."

Theresa looked up. Her face had grown pale. "How *terrible*, father! Did you know they were to hold the meeting?"

"I heard something about a debate at this precious club. What does that matter? Let them blaspheme in private as they please, it hurts nobody but themselves. But a public meeting at the Bishop's very door — and eighteen of his clergy!"

He paced the room up and down, in an excitement he could hardly control. "The poor, poor Bishop!" said Theresa, softly, the tears in her eyes.

"He will have the triumph of his life!" exclaimed Barron, looking up. "If there are dry bones on our side, this will put life into them. Those fellows have given themselves into our hands!"

He paused in his walk, falling into a profound reverie in which he lost all sense of his daughter's presence. She dared not rouse him; and indeed the magnitude of the scandal and distress left her speechless. She could only think of the Bishop — their frail, saintly Bishop whom every one loved. At last a clock struck. She said gently:

"Father, I think it is time to go."

Barron started, drew a long breath, gathered up the newspaper, and took a letter from his pocket.

"That is for Maurice. Put in anything you like, but don't miss the morning post."

"Do you see the Bishop this morning, father?"

"No — this afternoon.   But there will be plenty to do this morning." He named two or three heads of the church party in Markborough on whom he must call. He must also see his solicitor, and find out whether the counsel whom the promoters of the writ against Meynell desired to secure had been already retained.

He kissed his daughter absently and departed, settling all his home business before he left the house in his usual peremptory manner, leaving behind him indeed in the minds of his butler and head gardener, who had business with him, a number of small but smarting wraths, which would ultimately have to be smoothed away by Theresa.

But when Theresa explored the open envelope he had given her for her brother, she found in it a cheque for £50, and a letter which seemed to Maurice's sister — unselfish and tender as she was — deplorably lacking in the scolding it ought to have contained.   If only her father had ever shown the same affection for Stephen!

Meanwhile as Barron journeyed to Markborough, under the shadow of the great Cathedral, quite another voice than his was in possession of the episcopal ear.   Precisely at eleven o'clock Richard Meynell appeared on the doorstep of the Palace, and was at once admitted to the Bishop's study.

As he entered tne large book-lined room his name was announced in a tone which did not catch the Bishop's attention, and Meynell, as he hesitatingly advanced, became the spectator of a scene not intended for his

"Meynell, as he hesitatingly advanced, became the spectator
of a scene not intended for his eyes"

eyes. On the Bishop's knee sat a little girl of seven or eight. She was crying bitterly, and the Bishop had his arms round her and was comforting her.

"There *was* bogies, grandfather! — there *was!* — and Nannie said I told lies — and I didn't tell lies."

"Darling, there aren't bogies anywhere — but I'm sure you didn't tell lies. What did you think they were like?"

"Grandfather, they was all black — and they jumped — and wiggled — and spitted — o-o-oh!"

And the child went off in another wail, at which moment the Bishop perceived Meynell. His delicate cheek flushed, but he held up his hand, in smiling entreaty; and Meynell disappeared behind a revolving bookcase.

The Bishop hastily returned to the charge, endeavouring to persuade his little granddaughter that the "bogie" had really been "cook's black cat," generally condemned to the kitchen and blackbeetles, but occasionally let loose to roam the upper floors in search of nobler game. The child dried her eyes, and listened, gravely weighing his remarks. Her face gradually cleared, and when at the end he said slyly, "And even if there were bogies, little girls shouldn't throw hairbrushes at their Nannies!" she nodded a judicial head, adding plaintively:

"But then Nannies mustn't talk *all* the time, grandfather! Little girls must talk a itty itty bit. If Nannies not let them, little girls *must* frow somefing at Nannies."

The Bishop laughed — a low, soft sound, from which Meynell in the distance caught the infection of mirth.

A few murmured words — no doubt a scolding — and then:

"Are you good, Barbara?"

"Ye-s," said the child, slowly — "not very."

"Good enough to say you're sorry to Nannie?"

The child smiled into his face.

"Go along then, and say it!" said the Bishop, "and mind you say it nicely."

Barbara threw her arm round his neck and hugged him passionately. Then he set her down, and she ran happily away, through a door at the farther end of the room.

Meynell advanced, and the Bishop came to meet him. Over both faces, as they approached each other, there dropped a sudden shadow — a tremor as of men who knew themselves on the brink of a tragical collision — decisive of many things. And yet they smiled, the presence of the child still enwrapping them.

"Excuse these domesticities," said the Bishop, "but there was such woe and lamentation just before you came. And childish griefs go deep. Bogies — of all kinds— have much to answer for!"

Then the Bishop's smile disappeared. He beckoned Meynell to a chair, and sat down himself.

Francis Craye, Bishop of Markborough, was physically a person of great charm. He was small — not more than five foot seven; but so slenderly and perfectly made, so graceful and erect in bearing, that his height, or lack of it, never detracted in the smallest degree from his dignity, or from the reverence inspired by the innocence and un-

worldliness of his character.   A broad brow, overshadowing and overweighting the face, combined, with extreme
delicacy of feature, a touch of emaciation, and a pure
rose in the alabaster of the cheeks, to produce the aspect
of a most human ghost — a ghost which had just tasted
the black blood, and recovered for an hour all the vivacity
of life.   The mouth, thin-lipped and mobile to excess,
was as apt for laughter as for tenderness; the blue eyes
were frankness and eagerness itself.   And when the
glance of the spectator pursued the Bishop downward,
it was to find that his legs, in the episcopal gaiters, were
no less ethereal than his face; while his silky white hair
added the last touch of refinement to a personality of
spirit and fire.

Meynell was the first to speak.

"My lord! let me begin this conversation by once
more thanking you — from my heart — for all the personal kindness that you have shown me in the last few
months, and in the correspondence of the last fortnight."

His voice wavered a little.   The Bishop made no sign.

"And perhaps," Meynell resumed, "I felt it the kindest
thing of all that — after the letters I have written you
this week — after the meeting of yesterday — you should
have sent me that telegram last night, saying that you
wished to see me to-day.   That was like you — that
touched me indeed!"   He spoke with visible emotion.

The Bishop looked up.

"There can be no question, Meynell, of any personal
enmity between yourself and me," he said gravely.   "I

shall act in the matter entirely as the responsibilities of my office dictate — that you know. But I have owed you much in the past — much help — much affection. This diocese owes you much. I felt I must make one last appeal to you — terrible as the situation has grown. You could not have foreseen that meeting of yesterday!" he added impetuously, raising his head.

Meynell hesitated.

"No, I had no idea we were so strong. But it might have been foreseen. The forces that brought it about have been rising steadily for many years."

There was no answer for a moment. The Bishop sat with clasped hands, his legs stretched out before him, his white head bent. At last, without moving, he said :

"There are grave times coming on this diocese, Meynell — there are grave times coming on the Church!"

"Does any living church escape them?" said Meynell, watching him — with a heavy heart.

The Bishop shook his head.

"I am a man of peace. Where you see a hope of victory for what you think, no doubt, a great cause, I see above the mêlée, Strife and Confusion and Fate — "red with the blood of men." What can you — and those who were at that meeting yesterday — hope to gain by these proceedings? If you could succeed, you would break up the Church, the strongest weapon that exists in this country against sin and selfishness — and who would be the better?"

"Believe me — we sha'n't break it up."

"Certainly you will! Do you imagine that men who are the spiritual sons and heirs of Pusey and Liddon are going to sit down quietly in the same church with you and the eighteen who started this League yesterday? They would sooner die."

Meynell bore the onslaught quietly.

"It depends upon our strength," he said slowly, "and the strength we develop, as the fight goes on."

"Not at all! — a monstrous delusion!" The Bishop raised an indignant brow. "If you overwhelmed us — if you got the State on your side, as in France at the Revolution—you would still have done nothing toward your end — nothing whatever! We refuse — we shall always refuse — to be unequally yoked with those who deny the fundamental truths of the Faith!"

"My lord, you are so yoked at the present moment," said Meynell firmly — the colour had flashed back into his cheeks — "it is the foundation of our case that half the educated men and women we gather into our churches to-day are — in our belief — Modernists already. Question them! — they are with us — not with you. That is to say, they have tacitly shaken off the old forms — the Creeds and formularies that bind the visible, the legal, church. They do not even think much about them. Forgive me if I speak plainly! They are not grieving about the old. Their soul — those of them, I mean that have the gift of religion — is travailing — dumbly travailing — with the new. Slowly, irresistibly, they are evolving for themselves new forms, new creeds, whether they know it or not. You — the traditional party — you, the bishops and the orthodox majority — can help them, or hinder them. If you deny them organized expression and outlet, you prolong the dull friction between them and the current Christianity. You waste where you might gather — you quench where you might kindle. But there they are — in the same church with you — and you cannot drive them out!"

The Bishop made a sound of pain.

"I wish to drive no one out," he said, lifting a diaphanous hand. "To his own master let each man stand or fall. But you ask us — *us*, the appointed guardians of the Faith — the *ecclesia docens* — the historic episcopate — to deny and betray the Faith! You ask us to assent formally to the effacing of all difference between Faith and Unfaith — you bid us tell the world publicly that belief matters nothing — that a man may deny all the Divine Facts of Redemption, and still be as good a Christian as any one else. History alone might tell you — and I am speaking for the moment as a student to a student — that the thing is inconceivable!"

"Unless — *solvitur vivendo!*" said Meynell in a low voice. "What great change in the religious life of men has not seemed inconceivable — till it happened? Think of the great change that brought this English Church into being! Within a couple of generations men had to learn to be baptized, and married, and buried, with rites unknown to their fathers — to stand alone and cut off from the great whole of Christendom — to which they

had once belonged — to see the Mass, the cult of Our
Lady and the Saints, disappear from their lives. What
change that any Modernist proposes could equal that?
But England lived through it! — England emerged! —
she recovered her equilibrium. Looking back upon it
all now, we see — you and I agree there — that it was
worth while — that the energizing, revealing power
behind the world was in the confusion and the dislocation;
and that England gained more than she lost when she
made for herself an English and a national Church in
these islands, out of the shattered débris of the Roman
system."

He bent forward, and looked intently into the Bishop's
face. "What if another hour of travail be upon us?
And is any birth possible without pain?"

"Don't let us argue the Reformation!" said the Bishop,
with a new sharpness of note. "We should be here all
night. But let me at least point out to you that the
Church kept her Creeds! — the Succession! — the four
great Councils! — the unbroken unity of essential dogma.
But you" — he turned with renewed passion on his
companion — "what have you done with the Creeds?
Every word in them steeped in the heart's blood of generations! — and you put them aside as a kind of theological
bric-à-brac that concerns us no more. Meynell! — you
have no conception of the forces that this movement
of yours, if you persist in it, will unchain against you!
You are like children playing with the lightning!"

Denunciation and warning sat with a curious majesty

on the little Bishop as he launched these words.   It was with a visible effort that Meynell braced himself against them.

"Perhaps I estimate the forces for and against differently from yourself, Bishop.   But when you prophesy war, I agree.   There will be war! — and that makes the novelty of the situation.   Till now there has never been equality enough for war.   The heretic has been an excrescence to be cut away.   Now you will have to make some terms with him!   For the ideas behind him have invaded your inmost life.   They are all about you and around you — and when you go out to fight him, you will discover that you are half on his side!"

"If that means," said the Bishop impatiently, "that the Church is accessible to new ideas — that she is now, as she has always been, a learned Church — the Church of Westcott and Lightfoot, of a host of younger scholars who are as well acquainted with the ideas and contentions of Modernism — as you call it — as any Modernist in Europe — and are still the faithful servants and guardians of Christian dogma — why, then, you say what is true!   We perfectly understand your positions — and we reject them."

Through Meynell's expression there passed a gleam — slight and gentle — of something like triumph.

"Forgive me! — but I think you have given me my point.   Let me recall to you the French sayings — 'Comprendre, c'est pardonner — Comprendre, c'est aimer.'   It is because for the first time you do under-

stand them — that, for the first time, the same arguments
play upon you as play upon us — it is for that very reason
that we regard the field as half won, before the battle
is even joined."

The Bishop gazed upon him with a thin, dropping lip —
an expression of suffering in the clear blue eyes.

"That Christians" — he said under his breath —
"should divide the forces of Christ — with the sin and
misery of this world devouring and defiling our brethren
day by day!"

"What if it be not 'dividing' — but doubling —
the forces of Christ!" said Meynell, with pale resolution.
"All that we ask is the Church should recognize existing
facts — that organization should shape itself to reality.
In our eyes, Christendom is divided to-day — or is rapidly
dividing itself — into two wholly new camps. The division between Catholic and Protestant is no longer the
supreme division; for the force that is rising affects both
Protestant and Catholic equally. Each of the new divisions has a philosophy and a criticism of its own; each
of them has an immense hold on human life, though
Modernism is only now slowly realizing and putting out
its power. Two camps! — two systems of thought! —
both of them *Christian* thought. Yet one of them, one
only, *is in possession* of the churches, the forms, the
institutions; the other is everywhere knocking at the
gates. 'Give us our portion!' — we say — 'in Christ's
name.' But *only our portion!* We do not dream of
dispossessing the old — it is the last thing, even, that we

desire. But for the sake of souls now wandering and desolate, we ask to live side by side with the old — in brotherly peace, in equal right — sharing what the past has bequeathed! Yes, even the loaves and fishes! — they ought to be justly divided out like the rest. But, above all, the powers, the opportunities, the trials, the labours of the Christian Church!"

"In other words, so far as the English Church is concerned, you propose to reduce us within our own borders to a peddling confusion of sects, held together by the mere physical link of our buildings and our endowments!" said the Bishop, as he straightened himself in his chair.

He spoke with a stern and contemptuous force which transformed the small body and sensitive face. In the old room, the library of the Palace, with its rows of calf-bound folios, and its vaulted fifteenth century roof, he sat as the embodiment of ancient, inherited things, his gentleness lost in that collective, that corporate, pride which has been at once the noblest and the deadliest force in history.

Meynell's expression changed, in correspondence. It, too, grew harder, more challenging.

"My lord — is there no loss already to be faced, of another kind? — is all well with the Church? How often have I found you here — forgive me! — grieving for the loss of souls — the decline of faith — the empty churches — the dwindling communicants — the spread of secularist literature — the hostility of the workmen!

And yet what devotion, what zeal, there is in this diocese, beginning with our Bishop. Have we not often asked ourselves what such facts could possibly mean — why God seemed to have forsaken us?"

"They mean luxury and selfishness — the loss of discipline at home and abroad," said the Bishop, with bitter emphasis. "It is hard indeed to turn the denial of Christ into an argument against His Gospel!"

Meynell was silent. His heart was burning within him with a passionate sense at once of the vast need and hungry unrest so sharply dismissed by the Bishop, and of the efficacy of that "new teaching" for which he stood. But he ceased to try and convey it by argument. After a few moments he began in his ordinary voice to report various developments of the Movement in the diocese of which he believed the Bishop to be still ignorant.

"We wish to conceal nothing from you," he said at last with emotion; "and consistently with the trial of strength that must come, we desire to lighten the burden on our Bishop as much as we possibly can. This will be a solemn testing of great issues — we on our side are determined to do nothing to embitter or disgrace it."

The Bishop, now grown very white, looked at him intently.

"I make one last appeal, Meynell, to your obedience — and to the promises of your ordination."

"I was a boy then" — said Meynell slowly — "I am a man now. I took those vows sincerely, in absolute good faith; and all the changes in me have come about, as it seems to me, by the inbreathing of a spirit not my own — partly from new knowledge — partly in trying to help my people to live — or to die. They represent to me things lawfully — divinely — learnt. So that in the change itself, I cannot acknowledge or feel wrongdoing. But you remind me — as you have every right to do — that I accepted certain rules and conditions. Now that I break them, must I not resign the position dependent on them? Clearly, if it were a question of any ordinary society. But the Christian Church is not an ordinary society! It is the sum of Christian life!"

The Bishop raised a hand of protest, but without speaking. Meynell resumed:

"And that Life makes the Church — moulds it afresh, from age to age. There are times — we hold — when the Church very nearly expresses the Life; there are others when there are great discordances between the Life, and its expression in the Church. We believe that there are such discordances now because — once more — of a New Learning. And we believe that to withdraw from the struggle to make the Church more fully represent the Life would be sheer disloyalty and cowardice. We must stay it out, and do our best. We are not dishonest, for, unlike many Liberals of the past and the present — we speak out! We are inconsistent indeed with a past pledge; but are we any more inconsistent than the High Churchman who repudiates the 'blasphemous fables' of the Mass when he signs the Articles, and then encourages adoration of the Reserved Sacrament in his church?"

The Bishop made no immediate reply. He was at that moment involved in a struggle with an incumbent in Markborough itself who under the very shadow of the Cathedral had been celebrating the Assumption of the Blessed Virgin in flat disobedience to his diocesan. His mind wandered for a minute or two to this case. Then, rousing himself, he said abruptly, with a keen look at Meynell:

"I know of course that, in your case, there can be no question of clinging to the money of the Church."

Meynell flushed.

"I had not meant to speak of it — but your lordship knows that all I receive from my living is given back to church purposes. I support myself by what I write. There are others of us who risk much more than I — who risk indeed their all!"

"You have done a noble work for your people, Meynell." The Bishop's voice was not unlike a groan.

"I have done nothing but what was my bounden duty to do."

"And practically your parish is with you in this terrible business?"

"The church people in it, by an immense majority — and some of the dissenters. Mr. Barron, as you know, is the chief complainant, and there are of course some others with him."

"I expect to see Mr. Barron this afternoon," remarked the Bishop, frowning.

Meynell said nothing.

The Bishop rose.

"I understand from your letter this morning that you have no intention of repeating the service of last Sunday?"

"Not at present. But the League will go to work at once on a revised service-book."

"Which you propose to introduce on a given Sunday — in all the Reformers' churches?"

"That is our plan."

"You are quite aware that this whole scheme may lead to tumults — breaches of the peace?"

"It may," said Meynell reluctantly.

"But you risk it?"

"We must," said Meynell, after a pause.

"And you refuse — I ask you once more — to resign your living, at my request?"

"I do — for the reasons I have given."

The Bishop's eyes sparkled.

"As to my course," he said, dryly, "Letters of Request will be sent at once to the Court of Arches preferring charges of heretical teaching and unauthorized services against yourself and two other clergy. I shall be represented by so-and-so." He named the lawyers.

They stood, exchanging a few technical informations of this kind for a few minutes. Then Meynell took up his hat. The Bishop hesitated a moment, then held out his hand.

Meynell grasped it, and suddenly stooped and kissed the episcopal ring.

"I am an old man" — said the Bishop brokenly — "and a weary one. I pray God that He will give me strength to bear this burden that is laid upon me."

Meynell went away, with bowed head. The Bishop was left alone. He moved to the window and stood looking out. Across the green of the quadrangle rose the noble mass of the Cathedral. His lips moved in prayer; but all the time it was as though he saw beside the visible structure — its ordered beauty, its proud and cherished antiquity — a ruined phantom of the great church, roofless and fissured, its sacred places open to the winds and rains, its pavements broken and desolate.

The imagination grew upon him, and it was only with a great effort that he escaped from it.

"My bogies are as foolish as Barbara's," he said to himself with a smile as he went back to the daily toil of his letters.

CHAPTER VI

MEYNELL left the Palace shaken and exhausted. He carried in his mind the image of his Bishop, and he walked in bitterness of soul. The quick, optimistic imagination which had alone made the action of these last weeks possible had for the moment deserted him, and he was paying the penalty of his temperament.

He turned into the Cathedral, and knelt there some time, conscious less of articulate prayer than of the vague influences of the place; the warm gray of its shadows, the relief of its mere space and silence, the beauty of the creeping sunlight — gules, or, and purple — on the spreading pavements. And vaguely — while the Bishop's grief still, as it were, smarted within his own heart — there arose the sense that he was the mere instrument of a cause; that personal shrinking and compunction were not allowed him; that he was the guardian of nascent rights and claims far beyond anything affecting his own life. Some such conviction is essential to the religious leader — to the enthusiast indeed of any kind; and it was not withheld from Richard Meynell.

When he rose and went out, he saw coming toward him a man he knew well — Fenton, the Vicar of a church on the outskirts of Markborough, famous for its "high" doctrine and services; a young boyish fellow, curly haired, in whom the "gayety" that Catholicism, Anglican or Roman, prescribes to her most devout children was as conspicuous as an ascetic and labourious life. Meynell loved and admired him. At a small clerical meeting the two men had once held an argument that had been long remembered — Fenton maintaining hotly the doctrine of an intermediate and purgatorical state after death, basing it entirely on a vision of Saint Perpetua recorded in the Acta of that Saint. Impossible, said the fair-haired, frank-eyed priest — who had been one of the best wicket-keeps of his day at Winchester — that so solemn a vision, granted to a martyr, at the moment almost of death, could be misleading. Purgatory therefore must be accepted and believed, even though it might not be expedient to proclaim it publicly from an Anglican pulpit. "Since the evening when I first read the Acta of SS. Perpetua and Felicitas," said the speaker, with an awed sincerity, "I have never doubted for myself, nor have I dared to hide from my penitents what is my own opinion."

In reply, Meynell, instead of any general argument, had gently taken the very proof offered him — *i.e.*, the vision — dissecting it, the time in which it arose, and the mind in which it occurred, with a historical knowledge and a quick and tender penetration which had presently absorbed the little company of listeners, till Fenton said abruptly, with a frown of perplexity:

"In that way, one might explain anything — the Trans-figuration for instance — or Pentecost."

Meynell looked up quickly.

"Except — the mind that dies for an idea!"

Yet the encounter had left them friends; and the two men had been associated not long afterward in a heroic attempt to stop some dangerous rioting arising out of a strike in one of the larger collieries.

Meynell watched the young figure of Fenton approaching through the bands of light and shadow in the great nave. As it came nearer, some instinct made him stand still, as though he became the mere spectator of what was about to happen. Fenton lifted his head; his eyes met Meynell's, and, without the smallest recognition, his gaze fixed on the pavement, he passed on toward the east end of the Cathedral.

Meynell straightened himself for a minute's "recollection," and went his way. On the pavement outside the western portal he ran into another acquaintance — a Canon of the Cathedral — hurrying home to lunch from a morning's work in the Cathedral library. Canon France looked up, saw who it was, and Meynell, every nerve strained to its keenest, perceived the instant change of expression. But there was no ignoring him, though the Canon did not offer to shake hands.

"Ah! Meynell, is that you? A fine day at last!"

"Yes, we may save the harvest yet!" said Meynell, pausing in his walk.

A kind of nervous curiosity bade him try and detain

the Canon. But France — a man of sixty-five, with a large Buddha-like face, and a pair of remarkably shrewd and humorous black eyes — looked him quickly over from top to toe, and hurried on, throwing a "good-bye" over his shoulder. When he and Meynell had last met it had been to talk for a friendly hour over Monseigneur Duchesne's last book and its bearing on Ultramontane pretensions; and they had parted with a cordial grip of the hand, promising soon to meet again.

"Yet he knew me for a heretic then!" thought Meynell. "I never made any secret of my opinions."

All the same, as he walked on, he forced himself to acknowledge to the full the radical change in the situation. Acts of war suspend the normal order; and no combatant has any right to complain.

Then a moment's weariness seized him of the whole train of thought to which his days and nights were now committed, and he turned with eagerness to look at the streets of Markborough, full of a market-day crowd, and of "the great mundane movement." Farmers and labourers were walking up and down; oxen and sheep in the temporary pens of the market-place were waiting for purchasers; there was a Socialist lecturer in one corner, and a Suffragist lady on a wagon in another. The late August sun shone upon the ruddy faces and broad backs of men to whom certainly it did not seem to be of great importance whether the Athanasian Creed were omitted from the devotions of Christian people or no. There was a great deal of chaffering going on; a little courting, and some cheating. Meynell recognized some of his parishioners, spoke to a farmer or two, exchanged greeting with a sub-agent of the miners' union, and gave some advice to a lad of his choir who had turned against the pits and come to "hire" himself at Markborough.

It was plain to him, however, after a little, that although he might wish to forget himself among the crowd, the crowd was on the contrary rather sharply aware of the Rector of Upcote. He perceived as he moved slowly up the street that he was in fact a marked man. Looks followed him; and the men he knew greeted him with a difference.

A little beyond the market-place he turned down a narrow street leading to the mother church of the town — an older foundation even than the Cathedral. Knocking at the door in the wall, he was admitted to an old rectory house, adjacent to the church, and in its low-ceiled dining-room he found six of the already famous "eighteen" assembled, among them the two other clergy who with himself had been singled out for the first testing prosecution. A joint letter was being drawn up for the press.

Meynell was greeted with rejoicing — a quiet rejoicing, as of men occupied with grave matters, that precluded any ebullience of talk. With Meynell's appearance, the meeting became more formal, and it was proposed to put the Vicar of the ancient church under whose shadow they were gathered, into the chair. The old man, Treherne by name, had been a double-first in days when double-firsts were everything, and in a class-list not much more modern than Mr. Gladstone's. He was a gentle, scholarly person, silent and timid in ordinary life, and his adhesion to the "eighteen" had been an astonishment to friends and foes. But he was not to be inveigled into the "chair" on any occasion, least of all in his own dining-room.

"I should keep you here all night, and you would get nothing done," he said with a smiling wave of the hand. "Besides — *excludat jurgia finis!* — let there be an age-limit in all things! Put Meynell in. It is he that has brought us all into this business."

So, for some hours or more, Meynell and the six grappled with the letter that was to convey the challenge of the revolted congregations to the general public through the *Times*. It was not an easy matter, and some small jealousies and frictions lifted their heads that had been wholly lost sight of in the white-hot feeling of the inauguration meeting.

Yet on the whole the seven men gathered in this room were not unworthy to lead the "forlorn hope" they had long determined on. Darwen — young, handsome, spiritual, a Third Classic, and a Chancellor's medallist; Waller, his Oxford friend, a man of the same type, both representing the recent flowing back of intellectual forces into the Church which for nearly half a century had abandoned her; Petitôt, Swiss by origin, small, black-eyed, irrepressible, with a great popularity among the hosiery operatives of whom his parish was mainly composed; Derrick, the Socialist, of humble origin and starved education, yet possessed of a natural sway over men, given him by a pair of marvellous blue eyes, a character of transparent simplicity, a tragic honesty and the bitter-sweet gift of the orator; Chesham, a man who had left the army for the Church, had been grappling for ten years with a large parish of secularist artisans, and was now preaching Modernism with a Franciscan fervour and success; and Rollin, who owned a slashing literary style, was a passionate Liberal in all fields, had done excellent work in the clearing and cleaning of slums, with much loud and unnecessary talk by the way, and wrote occasionally for the *Daily Watchman*. Chesham and Darwen were Meynell's co-defendants in the suit brought by the Bishop.

Rollin alone seemed out of place in this gathering of men, drawing tense breath under a new and almost unbearable responsibility. He was so in love with the sensational, notoriety side of the business, so eager to pull wires, and square editors, so frankly exultant in the "big row" coming on, that Meynell, with the Bishop's face still in his mind, could presently hardly endure him. He felt as Renan toward Gavroche. Was it worth while to go through so much that Rollin might cut a figure, and talk at large about "modern thought?"

However Darwen and Waller, Derrick also, were just as determined as Meynell to keep down the frothy self-advertising element in the campaign to the minimum that human nature seems unable to do without. So that

Rollin found himself gradually brought into line, being not a bad fellow, but only a common one; and he abandoned with much inward chagrin the project of a flaming "interview" for the *Daily Watchman* on the following day.

And indeed, as this handful of men settled down to the consideration of the agenda for a large conference to be held in Markborough the following week, there might have been discerned in six of them, at least, a temper that glorified both them and their enterprise; a temper of seriousness, courage, unalterable conviction, with such delicacy of feeling as befits men whose own brethren and familiar companions have become their foes.   They were all pastors in the true sense, and every man of them knew that in a few months he would probably have lost his benefice and his prospects.   Only Treherne was married, and only he and Rollin had private means.

Meynell was clearly their leader.   Where the hopefulness of the others was intermittent his was constant; his knowledge of the English situation generally, as well as of the lie of forces in the Markborough district, was greater than theirs; and his ability as a writer made him their natural exponent.   It was he who drew up the greater part of their "encyclical" for the press; and by the time the meeting was over he had so heightened in them the sense of mission, so cheered them with the vision of a wide response from the mind of England, that all lesser thoughts were sunk, and they parted in quietness and courage.

Meynell left the outskirts of Markborough by the Maudeley road, meaning to walk to Upcote by Forkéd Pond and Maudeley Park.

It was now nearly a fortnight since he had seen Mary Elsmere, and for the first time, almost, in these days of storm and stress could the mind make room for some sore brooding on the fact. He had dined at Maudeley, making time with infinite difficulty; Mrs. Elsmere and her daughter were not there. He had asked Mrs. Flaxman to tea at the Rectory, and had suggested that she should bring her sister and her niece. Mr. and Mrs. Flaxman appeared — without companions. Once or twice he had caught sight of Mary Elsmere's figure in the distance of Miss Puttenham's garden. Yet he had not ventured to intrude upon the two friends. It had seemed to him by then it must be her will to avoid him, and he respected it.

As to other misgivings and anxieties, they were many. As Meynell entered the Maudeley lane, with the woods of Sandford Abbey on his left, and the little trout-stream flashing and looping through the water meadows on his right, his mind was often occupied by a conversation between himself and Stephen Barron which had taken place the night before. Meynell could not but think of it remorsefully.

"And I can explain nothing — to make it easier for the poor old fellow — nothing! He thinks if we had allowed the engagement, it would all have come right — he would have got a hold upon her, and been able to shape her.

Oh, my dear boy — my dear boy! Yet, when the time comes, Stephen shall have any chance, any help, I can give him — unless indeed she has settled her destiny for herself by then, without any reference to us. And Stephen shall know — what there is to know!"

As to Hester herself, she seemed to have been keeping the Fox-Wilton household in perpetual fear. She went about in her mocking, mysterious way, denying that she knew anything about Sir Philip Meryon, or had any dealings with him. Yet it was shrewdly suspected that letters had passed between them, and Hester's proceedings were so quick-silverish and incalculable that it was impossible to keep a constant watch upon her. In the wilderness of Maudeley Park, which lay directly between the two houses, they might quite well have met — they probably had met. Meynell noticed and rebuked in himself a kind of settled pessimism as to Hester's conduct and future. "Do what you will," it seemed to say — "do all you can — but that life has in it the ferments of tragedy."

Had they at least been doing all they could? he asked himself anxiously, vowing that no public campaign must or should distract him from a private trust much older than it, and no less sacred. In the midst of the turmoil of these weeks he had been corresponding on Lady Fox-Wilton's behalf with a lady in Paris to whom a girl of Hester's age and kind might be safely committed for the perfecting of her French and music. It had been necessary to warn the lady that in the case of such a pensionnaire as Hester the male sex might give trouble; and Hester had not yet signified her gracious consent to go.

But she would go — she must go — and either he or Alice Puttenham would take her over and install her. Good heavens, if one had only Edith Fox-Wilton to depend on in these troubles!

As for Philip Meryon, he was, of course, now and always, a man of vicious habits and no scruples. He seemed to be staying at Sandford with the usual crew of flashy, disreputable people, and to allow Hester to run any risks with regard to him would be simply criminal. Yet with so inefficient a watch-dog as Lady Fox-Wilton, who could guarantee anything? Alice, of course, thought of nothing else than Hester, night and day. But it was part of the pathos of the situation that she had so little influence on the child's thoughts and deeds.

Poor, lonely woman! In Alice's sudden friendship for Mary Elsmere, her junior by some twelve years, the Rector, with an infinite pity, read the confession of a need that had become at last intolerable. For these seventeen years he had never known her make an intimate friend, and to see her now with this charming, responsive girl was to realize what the long hunger for affection must have been. Yet even now, how impossible to satisfy it, as other women could satisfy it! What ghosts and shadows about the path of friendship!

"A dim and perilous way," his mind went sounding back along the intricacies of Alice Puttenham's story.

The old problems arose in connection with it — problems now of ethics, now of expediency. And interfused with them a sense of dull amazement and yet of intolerable repetition — in this difficulty which had risen with regard to Hester. The owner of Sandford — *and Hester!* When he had first seen them together, it had seemed a thing so sinister that his mind had refused to take it seriously. A sharp word to her, a word of warning to her natural guardians — and surely all was mended. Philip never stayed more than three weeks in the old house; he would very soon be gone, and Hester's fancy would turn to something else.

But that the passing shock should become anything more! There rose before Meynell's imagination a vision of the two by the river, not in the actual brightness of the August afternoon, but bathed, as it were, in angry storm-light; behind them, darkness, covering "old, unhappy, far-off things." From that tragical gloom it seemed as though their young figures had but just emerged, unnaturally clear; and yet the trailing clouds were already threatening the wild beauty of the girl.

He blamed himself for lack of foresight. It should have been utterly impossible for those two to meet! Meryon generally appeared at Sandford three times a year, for various sporting purposes. Hester might easily have been sent away during these descents. But the fact was she had grown up so rapidly — yesterday a mischievous child, to-day a woman in her first bloom — that they had all been taken by surprise. Besides, who could have imagined any communication whatever between the Fox-Wilton household and the riotous party at Sandford Abbey?

As to the girl herself, Meynell was always conscious of being engaged in some long struggle to save and protect his ward against her will.   There were circumstances connected with Hester that should have stirred in the few people who knew them a special softness of heart in regard to her.   But it was not easy to feel it.   The Rector had helped two women to watch over her upbringing; he had brought her to her first communion, and tried hard, and quite in vain, to instil into her the wholesome mysticisms of the Christian faith; and the more efforts he made, the more sharply was he aware of the hard, egotistical core of the girl's nature, of Hester's fatal difference from other girls.

And yet, as he thought of her with sadness and perplexity, there came across him the memory of Mrs. Elsmere's sudden movement toward Hester; how she had drawn the child to her and kissed her — she, so unearthly and so spiritual, whose very aspect showed her the bondswoman of Christ.

The remembrance rebuked him, and he fell into fresh plans about the child.   She must be sent away at once!— and if there were really any sign of entanglement he must himself go to Sandford and beard Philip in his den. There was knowledge in his possession that might be used to frighten the fellow.   He thought of his cousin with loathing and contempt.

But — to do him justice — Meryon knew nothing of those facts that gave such an intolerable significance to any contact whatever between his besmirched life and that of Hester Fox-Wilton.

Meryon knew nothing — and Stephen knew nothing — nor the child herself. Meynell shared his knowledge with only two other persons — no! — three. Was that woman, that troublesome, excitable woman, whose knowledge had been for years the terror of three lives — was she alive still? Ralph Fox-Wilton had originally made it well worth her while to go to the States. That was in the days when he was prepared to pay anything. Then for years she had received an allowance, which, however, Meynell believed had stopped sometime before Sir Ralph's death. Meynell remembered that the stopping of it had caused some friction between Ralph and his wife. Lady Fox-Wilton had wished it continued. But Ralph had obstinately refused to pay any more. Nothing had been heard of her, apparently, for a long while. But she had still a son and grand-children living in Upcote vilage.

Meynell opened the gate leading into the Forkéd Pond enclosure. The pond had been made by the damming of part of the trout stream at the point where it entered the Maudeley estate, and the diversion of the rest to a new channel. The narrow strip of land between the pond and the new channel made a little waterlocked kingdom of its own for the cottage, which had been originally a fishing hut, built in an Izaak Walton-ish mood by one of the owners of Maudeley. But the public footpath through the park ran along the farther side of the pond, and the doings of the inhabitants of the cottage, thick though the leafage was, could sometimes be observed from it.

Involuntarily Meynell's footsteps lingered as the little thatched house became visible, its windows set wide to the sounds and scents of the September day. There was conveyed to him a sense of its warm loneliness in the summer nights, of the stars glimmering upon it through the trees, of the owls crying round it. And within — in one of those upper rooms — those soft deep eyes, at rest in sleep? — or looking out, perhaps, into the breathing glooms of the wood? — the sweet face propped on the slender hand.

He felt certain that the inner life of such a personality as Mary Elsmere was rich and passionate. Sometimes, in these lonely hours, did she think of the man who had told her so much of himself on that, to him, memorable walk? Meynell looked back upon the intimate and autobiographical talk into which he had been led, with some wonder and a hot cheek. He had confessed himself partly to Elsmere's daughter, on a hint of sympathy, as to one entitled to such a confidence, so to speak, by inheritance, should she desire it; but still more — he owned it — to a delightful woman. It was the first time in Meynell's strenuous life, filled to the brim with intellectual and speculative effort on the one hand, and with the care of his parish on the other, that he had been conscious of any such feeling as now possessed him. In his first man-hood it had been impossible for him to marry, because he had his brothers to educate. And when they were safely out in the world the Rector, absorbed in the curing of sick bodies and the saving of sick souls, could not dream of spending the money thus set free on a household for himself.

He had had his temptations of the flesh, his gusts of inclination, like other men. But he had fought them down victoriously, for conscience sake; and it was long now since anything of the sort had assailed him.

He paused a moment among the trees, just before the cottage passed out of sight. The sun was sinking in a golden haze, the first prophecy of autumnal mists. Broad lights lay here and there upon the water, to be lost again in depths of shadow, wherein woods of dream gave back the woods that stooped to them from the shore. Every-thing was so still he could hear the fish rising, the run of a squirrel along a branch, the passage of a coot through the water.

The very profoundity of nature's peace suddenly showed him to himself. A man engaged in a struggle beyond his power! — committed to one of those tasks that rend and fever the human spirit even while they ennoble it! He had talked boldly to Stephen and the Bishop of "war" — "inevitable" and "necessary war." At the same time there was no one who would suffer from war more than he. The mere daily practice of Christianity, as a man's life-work, is a daily training in sensitiveness, involves a daily refining of the nerves. When a man so trained, so refined, takes up the public tasks of leadership and organization, in this noisy, hard-hitting world, his nature is set at enmity with itself. Meynell did not yet know whether the mystic in him would allow the fighter in him to play his part.

If the memory of Fenton's cold, unrecognizing eyes and rigid mouth, as they passed each other in the silence of the Cathedral, had power to cause so deep a stab of pain, how was he to brace himself in the future to what must come? — the alienation of friend after friend, the condemnation of the good, the tumult, the poisoned feeling, the abuse, public and private.

Only by the help of that Power behind the veil of things, perceived by the mind of faith! " '*Thou, Thou art being and breath!*' — Thine is this truth, which, like a living hand, bridles and commands me. Grind my life as corn in Thy mill! — but forsake me not! Nay, Thou wilt not, Thou canst not forsake me!"

No hope for a man attempting such an enterprise as Meynell's but in this simplicity, this passion of self-surrender. Without it no adventure in the spiritual fight has ever touched and fired the heart of man. Meynell was sternly and simply aware of it.

But how is this temper, this passion, kindled?

The answer flashed. Everywhere the divine ultimate Power mediates itself through the earthly elements and forces, speaks through small, childish things, incarnates itself in lover, wife, or friend — flashing its mystic fire through the web of human relations.   It seemed to Meynell, as he stood in the evening stillness by the pond, hidden from sight by the light brushwood round him, that, absorbed as he had been from his youth in the symbolism and passion of the religious life, as other men are absorbed in art or science, he had never really understood one of these great words by which he imagined himself to live — Love, or Endurance, or Sacrifice, or Joy — because he had never known the most sacred, the most intimate, things of human life out of which they grow.

And there uprose in him a sudden yearning — a sudden flame of desire — for the revealing love of wife and child.   As it thrilled through him, he seemed to be looking down into the eyes — so frank, so human — of Mary Elsmere.

Then while he watched, lost in feeling, yet instinctively listening for any movement in the wood, there was a flicker of white among the trees opposite.   A girl, book in hand, came down to the water's edge, and paused there a little, watching the glow of sunset on the water.   Meynell retreated farther into the wood; but he was still able to see her.   Presently she sat down, propping herself against a tree, and began to read.

Her presence, the grace of her bending neck, informed the silence of the woods with life and charm.   Meynell watched her a few moments in a trance of pleasure. But memory broke in upon the trance and scattered all his pleasure.   What reasonable hope of winning the daughter of that quiet, indomitable woman, who, at their first meeting, had shown him with such icy gentleness the gulf between himself and them?

And yet between himself and Mary he knew that there was no gulf. Spiritually she was her father's child, and not her mother's.

But to suppose that she would consent to bring back into her mother's life the same tragic conflict, in new form, which had already rent and seared it, was madness. He read his dismissal in her quiet avoidance of him ever since she had been a witness of her mother's manner toward him.

No. Such a daughter would never inflict a second sorrow, of the same kind, on such a mother. Meynell bowed his head, and went slowly away. It was as though he left youth and all delightfulness behind him, in the deepening dusk of the woods.

While Meynell was passing through the woods of Forkéd Pond a very different scene, vitally connected with the Rector and his fortunes, was passing a mile away, in a workman's cottage at Upcote Minor.

Barron had spent an agitated day. After his interview with the Bishop, in which he was rather angrily conscious that his devotion and his zeal were not rewarded with as much gratitude or as complete a confidence on the Bishop's part as he might have claimed, he called on Canon France.

To him he talked long and emphatically on the situation, on the excessive caution of the Bishop, who had entirely refused to inhibit any one of the eighteen, at present, lest there should be popular commotions; on the measures that he and his friends were taking, and on the strong feeling that he believed to be rising against the Modernists. It was evident that he was discontented with the Bishop, and believed himself the only saviour of the situation.

Canon France watched him, sunk deep in his armchair, the plump fingers of one hand playing with certain charter rolls of the fourteenth century, with their seals attached, which lay in a tray beside him. He had just brought them over from the Cathedral Library, and was longing to be at work on them. Barron's conversation did not interest him in the least, and he even grudged him his second cup of tea. But he did not show his impatience. He prophesied a speedy end to a ridiculous movement; wondered what on earth would happen to some of the men, who had nothing but their livings, and finally said, with a humorous eye, and no malicious intention:

"The Romanists have always an easy way of settling these things. They find a scandal or invent one. But Meynell, I suppose, is immaculate."

Barron shook his head.

"Meynell's life is absolutely correct, outwardly," he said slowly. "Of course the Upcote people whom he has led away think him a saint."

"Ah, well," said the Canon, smiling, "no hope then —

that way. I rejoice, of course, for Meynell's sake. But the goodness of the unbeliever is becoming a great puzzle to mankind."

"Apparent goodness," said Barron hotly.

The Canon smiled again. He wished — and this time more intensely — that Barron would go, and let him get to his charters.

And in a few minutes Barron did take his departure. As he walked to the inn to find his carriage he pondered the problem of the virtuous unbeliever. A certain Bampton lecture by a well-known and learned Bishop recurred to him, which most frankly and drastically connected "Unbelief" with "Sin." Yet somehow the view was not borne out, as in the interests of a sound theology it should have been, by experience.

After all, he reached Upcote in good time before dinner, and remembering that he had to inflict a well-deserved lecture on the children who had been caught injuring trees and stealing wood in his plantations, he dismissed the carriage and made his way, before going home, to the cottage, which stood just outside the village, on the way from Maudeley to the Rectory and the church.

He knocked peremptorily. But no one came. He knocked again, chafing at the delay. But still no one came, and after going round the cottage, tapping at one of the windows, and getting no response, he was just going away, in the belief that the cottage was empty, when there was a rattling sound at the front door. It opened, and an old woman stood in the doorway.

"You've made a pretty noise," she said grimly, "but there's no one in but me."

"I am Mr. Barron," said her visitor, sharply. "And I want to see John Broad. My keepers have been complaining to me about his children's behaviour in the woods."

The woman before him shook her head irritably.

"What's the good of asking me? I only came off the cars here last night."

"You're a lodger, I suppose?" said Barron, eying her suspiciously. He did not allow his tenants to take in lodgers.

And the more he examined her the stranger did her aspect seem. She was evidently a woman of seventy or upward, and it struck him that she looked haggard and ill. Her grayish-white hair hung untidily about a thin, bony face; the eyes, hollow and wavering, infected the spectator with their own distress; yet the distress was so angry that it rather repelled than appealed. Her dress was quite out of keeping with the labourer's cottage in which she stood. It was a shabby blue silk, fashionably cut, and set off by numerous lockets and bangles.

She smiled scornfully at Barron's questions.

"A lodger? Well, I daresay I am. I'm John's mother."

"His mother?" said Barron, astonished. "I didn't know he had a mother alive." But as he spoke some vague recollection of Theresa's talk in the morning came back upon him.

The strange person in the doorway looked at him oddly.

"Well, I daresay you didn't. There's a many as would say the same. I've been away this eighteen year, come October."

Barron, as she spoke, was struck with her accent, and recalled her mention of "the cars."

Why, you've been in the States," he said.

"That's it — eighteen year." Then suddenly, pressing her hand to her forehead, she said angrily: "I don't know what you mean. What do you come bothering me for? I don't know who you are — and I don't know nothing about your trees. Come in and sit down. John'll be in directly."

She held the door open, and Barron, impelled by a sudden curiosity, stepped in. He thought the woman was half-witted; but her silk dress, and her jewellery, above all her sudden appearance on the scene as the mother of a man whom he had always supposed to be alone in the world, with three motherless, neglected children, puzzled him.

So as one accustomed to keep a sharp eye on the morals and affairs of his cottage tenants, he began to question her about herself. She had thrown herself confusedly on a chair, and sat with her head thrown back, and her eyes half closed — as though in pain. The replies he got from her were short and grudging, but he made out from them that she had married a second time in the States, that she had only recently written to her son, who for some years had supposed her dead, and had now come home to him, having no other relation left in the world.

He soon convinced himself that she was not normally sane. That she had no idea as to his own identity was not surprising, for she had left Upcote for the States years before his succession to the White House estate. But her memory in all directions was confused, and her strange talk made him suspect drugs. She had also, it seemed, the usual grievances of the unsound mind, and believed herself to be injured and assailed by persons to whom she darkly alluded.

As they sat talking, footsteps were heard in the road outside. Mrs. Sabin — so she gave her name — at once hurried to the door and looked out. The movement betrayed her excited, restless state — the state of one just returned to a scene once familiar and trying, with a clouded brain, to recover old threads and clues.

Barron heard a low cry from her, and looked round.

"What's the matter?"

He saw her bent forward and pointing, her wrinkled face expressing a wild astonishment.

"That's her! — that's my Miss Alice!"

Barron, following her gesture, perceived through the half-open door two figures standing in the road on the farther side of a bit of village green. Meynell, who had just emerged from Maudeley Park upon the highroad, had met Alice Puttenham on her way to pay an evening visit to the Elsmeres, and had stopped to ask a question about some village affairs. Miss Puttenham's face was turned toward John Broad's cottage; the Rector had his back to it. They were absorbed in what they were talking about, and had of course no idea that they were watched.

"Why do you say my Miss Alice?" Barron inquired in astonishment.

Mrs. Sabin gave a low laugh. And at the moment, Meynell turned so that the level light now flooding the village street shone full upon him. Mrs. Sabin tottered back from the door, with another stifled cry, and sank into her chair. Her eyes seemed to be starting out of her head. "But — but they told me he was dead. He'll have married her then?"

She raised herself, peering eagerly at her companion.

"Married whom?" said Barron, utterly mystified, but affected himself, involuntarily, by the excitement of his strange companion.

"Why — Miss Alice!" she said gasping.

"Why should he marry her?"

Mrs. Sabin tried to control herself. "I'm not to talk about that — I know I'm not. But they give me my money for fifteen year — and then they stopped giving it — three year ago. I suppose they thought I'd never be back here again. But John's my flesh and blood, all the same. I made Mr. Sabin write for me to Sir Ralph. But there came a lawyer's letter and fifty pounds — and that was to be the last, they said. So when Mr. Sabin died, I said I'd come over and see for myself. But I'm ill — you see — and John's a fool — and I must find

some one as 'ull tell me what to do.   If you're a gentleman living here" — she peered into his face — "perhaps
you'll tell me?   Lady Fox-Wilton's left comfortable,
I know.   Why shouldn't she do what's handsome?
Perhaps you'll give me a word of advice, sir?   But you
mustn't tell! — not a word to anybody.   Perhaps they'll
be for putting me in prison?"

She put her finger to her mouth; and then once more
she bent forward, passionately scrutinizing the two people
in the distance.   Barron had grown white.

"If you want my advice you must try and tell me
plainly what all this means," he said, sternly.

She looked at him — with a mad expression flickering
between doubt and desire.

"Then you must shut the door, sir," she said at last.
Yet as he moved to do so, she bent forward once more to
look intently at the couple outside.

"And what did they tell me that lie for?" she repeated,
in a tone half perplexed, half resentful.   Then she turned
peremptorily to Barron.

"Shut the door!"

Half an hour later Barron emerged into the road, from
the cottage.   He walked like a man bewildered.   All
that was evil in him rejoiced; all that was good sorrowed.
He felt that God had arisen, and scattered his enemies;
he also felt a genuine horror and awe in the presence of
human frailty.

All night long he lay awake, pondering how to deal

with the story which had been told him; how to clear up its confusions and implications; to find some firm foothold in the mad medley of the woman's talk — some reasonable scheme of time and place. Much of what she had told him had been frankly incoherent; and to press her had only made confusion worse. He was tolerably certain that she was suffering from some obscure brain trouble. The effort of talking to him had clearly exhausted her; but he had not been able to refrain from making her talk. At the end of the half hour he had advised her — in some alarm at her ghastly look — to see a doctor. But the suggestion had made her angry, and he had let it drop.

In the morning news was brought to him from Broad's cottage that John Broad's mother, Mrs. Richard Sabin, who had arrived from America only forty-eight hours before, had died suddenly in the night. The bursting of an unsuspected aneurism in the brain was, according to the doctor called in, the cause of death.

BOOK II

HESTER

" Light as the flying seed-balls is their play
The silly maids! "

"Who see in mould the rose unfold,
The soul through blood and tears."

CHAPTER VII

"I CANNOT get this skirt to hang a Lady Edith's did," said Sarah Fox-Wilton discontentedly.

"Spend twenty guineas on it, my dear, as Lady Edith did on hers, and it'll be all right," said a mocking voice.

Sarah frowned. She went on pinning and adjusting a serge skirt in the making, which hung on the dummy before her. "Oh, we all know what *you* would like to spend on your dress, Hester!" she said angrily, but indistinctly, as her mouth was full of pins.

"Because really nice frocks are not to be had any other way," said Hester coolly. "You pay for them — and you get them. But as for supposing you can copy Lady Edith's frocks for nothing, why, of course you can't, and you don't!"

"If I had ever so much money," said Sarah severely, "I shouldn't think it *right* to spend what Lady Edith does on her dress."

"Oh, wouldn't you!" said Hester with a laugh and a yawn. "Just give *me* the chance — that's all!" Then she turned her head — "Lulu! — you mustn't eat any more toffy!" — and she flung out a mischievous hand and captured a box that was lying on the table, before a girl,

who was sitting near it with a book, could abstract from
it another square of toffy.

"Give it me!" said Lulu, springing up, and making
for her assailant. Hester laughingly resisted, and they
wrestled for the box a little, till Hester suddenly let it go.

"Take it then — and good luck to you! I wouldn't
spoil my teeth and my complexion as you do — not for
tons of sweets. Hullo!" — the speaker sprang up —
"the rain's over, and it's quite a decent evening. I
shall go out for a run and take Roddy."

"Then I shall have to come too," said Sarah, getting
up from her knees, and pulling down her sleeves. "I
don't want to at all, but mamma says you are not to
go out alone."

Hester flushed. "Do you think I can't escape you
all — if I want to? Of course I can. What geese you
are! None of you will ever prevent me from doing what
I want to do. It really would save such a lot of time
and trouble if you would get that into your heads."

"Where do you mean to go?" said Sarah stolidly,
without taking any notice of her remark. "Because if
you'll go to the village, I can get some binding I want."

"I have no intention whatever of going out for your
convenience, thank you!" said Hester, laughing angrily.
"I am going into the garden, and you can come or not
as you please." She opened the French window as she
spoke and stepped out.

"Has mamma heard from that Paris woman yet?"
asked Lulu, looking after Hester, who was now standing

on the lawn playing with a terrier-puppy she had lately
brought home as a gift from a neighbouring farmer —
much to Lady Fox-Wilton's annoyance. Hester had an
absurd way of making friends with the most unsuitable
people, and they generally gave her things.

"The Rector expected to hear to-day."

"I don't believe she'll go," said Lulu, beginning again
on the toffy. She was a heavily made girl of twenty, with
sleepy eyes and a dull complexion. She took little exercise, was inordinately fond of sweet things, helped her
mother a little in the housekeeping, and was intimately
acquainted with all the gossip of the village. So was
Sarah; but her tongue was sharper than Lulu's, and her
brain quicker. She was therefore the unpopular sister;
while for Lulu her acquaintances felt rather a contemptuous indulgence. Sarah had had various love affairs,
which had come to nothing, and was regarded as "disappointed" in the village. Lulu was not interested in
young men, and had never yet been observed to take any
trouble to capture one. So long as she was allowed
sufficient sixpenny novels to read, and enough sweet
things to eat, she was good-humoured enough, and could
do kind things on occasion for her friends. Sarah was
rarely known to do kind things; but as her woman friends
were much more afraid of her than of Lulu, she was in
general treated with much more consideration.

Still it could not be said that Lady Fox-Wilton was to
be regarded as blessed in either of her two elder daughters.
And her sons were quite frankly a trouble to her. The

eldest, Sarah's junior by a year and a half, had just left Oxford suddenly and ignominiously, without a degree, and was for the most part loafing at home. The youngest, a boy of fifteen, was supposed to be delicate, and had been removed from school by his mother on that account. He too was at home, and a tutor who lodged in the village was understood to be preparing him for the Civil Service. He was a pettish and spiteful lad, and between him and Hester existed perpetual feud.

But indeed Hester was at war with each member of the family in turn; sometimes with all of them together. And it had been so from her earliest childhood. They all felt instinctively that she despised them and the slow, lethargic temperament which was in most of them an inheritance from a father cast in one of the typical moulds of British Philistinism. There was some insurmountable difference between her and them. In the first place, her beauty set her apart from the rest; and, beside her, Sarah's sharp profile, and round apple-red cheeks, or Lulu's clumsiness, made, as both girls were secretly aware, an even worse impression than they need have made. And in the next, there were in her strains of romantic, egotistic ability to which nothing in them corresponded. She could play, she could draw — brilliantly, spontaneously — up to a certain point, when neither Sarah nor Lulu could stumble through a "piece," or produce anything capable of giving the smallest satisfaction to their drawing-master. She could chatter, on occasion, so that a room full of people instinctively listened. And she had read voraciously, especially poetry, where they were content with picture-papers and the mildest of novels. Hester brought nothing to perfection; but there could be no question that in every aspect of life she was constantly making, in comparison with her family, a dashing or dazzling effect all the more striking because of the unattractive *milieu* out of which it sprang.

The presence of Lady Fox-Wilton, in particular, was needed to show these contrasts at their sharpest.

As Hester still raced about the lawn, with the dog, that lady came round the corner of the house, with a shawl over her head, and beckoned to the girl at play. Hester carelessly looked round.

"What do you want, mamma!"

"Come here. I want to speak to you."

Hester ran across the lawn in wide curves, playing with the dog, and arrived laughing and breathless beside the newcomer. Edith Fox-Wilton was a small, withered woman, in a widow's cap, who more than looked her age, which was not far from fifty. She had been pretty in youth, and her blue eyes were still appealing, especially when she smiled. But she did not smile often, and she had the expression of one perpetually protesting against all the agencies — this-worldly or other-worldly — which had the control of her existence. Her weak fretfulness depressed all the vitalities near her; only Hester resisted.

At the moment, however, her look was not so much fretful as excited. Her thin cheeks were much redder than usual; she constantly looked round as though expecting or dreading some interruption; and in a hand which shook she held a just opened letter.

"What is the matter, mamma?" asked Hester, a sharp challenging note in her gay voice. "You look as though something had happened."

"Nothing has happened," said Lady Fox-Wilton hastily. "And I wish you wouldn't romp with the puppy in that way, Hester. He's always doing some damage to the flowers. I'm going out, and I wished to give you a message from the Rector."

"Is that from Uncle Richard?" said Hester, glancing carelessly at the letter.

Lady Fox-Wilton crushed it in her hand.

"I told you it was. Why do you ask unnecessary questions? The Rector has heard from the lady in Paris and he wants you to go as soon as possible. Either he or Aunt Alice will take you over. We have had the best possible recommendations. You will enjoy it very much. They can get you the best lessons in Paris, they say. They know everybody."

"H'm —" said Hester, reflectively. Then she looked at the speaker. "Do you know, mamma, that I happen to be eighteen this week?"

"Don't be silly, Hester! Of course I know!"

"Well, you see, it's rather important. Am I or am I not obliged to do what you and Mr. Meynell want me to do? I believe I'm not obliged. Anyway, I don't quite see how you're going to make me do it, if I don't want to."

"You can behave like a naughty, troublesome girl, without any proper feeling, of course! — if you choose," said Lady Fox-Wilton warmly. "But I trust you will do nothing of the kind. We are your guardians till you are twenty-one; and you ought to be guided by us."

"Well, of course I can't be engaged to Stephen, if you say I mayn't — because there's Stephen to back you up. But if Queen Victoria could be a queen at eighteen, I don't see why *I* shouldn't be fit at eighteen to manage my own wretched affairs! Anyway — I — am — not — going to Paris — unless I want to go. So I don't advise you to promise that lady just yet. If she keeps her room empty, you might have to pay for it!"

"Hester, you are really the plague of my life!" cried Lady Fox-Wilton helplessly. "I try to keep you — the Rector tries to keep you — out of mischief that any girl ought to be ashamed — of — and ——"

"What mischief?" demanded Hester peremptorily. "Don't run into generalities, mamma."

"You know very well what mischief I mean!"

"I know that you think I shall be running away some day with Sir Philip Meryon!" said the girl, laughing, but with a fierce gleam in her eyes. "I have no intention at present of doing anything of the kind. But if anything could make me do it, it would be the foolish way in which you and the others behave. I don't believe the Rector ever told you to set Sarah and Lulu on to dog me wherever I go!"

"He told me you were not to be allowed to meet that

man. You won't promise me not to meet him — and what can we do? You know what the Rector feels. You know that he spent an hour yesterday arguing and pleading with you, when he had been up most of the night preparing papers for this commission. What's the matter with you, Hester? Are you quite in your right senses?"

The girl had clasped her hands behind her back, and stood with one foot forward, "on tiptoe for a flight," her young figure and radiant look expressing the hot will which possessed her. At the mention of Meynell's name she clearly hesitated, a frown crossed her eyes, her lip twitched. Then she said with vehemence :

"Who asked him to spend all that time? Not I. Let him leave me alone. He does not care twopence about me, and it's mere humbug and hypocrisy all his pretending to care."

"And your Aunt Alice — who's always worshipped you? Why, she's just miserable about you!"

"She says exactly what you and Uncle Richard tell her to say — she always has! Well, I don't know about Paris, mamma — I'll think about it. If you and Sarah will just let me be, I'll take Roddy for a stroll, and then after tea I'll tell you what I'll do." And, turning, she beckoned to a fine collie lazily sunning himself on the drawing-room steps, and he sprang up, gambolling about her.

"Promise you won't meet that man!" said Lady Fox-Wilton, in agitation.

"I believe he went up to Scotland to-day," said Hester, laughing. "I haven't the smallest intention of meeting him. Come, Roddy!"

The eyes of the two met — in those of the older woman, impatience, a kind of cold exasperation; in Hester's, defiance. It was a strange look to pass between a mother and daughter. Hester turned away, and then paused:

"Oh, by the way, mamma — where are you going?"

Lady Fox-Wilton hesitated unaccountedly.

"Why do you ask?"

Hester opened her eyes.

"Why shouldn't I? Is it a secret? I wanted you to tell Aunt Alice something if you were going that way."

"Mamma!"

Sarah suddenly emerged from the schoolroom window and ran excitedly across the lawn toward her mother. "Have you heard this extraordinary story about John Broad's mother? Tibbald has just told me."

Tibbald was the butler, and Sarah's special friend and crony.

"What story? I wish you wouldn't allow Tibbald to gossip as you do, Sarah!" said Lady Fox-Wilton angrily. But a close observer might have seen that her bright colour precipitately left her.

"Why, what harm was it?" cried Sarah, wondering. "He told me, because it seems Mrs. Sabin used to be a servant of ours long ago. Do you remember her, mamma?"

Again Lady Fox-Wilton stumbled perceptibly in replying. She turned away, and, with the garden scissors at her waist, she began vaguely to clip off some dead roses from some bushes near her.

"We once had a maid — for a very short time," she said over her shoulder, "who married some one of that name. What about her?"

"Well, she came back from America two days ago. John Broad thought she was dead. He hadn't heard of her for four years. But she turned up on Tuesday — the queerest old woman! She sat there boasting and chattering — in a silk dress with gold bracelets! — they thought she was going to make all their fortunes. But she must just have been off her head, for she died last night in her sleep, and there were only a few shillings on her — not enough to bury her. There's to be an inquest this evening, they say."

"Don't spend all your time chattering in the village, Sarah," said Lady Fox-Wilton severely, as, still with her back toward the girls, she moved away in the direction of the drive. "You'll never get your dress done if you do."

"I say — what's wrong with mamma?" said Hester coolly, looking after her. "I suppose Bertie's been getting into some fresh bother."

Bertie was the elder brother, who was Sarah's special friend in the family. So that she at once resented the remark.

"If she's worrying about anything, she's worrying about you," said Sarah tartly, as she went back to the house. "We all know that."

Hester, with her dog beside her, went strolling leisurely through the village street, past Miss Puttenham's cottage on the one hand and the Rectory gates on the other, making for a footpath that led from the back of the village, through fields and woods, on to the Chase.

As she passed beneath the limes that overhung Miss Puttenham's railings she perceived some distant figures in the garden. Uncle Richard, with mamma and Aunt Alice on either side of him. They were walking up and down in close conversation; or, rather, Uncle Richard seemed to be talking earnestly, addressing now one lady, now the other.

What a confabulation! No doubt all about her own crimes and misdemeanours. What fun to creep into the garden and play the spy. "That's what Sarah would do — but I'm not Sarah." Instead, she turned into the footpath and began to mount toward the borders of the Chase. It was a brilliant September afternoon, and the new grass in the shorn hayfields was vividly green. In front rose the purple hills of the Chase, while to the left, on the far borders of the village, the wheels and chimneys of two collieries stood black against a blaze of sun. But the sharp emphasis of light and colour, which in general would have set her own spirits racing, was for a while lost on Hester. As soon as she was out of sight of the village, or any passers-by, her aspect changed. Once or twice she caught her breath in what was very like a sob; and there were moments when she could only save herself from the disgrace of tears by a

wild burst of racing with Roddy. It was evident that
her brush with Lady Fox-Wilton had not left her as
callous as she seemed.

Presently the path forsook the open fields and entered
a plantation of dark and closely woven trees where the
track was almost lost in the magnificence of the bracken.
Beyond this, a short climb of broken slopes, and Hester
was out on the bare heath, with the moorland wind blowing about her.

She sat down on a bank beneath a birch tree, twisted
and tortured out of shape by the northwesterly gales
that swept the heath in winter. All round her a pink
and purple wilderness, with oases of vivid green and
swaying grass. Nothing in sight but a keeper's hut, and
some grouse butts far away; an ugly red building on the
horizon, in the very middle of the heath, the Markborough isolation hospital; and round the edge of the
vast undulating plateau in all directions the faint smoke
of the colliery chimneys. But the colour of the heath
was the marvel. The world seemed stained in crimson,
and in every shade and combination of it. Close at hand
the reds and pinks were diapered with green and gold
as the bilberries and the grasses ran in and out of the
heather; but on every side the crimson spread and bil-
lowed to the horizon, covering the hollows and hills of the
Chase, absorbing all lesser tones into itself. After the
rain of the morning, the contours of the heath, the dis-
tances of the plain, were unnaturally clear; and as the
sunshine, the high air, the freshly moving wind, played

upon Hester, her irritation passed away in a sensuous delight.

"Why should I let them worry me? I won't! I am here! I am alive! I am only eighteen! I am going to manage my life for myself — and get out of this coil. Now let me think!"

She slid downward among the heather, her face propped on her hands. Close beneath her eyes was an exquisite tuft of pink bell-heather intergrown with bunchberries. And while a whole vague series of thoughts and memories passed through her mind she was still vividly conscious of the pink bells, the small bright leaves. Sensation in her was exceptionally keen, whether for pleasure or pain. She knew it and had often coolly asked herself whether it meant that she would wear out — life and brain — quicker than other people — burn faster to the socket. So much the better if it did.

What was it she really wanted? — what did she mean to do? Proudly, she refused to admit any other will in the matter. The thought of Meynell, indeed, touched some very sore and bitter chords in her mind, but it did not melt her. She knew very well that she had nothing to blame her guardian for; that year after year from her childhood up she had repelled and resisted him, that her whole relation to him had been one of stubbornness and caprice. Well, there were reasons for it; she was not going to repent or change.

Of late his conduct with regard to Stephen's proposal had stirred in her a kind of rage. It was not that she imagined herself in love with Stephen; but she had chosen to be engaged to him; and that any one should affect to control her in such a matter, should definitely and decidedly cross her will, was intolerable to her wild pride. If Stephen had rebelled with her, she might have fallen fiercely in love with him — for a month. But he had submitted — though it was tolerably plain what it had cost him; and all her careless liking for him, the fruit of years of very poorly requited devotion on his part, seemed to have disappeared in a night.

Why shouldn't she be engaged at seventeen — within two months of eighteen, in fact? Heaps of girls were. It was mere tyranny and nonsense. She recalled her interview with Meynell, in which the Rector had roused in her a new and deeper antagonism than any she had yet felt toward his efforts to control her. It was as though he did not altogether believe in his own arguments; as though there were something behind which she could not get at. But if there were something behind, she had a right to know it. She had a right to know the meaning of her father's extraordinary letter to Meynell — the letter attached to his will — in which she had been singled out by name as needing the special tutelage of the Rector. So far as the Rector's guardianship of the other children was concerned, it was almost a nominal thing. Another guardian had been named in the will, Lady Fox-Wilton's elder brother, and practically everything that concerned the other children was settled by him, in concert with the mother. The Rector never interfered, was never indeed consulted, except on purely formal matters of business. But for her — for her only — Uncle Richard — as she always called her guardian — was to be the master — the tyrant! — close at hand. For so Sir Ralph had laid it down, in his testamentary letter — "I commend Hester to your special care. And in any difficulties that may arise in connection with her, I beg for our old friendship's sake that you will give my wife the help and counsel that she will certainly need. She knows it is my wish she should rely entirely upon you."

Why had he written such a letter? Since Sir Ralph's death, two years before, the story of it had got about; and the injustice, as she held, of her position under it had sunk deep into the girl's passionate sense, and made her infinitely more difficult to manage than she had been before. Of course everybody said it was because of her temper; because of the constant friction between her and her father; people believed the hateful things he used sometimes to say about her.

Nor was it only the guardianship — there was the money too! Provision made for all of them by name — and nothing for her! She had made Sarah show her a copy of the will — she knew! Nothing indeed for any of them — the girls at least — till Lady Fox-Wilton's death, or till they married; but nothing for *her*, under any circumstances.

"Well, why should there be?" Sarah had said. "You know you'll have Aunt Alice's money. *She* won't leave a penny to us."

All very well! The money didn't matter! But to be singled out and held up to scorn by your own father!

A flood of bitterness surged in the girl's heart. And then they expected her to be a meek and obedient drudge to her mother and her elder sisters; to open her mouth and take what they they chose to send her. She might not be engaged to Stephen — for two years at any rate; and yet if she amused herself with any one else she was to be packed off to Paris, to some house of detention or other, under lock and key.

Her cheeks flamed. When had she first come across Philip Meryon? Only the day before that evening when Uncle Richard had found her fishing with him. She knew very well that he was badly spoken of; trust Upcote for gossip and scandal! Well, so was she! — they were outcasts together. Anyway, he was more amusing to walk and talk with than her sisters, or the dreadful young men they sometimes gathered about them. Why shouldn't she walk and talk with him? As if she couldn't protect herself! As if she didn't know a great deal more of the world than her stupid sisters did, who never read a book or thought of anything beyond the tittle-tattle of their few local friends.

But Philip Meryon had read lots of books, and liked those that she liked. He could read French too, as she could. And he had lent her some French books, which she had read eagerly — at night or in the woods — wherever she could be alone and unobserved. Why shouldn't she read them? There was one among them — "Julie de Trécœur," by Octave Feuillet, that still seemed running, like a great emotion, through her veins. The tragic leap of Julie, as she sets her horse to the cliff and thunders to her death, was always in Hester's mind. It was so that she herself would like to die, spurning submission and patience, and all the humdrum virtues.

She raised herself, and the dog beside her sprang up and barked. The sun was just dropping below a bank of fiery cloud, and a dazzling and garish light lay on the red undulations of the heath. As she stood up she suddenly perceived the figure of a man about a hundred yards off emerging from a gully—a sportsman with his gun over his shoulder. He had apparently just parted from the group with whom he had been shooting, who were disappearing in another direction.

Philip Meryon! Now she remembered! He and two other men had taken the shooting on this side of the Chase. Honestly she had forgotten it; honestly her impression was that he had gone to Scotland. But of course none of her family would ever believe it. They would insist she had simply come out to meet him.

What was she to do? She was in a white serge dress, and with Roddy beside her, on that bare heath, she was an object easily recognized. Indeed, as she hesitated, she heard a call in the distance, and saw that Meryon was waving to her and quickening his pace. Instantly, with a leaping pulse, she turned and fled, Roddy beside her, barking his loudest. She ran along the rough track of the heath, as though some vague wild terror had been breathed into her by the local Pan. She ran fleet and light as air — famous as a runner from her childhood. But the man behind her had once been a fine athlete, and he gained upon her fast. Soon she could hear his laugh behind her, his entreaties to her to stop. She had reached the edge of the heath, where the wood began, and the path ran winding down it, with banks of thick fern on either hand.

If it had not been for the dog she could have slipped under the close-set trees, whence the light had already departed, and lain close among the fern. But with Roddy — no chance! She suddenly turned toward her pursuer, and with her hand on the dog's neck awaited him.

"Caught — caught! — by Jove!" cried Philip Meryon, plunging to her through the fern. "Now what do you deserve — for running away?"

"A *gentleman* would not have tried to catch me!" she said haughtily, as she faced him, with dilating nostrils.

"Take care! — don't be rude to me — I shall take my revenge!"

As he spoke, Meryon was fairly dazzled, intoxicated by the beauty of the vision before him — this angry wood-nymph, half-vanishing like another Daphne into the deep fern amid which she stood. But at the same time he was puzzled — and checked — by her expression. There was no mere provocation in it, no defiance that covers a yielding mind; but, rather, an energy of will, a concentrated force, that held at bay a man whose will was the mere register of his impulses.

"You forget," said Hester coolly, "that I have Roddy with me." And as she spoke the dog couching at her side poked up his slender nose through the fern and growled. He did not like Sir Philip.

Meryon looked upon her smiling — his hands on his sides. "Do you mean to say that when you ran you did not mean me to follow?"

"On the contrary, if I ran, it was evidently because I wished to get away."

"Then you were very ungrateful and unkind; for I have at this moment in my pocket a book you asked me to get for you. That's what I get for trying to please you."

"I don't remember that I asked you to get anything for me."

"Well, you said you would like to see some of George Sand's novels, which — for me — was just the same. So when I went to London yesterday I managed to borrow it, and there it is." He pointed triumphantly to a yellow-paper-bound volume sticking out of his coat pocket. "Of course you know George Sand is a sort of old Johnnie now; nobody reads her. But that's your affair. Will you have it?" He offered it.

The excitement, the wild flush in the girl's face, had subsided. She looked at the book, and at the man holding it out.

"What is it?" She stooped to read the title — "Mauprat." "What's it about?"

"Some nonsense about a cad tamed by a sentimental young woman." He shrugged his shoulders. "I tried to read it, and couldn't. But they say it's one of her best. If you want it, there it is."

She took it reluctantly, and moved on along the downward path, he following, and the dog beside them.

"Have you read the other book?" he asked her.

"'Julie de Trécœur?' Yes."

"What did you think of it?"

"It was magnificent!" she said shortly, with a quickened breath. "I shall get some more by that man."

"Well, you'd better be careful!" He laughed. "I've got some others, but I didn't want to recommend them to you. Lady Fox-Wilton wouldn't exactly approve."

"I don't tell mamma what I read." The girl's young voice sounded sharply beside him in the warm autumnal dusk. "But if you lent me anything you oughtn't to lend me I would never speak to you again!"

Meryon gave a low whistle.

"My goodness! I shall have to mind my p's and q's. I don't know that I ought to have lent you 'Julie de Trécœur' if it comes to that."

"Why not?" Hester turned her great, astonished eyes upon him. "One might as well not read Byron as not read that."

"Hm — I don't suppose you read all Byron."

He threw her an audacious look.

"As much as I want to," she said, indifferently. "Why aren't you in Scotland?"

"Because I had to go to London instead. Beastly

nuisance! But there was some business I couldn't get out of."

"Debts?" she said, raising her eyebrows.

The self-possession of this child of eighteen was really amazing. Not a trace in her manner of timidity or tremor. In spite of her flight from him he could not flatter himself that he had made any impression on her nerves. Whereas her beauty and her provocative way were beginning to tell deeply on his own.

"Well, I daresay!" His laugh was as frank as her question. "I'm generally in straits."

"Why don't you do some work, and earn money?" she asked him, frowning.

"Frankly — because I dislike work."

"Then why did you write a play?"

"Because it amused me. But if it had been acted and made money, and I had had to write another, that would have been work; and I should probably have loathed it."

"That I don't believe," she said, shaking her head. "One can always do what succeeds. It's like pouring petrol into the motor."

"So you think I'm only idle because I'm a failure?" he asked her, his tone betraying a certain irritation.

"I wonder why you *are* idle — and why you *are* a failure?" she said, turning upon him a pair of considering eyes.

"Take care, Mademoiselle!" he said, gasping a little. "I don't know why you allow yourself these *franchises!*"

"Because I am interested in you — rather. Why won't the neighbourhood call on you — why do you have disreputable people to stay with you? It is all so foolish!" she said, with childish and yet passionate emphasis. "You needn't do it!"

Meryon had turned rather white.

"When you grow a little older," he said severely, "you will know better than to believe all the gossip you hear. I choose the friends that suit me — and the life too. My friends are mostly artists and actors — they are quite content to be excluded from Upcote society — so am I. I don't gather you are altogether in love with it yourself."

He looked at her mockingly.

"If it were only Sarah — or mamma," she said doubtfully.

"You mean I suppose that Meynell — your precious guardian — my very amiable cousin — allows himself to make all kinds of impertinent statements about me. Well, you'll understand some day that there's no such bad judge of men as a clergyman. When he's not ignorant he's prejudiced — and when he's not prejudiced he's ignorant."

A sudden remorse swelled in Hester's mind.

"He's not prejudiced! — he's not ignorant! How strange that you and he should be cousins!"

"Well, we do happen to be cousins. And I've no doubt that you would like me to resemble him. Unfortunately I can't accommodate you. If I am to take a relation for a model, I prefer a very different sort of per-

son — the man from whom I inherited Sandford. But
Richard, I am sure, never approved of him either."

"Who was he? — I never heard of him." And, with
the words, Hester carelessly turned her head to look at a
squirrel that had run across the glade and was now
peeping at the pair from the first fork of an oak tree.

"My uncle? Well, he was an awfully fine fellow —
whatever Meynell may say. If the Abbey wasn't taboo,
I could show you a portrait of him there — by a French-
man — that's a superb thing. He was the best fencer in
England — and one of the best shots. He had a beautiful
voice — he could write — he could do anything he pleased.
Of course he got into scrapes — such men do — and if
Richard ever talked to you about him, of course he'd
crab him. All the same, if one must be like one's relations — which is, of course, quite unnecessary — I should
prefer to take after Neville than after Richard."

"What was his name?"

"Neville — Sir Neville Flood." Hester looked puzzled.

"Well! — if you want the whole genealogical tree,
here it is: There was a certain Ralph Flood, my grandfather, an old hunting squire, a regular bad lot! Oh!
I can tell you the family history doesn't give me much
chance! He came from Lincolnshire originally, having
made the county there too hot to hold him, and bought
the Abbey, which he meant to restore and never did.
He worried his wife into her grave, and she left him
three children: Neville, who succeeded his father; and
two daughters — Meynell's mother, who was a good

deal older than Neville and married Colonel Meynell, as he was then; and my mother, who was much the youngest, and died three years ago. She was Neville's favourite sister, and as he knew Richard didn't want the Abbey, he left it to me. A precious white elephant — not worth a fiver to anybody. I was only thirteen when Neville was drowned ——"

"Drowned?"

Meryon explained that Neville Flood had lost his life in a storm on an Irish lough; a queer business, which no one had ever quite got to the bottom of. Many people had talked of suicide. There was no doubt he was in very low spirits just before it happened. He was unhappily married, mainly through his own fault. His wife could certainly have got a divorce from him if she had applied for it. But very soon after she separated from Flood she became a Catholic, and nothing would induce her to divorce him. And against her there was never a breath. It was said of course that he was in love with some one else, and broken-hearted that his wife refused to lend herself to a divorce. But nobody knew anything.

"And, by Jove, I wonder why I'm telling you all these shady tales. You oughtn't to know anything about such things," Meryon broke off suddenly.

Hester's beautiful mouth made a scornful movement.

"I'm not a baby — and I intend to know what's *true*. I should like to see that picture."

"What — of my Uncle Neville?"

Meryon eyed her curiously, as they strolled on through the arched green of the woodland. Every now and then there were openings through which poured a fiery sun, illuminating Hester's face and form.

"Do you know" — he said at last — "there is an uncommonly queer likeness between you and that picture?"

"Me?" Hester opened her eyes in half-indifferent astonishment. "People say such absurd things. Heaps of people think I am like Uncle Richard — not complimentary, is it? I hope his uncle was better looking. And, anyway, I am no relation of either of them."

"Neville and Richard were often mistaken for one another — though Neville was a deal handsomer than old Richard. However, nobody can account for likenesses. If you come to think of it, we are all descended from a small number of people. But it has often struck me ——" He looked at her again attentively. "The setting of the ear — and the upper lip — and the shape of the brow — I shall bring you a photograph of the picture."

"What does it matter!" said Hester impatiently. "Besides, I am going away directly — to Paris."

"To Paris! — why and wherefore?"

"To improve my French — and" — she turned and looked at him in the face, laughing — "to make sure I don't go walks with you!"

He was silent a moment, twisting his lip.

"When do you go?"

"In a week or two — when there's room for me."
He laughed.

"Oh! come then — there's time for a few more talks.
Listen — you think I'm such an idle dog. I'm nothing
of the sort. I've nearly finished a whole new play. Only
— well, I couldn't talk to you about it — it's not a play for
jeunes filles. But after all I might read you a few scenes.
That wouldn't do any harm. You're so deuced clever!
— your opinion would be worth having. I can tell you
the managers are all after it! I'm getting letters by every
post asking for parts. What do you say? Can you meet
me somewhere? I'll choose some of the best bits. Just
name your time!"

Her face had kindled, answering to the vivacity — the
peremptoriness — in his. Her vanity was flattered at
last; and he saw it.

"Send me a word!" he said under his breath. "That
little schoolroom maid — is she safe?"

"Quite!" said Hester, also under her breath, and
smiling.

"You beautiful creature!" he spoke with low intensity. "You lovely, wild thing!"

"Take care!" Hester sprang away from him as he put
out an incautious hand. "Come, Roddy! Good night!"

In a flash the gloom of the wood closed upon her, and
she was gone.

Meryon walked on laughing to himself, and twisting
his black moustache. After some years of bad company

and easy conquests, Hester's proud grace, her reckless beauty, her independent, satiric ways had sent a new stimulus through jaded nerves. Had he met her in London on equal terms with other men he knew instinctively that he would have had but small chance with her. It was the circumstances of this quiet country place, where young men of Hester's class were the rarest of apparitions, and where Philip, flying from his creditors and playing the part of a needy Don Juan amid the picturesque dilapidations of the Abbey, was gravelled day after day for lack of occupation — it was these surroundings that had made the flirtation possible. Well, she was a handsome daredevil little minx. It amused him to make love to her, and in spite of his parsonical cousin, he should continue to do so. And that the proceeding annoyed Richard Meynell made it not less, but more, enticing. Parsons, cousins or no, must be kept in their place.

Hester ran home, a new laugh on her lip, and a new red on her cheek. Several persons turned to look at her in the village street, but she took no notice of any one till, just as she was nearing the Cowroast, she saw groups round the door of the little inn, and a stream of men coming out. Among them she perceived the Rector. He no sooner saw her than with an evident start he altered his course and came up to her.

"Where have you been, Hester?"

She chose to be offended by the inquiry, and answered pettishly that for once she had been out by herself without a keeper. He took no notice of her tone, and walked on beside her, his eyes on the ground. Presently she wondered whether he had heard her reply at all, he was so evidently thinking of something else. In her turn she began to ask questions.

"What's happening in the village? Why are those people coming out of the Cowroast?"

"There's been an inquest there."

"On that old woman who was once a servant of ours?"

The Rector looked up quickly.

"Who told you anything about her?"

"Oh, Sarah heard from Tibbald — trust him for gossip! Was she off her head?"

"She died of disease of the brain. They found her dead in her bed."

"Well, why shouldn't she? An excellent way to die! Good night, Uncle Richard — good night! You go too slow for me."

She walked away with a defiant air, intended to show him that he was in her black books. He stood a moment looking after her, compunction and sad affection in his kind eyes.

CHAPTER VIII

MEANWHILE, for Catharine Elsmere and Mary these days of early autumn were passing in a profound external quiet which bore but small relation to the mental history of mother and daughter.

The tranquillity indeed of the little water-locked cottage was complete. Mrs. Flaxman at the big house took all the social brunt upon herself. She set no limit to her own calls, or to her readiness to be called upon. The Flaxman dinner and tennis parties were soon an institution in the neighbourhood; and the distinguished persons who gathered at Maudeley for the Flaxman week-ends shed a reflected lustre on Upcote itself. But Rose Flaxman stoutly protected her widowed sister. Mrs. Elsmere was delicate and in need of rest; she was not to be expected to take part in any social junketings, and callers were quite plainly warned off.

For all of which Catharine Elsmere was grateful to a younger sister, grotesquely unlike herself in temperament and character, yet brought steadily closer to her by the mere passage of life. Rose was an artist and an optimist. In her youth she had been an eager and exquisite musician; in her middle life she was a loving and a happy woman, though she too had known a tragic moment in her first

187

youth. Catharine, her elder by some years, still maintained, beneath an exquisite refinement, the strong north-
country characteristics of the Westmoreland family
to which the sisters belonged. Her father had been an
Evangelical scholar and headmaster; the one slip of
learning in a rude and primitive race. She had been
trained by him; and in spite of her seven years of married
life beside a nature so plastic and sensitive as Elsmere's,
and of her passionate love for her husband, it was the
early influences on her character which had in the end
proved the more enduring.

For years past she had spent herself in missionary
work for the Church, in London; and though for Robert's
sake she had maintained for long a slender connection
that no one misunderstood with the New Brotherhood, the
slow effect of his withdrawal from her life made itself
inevitably felt. She stiffened and narrowed intellectually;
while for all sinners and sufferers, within the lines of
sympathy she gradually traced out for herself, she would
have willingly given her body to be burned, so strong was
the Franciscan thirst in her for the self-effacement and
self-sacrifice that belong to the Christian ideal, carried
to intensity.

So long as Mary was a child, her claim upon her mother
had to some extent balanced the claims of what many
might have thought a devastating and depersonalizing
charity. Catharine was a tender though an austere
mother; she became and deserved to become the idol of
her daughter. But as Mary grew up she was drawn

inevitably into her mother's activities; and Catharine, in the blindness of her ascetic faith, might have injured the whole spring of the girl's youth by the tremendous strain thus put upon it by affection on the one hand and pity on the other.

Mercifully, perhaps, for them both, Catharine's nerve and strength suddenly gave way; and with them that abnormal exaltation and clearness of spiritual vision which had carried her through many sorrowing years. She entered upon a barren and darkened path; the Christian joy deserted her, and there were hours and days when little more than the Christian terrors remained. It was her perception of this which roused such a tender and desperate pity in Mary. Her mother's state fell short indeed of religious melancholy; but for a time it came within sight of it. Catharine dreaded to be found herself a castaway; and the memory of Robert's denials of the faith — magnified by her mental state, like trees in mist — had now become an ever-haunting misery which tortured her unspeakably. Her mind was possessed by the parables of judgment — the dividing of the sheep from the goats, the shutting of the door of salvation on those who had refused the heavenly offers, and by all those sayings of the early Church that make "faith" the only passport to eternal safety.

Her saner mind struggled in vain against what was partly a physical penalty for defied physical law. And Mary also, her devoted companion, whose life depended hour by hour on the aspects and changes of her mother, must needs be drawn within the shadow of Catharine's dumb and phantom-ridden pain. The pain itself was dumb, because it concerned the deepest feelings of a sternly reserved woman. But mingled with the pain were other matters — resentments, antagonisms — the expression of which often half consciously relieved it. She rose in rebellion against those sceptical and deadly forces of the modern world which had swept her beloved from the narrow way. She fled them for herself; she feared them for Mary, in whom she had very early divined the working of Robert's aptitudes and powers.

And now — by ill-fortune — a tired and suffering woman had no sooner found refuge and rest in the solitude of Forkéd Pond than, thanks partly to the Flaxmans' new friendship for Upcote's revolutionary parson, and partly to all the public signs, not to be escaped, of the commotion brewing in the diocese, and in England generally, the same agitations, the same troubles which had detroyed her happiness and peace of mind in the past, came clattering about her again.

Every one talked of them; every one took a passionate concern in them; the newspapers were full of them. The personality of Meynell, or that of the Bishop; the characters and motives of his opponents; the chances of the struggle — and the points on which it turned; even in the little solitary house between the waters Catharine could not escape them. The Bishop, too, was an old friend; before his promotion he had been the incumbent of a London parish in which Catharine had worked. She

was no sooner settled at Forkéd Pond than he came to
see her; and what more natural than he should speak of
the anxieties weighing upon him to one so able to feel
for them?

Then! — the first involuntary signs of Mary's interest
in, Mary's sympathy with, the offender! In Catharine's
mind a thousand latent terrors sprang at once to life.
For a time — some weeks — she had succeeded in checking all developments. Invitations were refused; meetings
were avoided. But gradually the situation changed.
Points of contact began inevitably to multiply between
Mary and the disturber of Christ's peace in Upcote.
Mary's growing friendship for Alice Puttenham, her
chance encounters with Meynell there, or in the village,
or in the Flaxmans' drawing-room, were all distasteful
and unwelcome to Catharine Elsmere. At least her
Robert had sacrificed himself — had done the honest
and honourable thing. But this man — wounding the
Church from within — using the opportunities of the
Church for the destruction of the Church — who would
make excuses for such a combatant?

And the more keenly she became aware of the widen-
ing gulf between her thoughts and Mary's — of Mary's
involuntary, instinctive sympathy with the enemy —
the greater was her alarm.

For the first time in all her strenuous, self-devoted life
she would sometimes make much of her physical weakness
in these summer days, so as to keep Mary with her, to
prevent her from becoming more closely acquainted with

Meynell and Meynell's ideas. And in fact this new anxiety interfered with her recovery; she had only to let herself be ill, and ill most genuinely she was.

Mary understood it all, and submitted. Her mother's fears were indeed amply justified! Mary's secret mind was becoming absorbed, from a distance, in Meynell's campaign; Meynell's personality, through all hindrance and difficulty — nay, perhaps, because of them — was gradually seizing upon and mastering her own; and processes of thought that, so long as she and her mother were, so to speak, alone in the world together, were still immature and potential, grew apace. The woods and glades of Maudeley, the village street, the field paths, began to be for her places of magic, whence at any moment might spring flowers of joy known to her alone. To see him pass at a distance, to come across him in a miner's cottage, or in Miss Puttenham's drawing-room — these rare occasions were to her the events of the summer weeks. Nevertheless, when September arrived, she had long since forbidden herself to hope for anything more.

Meanwhile, Rose Flaxman was the only person who ever ventured to feel and show the irritation of the natural woman toward her sister's idiosyncrasies.

"Do for heaven's sake stop her reading these books!" she said impatiently one evening to Mary, when she had taken leave of Catharine, and her niece was strolling back with her toward Maudeley.

"What books?"

"Why, lives of bishops and deans and that kind of

thing! I never come but I find a pile of them beside her. It should be made absolutely illegal to write the life of a clergyman! My dear, your mother would be well in a week if we could only stop it and put her on a course of Gaboriau!"

Mary smiled rather sadly.

"They seem to be the only things that interest her now."

"What, the deans? I know. It's intolerable. She went to speak to the postman just now while I was with her, and I looked at the book she had been reading with her mark in it. I should like to have thrown it into the pond! Some tiresome canon or other writing to a friend about Eternal Punishment. What does he know about it? I should like to ask! I declare I hope he may know something more about it some day! There was your mother as white as her ruffles, with dark lines under her eyes. I tell you clerical intimidation should be made a punishable offence. It's just as bad as any other!"

Mary let her run on. She moved silently along the grassy path, her pretty head bent, her hands clasped behind her. And presently her aunt resumed: "And the strange thing is, my dear, saving your presence — that your beloved mother is quite lax in some directions, while she is so strict in others. I never can make her pay the smallest attention to the things I tell her about Philip Meryon, for instance, that Hugh tells me. 'Poor fellow!' she always calls him, as though his abominable ways were like the measles — something you couldn't

help.   And as for that wild minx Hester! — she has
positively taken a fancy to her.   It reminds me of what
an old priest said to me once in Rome — 'Sins, madame!
— the only sins that matter are those of the intellect!'
There! — send me off — before I say any more *incon-
venances*!"

Mary waved farewell to her vivacious aunt, and walked
slowly back to the cottage.   She was conscious of inner
smart and pain; conscious also for the first time of a
critical mind toward the mother whose will had been the
law of her life.   It was not that she claimed anything
for herself; but she claimed justice for a man misread.

"If they could only know each other!" — she found
herself saying at last aloud — with an impetuous energy;
and then, with a swift return upon herself — "Mother,
darling! — mother, who has no one in the world —
but me!"

As the words escaped her, she came in sight of the
cottage, and saw that her mother was sitting in her usual
place beside the water.   Catharine's hands were resting
on a newspaper they had evidently just put down, and
she was gazing absently across the lights and shadows,
the limpid blues and browns of the tree-locked pool
before her.

Mary came to sit on the grass beside her

"Have you been reading, dearest?"

But as she spoke she saw, with discomfort, that the
newspaper on her mother's knee was the *Church Guardian*,
in which a lively correspondence on the subject of Mey-

nell and the Modernist Movement generally was at the moment proceeding.

"Yes, I have been reading," said Catharine slowly — "and I have been very sad."

"Then I wish you wouldn't read!" cried Mary, kissing her hand. "I should like to burn all the newspapers!"

"What good would that do?" said Catharine, trying to smile. "I have been reading Bishop Craye's letter to the *Guardian*. Poor Bishop! — what a cruel, cruel position!"

The words were spoken with a subdued but passionate energy, and when Mrs. Elsmere perceived that Mary made no reply, her hand slipped out of her daughter's.

There was silence for a little, broken by Catharine, speaking with the same quiet vehemence:

"I cannot understand how you, Mary, or any one else can defend what this man — Mr. Meynell — is doing. If he cannot agree with the Church, let him leave it. But to stay in it — giving this scandal — and this offence ——"

Her voice failed her. Mary collected her thoughts as best she could.

At last she said, with difficulty:

"Aren't you thinking only of the people who may be hurt — or scandalized? But after all, there they are in the Church, with all its privileges and opportunities — with everything they want. They are not asked to give anything up — nobody thinks of interfering with them — they have all the old dear things, the faiths and the practices they love — and that help *them*. They are only asked to tolerate other people who want different things. Mr. Meynell stands — I suppose — for the people — who are starved, whose souls wither, or die, for lack of the only food that could nourish them."

"'I am the bread of life,'" said Catharine with an energy that shook her slight frame. "The Church has no other food to give. Let those who refuse it go outside. There are other bodies, and other means."

"But, mother, this is the *National* Church!" pleaded Mary, after a moment. "The Modernists too say — don't they? — that Christ — or what Christ stands for — is the bread of life. Only they understand the words — differently from you. And if" — she came closer to her mother, and putting her hands on Catharine's knees, she looked up into the elder woman's face — "if there were only a few here and there, they could of course do nothing; they could only suffer, and be silent. But there are so many of them — so many! What is the 'Church' but the living souls that make it up? And now thousands of these living souls want to change things in the Church. Their consciences are hurt — they can't believe what they once believed. What is the justice of driving them out — or leaving them starved — forever? They were born in the Church; baptized in the Church! They love the old ways, the old buildings, the old traditions. 'Comfort our consciences!' they say; 'we will never tyrannize over yours. Give us the teaching and the expression we want; you will always have what you want! Make room for us — beside you. If your own faith is strong it will only be the stronger because you let ours speak and live — because you give us our bare rights, as free spirits, in this Church that belongs to the whole English people.' Dear mother, you are so just always — so loving — doesn't that touch you — doesn't it move you — at all?"

The girl's charming face had grown pale. So had Catharine's.

"This, I suppose, is what you have heard Mr. Meynell say," she answered slowly.

Mary turned away, shading her eyes with her hand.

"Yes," she said, with shrinking; "at least I know it is what he would say."

"Oh, Mary, I wish we had never come here!" It was a cry of bitterness, almost of despair. Mary turned and threw her arms round the speaker's neck.

"I will never hurt you, my beloved! you know I won t."

The two gazed into each other's eyes, questions and answers, unspoken yet understood, passing between them. Then Catharine disengaged herself, rose, and went away.

During the night that followed Mary slept little. She was engaged in trying to loosen and tear away those tendrils of the heart that had begun to climb and spread more than she knew. Toward the early dawn it seemed to her she heard slight sounds in her mother's room. But immediately afterward she fell asleep.

The next day, Mary could not tell what had happened; but it was as though, in some inexplicable way, doors had been opened and weights lifted; as though fresh winds had been set blowing through the House of Life. Her mother seemed shaken and frail; Mary hovered about her with ministering tenderness. There were words begun and left unfinished, movements and looks that strangely thrilled and bewildered the younger woman. She had no key to them; but they seemed to speak of change — of something in her mother that had been beaten down, and was still faintly, pitifully striving. But she dared say nothing. They read, and wrote letters, and strolled as usual; till in the evening, while Mary was sitting by the water, Catherine came out to her and stood beside her, holding the local paper in her hand.

"I see there is to be a meeting in the village next Friday — of the Reformers' League. Mr. Meynell is to speak."

Mary looked up in amazement.

"Yes?"

"You would perhaps like to go. I will go with you."

"Mother!" Mary caught her mother's hand and kissed it, while the tears sprang to her eyes. "I want to go nowhere — to do nothing — that gives you pain!"

"I know that," said Catharine quietly. "But I — I should like to understand him."

And with a light touch of her hand on Mary's red-gold hair, she went back into the house. Mary wandered away by herself into the depths of the woods, weeping, she scarcely knew why. But some sure instinct, lost in wonder as she was, bade her ask her mother no questions; to let time show.

The day of the League meeting came. It happened also to be the date on which the Commission of Inquiry into the alleged heresies and irregularities of the Rector of Upcote was holding its final meeting at Markborough. The meetings of the commission were held in the Library of the Cathedral, once a collegiate church of the Cistercian order. All trace of the great monastery formerly connected with it had disappeared, except for the Library and a vaulted room below it which now made a passageway from the Deanery to the north transept.

The Library offered a worthy setting for high themes. The walls were, of course, wreathed in the pale golds and dignified browns of old books. A light gallery ran round three sides of the room, while a large perpendicular window at the farther end contained the armorial bearings of various benefactors of the see. Beneath the window was a bookcase containing several chained books — a Vulgate, a Saint Augustine, the *Summa* of St. Thomas; precious possessions, and famous in the annals of early printing. And wherever there was a space of wall left free, pictures or engravings of former bishops and dignitaries connected with the Cathedral enforced the message and meaning of the room.

A seemly, even beautiful place — pleasantly scented with old leather, and filled on this September afternoon with the sunshine which, on the Chase, was at the same moment kindling the heather into a blood-red magnificence. Here the light slipped in gently, subdued to the quiet note and standard of the old Library.

The Dean was in the Chair. He was a man of seventy who had only just become an old man, submitting with difficulty, even with resentment, to the weight of his years. He wore a green shade over his eyes, beneath which his long sharp nose and pointed chin — in the practical absence of the eyes — showed with peculiar emphasis. He was of heavy build, and suffered from chronic hoarseness. In his youth he had been a Broad churchman and a Liberal, and had then passed, through stages mysterious to his oldest friends, into an actively dogmatic and ecclesiastical phase. It was rumoured that he had had strange spiritual experiences; a "vision" was whispered; but all that was really known was that from an "advanced" man, in the Liberal sense, he had become the champion of high orthodoxy in the Chapter, and an advocate of disestablishment as the only means of restoring "Catholic liberty" to the Church.

The Dean's enemies, of whom he had not a few, brought various charges against him. It was said that he was a worldling with an undue leaning to notabilities. And indeed in every gathering, social or ecclesiastical, the track of the Dean's conversation sufficiently indicated the relative importance of the persons present. Others declared that during his long tenure of a country living he had left the duties of it mainly to a curate, and had found it more interesting to live in London, conferring with Cabinet Ministers on educational reform; while the women-folk of the Chapter pitied his wife, whose subdued or tremulous aspect certainly suggested that the Dean's critical and sarcastic temper sharpened itself at home for conflicts abroad.

On the Dean's right hand sat Canon Dornal, a man barely forty, who owed his canonry to the herculean work he had done for fourteen years in a South London parish, work that he would never have relinquished for the comparative ease of the Markborough precincts but for a sudden failure in health which had pulled him up in mid-career, and obliged him to think of his wife and children. He had insisted, however, on combining with his canonry a small living in the town, where he could still slave as he pleased; and his sermons in the Cathedral were generally held to be, next to the personality of the Bishop, all that was noblest in Markborough Christianity. His fine head, still instinct with the energy of youth, was covered with strong black hair; dark brows shadowed Cornish blue eyes, simple, tranquil, almost *naïf*, until of a sudden there rushed into them the passionate or tender feeling that was in truth the heart of the man. The mouth and chin were rather prominent, and, when at rest, severe. He was a man in whom conscience was a gadfly, remorseless and tormenting. He was himself overstrained and his influence sometimes produced in others a tension on which they looked back with resentment. But he was a saint; open, pure, and loving as a child; yet often tempest-driven with new ideas, since he possessed at once the imagination that frees a man from tradition, and the piety which clings to it.

Beside him sat a University professor, the young holder of an important chair, who had the face, the smile, the curly hair of a boy of twenty, or appeared to have them, till you came to notice the subtleties of the mouth and the crow's-feet which had gathered round the eyes. And the paradox of his aspect only repeated the paradox within. His "History and the Gospels," recently published, would have earned him excommunication under any Pope; yet no one was a more rigid advocate of tests and creeds, or could be more eloquent in defence of damnatory clauses. The clergy who admired and applauded him did not read his books. It was rumoured indeed that there were many things in them which were unsound; but the rumour only gave additional zest to the speeches in which at Church Congresses and elsewhere he flattered clerical prejudice, and encouraged clerical ignorance. To him there was no more "amusing" study — using "amusing" in the French sense as meaning something that keeps a man intellectually happy and awake — than the study of the Gospels. They presented an endless series of riddles, and riddles were what he liked. But the scientific treatment of these riddles had, according to him, nothing to do with the discipline of the Church; and to the discipline of the Church this young man, with the old eyes and mouth, was rigorously attached. He was a bachelor and a man of means — facts which taken together with his literary reputation and his agreeable aspect made him welcome among women; of which he was well aware.

The Archdeacon, Doctor Froswick, and the Rural Dean, Mr. Brathay, who completed the Commission of Inquiry, were both men of middle age; the Archdeacon, fresh-coloured and fussy, a trivial, kindly person of no great account; the Rural Dean, broad-shouldered and square-faced, a silent, trustworthy man, much beloved in a small circle.

A pile of books, MSS., and letters lay to tne Chairman s right hand. On the blotting-pad before him was the voluminous written report of the commission which only awaited the signatures of the Commissioners, and — as to one paragraph in it — a final interview with Meynell himself, which had been fixed for noon. Business was now practically over till he arrived, and conversation had become general.

"You have seen the leader in the *Oracle* this morning?" asked the Archdeacon, nervously biting his quill. "Perfectly monstrous, I think! I shall withdraw my subscription."

"With the *Oracle*," said the Professor, "it will be a mere question of success or failure. At present they are inclined to back the rebellion."

"And not much wonder!" put in the Dean's hoarse voice. "The news this morning is uncommonly bad. Four more men joined the League here — a whole series of League meetings in Yorkshire! — half the important newspapers gone over or neutral — and a perfectly scandalous speech from the Bishop of Dunchester!"

"I thought we should hear of Dunchester before long,"

said the Professor, with a sarcastic lip. "Anything that annoys his brethren has his constant support. But if the Church allows a Socinian to be put over her, she must take the consequences!"

"What can the Church do?" said the Dean, shrugging his shoulders. "If we had accepted Disestablishment years ago, Dunchester would never have been a bishop. And now we may have missed our chance."

"Of what?" — Canon Dornal looked up — "of Disestablishment?"

The Dean nodded.

"The whole force of *this* Liberal movement," he said slowly, "will be thrown against Disestablishment. There comes the dividing line between it and the past. I say again, we have missed our chance. If the High Churchmen had known their own minds — if they had joined hands boldly with the Liberation society, and struck off the State fetters — we should at least have been left in quiet possession of what remained to us. We should not have been exposed to this treachery from within. Or, at least, we should have made short work of it."

"That means, that you take for granted we should have kept our endowments and our churches?" said Canon Dornal.

The Dean flushed.

"We have been called a nation of shopkeepers," he said vehemently, "but nobody has ever called us a nation of thieves."

The Canon was silent. Then his eye caught the

bulky MS. report lying before the Dean, and he made a restless movement as though the sight of it displeased him.

"The demonstrations the papers report this morning are not all on one side," said the Rural Dean slowly but cheerfully, as though from a rather unsatisfactory reverie this fact had emerged.

"No — there seems to have been something like a riot at Darwen's church," observed the Archdeacon. "What can they expect? You don't outrage people's dearest feelings for nothing. The scandal and misery of it! Of course we shall put it down — but the Church won't recover for a generation. And all that this handful of agitators may advertise themselves and their opinions!"

Canon Dornal frowned and fidgeted.

"We must remember," he said, "that — unfortunately — they have the greater part of European theology behind them."

"European theology!" cried the Archdeacon. "I suppose you mean German theology?"

"The same thing — almost," said the Canon, smiling a little sadly.

"And what on earth does German theology matter to us?" retorted the Archdeacon. "Haven't we got theologians of our own? What have the Germans ever done but set up one mare's nest after another, for us to set right? They've no sooner launched some cocksure theory or other than they have to give it up. I don't read German," said the Archdeacon, hastily, "but that's what I understand from the Church papers."

Silence a moment. The Professor looked at the ceiling, a smile twitching the corners of his mouth. The green shade concealed the Dean's expression. He also knew no German, but it did not seem necessary to say so. Canon Dornal looked uncomfortable.

"Do you see who it was that protected Darwen from the roughs outside his church?" he said presently

Brathay looked up.

"A party of Wesleyans? — class-leaders? Yes, I saw. Oh! Darwen has always been on excellent terms with the Dissenters!"

"Meynell too," said the Professor. "That of course is their game. Meynell has always gone for the inclusion of the Dissenters."

"Well, it was Arnold's game!" said the Canon, his look kindling. "Don't let's forget that. Meynell's dream is not unlike his — to include everybody that would be included."

"Except the Unitarians," said the Professor with emphasis — "the deniers of the Incarnation. Arnold drew the line there. So must we."

He spoke with a crisp and smiling decision — as of one in authority All kinds of assumptions lay behind his manner. Dornal looked at him with a rather troubled and hostile eye. This whole matter of the coming trial was to him deeply painful. He would have given anything to avoid it; but he did not see how it could be avoided. The extraordinary spread of the Movement indeed had made it impossible.

At this moment one of the vergers of the Cathedral entered the room to say that Mr. Meynell was waiting below. The Dean directed that he should be shown up, and the whole commission dropped their conversational air and sat expectant.

Meynell came in, rather hastily, brushing his hair back from his forehead. He shook hands with the Dean and the Archdeacon, and bowed to the other members of the commission. As he sat down, the Archdeacon, who was very sensitive to such things, and was himself a model of spick-and-span-ness, noticed that the Rector's coat was frayed, and one of the buttons loose. Anne indeed was not a very competent valet of her master; and nothing but a certain esthetic element in Meynell preserved him from a degree of personal untidiness which might perhaps have been excused in a man alternating, hour by hour, between his study-table and the humblest practical tasks among his people.

The other members of the commission observed him attentively. Perhaps all in their different ways and degrees were conscious of change in him: the change wrought insensibly in a man by some high pressure of emotion and responsibility — the change that makes a man a leader of his fellows, consecrates and sets him apart. Canon Dornal watched him with a secret sympathy and pity. The Archdeacon said to himself with repugnance that Meynell now had the look of a fanatic.

The Dean took a volume from the pile beside him, and opened it at a marked page.

"Before concluding our report to the Bishop, Mr. Meynell, we wished to have your explanation of an important passage in one of your recent sermons; and you have been kind enough to meet us with a view to giving us that explanation. Will you be so good as to look at the passage?"

He handed the book to Meynell, who read it in silence. The few marked sentences concerned the Resurrection.

"These Resurrection stories have for our own days mainly a symbolic, perhaps one might call it a sacramental, importance. They are the 'outward and visible' sign of an inward mystery. As a simple matter of fact the continuous life of the spirit of Christ in mankind began with the death of Jesus of Nazareth. The Resurrection beliefs, so far as we can see, were the natural means by which that Life was secured."

"Are we right in supposing, Mr. Meynell," said the Dean, slowly, "that in those sentences you meant to convey that the Resurrection narratives of the New Testament were not to be taken as historical fact, but merely as mythical — or legendary?"

"The passage means, I think, what it says, Mr. Dean."

"It is not, strictly speaking, logically incompatible," said the Professor, bending forward with a suave suggestiveness, "with acceptance of the statement in the Creed?"

"He shook hands with the Dean"

Meynell threw him a slightly perplexed look, and did not reply immediately. The Dean sharply interposed.

"Do you in fact accept the statements of the Creed? In that case we might report to the Bishop that you felt you had been misinterpreted — and would withdraw the sermon complained of, in order to allay the scandal it has produced?"

Meynell looked up.

"No," he said quietly, "no; I shall not withdraw the sermon. Besides" — the faintest gleam of a smile seemed to flit through the speaker's tired eyes — "that is only one of so many passages."

There was a moment's silence. Then Canon Dornal said:

"Many things — many different views — as we all know, are permitted, must be permitted, nowadays. But the Resurrection — is vital!"

"The physical fact?" said Meynell gently. His look met that of Dornal; some natural sympathy seemed to establish itself at once between them.

"The *historical* fact. If you could see your way to withdraw some of the statements in these volumes on this particular subject, much relief would be given to many — many wounded consciences."

The voice was almost pleading. The Dean moved abruptly in his chair. Dornal's tone was undignified and absurd. Every page of the books teemed with heresy!

But Meynell was for the moment only aware of his

questioner.   He leaned across the table as though addressing him alone.

"To us too — the Resurrection is vital — the transposi-
tion of it, I mean — from the natural, or physical to
the spiritual order."

Dornal did not of course attempt to argue.   But as
Meynell met the sensitive melancholy of his look the
Rector remembered that during the preceding year Dornal
had lost a little son, a delicate, gifted child, to whom he
had been peculiarly attached.   And Meynell's quick
imagination realized in a moment the haunted imagination of the other — the dear ghost that lived there —
and the hopes that grouped themselves about it.

A long wrestle followed between Meynell and the Professor.   But Meynell could not be induced to soften or
recant anything.   He would often say indeed with an
eager frown, when confronted with some statement of
his own, "That was badly put!   It should be so-and-
so."   And then would follow some vivid correction or
expansion, which sometimes left the matter worse than
before.   The hopes of the Archdeacon, for one set of
reasons, and of Dornal, for another, that some bridge of
retreat might be provided by the interview, died away.
The Dean had never hoped anything, and Mr. Brathay
sat open-mouthed and aghast, while Meynell's voice
and personality drove home ideas and audacities which
on the printed page were but dim to him.   Why had
the Anglican world been told for the last fifteen years

that the whole critical onslaught — especially the German onslaught — was a beaten and discredited thing? It seemed to him terribly alive!

The library door opened again, and Meynell disappeared — ceremoniously escorted to the threshold by the Professor. When that gentleman was seated again, the Dean addressed the meeting.

"A most unsatisfactory interview! There is nothing for it, I fear, but to send in our report unaltered to the Bishop. I must therefore ask you to append your signatures."

All signed, and the meeting broke up.

"Do you know at all when the case is likely to come on?" said Dornal to the Dean.

"Hardly before November. The Letters of Request are ready. Then after the Arches will come the appeal to the Privy Council. The whole thing may take some time."

"You see the wild talk in some of the papers this morning," said the Professor, interposing, "about a national appeal to Parliament to 'bring the Articles of the Church of England into accordance with modern knowledge.' If there is any truth in it, there may be an Armageddon before us."

Dornal looked at him with distaste. The speaker's light tone, the note of relish in it, as of one delighting in the drama of life, revolted him.

On coming out of the Cathedral Library, Dornal walked

across to the Cathedral and entered. He found his way
to a little chapel of St. Oswald on the north side, where
he was often wont to sit or kneel for ten minutes' quiet
in a busy day. As he passed the north transept he saw
a figure sitting motionless in the shadow, and realized
that it was Meynell.

The silence of the great Cathedral closed round him.
He was conscious of nothing but his own personality, and,
as it seemed, of Meynell's. They two seemed to be alone
together in a world outside the living world. Dornal
could not define it, save that it was a world of reconciled
enmities and contradictions. The sense of it alternated
with a disagreeable recollection of the table in the
Library and the men sitting round it, especially the
cherubic face of the Professor; the thought also of the
long, signed document which reported the "heresy" of
Meynell.

He had been quite right to sign it. His soul went out
in a passionate adhesion to the beliefs on which his own
life was built. Yet still the strange reconciling sense
flowed in and round him, like the washing of a pure stream.
He was certain that the Eternal Word had been made
flesh in Jesus of Nazareth, had died and risen, and been
exalted; that the Church was now the mysterious channel
of His risen life. He must, in mere obedience and loyalty,
do battle for that certainty — guard it as the most
precious thing in life for those that should come after.
Nevertheless he was conscious that there was in him none
of the righteous anger, none of the moral condemnation,

that his father or grandfather might have felt in the same case. As far as *feeling* went, nothing divided him from Meynell. They two across the commission table — as accuser and accused — had recognized, each in the other, the man of faith. The same forces played on both, mysteriously linking them, as the same sea links the headland which throws back its waves with the harbour which receives them.

Meynell too was conscious of Dornal as somewhere near him in the still, beautiful place, but only vaguely. He was storm-beaten by the labour and excitement of the preceding weeks, and these moments of rest in the Cathedral were sometimes all that enabled him to go through his day. He endeavoured often at such times to keep his mind merely vacant and passive, avoiding especially the active religious thoughts which were more than brain and heart could continuously bear. "One cannot always think of it — one must not!" he would say to himself impatiently. And then he would offer himself eagerly to the mere sensuous impressions of the Cathedral — its beauty, its cool prismatic spaces, its silences.

He did so to-day, though always conscious beyond the beauty, and the healing quiet, of the mysterious presence on which he "propped his soul." . . .

Conscious, too, of a dear human presence, closely interwoven now with his sense of things ineffable.

Latterly, as we have seen, he had not been without

some scanty opportunities of meeting Mary Elsmere. In Miss Puttenham's drawing-room, whither the common anxiety about Hester had drawn him on many occasions, he had chanced once or twice on Miss Puttenham's new friend. In the village, Mrs. Flaxman was beginning to give him generous help; the parish nurse was started. And sometimes when she came to consult, her niece was with her, and Meynell, while talking to the aunt either of his people or of the progress of the heresy campaign, was always keenly aware of the girlish figure beside her — of the quick, shy smile — the voice and its tones.

She was with him in spirit — that he knew — passionately knew. But the barriers between them were surely insurmountable. Her sympathy with him was like some warm, stifled thing — some chafing bird "beating up against the wind."

For a time, indeed, he had tried to put love from him, in the name of his high enterprise and its claims upon him. But as he sat tranced in the silence of the Cathedral that attempt finally gave way. His longing was hopeless, but it enriched his life. For it was fused with all that held him to his task; all that was divinest and sincerest in himself.

One of the great bells of the Cathedral struck the quarter. His moment of communion and of rest broke up. He rose abruptly and left the Cathedral for the crowded streets outside, thinking hard as he walked of quite other things.

The death of Mrs. Sabin in her son's cottage had been to Meynell like a stone flung into some deep shadowed pool — the ripples from it had been spreading through the secret places of life and thought ever since.

He had heard of the death on the morning after it occurred. John Broad, an inarticulate, secretive fellow, had come to the Rectory in quest of the Rector within a few hours of its occurrence. His mother had returned home, he said, unexpectedly, after many years of wanderings in the States; he had not had very much conversation with her, as she had seemed ill and tired and "terrible queer" when she arrived. He and his boys had given up their room to her for the night, and she had been very late in coming downstairs the following morning. He had had to go to his work, and when he came back in the evening he found her in great pain and unable to talk to him. She would not allow him to call any doctor, and had locked herself in her room. In the morning he had forced the door and had found her dead. He did not know that she had seen anybody but himself and his boys since her arrival.

But she had seen some one else. As the Rector walked along the street he had in his pocket a cutting from the Markborough *Post*, containing the report of the inquest, from which it appeared — the Rector of course was well aware of it — that Mr. Henry Barron of the White House, going to the cottage to complain of the conduct of the children in the plantation, had found her there, and had talked to her for some time. "I thought

her excited — and overtired — no doubt by the journey,"
he had said to the Coroner. "I tried to persuade her
to let me send in a woman to look after her, but she
refused."

In Barron's evidence at the inquest, to which Meynell had given close attention, there had been no hint
whatever as to the nature of his conversation with
Mrs. Sabin. Nor had there been any need to inquire.
The medical evidence was quite clear as to the cause
of death — advanced brain disease, fatally aggravated
by the journey.

Immediately after his interview with John Broad the
Rector had communicated the news of Mrs. Sabin's unexpected arrival and sudden death to two other persons
in the village. He still thought with infinite concern
of the effect it had produced on one of them. Since
his hurried note telling her of Barron's evidence before
the Coroner, and of his own impressions of it, he had
not seen her. But he must not leave her too much
to herself. A patient and tender pity, as of one on
whom the burden of a struggling and suffering soul
has long been thrown, dictated all his thoughts of her.
He had himself perceived nothing which need alarm her
in Barron's appearance at the inquest. Barron's manner
to himself had been singularly abrupt and cold when they
happened to run across each other, outside the room in
which the inquest was held; but all that was sufficiently
explained by the position of the heresy suit.

Still anxiously pondering, Meynell passed the last

houses in the Cathedral Close. The last of all belonged
to Canon France, and Meynell had no sooner left it
behind him than a full and portly figure emerged from its
front door.

Barron — for it was he — stood a moment looking
after the retreating Rector. A hunter's eagerness gave
sharpening, a grim sharpening, to the heavy face; yet
there was perplexity mixed with the eagerness. His
conversation with France had not been very helpful.
The Canon's worldly wisdom and shrewd contempt for
enthusiasts had found their natural food in the story
which Barron had brought him. His comments had been
witty and pungent enough. But when it had come to
the practical use of the story, France had been of little
assistance. His advice inclined too much to the Mel-
bourne formula — "Can't you let it alone?"   He had
pointed out the risks, difficulties, and uncertainties of the
matter with quite unnecessary iteration. Of course
there were risks and difficulties; but was a man of the
type of Richard Meynell to be allowed to play the hypocrite, as the rapidly emerging leader of a religious movement — a movement directed against the unity and
apostolicity of the English Church — when there were
those looking on who were aware of the grave suspicions
resting on his private life and past history?

CHAPTER IX

ON THE same afternoon which saw the last meeting of the Commission of Inquiry at Markborough, the windows of Miss Puttenham's cottage in Upcote Minor were open to the garden, and the sun stealing into the half darkened drawing-room touched all the many signs it contained of a woman's refinement and woman's tastes. {The room was a little austere. Not many books, but those clearly the friends and not the passing acquaintance of its mistress; not many pictures, and those rather slight suggestions on the dim blue walls than finished performances; a few "notes" in colour, or black and white, chosen from one or other of those moderns who can in a sensitive line or two convey the beauty or the harshness of nature. Over the mantelpiece there was a pencil drawing by Domenichino, of the Madonna and Child; a certain ecstatic languor in the Madonna, and, in all the lines of form and drapery, an exquisite flow and roundness.

The little maidservant brought in the afternoon letters and with them a folded newspaper — the Markborough *Post*. A close observer might have detected that it had been already opened, and hurriedly refolded in the old folds. There was much interest felt in Upcote Minor in the inquest held on John Broad's mother; and the kitchen had taken toll before the paper reached the drawing-room.

As though the maid's movement downstairs had been immediately perceived by a listening ear overhead, there was a quick sound of footsteps. Miss Puttenham ran downstairs, took the letters and the newspaper from the hands of the girl, and closed the door behind her.

She opened the paper with eagerness, and read the account it gave of the Coroner's inquiry held at the Cowroast a week before. The newspaper dropped to the ground. She stood a moment, leaning against the mantelpiece, every feature in her face expressing the concentration of thought which held her; then she dropped into a chair, and raising her two hands to her eyes, she pressed the shut lids close, lifting her face as though to some unseen misery, while a little sound — infinitely piteous — escaped her.

She saw a bedroom in a foreign inn — a vague form in the bed — a woman moving about in nurse's dress, the same woman who had just died in John Broad's cottage — and her sister Edith sitting by the fire. The door leading to the passage is ajar, and she is watching. . . . Or is it the figure in the bed that is watching? — a figure marred by illness and pain? Through the door comes hastily a form — a man. With his entrance, movement and life, like a rush of mountain air, come into the ugly shaded room. He is tall, with a long face, refined and yet violent, instinct with the character and the pride of an old hectoring race. He comes to the bed, kneels down, and the figure there throws itself on his breast. There is a sound of bitter sobbing, of low words ——

Alice Puttenham's hands dropped from her face — and lay outstretched upon her knee. She sat, staring before her, unconscious of the garden outside, or of the passage of time. In some ways she was possessed of more beauty at thirty-seven than she had been at twenty. And yet from childhood her face had been a winning one — with its childish upper lip and its thin oval, its delicate brunette colour, and the lovely clearness of its brown eyes. In youth its timid sweetness had been constantly touched with laughter. Now it shrank from you and appealed to you in one. But the departure of youth had but emphasized a certain distinction, a certain quality. Laughter was gone, but grace and character remained, imprinted also on the fragile body, the beautiful arms and hands. The only marring of the general impression came from an effect of restlessness and constraint. To live with Alice Puttenham was to conceive her as a creature subtly ill at ease, doing her best with a life which was, in some hidden way, injured at the core.

She thought herself quite alone this quiet afternoon, and likely to remain so. Hester, who had been lunching with her, had gone shopping into Markborough with the schoolroom maid, and was afterward to meet Sarah and Lulu at a garden party in the Cathedral Close. Lady Fox-Wilton had just left her sister's house after a long, querulous, excited visit, the latest of many during the past week. How could it be her — Alice's — fault, that Judith Sabin had come home in this sudden, mysterious way? Yet the event had reopened all the old wounds in Edith's mind, revived all the old grievances and terrors. Strange that a woman should be capable of one supreme act of help and devotion, and should then spend her whole after life in resenting it!

"It was you and your story — that shocking thing we had to do for you — that have spoilt my life — and my husband's. Tom never got over it — and I never shall. And it will all come out — some day — and then what'll be the good of all we've suffered!"

That was Edith's attitude — the attitude of a small, vindictive soul. It never varied year by year; it showed itself both in trifles and on great occasions; it hindered all sisterly affection; and it was the explanation of her conduct toward Hester — it had indeed made Hester what she was.

Again the same low sound of helpless pain broke from Alice Puttenham's lips. The sense of her unloved, solitary state, of all that she had borne and must still bear, roused in her anew a flame of memory. Torch-like it ran through the past, till she was shaken with anguish and revolt. She had been loved once! It had brought her to what the world calls shame. She only knew, at moments of strong reaction or self-assertion like the present, that she had once had a man at her feet who had been the desired and adored of his day; that she had breathed her heart out in the passion of youth on his breast; that although he had wronged her, he had suffered because of her, had broken his heart for her, and had probably died because circumstances denied him the power to save and restore her, and he was not of the kind that bears patiently either thwarting from without or reproach from within.

For his selfish passion, his weakness and his suffering, and her own woman's power to make him suffer; for his death, no less selfish indeed than his passion, for it had taken from her the community of the same air, and the same earth with him, the sense that somewhere in the world his warm life beat with hers, though they might be separated in bodily presence forever — for each and all of these things she had loved him. And there were still times when, in spite of the years that had passed away, and of other and perhaps profounder feelings that had supervened, she felt within her again the wild call of her early love, responding to it like an unhappy child, in vain appeal against her solitude, her sister's unkindness, and the pressure of irrevocable and unforgotten facts.

Suddenly, she turned toward a tall and narrow chest of drawers that stood at her left hand. She chose a key from her watch-chain, a small gold key that in their childhood had been generally mistaken by her nieces and nephews for one of the bunch of charms they were allowed to play with on "Aunt Alsie's" lap. With it she unlocked a drawer within her reach. Her hand slipped in; she threw a hasty look round her, at the window,

the garden. Not a sound of anything but the evening
wind, which had just risen, and was making a smart
rustling among the shrubs just outside. Her hand, a
white, furtive thing, withdrew itself, and in it lay a packet,
wrapped in some faded, green velvet. Hurriedly —
with yet more pauses to listen and to look — the wrapping
was undone; the case within fell open.

It contained a miniature portrait of a man — French
work, by an excellent pupil of Meissonier. The detail
of it was marvellous; so, in Alice Puttenham's view, was
the likeness. She remembered when and how it had been
commissioned — the artist, and his bare studio in a street
on the island, near Notre Dame; the chestnuts in the
Luxembourg garden as they walked home; the dust of
the falling blossoms, and the children playing in the
alleys. And through it all, what passionate, guilty
happiness — what dull sense of things irreparable! —
what deliberate shutting out of the future!

It was as good a likeness as the Abbey picture, only
more literal, less "arranged." The Abbey picture, also
by a French artist of another school, was younger, and
had a fine, romantic, René-like charm. "René" had been
her laughing name for him — her handsome, melancholy,
eloquent *poseur!* Like many of his family, he was proud
of his French culture, his French accent, and his knowledge of French books. The tradition that came originally from a French marriage had been kept up from
father to son. They were not a learned or an industrious
race, but their tongue soon caught the accent of the

boulevards — of the Paris they loved and frequented. Her hand lifted the miniature the better to catch the slanting light.

As she did so she was freshly struck with a resemblance she had long ceased to be conscious of. Familiarity with a living face, as so often happens, had destroyed for her its likeness — likeness in difference — to a face of the dead. But to-night she saw it — was indeed arrested by it.

"And yet Richard was never one tenth as good-looking!"

The portrait was set in pearls, and at the foot was an inscription in blue enamel —

"*A ma mie!*"

But before she could see it she must with her cold, quick fingers remove the fragment of stained paper that lay upon it like a veil. The half of a page of Molière — turned down—like that famous page of Shelley's "Sophocles" — and stained with sea water, as that was stained.

She raised the picture to her lips and kissed it — not with passion — but clingingly, as though it represented her only wealth, amid so much poverty. Then her hand, holding it, dropped to her knee again; the other hand came to close over it; and her eyes shut. Tears came slowly through the lashes.

Amazing! — that that woman should have come back — and died — within a few hundred yards, and she, Alice, know nothing! In spite of all Richard's persuasions she tortured herself anew with the thought of the interview between Judith and Mr. Barron.   What could they have talked about — so long?   Judith was always an excitable, hot-tempered creature.   Her silence had been heavily and efficiently bought for fifteen years.   Then steps had been taken — insisted upon — by Sir Ralph Fox-Wilton.   His wife and his sister-in-law had opposed him in vain.   And Ralph had after all triumphed in Judith's apparent acquiescence.

Supposing she had now come home, perhaps on a sudden impulse, with a view to further blackmail, would not her wisest move be to risk some indiscretion, some partial disclosure, so that her renewed silence afterward might have the higher price?   An hour's *tête-à-tête* with that shrewd, hard-souled man, Henry Barron!   Alice Puttenham guessed that her own long-established dislike of him as acquaintance and neighbour was probably returned with interest; that he classed her now as one of "Meynell's lot," and would be only too glad to find himself possessed of any secret information that might, through her, annoy and harass Richard Meynell, her friend and counsellor.

Was it conceivable that nothing should have been said in that lengthy interview as to the causes for Judith's coming home? — or of the reasons for her original departure?   What else could have accounted for so prolonged a conversation between two persons, so different in social grade, and absolute strangers to each other?

Richard had told her, indeed, and she saw from the *Post*, that at the inquest Barron had apparently accounted for the conversation. "She gave me a curious history of her life in the States. I was interested by her strange personality — and touched by her physical condition."

Richard was convinced that there was no reasonable cause for alarm. But Richard was always the consoler — the optimist—where she was concerned. Could she have lived at all — if it had not been so?

And then, for the second time, the rush of feeling rose, welling up, not from the springs of the past, but from the deepest sources of the present.

Richard!

That little villa on the Cap Martin — the steep pathway to it — and Richard mounting it, with that pale look, those tattered, sea-stained leaves in his hand — and the tragedy that had to be told, in his eyes, and on his lips. Could any other human being have upheld her as he did through that first year — through the years after? Was it not to him that she owed everything that had been recovered from the wreck; the independence and freedom of her daily life; protection from her hard brother-in-law, and from her sister's reproaches; occupation — hope — the gradual healing of intolerable wounds — the gradual awakening of a spiritual being?

Thus — after passion — she had known friendship; its tenderness, its disinterested affection and care.

Tenderness? Her hand dashed away some more impetuous tears, then locked itself in the other, the tension of the muscles answering to the inward effort for self-control. Thank God, she had never asked him for more; had often seemed indeed to ask him for much less; had made herself irresponsive, difficult, remote. At least she had never lost her dignity in his eyes — (ah! in whose eyes but his had she ever possessed it?) — she had never forfeited — never risked even — her sacred place in his life, as the soul he had helped through dark places, true servant as he was of the Master of Pity.

The alarms of the week died away, as this emotion gained upon her. She bethought her of certain central and critical years, when, after long dependence on him as comrade and friend, suddenly, she knew not how, her own pulse had quickened, and the sharpest struggle of her life had come upon her. It was the crisis of the mature woman, as compared with that of the innocent and ignorant girl; and in the silent mastering of it she seemed to have parted with her youth.

But she had never parted with self-controı and self-respect. She had never persuaded herself that the false was true. She had kept her counsel, and her sanity, and the wage of it had not been denied her. She had emerged more worthy of his friendship, more capable of rewarding it.

Yes, but with a clear and sad perception of the necessities laid upon her — of the sacrifices involved.

He believed her — she knew it — indifferent to the great cause of religious change and reform which he had at heart. In these matters, indeed, she had quietly, unwaveringly held aloof. There are efforts and endurances that can only be maintained — up to a point. Beyond that point resistance breaks. The life that is fighting emotion must not run too many risks of emotion. At the root of half the religious movements of the world lies the appeal of the preacher and the prophet — to women. Because women are the creatures and channels of feeling; and feeling is to religion as air to life.

But *she* — must starve feeling — not feed and cherish it. Richard's voice was too powerful with her already. To hear it dealing with the most intimate and touching things of the soul would have tested the resistance of her will too sorely. Courage and honour alike told her that she would be defeated and undone did she attempt to meet and follow him — openly — in the paths of religion. *Entbehren sollst du — sollst entbehren!*

So, long before this date, she had chosen her line of action. She took no part in the movement, and she rarely set foot in the village church, which was close to her gates. Meynell sadly believed her unshakeable — one of the natural agnostics or pessimists of the world who cannot be comforted through religion.

And meanwhile secretly, ardently, she tracked all the footsteps of his thoughts, reading what he read, thinking as far as possible what he thought, and revealing nothing.

Except that, lately, she had been indiscreet sometimes in talk with Mary Elsmere. Mary had divined her — had expressed her astonishment that her friend should declare herself and her sympathies so little; and Alice had set up some sort of halting explanation.

But in this nascent friendship it was not Mary alone who had made discoveries. . . .

Alice Puttenham sat very still, in the quiet shadowy room, her eyes closed, her hands crossed over the miniature, the Markborough paper lying on the floor beside her. As the first activity of memory, stirred and goaded by an untoward event, lost its poignancy; as she tried in obedience to Meynell to put away her terrors, with regard to the past, her thoughts converged ever more intensely on the present — on herself — and Mary. . . .

There was in the world, indeed, another personality rarely or never absent from Alice Puttenham's consciousness. One face, one problem, more or less acutely realized, haunted her life continuously. But this afternoon they had, for the moment, receded into the background. Hester had been, surely, more reasonable, more affectionate lately. Philip Meryon had now left Sandford; a statement to that effect had appeared in the *Post;* and Hester had even shown some kindness to poor Stephen. She had at last declared her willingness to go to Paris, and the arrangements were all made. The crisis in her of angry revolt, provoked apparently by the refusal of her guardian to allow her engagement to Stephen, seemed to be over.

So that for once Alice Puttenham was free to think and feel for her own life and what concerned it. From the events connected with Judith Sabin's death — through the long history of Meynell's goodness to her

— the mind of this lonely woman travelled on, to be filled and arrested by the great new fact of the present. She had made a new friend. And at the same moment she had found in her — at last — the rival with whom her own knowledge of life had threatened her these many years. A rival so sweet — so unwitting! Alice had read her. She had scarcely yet read herself.

Alice opened her eyes — to the quiet room, and the windy sky outside. She was very pale, but there were no tears. "It is not renouncing" — she whispered to herself — "for I never possessed. It is accepting — loving — giving — all one has to give."

And vaguely there ran through her mind immortal words —"*good measure — pressed down, and running over.*"

A smile trembled on her lip. She closed her eyes again, lost in one of those spiritual passions accessible only to those who know the play and heat of the spiritual war. The wind was blowing briskly outside, and from the wood-shed in the back garden came a sound of sawing. Miss Puttenham did not hear a footstep approaching on the grass outside.

Hester paused at the window — smiling. There was wildness — triumph — in her look, as though for her this quiet afternoon had seen some undisclosed adventure. Her cheek was hotly flushed, her loosened hair made a glory in the evening sun. Youth, selfishly pitiless — youth, the supplanter and destroyer — stood embodied in the beautiful creature looking down upon Alice Puttenham, on the still intensity of the plaintive face, the closed eyes, the hands holding the miniature.

Mischievously the girl came closer. She took the stillness before her for sleep.

"Auntie! Aunt Alsie!"

With a start, Alice Puttenham sprang up. The miniature dropped from her hands to the floor, opening as it fell. Hester looked at it astonished — and her hand stooped for it before Miss Puttenham had perceived her loss.

"Were you asleep, Aunt Alsie?" she asked, wondering. "I got tired of that stupid party — and I — well, I just slipped away" — the clear high voice had grown conscious — "and I looked in here, because I left a book behind me — Auntie, who is it?" She bent eagerly over the miniature, trying to see it in the dim light.

Miss Puttenham's face had faded to a gray-white.

"Give it to me, Hester!" She held out her hand imperiously.

"Mayn't I know even who it is?" asked Hester, as she unwillingly returned it. In the act she caught the inscription and her face kindled.

Impetuously throwing herself down beside Miss Puttenham, the girl looked up at her with an expression half mockery, half sweetness, while Alice, with unsteady fingers, replaced the case and locked the drawer.

"What an awfully handsome fellow!" said Hester in a low voice, "though you wouldn't let me see it properly. I say, Auntie, won't you tell me ——?"

"Tell you what?"

"Who he was — and why I never saw it before?   I
thought I knew all your things by heart — and now you've
been keeping something from me!"   The girl's tone had
changed to one of curious resentment.   "You know how
you scold *me* when you think I've got a secret."

"That is quite different, Hester."

Miss Puttenham tried to rise, but Hester, who was
leaning against her knee, prevented it.

"Why is it different?" she said, audaciously.   "You
always say you — you — want to be everything to me
— and then you hide things from me — and I ——"

She raised herself, sitting upright on the floor, her
hands round her knees, and spoke with extraordinary
animation and sparkling eyes.

"Why, I should have loved you twice as much, Aunt
Alice — and you know I *do* love you! — if you'd told me
more about yourself.   The people *I* care about are the
people who *live* — and feel — and do things!   There's
verse in one of your books" — she pointed to a little
bookshelf of poets on a table near — "I always think
of it when mamma reads the 'Christian Year' to us on
Sunday evenings —

> "Out of dangers, dreams, disasters
> *We* arise, to be your masters!'

We — the people who want to know, and feel, and *fight!*
We who loathe all the humdrum *bourgeois* talk — 'don't
do this — don't do that!'   Aunt Alsie, there's a German
line, too, you know it — '*Was uns alle bändigt, das*

Gemeine' — don't you hate it too — *das Gemeine?*" the word came with vehemence through the white teeth. "And how can we escape it — we women — except through freedom — through asserting ourselves — through love, of course? It all comes to love! — love that mamma says one ought not to talk about. I wouldn't talk about it, if it only meant what it means to Sarah and Lulu — I'd scorn to!"

She stopped — and looked with her blazing and wonderful eyes at her companion — her lips parted. Then she suddenly stooped and kissed the cold hand trying to withdraw itself from hers.

"Who was he, dear?" — she laid the hand caressingly against her cheek — "I'm good at secrets!"

Alice Puttenham wrenched herself free, and rose tottering to her feet.

"He is dead, Hester — and you mustn't speak of it to me — or any one — again."

She leant against the mantelpiece trying to recover herself — but in vain.

"I'm rather faint," she said at last, putting out a groping hand. "No, don't come! — I'm all right — I'll go upstairs and rest. I got overtired this morning."

And she went feebly toward the door.

Hester looked after her, panting and wounded. Aunt Alsie repel — refuse her! — Aunt Alsie! — who had always been her special possession and chattel. It had been taken for granted in the family, year after year, that if no one else was devoted to Hester, Aunt Alsie's

devotion, at least, never failed. Hester's clothes were
Miss Puttenham's special care; it was for Hester that
she stitched and embroidered. Hester was to inherit
her jewels and her money. In all Hester's scrapes it
was Aunt Alice who stood by her, who had often carried
her off bodily out of reach of the family anger, to the
Lakes, to the sea — once even, to Italy.

And from her childhood Hester had coolly taken it
all for granted, had never been specially grateful, or
much more amenable to counsels from Aunt Alice than
from anybody else. The slender, graceful woman, so
gentle, plaintive and reserved, so easily tyrannized over,
had never seemed to mean much to her. Yet now, as
she stood looking at the door through which Miss Puttenham had disappeared, the girl was conscious of a profound
and passionate sense of grievance, and of something
deeper, beneath it. The sensation that held her was new
and unbearable.

Then in a moment her temperament turned pain into
anger. She ran to the window and down the steps
into the garden.

"If she had told me" — she said to herself, with the
childish fury that mingled in her with older and maturer
things — "I might have told *her*. Now — I fend for
myself!"

CHAPTER X

MEANWHILE, in the room upstairs, Alice Puttenham lying with her face pressed against the back
of the chair into which she had feebly dropped,
heard Hester run down the steps, tried to call, or rise,
and could not. Since the death of Judith Sabin she
had had little or no sleep, and much less food than
usual, with — all the while — the pressure of a vague
corrosive terror on nerve and brain. The shock of that
miniature in Hester's hands had just turned the scale;
endurance had given way.

The quick footsteps receded. Yet she could do nothing
to arrest them. Her mind floated in darkness.

Presently out of the darkness emerged a sound, a
touch — a warm hand on hers.

"Dear — dear Miss Puttenham!"

"Yes."

Her voice seemed to herself a sigh — the faintest —
from a great distance.

"The servants said you were here. Ellen came up
to knock, and you did not hear. I was afraid you were
ill — so I came in — you'll forgive me."

"Thank you."

Silence for a while. Mary brought cold water, chafed

her friend's hands, and rendered all the services that women in such straits know how to lavish on a sufferer. Gradually Alice mastered herself, but more than a broken word or two still seemed beyond her, and Mary waited in patience. She was well aware that some trouble of a nature unknown to her had been weighing on Miss Puttenham for a week or more; and she realized too, instinctively, that she would get no light upon it.

Presently there was a knock at the door, and Mary went to open it. The servant whispered, and she returned at once.

"Mr. Meynell is here," she said, hesitating. "You will let me send him away?"

Alice Puttenham opened her eyes.

"I can't see him. But please — give him some tea. He'll have walked — from Markborough."

Mary prepared to obey.

"I'll come back afterward."

Alice roused herself further.

"No — there is the meeting afterward. You said you were going."

"I'd rather come back to you."

"No, dear — no. I'm — I'm better alone. Good night, kind angel. It's nothing" — she raised herself in the chair — "only bad nights! I'll go to bed — that'll be best. Go down — give him tea. And Mrs. Flaxman's going with you?"

"No. Mother said she wished to go," said Mary, slowly. "She and I were to meet in the village."

Alice nodded feebly, too weak to show the astonishment she felt.

"Just time. The meeting is at seven."

Then with a sudden movement — "Hester! — is she gone?"

"I met her and the maid — in the village — as I came in."

A silence — till Alice roused herself again — "Go dear, don't miss the meeting. I — I want you to be there. Good night."

And she gently pushed the girl from her, putting up her pale lips to be kissed, and asking that the little parlour-maid should be sent to help her undress.

Mary went unwillingly. She gave Miss Puttenham's message to the maid, and when the girl had gone up to her mistress she lingered a moment at the foot of the stairs, her hands lightly clasped on her breast, as though to quiet the stir within.

Meynell, expecting to see the lady of the house, could not restrain the start of surprise and joy with which he turned toward the incomer. He took her hand in his — pressing it involuntarily. But it slipped away, and Mary explained with her soft composure why she was there alone — that Miss Puttenham was suffering from a succession of bad nights and was keeping her room — that she sent word the Rector must please rest a little before going home, and allow Mary to give him tea.

Meynell sank obediently into a chair by the open window, and Mary ministered to him. The lines of his strong worn face relaxed. His look returned to her again and again, wistfully, involuntarily; yet not so as to cause her embarrassment.

She was dressed in some thin gray stuff that singularly became her; and with the gray dress she wore a collar or ruffle of soft white that gave it a slight ascetic touch. But the tumbling red-gold of the hair, the frank dignity of expression, belonged to no mere cloistered maid.

Meynell heard the news of Miss Puttenham's collapse with a sigh — checked at birth. He asked few questions about it; so Mary reflected afterward. He would come in again on the morrow, he said, to inquire for her. Then, with some abruptness, he asked whether Hester had been much seen at the cottage during the preceding week.

Mary reported that she had been in and out as usual, and seemed reconciled to the prospect of Paris.

"Are you — is Miss Puttenham sure that she hasn't still been meeting that man?"

Mary turned a startled look upon him.

"I thought he had gone away?"

"There may be a stratagem in that. I have been keeping what watch I could — but at this time — what use am I?"

The Rector threw himself back wearily in his chair, his hands behind his head. Mary was conscious of some deep throb of feeling that must not come to words. Even since she had known it the face had grown older — the lines deeper — the eyes finer. She stooped forward a little.

"It is hard that you should have this anxiety too. Oh! but I *hope* there is no need!"

He raised himself again with energy.

"There is always need with Hester. Oh! don't suppose I have forgotten her! I have written to that fellow, my cousin. I went, indeed, to see him the day before yesterday, but the servants at Sandford declared he had gone to town, and they were packing up to follow. Lady Fox-Wilton and Miss Alice here have been keeping a close eye on Hester herself, I know; but if she chose, she could elude us all!"

"She couldn't give such pain — such trouble!" cried Mary indignantly.

The Rector shook his head sadly. Then he looked at his companion.

"Has she made a friend of you? I wish she would."

"Oh! she doesn't take any account of me," said Mary, laughing. "She is quite kind to me — she tells me when she thinks my frock is hideous — or my hat's impossible — or she corrects my French accent. She is quite kind, but she would no more think of taking advice from me than from the sofa-cushion."

Meynell shrugged his shoulders.

"She has no bump of respect — never had!" and he began to give a half humorous account of the troubles and storms of Hester's bringing up. "I often ask myself whether we haven't all — whether I, in particular, haven't been a first-class bungler and blundered all through with regard to Hester. Did we choose the wrong governesses? They seemed most estimable people. Did we thwart her unnecessarily? I can't remember a time when she didn't have everything she wanted!"

"She didn't get on very well with her father?" suggested Mary timidly.

Meynell made a sudden movement, and did not answer for a moment.

"Sir Ralph and she were always at cross-purposes," he said at last. "But he was kind to her — according to his lights; and — he said some very sound and touching things to me about her — on his death-bed."

There was a short silence. Meynell had covered his eyes with his hand. Mary was at a loss how to continue the conversation, when he resumed:

"I wonder if you will understand how strangely this anxiety weighs upon me — just now."

"Just now?"

"Here am I preaching to others," he said slowly, "leading what people call a religious movement, and this homely elementary task seems to be all going wrong. I don't seem to be able to protect this child confided to me."

"Oh, but you will protect her!" cried Mary, "you will! She mayn't seem to give way — when you talk to her; but she has said things to me — to my mother too ——"

"That shows her heart isn't all adamant? Well, well! — you're a comforter, but ——"

"I mean that she knows — I'm sure she does — what you've done for her — how you've cared for her," said Mary, stammering a little.

"I have done nothing but my plainest, simplest duty. I have made innumerable mistakes; and if I fail with her, it's quite clear that I'm not fit to teach or lead anybody."

The words were spoken with an impatient emphasis to which Mary did not venture a reply. But she could not restrain an expression in her gray eyes which was a balm to the harassed combatant beside her.

They said no more of Hester. And presently Mary's hunger for news of the Reform Movement could not be hid. It was clear she had been reading everything she could on the subject, and feeding upon it in a loneliness, and under a constraint, which touched Meynell profoundly. The conflict in her between a spiritual heredity — the heredity of her father's message — and her tender love for her mother had never been so plain to him. Yet he could not feel that he was abetting any disloyalty in allowing the conversation. She was mature. Her mind had its own rights!

Mary indeed, unknown to him, was thrilling under a strange and secret sense of deliverance. Her mother's spiritual grip upon her had relaxed; she moved and spoke with a new though still timid sense of freedom.

So once again, as on their first meeting, only more

intimately, her sympathy, her quick response, led him on. Soon lying back at his ease, his hands behind his head, he was painting for her the progress of the campaign; its astonishing developments; the kindling on all sides of the dry bones of English religion.

The new — or re-written — Liturgy of the Reform was, it seemed, almost completed. From all parts: from the Universities, from cathedral cloisters, from quiet country parishes, from the clash of life in the great towns, men had emerged as though by magic to bring to the making of it their learning and their piety, the stored passion of their hearts. And the mere common impulse, the mere release of thoughts and aspirations so long repressed, had brought about an extraordinary harmony, a victorious selflessness, among the members of the commission charged with the task. The work had gone with rapidity, yet with sureness, as in those early years of Christianity, which saw so rich and marvellous an upgrowth from the old soil of humanity. With surprising ease and spontaneity the old had passed over into the new; just as in the first hundred years after Christ's death the psalms and hymns and spiritual songs of the later Judaism had become, with but slight change, the psalms and hymns of Christianity; and a new sacred literature had flowered on the stock of the old.

"To-night — here! — we submit the new marriage service and the new burial service to the Church Council. And the same thing will be happening, at the same moment, in all the churches of the Reform — scattered through England."

"How many churches now?" she asked, with a quickened breath.

"Eighteen in July — this week, over a hundred. But before our cases come on for trial there will be many more. Every day new congregations come in from new dioceses. The beacon fire goes leaping on, from point to point!"

But the emotion which the phrase betrayed was instantly replaced by the business tone of the organizer as he went on to describe some of the practical developments of the preceding weeks: the founding of a newspaper; the collection of propagandist funds; the enrolment of teachers and missionaries, in connection with each Modernist church. Yet, at the end of it all, feeling broke through again.

"They have been wonderful weeks! — wonderful! Which of us could have hoped to see the spread of such a force in the dusty modern world! You remember the fairy story of the prince whose heart was bound with iron bands — and how one by one, the bands give way? I have seen it like that — in life after life."

"And the fighting?"

She had propped her face on her hands, and her eyes, with their eager sympathy, their changing lights, rained influence on the man beside her; an influence insensibly mingling with and colouring the passion for ideas which held them both in its grip.

" — Has been hot — will be of course infinitely hotter still! But yet, again and again, with one's very foes, one grasps hands. They seem to feel with us 'the common wave' — to be touched by it — touched by our hope. It is as though we had made them realize at last how starved, how shut out, we have been — we, half the thinking nation! — for so long!"

"Don't — don't be too confident!" she entreated. "Aren't you — isn't it natural you should miscalculate the forces against you? Oh! they are so strong! and — and so noble."

She drew in her breath, and he understood her.

"Strong indeed," he said gravely. "But —— "

Then a smile broke in.

"Have I been boasting? You see some signs of swelled head? Perhaps you are right. Now let me tell you what the other side are doing. That chastens one! There is a conference of Bishops next week; there was one a week ago. These are of course thundering resolutions in Convocation. The English Church Union has an Albert Hall meeting; it will be magnificent. A 'League of the Trinity' has started against us, and will soon be campaigning all over England. The orthodox newspapers are all in full cry. Meanwhile the Bishops are only waiting for the decision of my case — the test case — in the lower court to take us all by detachments. Every case, of course, will go ultimately to the Supreme Court — the Privy Council. A hundred cases — that will take time! Meanwhile — from us — a monster petition — first to the Bishops

for the assembling of a full Council of the English
Church, then to Parliament for radical changes in the
conditions of membership of the Church, clerical and
lay."

Mary drew in her breath.

"You *can't* win! you *can't* win!"

And he saw in her clear eyes her sorrow for him and
her horror of the conflict before him.

"That," he said quietly, "is nothing to us. We are
but soldiers under command."

He rose; and, suddenly, she realized with a fluttering
heart how empty that room would be when he was gone.
He held out his hand to her.

"I must go and prepare what I have to say to-night.
The Church Council consists of about thirty people —
two thirds of them will be miners."

"How is it *possible* that they can understand you?"
she asked him, wondering.

"You forget that half of them I have taught
from their childhood. They are my spiritual brothers,
or sons — picked men — the leaders of their fellows —
far better Christians than I. I wish you could see
them — and hear them." He looked at her a little
wistfully.

"I am coming," she said, looking down.

His start of pleasure was very evident.

"I am glad," he said simply; "I want you to know
these men."

"And my mother is coming with me."

Her voice was constrained. Meynell felt a natural surprise. He paused an instant, and then said with gentle emphasis:

"I don' think there will be anything to wound her. At any rate, there will be nothing new, or strange— to *her* — in what is said to-night."

"Oh, no!" Then, after a moment's awkwardness, she said, "We shall soon be going away."

His face changed.

"Going away? I thought you would be here for the winter!"

"No. Mother is so much better, we are going to our little house in the Lakes, in Long Whindale. We came here because mother was ill — and Aunt Rose begged us. But ——"

"Do you know" — he interrupted her impetuously — "that for six months I've had a hunger for just one fortnight up there among the fells?"

"You love them?" Her face bloome with pleasure. "You know the dear mountains?"

He smiled.

"It doesn't do to think of them, does it? You should see the letters on my table! But I may have to take a few days' rest, some time. Should I find you in Long Whindale — if I dropped down on you — over Goat Scar?"

"Yes — from December till March!" Then she suddenly checked the happiness of her look and tone. "I needn't warn you that it rains."

"Doesn't it rain! And everybody pretends it doesn't. The lies one tells!"

She laughed.

They stood looking at each other. An atmosphere seemed to have sprung up round them in which every tone and movement had suddenly become magnified — significant.

Meynell recovered himself. He held out his hand in farewell, but he had scarcely turned away from her, when she made a startled movement toward the open window.

"What is that?"

There was a sound of shouting and running in the street outside. A crowd seemed to be approaching. Meynell ran out into the garden to listen. By this time the noise had grown considerably, and he thought he distinguished his own name among the cries.

"Something has happened at the colliery!" he said to Mary, who had followed him.

And he hurried toward the gate, bareheaded, just as a gray-haired lady in black entered the garden.

"Mother," cried Mary, in amazement.

Catharine Elsmere paused — one moment; she looked from her daughter to Meynell. Then she hurried to the Rector.

"You are wanted!" she said, struggling to get her breath. "A terrible thing has happened. They think four lives have been lost — some accident to the cage — and people blame the man in charge. They've got him shut up in the colliery office — and declare they'll kill him. The crowd looks dangerous — and there are very few police. I heard you were here — some one, the postman, saw you come in — you must stop it. The people will listen to you."

Her fine, pale face, framed in her widow's veil, did not so much ask as command. He replied by a gesture — then by two or three rapid inquiries. Mary — bewildered — saw them for an instant as allies and equals, each recognizing the other. Then Meynell ran to the gate, and was at once swallowed up in the moving groups which had gathered there, and seemed to carry him back with them toward the colliery.

Catharine Elsmere turned to follow — Mary at her side. Mary looked at her in anxiety, dreading the physical strain for one, of late, so frail.

"Mother darling! — ought you?"

Catharine took no heed whatever of the question.

"It is the women who are so terrible," she said in a low voice, as they hurried on; "their faces were like wild beasts. They have telephoned to Cradock for police. If Mr. Meynell can keep them in check for half an hour, there may be hope."

They ran on, swept along by the fringe of the crowd till they reached the top of a gentle descent at the farther end of the village. At the bottom of this hill lay the colliery, with its two huge chimneys, its shed and engine houses, its winding machinery, and its heaps of refuse. Within the enclosure, from the height where they stood, could be seen a thin line of police surrounding a small shed — the pay-office. On the steps of it stood the manager, and the Rector, to be recognized by his long coat and his bare head, had just joined him. Opposite to the police, and separated from the shed by about ten yards and a wooden paling, was a threatening and vociferating mob, which stretched densely across the road and up the hill on either side; a mob largely composed of women — dishevelled, furious women — their white faces gleaming amid the coal-blackened forms of the miners.

"They'll have 'im out," said a woman in front of Mary Elsmere. "Oh, my God! — they'll have 'im out! It was he caused the death of the boy — yo mind 'im — young Jimmy Ragg — a month sen; though the crowner's jury did let 'im off, more shame to them! An' now they say as how he signalled for 'em to bring up the men from the Albert pit afore he'd made sure as the cage in the Victory pit was clear!"

"Explain to me, please," said Mary, touching the woman's arm.

Half a dozen turned eagerly upon her.

"Why, you see, miss, as the two cages is like buckets in a well — the yan goes down, as the other cooms up. An' there's catches as yo mun knock away to let 'un go down — an' this banksman — ee's a devil! — he niver so much as walked across to the other shaft to see — an' theer was the catches fast — an' instead o' goin' down, theer was the cage stuck, an' the rope uncoilin' itsel', and fallin' off the drum — an' foulin' the other rope — An' then all of a suddent, just as them poor fellows wor nearin' top — the drum began to work t'other way — run backards, you unnerstan? — an' the engineman lost 'is head an' niver thowt to put on t' breaks — an' — oh! Lord save us! — whether they was drownt at t'bottom i' the sump, or killt afore they got theer — theer's no one knows yet — They're getten of 'em up now."

And as she spoke, a great shout which became a groan ran through the crowd. Men climbed up the railings at the side of the road that they might see better. Women stood on tiptoe. A confused clamour came from below, and in the colliery yard there could be seen a gruesome sight; four stretchers, borne by colliers, their burdens covered from view. Beside them were groups of women and children and in front of them the crowd made way. Up the hill they came, a great wail preceding and surrounding them; behind them the murmurs of an ungovernable indignation.

As the procession neared them Mary saw a gray-haired woman throw up her arm, and heard her cry out in a voice harsh and hideous with excitement:

"Let 'im as murdered them pay for't! What's t' good o' crowner's juries? — Let's settle it oursel's!"

Deep murmurs answered her.

"And it's this same Jenkins," said another fierce voice, "as had a sight to do wi' bringin' them blacklegs down here, in the strike, last autumn. He's been a

great man sense, has Jenkins, wi' the masters; but he
sha'n't murder our husbinds and sons for us, while he's
loafin' round an' playin' the lord — not he! Have they
got 'un safe?"

"Aye, he's in the pay-house safe enough," shouted
another — a man. "An' if them as is defendin' of 'un
won't give 'un up, there's ways o' makin' them."

The procession of the dead approached — all the men
baring their heads, and the women wailing. In front
came a piteous group — a young half-fainting wife,
supported by an older woman, with children clinging
to her skirts. Catharine went forward, and lifted a
baby or two that was being dragged along the ground.
Mary took up another child, and they both joined the
procession.

As they did so, there was a shout from below.

Mary, white as her dress, asked an elderly miner
beside her, who had shown no excitement whatever, to
tell her what had happened. He clambered up on the
bank to look and came back to her.

"They've beaten 'un back, miss," he said in her ear.
"They've got the surface men to help, and Muster
Meynell he's doing his best; if there's anybody can hold
'em, he can; but there's terrible few on 'em. It is time
as the Cradock men came up. They'll be trying fire
before long, an' the women is like devils."

On went the procession into the village, leaving the
fight behind them. In Mary's heart, as she was pushed
and pressed onward, burnt the memory of Meynell on the

steps — speaking, gesticulating — and the surging crowd in front of him.

There was that to do, however, which deadened fear. In the main street the procession was met by hurrying doctors and nurses. For those broken bodies indeed — young men in their prime — nothing could be done, save to straighten the poor limbs, to wash the coal dust from the strong faces, and cover all with the white linen of death. But the living — the crushed, stricken living — taxed every energy of heart and mind. Catharine, recognized at once by the doctors as a pillar of help, shrank from no office and no sight, however terrible. But she would not permit them to Mary, and they were presently separated.

Mary had a trio of sobbing children on her knee, in the living-room of one of the cottages, when there was a sudden tramp outside. Everybody in Miners' Row, including those who were laying out the dead, ran to the windows.

"The police from Cradock!" — fifty of them.

The news passed from mouth to mouth, and even those who had been maddest half an hour before felt the relief of it.

Meanwhile detachments of shouting men and women ran clattering at intervals through the village streets. Sometimes stragglers from them would drop into the cottages alongside — and from their panting talk, what had happened below became roughly clear. The police had arrived only just in time. The small band defending the office was worn out, the Rector had been struck, palings torn down; in another half-hour the rioters would have set the place on fire and dragged out the man of whom they were in search.

The narrator's story was broken by a howl—

"Here he comes!" And once again, as though by a rush of muddy water, the street filled up, and a strong body of police came through it, escorting the banksman who had been the cause of the accident. A hatless, hunted creature, with white face and loosened limbs, he was hurried along by the police, amid a grim silence that had suddenly succeeded to the noise.

Behind came a group of men, officials of the colliery, and to the right of them walked the Rector, bareheaded as before, a bandage on the left temple. His eyes ran along the cottages, and he presently perceived Mary Elsmere standing at an open door, with a child that had cried itself to sleep in her arms.

Stepping out of the ranks, he approached her. The people made way for him, a few here and there with sullen faces, but in the main with a friendly and remorseful eagerness.

"It's all over," he said in Mary's ear. "But it was touch and go. An unpopular man — suspected of telling union secrets to the masters last year. He was concerned in another accident to a boy — a month ago; they all think he was in fault, though the jury exonerated him. And now — a piece of abominable carelessness! — manslaughter at least. Oh! he'll catch it hot! But we weren't going to have him murdered on our hands. If he hadn't got safe into the office, the women alone would have thrown him down the shaft. By the way, are you learned in 'first aid'?"

He pointed, smiling, to his temple, and she saw that the wound beneath the rough bandage was bleeding afresh.

"It makes me feel a bit faint," he said with annoyance; "and there is so much to do!"

"May I see to it?" said her mother's voice behind her. And Catharine, who had just descended from an upper room, went quickly to a nurse's wallet which had been left on a table in the kitchen, and took thence an antiseptic dressing and some bandaging.

Meynell sat down by the table, shivering a little from shock and strain, while she ministered to him. One of the women near brought him brandy; and Catharine deftly cleaned and dressed the wound. Mary looked on, handing what was necessary to her mother, and in spite of herself, a ray of strange sweetness stole through the tragedy of the day.

In a very few minutes Meynell rose. They were in the cottage of one of the victims. The dead lay overhead, and the cries of wife and mother could be heard through the thin flooring.

"Don't go up again!" he said peremptorily to Catharine. "It is too much for you."

She looked at him gently.

"They asked me to come back again. It is not too much for me. Please let me."

He gave way. Then, as he was following her uptsairs,
he turned to say to Mary:

"Gather some of the people, if you can, outside. I
want to give a notice when I come down."

He mounted the ladder-stairs leading to the upper
room. Violent sounds of wailing broke out overhead,
and the murmur of his voice could be heard between.

Mary quietly sent a few messengers into the street.
Then she gathered up the sleeping child again in her
arms, and sat waiting. In spirit she was in the room
overhead. The thought of those two — her mother and
Meynell — beside a bed of death together, pierced her
heart.

After what seemed to her an age, she heard her mother's
step, and the Rector following. Catharine stood again
beside her daughter, brushing away at last a few quiet
tears.

"You oughtn't to face this any more, indeed you
oughtn't," said Meynell, with urgency, as he joined them.
"Tell her so, Miss Mary. But she has been doing wonders.
My people bless her!"

He held out his hand, involuntarily, and Catharine
placed hers in it. Then, seeing a small crowd already
collected in the street, he hurried out to speak to them.

Heanwhile evening had fallen, a late September
evening, shot with gold and purple. Behind the village
the yellow stubbles stretched up to the edge of the Chase

and drifts of bluish smoke from the colliery chimneys hung in the still air.

Meynell, standing on the raised footpath above the crowd, gave notice that a special service of mourning would be held in the church that evening. The meeting of the Church Council would of course be postponed. ;

During his few words Mary made her way to the farther edge of the gathering, looking over it toward the speaker. Behind him ran the row of cottages, and in the doorway opposite she saw her mother, with her arm tenderly folded round a sobbing girl, the sister of one of the dead. The sudden tranquillity, the sudden pause from tumult and anguish seemed to draw a "wind-warm space" round Mary, and she had time, for a moment, to think of herself and the strangeness of this tragic day.

How amazing that her mother should be here at all. This meeting of the Reformers' League to which she had insisted on coming — as a spectator of course, and with the general public — what did it mean? Mary did not yet know, long as she had pondered it.

How beautiful was the lined face! — so pale in the golden dusk, in its heavy frame of black. Mary could not take her eyes from it. It betrayed an animation, a passion of life, which had been foreign to it for months. In these few crowded hours, when every word and action had been simple, instructive, inevitable; love to God and man working at their swiftest and purest; through all the tragedy and the horror some burden seemed to have dropped from Catharine's soul. She met her daughter's eyes, and smiled.

When Meynell had finished, the crowd silently drifted away, and he came back to the Elsmeres. They noticed the village fly coming toward them — saw it stop in the roadway.

"I sent for it," Meynell explained rapidly. "You mustn't let your mother do any more. Look at her! Please, will you both go to the Rectory? My cook will give you tea; I have let her know. Then the fly will take you home."

They protested in vain — must indeed submit. Catharine flushed a little at being so commanded; but there was no help for it.

"I *would* like to come and show you my den!" said Meynell, as he put them into the carriage. "But there's too much to do here."

He pointed sadly to the cottages, shut the door, and they were off.

During the short drive Catharine sat rather stiffly upright. Saint as she was, she was accustomed to have her way.

They drove into the dark shrubbery that lay between the Rectory and the road. At the door of the little house stood Anne in a white cap and clean apron. But the white cap sat rather wildly on its owner's head; nor would she take any interest in her visitors till she had got from them a fuller account of the tumult at the pit than had yet reached her, and assurances that Meynell's wound was but slight.   But when these were given she pounced upon Catharine.

"Eh, but you're droppin'!"

And with many curious looks at them she hurried them into the study, where a hasty clearance had been made among the books, and a tea-table spread.

She bustled away to bring the tea.

Then exhaustion seized on Catharine.   She submitted to be put on the sofa after it had been cleared of its pile of books; and Mary sat by her a while, holding her hands. Death and the agony of broken hearts overshadowed them.

But then the dogs came in, discreet at first, and presently — at scent of currant cake—effusively friendly. Mary fed them all, and Catharine watched the colour coming back to her face, and the dumb sweetness in the gray eyes.

Presently, while her mother still rested, Mary took courage to wander round the room, looking at the books, the photographs on the walls, the rack of pipes, the carpenter's bench, and the panels of half-finished carving. Timidly, yet eagerly, she breathed in the message it seemed to bring her from its owner — of strenuous and frugal life.   Was that half-faded miniature of a soldier his father — and that sweet gray-haired woman his mother?   Her heart thrilled to each discovery.

Then Anne invaded them, for conversation, and while Catharine, unable to hide her fatigue, lay speechless, Anne chattered about her master.   Her indignation was boundless that any hand could be lifted against him in his own parish. "Why he strips himself bare for them, he does!"

And — with Mary unconsciously leading her — out came story after story, in the racy Mercian vernacular, illustrating a good man's life, and all

> His little nameless unremembered acts
> Of kindness and of love.

As they drove slowly home through the sad village street they perceived Henry Barron calling at some of the stricken houses. The squire was always punctilious, and his condolences might be counted on. Beside him walked a young man with a jaunty step, a bored sallow face, and a long moustache which he constantly caressed. Mary supposed him to be the squire's second son, "Mr. Maurice," whom nobody liked.

Then the church, looming through the dusk; lights shining through its fine perpendicular windows, and the sound of familiar hymns surging out into the starry twilight.

Catharine turned eagerly to her companion.

"Shall we go in?"

The emotion of one to whom religious utterance is as water to the thirsty spoke in her voice. But Mary caught and held her.

"No, dearest, no!— come home and rest." And when Catharine had yielded, and they were safely past the lighted church, Mary breathed more freely. Instinc-

tively she felt that certain barriers had gone down before the tragic tumult, the human action of the day; let
well alone!

And for the first time, as she sat in the darkness,
holding her mother's hand, and watching the blackness
of the woods file past under the stars, she confessed her
love to her own heart — trembling, yet exultant.

Meanwhile in the crowded church, men and women
who had passed that afternoon through the extremes
of hate and sorrow unpacked their hearts in singing
and prayer. The hymns rose and fell through the dim
red sandstone church — symbol of the endless plaint
of human life, forever clamouring in the ears of Time;
and Meynell's address, as he stood on the chancel steps,
almost among the people, the disfiguring strips of
plaster on the temple and brow sharply evident between
the curly black hair and the dark hollows of the eyes,
sank deep into grief-stricken souls. It was the plain
utterance of a man, with the prophetic gift, speaking to human beings to whom, through years of check-
ered life, he had given all that a man can give of
service and of soul. He stood there as the living
expression of their conscience, their better mind, conceived
as the mysterious voice of a Divine power in man; and
in the name of that Power, and its direct message to
the human soul embodied in the tale we call Christianity,
he bade them repent their bloodthirst, and hope in God
for their dead. He spoke amid weeping; and from that

night forward one might have thought his power unshake-able, at least among his own people.

But there were persons in the church who remained untouched by it. In the left aisle Hester sat a little apart from her sisters, her hard, curious look ranging from the preacher through the crowded benches. She surveyed it all as a spectacle, half thrilled, half critical. And at the western end of the aisle the squire and his son stood during the greater part of the service, showing plainly by their motionless lips and folded arms that they took no part in what was going on.

Father and son walked home together in close con-versation.

And two days later the first anonymous letter in the Meynell case was posted in Markborough, and duly de-livered the following morning to an address in Upcote Minor.

CHAPTER XI

"WHAT on earth can Henry Barron desire a private interview with me about?" said Hugh Flaxman looking up from his letters, as he and his wife sat together after breakfast in Mrs. Flaxman's sitting-room.

"I suppose he wants subscriptions for his heresy hunt? The Church party seem to be appealing for funds in most of the newspapers."

"I should have thought he knew I am not prepared to support him," said Flaxman quietly.

"Where are you, old man?" His wife laid a caressing hand on his shoulder —"I don't really quite know."

Flaxman smiled at her.

"You and I are not theologians, are we, darling?" He kissed the hand. "I don't find myself prepared to swear to Meynell's precise 'words' any more than I was to Robert's. But I am ready to fight to prevent his being driven out."

"So am I!" said Rose, erect, with her hands behind her.

"We want all sorts."

"Ye-es," said Rose doubtfully. "I don't think I want Mr. Barron."

"Certainly you do! A typical product — with just

as much right to a place in English religion as Meynell — and no more."

"Hugh! — you must behave very nicely to the Bishop to-night."

"I should think I must!— considering the *ominum gatherum* you have asked to meet him. I really do not think you ought to have asked Meynell."

"There we must agree to differ," said Rose firmly. "Social relations in this country must be maintained — in spite of politics — in spite of religion — in spite of everything."

"That's all very well — but if you mix people too violently, you make them uncomfortable."

"My dear Hugh!— how many drawing-rooms are there?" His wife waved a vague hand toward the folding doors on her right, implying the suite of Georgian rooms that stretched away beyond them; "one for every *nuance* if it comes to that. If they positively won't mix I shall have to segregate them. But they will mix." Then she fell into a reverie for a moment, adding at the end of it — "I must keep one drawing-room for the Rector and Mr. Norham ——"

"That I understand is what we're giving the party for. Intriguer!"

Rose threw him a cool glance.

"You may continue to play Gallio if you like. *I* am now a partisan."

"So I perceive. And you hope to turn Norham into one."

Rose nodded. Mr. Norham was the Home Secretary, the most important member in a Cabinet headed by a Prime Minister in rapidly failing health; to whose place, either by death or retirement it was generally expected that Edward Norham would succeed.

"Well, darling, I shall watch your manœuvres with interest," said Flaxman, rising and gathering up his letters — "and, *longo intervallo*, I shall humbly do my best to assist them. Are Catherine and Mary coming?"

"Mary certainly — and, I think, Catharine. The Fox-Wiltons of course, and that mad creature Hester, who goes to Paris in a few days — and Alice Puttenham. How that sister of hers bullies her — horrid little woman! *And* Mr. Barron!"— Flaxman made an exclamation — "and the deaf daughter — and the nice elder son — and the unpresentable younger one — in fact the whole menagerie."

Flaxman shrugged his shoulders.

"A few others, I hope, to act as buffers."

"Heaps!" said Rose. "I have asked half the neighbourhood — our first big party. And as for the weekenders, you chose them yourself." She ran through the list, while Flaxman vainly protested that he had never in their joint existence been allowed to do anything of the kind. "But to-night you're not to take any notice of them at all. Neighbours first! Plenty of time for you to amuse yourself to-morrow. What time does Mr. Barron come?"

"In ten minutes!" said Flaxman, hastily departing,

only, however, to be followed into his study by Rose, who breathed into his ear —

"And if you see Mary and Mr. Meynell colloguing — play up!"

Flaxman turned round with a start.

"I say! — is there really anything in that?"

Rose, sitting on the arm of his chair, did her best to bring him up to date. Yes — from her observation of the two — she was certain there was a good deal in it.

"And Catharine?"

Rose's eyebrows expressed the uncertainty of the situation.

"But such an odd thing happened last week! You remember the day of the accident — and the Church Council that was put off?"

"Perfectly."

"Catharine made up her mind suddenly to go to that Church Council — after not having been able to speak of Mr. Meynell or the Movement for weeks. *Why* — neither Mary nor I know. But she walked over from the cottage — the first time she has done it. She arrived in the village just as the dreadful thing had happened in the pit. Then of course she and the Rector took command. Nobody who knew Catharine would have expected anything else. And now she and Mary and the Rector are busy looking after the poor survivors. 'It's propinquity does it,' my dear!"

"Catharine could never — never — reconcile herself."

"I don't know," said Rose, doubtfully. "What did she want to go to that Council for?"

"Perhaps to lift up her voice?"

"No. Catharine isn't that sort. She would have suffered dreadfully — and sat still."

And with a thoughtful shake of the head, as though to indicate that the veins of meditation opened up by the case were rich and various, Rose went slowly away.

Then Hugh was left to his *Times*, and to speculations on the reasons why Henry Barron — a man whom he had never liked and often thwarted — should have asked for this interview in a letter marked "private." Flaxman made an agreeable figure, as he sat pondering by the fire, while the *Times* gradually slipped from his hands to the floor. And he was precisely what he looked — an excellent fellow, richly endowed with the world's good things, material and moral. He was of spare build, with grizzled hair; long-limbed, clean-shaven and gray-eyed. In general society he appeared as a person of polished manners, with a gently ironic turn of mind. His friends were more numerous and more devoted than is generally the case in middle age; and his family were rarely happy out of his company. Certain indeed of his early comrades in life were inclined to accuse him of a too facile contentment with things as they are, and a rather Philistine estimate of the value of machinery. He was absorbed in "business" which he did admirably. Not so much of the financial sort, although he was a trusted member of important boards. But for all that unpaid multiplicity of affairs — magisterial, municipal, social or charitable — which make the country gentleman's sphere Hugh Flaxman's appetite was insatiable. He was a born chairman of a county council, and a heaven-sent treasurer of a hospital.

And no doubt this natural bent, terribly indulged of late years, led occasionally to "holding forth"; at least those who took no interest in the things which interested Flaxman said so. And his wife, who was much more concerned for his social effect than for her own, was often nervously on the watch lest it should be true. That her handsome, popular Hugh should ever, even for a quarter of an hour, sit heavy on the soul even of a youth of eighteen was not to be borne; she pounced on each incipient harangue with mingled tact and decision.

But though Flaxman was a man of the world, he was by no means a worldling. Tenderly, unflinchingly, with a modest and cheerful devotion, he had made himself the stay of his brother-in-law Elsmere's harassed and broken life. His supreme and tyrannical common sense had never allowed him any delusions as to the ultimate permanence of heroic ventures like the New Brotherhood; and as to his private opinions on religious matters it is probable that not even his wife knew them. But outside the strong affections of his personal life there was at least one enduring passion in Flaxman which dignified his character. For liberty of experiment, and liberty of conscience, in himself or others, he would gladly

have gone to the stake.   Himself the loyal upholder of
an established order, which he helped to run decently,
he was yet in curious sympathy with many obscure rev-
olutionists in many fields.   To brutalize a man's conscience seemed to him worse than to murder his body.
Hence a constant sympathy with minorities of all sorts;
which no doubt interfered often with his practical effi-
ciency.   But perhaps it accounted for the number of his
friends.

"We shall, I presume, be undisturbed?"
The speaker was Henry Barron; and he and Flaxman
stood for a moment surveying each other after their first
greeting.
"Certainly.   I have given orders.   For an hour if
you wish, I am at your disposal."
"Oh, we shall not want so long."
Barron seated himself in the chair pointed out
to him.   His portly presence, in some faultlessly new
and formal clothes, filled it substantially; and his
colour, always high, was more emphatic than usual.
Beside him, Flaxman made but a thread-paper appearance.
"I have come on an unpleasant errand"— he said,
withdrawing some papers from his breast pocket — "but
— after much thought — I came to the conclusion that
there was no one in this neighbourhood I could consult
upon a very painful matter, with greater profit — than
yourself."

Flaxman made a rather stiff gesture of acknowledgment.

"May I ask you to read that?"

Barron selected a letter from the papers he held and handed it to his host.

Flaxman read it. His face changed and worked as he did so. He read it twice, turned it over to see if it contained any signature, and returned it to Barron.

"That's a precious production! Was it addressed to yourself?"

"No — to Dawes, the colliery manager. He brought it to me yesterday."

Flaxman thought a moment.

"He is — if I remember right — with yourself, one of the five aggrieved parishioners in the Meynell case?"

"He is. But he is by no means personally hostile to Meynell — quite the contrary. He brought it to me in much distress, thinking it well that we should take counsel upon it, in case other documents of the same kind should be going about."

"And you, I imagine, pointed out to him the utter absurdity of the charge, advised him to burn the letter and hold his tongue?"

Barron was silent a moment. Then he said, with slow distinctness:

"I regret I was unable to do anything of the kind."

Flaxman turned sharply on the speaker.

"You mean to say you believe there is a word of truth in that preposterous story?"

"I have good reason, unfortunately, to know that it cannot at once be put aside."

Both paused — regarding each other. Then Flaxman said, in a raised accent of wonder:

"You think it possible — *conceivable* — that a man of Mr. Meynell's character — and transparently blameless life — should have not only been guilty of an intrigue of this kind twenty years ago — but should have done nothing since to repair it — should actually have settled down to live in the same village side by side with the lady whom the letter declares to be the mother of his child — without making any attempt to marry her — though perfectly free to do so? Why, my dear sir, was there ever a more ridiculous, a more incredible tale!"

Flaxman sprang to his feet, and with his hands in his pockets, turned upon his visitor, impatient contempt in every feature.

"Wait a moment before you judge," said Barron dryly. "Do you remember a case of sudden death in this village a few weeks ago? — a woman who returned from America to her son John Broad, a labourer living in one of my cottages — and died forty-eight hours after arrival of brain disease?"

Flaxman's brow puckered.

"I remember a report in the *Post*. There was an inquest — and some curious medical evidence?"

Barron nodded assent.

"By the merest chance, I happened to see that woman the night after she arrived. I went to the cottage to remonstrate on the behaviour of John Broad's boys in my plantation. She was alone in the house, and she came to the door. By the merest chance also, while we stood there, Meynell and Miss Puttenham passed in the road outside. The woman — Mrs. Sabin — was terribly excited on seeing them, and she said things which astounded me. I asked her to explain them, and we talked — alone — for nearly an hour. I admit that she was scarcely responsible, that she died within a few hours of our conversation, of brain disease. But I still do not see — I wish to heaven I did! — any way out of what she told me — when one comes to combine it with — well, with other things. But whether I should finally have decided to make any use of the information I am not sure. But unfortunately"— he pointed to the letter still in Flaxman's hand — "that shows me that other persons — persons unknown to me — are in possession of some, at any rate, of the facts — and therefore that it is now vain to hope that we can stifle the thing altogether."

"You have no idea who wrote the letter?" said Flaxman, holding it up.

"None whatever," was the emphatic reply.

"It is a disguised hand" — mused Flaxman — "but an educated one — more or less. However — we will return presently to the letter. Mrs. Sabin's communication to you was of a nature to confirm the statements contained in it?"

"Mrs. Sabin declared to me that having herself — independently — become aware of certain facts, while she was a servant in Lady Fox-Wilton's employment, that lady — no doubt in order to ensure her silence — took her abroad with herself and her young sister, Miss Alice, to a place in France she had some difficulty in pronouncing — it sounded to me like Grenoble; that there Miss Puttenham became the mother of a child, which passed thenceforward as the child of Sir Ralph and Lady Fox-Wilton, and received the name of Hester. She herself nursed Miss Puttenham, and no doctor was admitted. When the child was two months old, she accompanied the sisters to a place on the Riviera, where they took a villa. Here Sir Ralph Wilton, who was terribly broken and distressed by the whole thing, joined them, and he made an arrangement with her by which she agreed to go to the States and hold her tongue. She wrote to her people in Upcote — she had been a widow for some years — that she had accepted a nurse's situation in the States, and Sir Ralph saw her off from Genoa for New York. She seems to have married again in the States; and in the course of years to have developed some grievance against the Fox-Wiltons which ultimately determined her to come home. But all this part of her story was so excited and incoherent that I could make nothing of it. Nor does it matter very much to the subject — the real subject — we are discussing."

Flaxman, who was standing in front of the speaker, intently listening, made no immediate reply. His eyes — half absently — considered the man before him. In Barron's aspect and tone there was not only the pompous self-importance of the man possessed of exclusive and sensational information; there were also indications of triumphant trains of reasoning behind that outraged his listener.

"What has all this got to do with Meynell?" said Flaxman abruptly.

Barron cleared his throat.

"There was one occasion"— he said slowly — "and one only, on which the ladies at Grenoble — we will say it was Grenoble — received a visitor. Miss Puttenham was still in her room. A gentleman arrived, and was admitted to see her. Mrs. Sabin was bundled out of the room by Lady Fox-Wilton. But it was a small wooden house, and Mrs. Sabin heard a good deal. Miss Puttenham was crying and talking excitedly. Mrs. Sabin was certain from what, according to her, she could not help overhearing, that the man ——"

"Must one go into this back-stairs story?" asked Flaxman, with repulsion.

"As you like," said Barron, impassively. "I should have thought it was necessary." He paused, looking quietly at his questioner.

Flaxman restrained himself with some difficulty.

"Did the woman have any real opportunity of seeing this visitor?"

"When he went away, he stood outside the house talking to Lady Fox-Wilton. Mrs. Sabin was at the window, behind the lace curtains, with the child in her arms. She watched him for some minutes."

"Well?" said Flaxman sharply.

"She had never seen him before, and she never saw him again, until — such at least was her own story — from the door of her son's cottage, while I was with her, she saw Miss Puttenham — and Meynell — standing in the road outside."

Flaxman took a turn along the room, and paused.

"You admit that she was ill at the time she spoke to you — and in a distracted, incoherent state?"

"Certainly I admit it." Barron drew himself erect, with a slight frown, as though tacitly protesting against certain suggestions in Flaxman's manner and voice. "But now let us look at another line of evidence. You as a newcomer are probably quite unaware of the gossip there has always been in this neighbourhood, ever since Sir Ralph Wilton's death, on the subject of Sir Ralph's will. That will in a special paragraph committed Hester Fox-Wilton to Richard Meynell's guardianship in remarkable terms; no provision whatever was made for the girl under Sir Ralph's will, and it is notorious that he treated her quite differently from his other children. From the moment also of the French journey, Sir Ralph's character and temper appeared to change. I have inquired of a good many persons as to this; of course with absolute discretion. He was a man of narrow Evangelical opinions" — at the word "narrow" Flaxman threw a sudden glance at the speaker — "and of strict veracity. My belief is that his later life was darkened by the falsehood to which he and his wife committed themselves. Finally, let me ask you to look at the young lady herself;

at the extraordinary difference between her and her supposed family; at her extraordinary likeness — to the Rector.

Flaxman raised his eyebrows at the last words, his aspect expressing disbelief and disgust even more strongly than before. Barron glanced at him, and then, after a moment, resumed in another manner, loftily explanatory:

"I need not say that personally I find myself mixed up in such a business with the utmost reluctance."

"Naturally," put in Flaxman dryly. "The risks attaching to it are simply gigantic."

"I am aware of it. But as I have already pointed out to you, by some strange means — connected I have no doubt with the woman, Judith Sabin, though I cannot throw any light upon them — the story is no longer in my exclusive possession, and how many people are already aware of it and may be aware of it we cannot tell. I thought it well to come to you in the first instance, because I know that — you have taken some part lately — in Meynell's campaign."

"Ah!" thought Flaxman — "now we've come to it!"

Aloud he said:

"By which I suppose you mean that I am a subscriber to the Reform Fund, and that I have become a personal friend of Meynell's? You are quite right. Both my wife and I greatly like and respect the Rector." He laid stress on the words.

"It was for that very reason — let me repeat — that

I came to you. You have influence with Meynell; and I want to persuade you, if I can, to use it." The speaker paused a moment, looking steadily at Flaxman. "What I venture to suggest is that you should inform him of the stories that are now current. It is surely just that he should be informed. And then — we have to consider the bearings of this report on the unhappy situation in the diocese. How can we prevent its being made use of? It would be impossible. You know what the feeling is — you know what people are. In Meynell's own interest, and in that of the poor lady whose name is involved with his in this scandal, would it not be desirable in every way that he should now quietly withdraw from this parish and from the public contest in which he is engaged? Any excuse would be sufficient — health — overwork — anything. The scandal would then die out of itself. There is not one of us — those on Meynell's side, or those against him — who would not in such a case do his utmost to stamp it out. But — if he persists — both in living here, and in exciting public opinion as he is now doing — the story will certainly come out! Nothing can possibly stop it."

Barron leant back and folded his arms. Flaxman's eyes sparkled. He felt an insane desire to run the substantial gentleman sitting opposite to the door and dismiss him with violence. But he restrained himself.

"I am greatly obliged to you for your belief in the power of my good offices," he said, with a very frosty smile, "but I am afraid I must ask to be excused. Of course if the matter became serious, legal action would be taken very promptly."

"How can legal action be taken?" interrupted Barron roughly. "Whatever may be the case with regard to Meynell and her identification of him, Judith Sabin's story is true. Of that I am entirely convinced."

But he had hardly spoken before he felt that he had made a false step. Flaxman's light blue eyes fixed him.

"The story with regard to Miss Puttenham?"

"Precisely."

"Then it comes to this: Supposing that woman's statement to be true, the private history of a poor lady who has lived an unblemished life in this village for many years is to be dragged to light — for what? In order — excuse my plain speaking — to blackmail Richard Meynell, and to force him to desist from the public campaign in which he is now engaged? These are hardly measures likely, I think, to commend themselves to some of your allies, Mr. Barron!"

Barron had sprung up in his chair.

"What my allies may or may not think is nothing to me. I am of course guided by my own judgment and conscience. And I altogether protest against the word you have just employed. I came to you, Mr. Flaxman, I can honestly say, in the interests of peace! — in the interests of Meynell himself."

"But you admit that there is really no evidence worthy of the name connecting Meynell with the story at all!" said Flaxman, turning upon him. "The crazy impression of a woman dying of brain disease — some gossip about Sir Ralph's will — a likeness that many people have never perceived! What does it amount to? Nothing! — nothing at all! — less than nothing!"

"I can only say that I disagree with you." The voice was that of a rancorous obstinacy at last unveiled. "I believe that the woman's identification was a just one — though I admit that the proof is difficult. But then perhaps I approach the matter in one way, and you in another. A man, Mr. Flaxman, in my belief, does not throw over the faith of Christ for nothing! No! Such things are long prepared. Conscience, my dear sir, conscience breaks down first. The man becomes a hypocrite in his private life before he openly throws off the restraints of religion. That is the sad sequence of events. I have watched it many times."

Flaxman had grown rather white. The man beside him seemed to him a kind of monstrosity. He thought of Meynell, of the eager refinement, the clean idealism, the visionary kindness of the man — and compared it with the "muddy vesture," mental and physical, of Meynell's accuser.

Nevertheless, as he held himself in with difficulty he began to perceive more plainly than he had yet done some of the intricacies of the situation.

"I have nothing to do," he said, in a tone that he endeavoured to make reasonably calm, "nor has anybody, with generalization of that kind, in a case like this. The point is — could Meynell, being what he is, what we all know him to be, have not only betrayed a young girl, but have then failed to do her the elementary justice of marrying her? And the reply is that the thing is incredible!"

"You forget that Meynell was extremely poor, and had his brothers to educate ——"

Flaxman shrugged his shoulders in laughing contempt.

"Meynell desert the mother of his child — because of poverty — because of his brothers' education! — *Meynell!* You have known him some years — I only for a few months. But go into the cottages here — talk to the people — ask them, not what he believes, but what he *is* — what he has been to them. Get one of them, if you can, to credit this absurdity!"

"The Rector's intimate friendship with Miss Puttenham has long been an astonishment — sometimes a scandal — to the village!" exclaimed Barron, doggedly.

Flaxman stared at him in a blank amazement, then flushed. He took a turn up and down the room, after which he returned to the fireside, composed. What was the use of arguing with such a disputant? He felt as though the mere conversation were an insult to Meynell, in which he was forced to participate.

He took a seat deliberately, and put on his magisterial manner, which, however, was much more delicately and unassumingly authoritative than that of other men.

"I think we had better clear up our ideas. You bring me a story — a painful story — concerning a lady with whom we are both acquainted, which may or may

not be true.   Whether it is true or not is no concern of ours.
Neither you nor I have anything to do with it, and legal
penalties would certainly follow the diffusion of it.   You
invite me to connect with it the name of a man for whom
I have the deepest respect and admiration; who bears an
absolutely stainless record; and you threaten to make
use of the charge in connection with the heresy trials
now coming on.   Now let me give you my advice — for
what it may be worth.   I should say — as you have asked
my opinion — have nothing whatever to do with the
matter!   If anybody else brings you anonymous letters,
tell them something of the law of libel — and something
too of the guilt of slander!   After all, with a little good
will, these are matters that are as easily quelled as raised.
A charge so preposterous has only to be firmly met to
die away.   It is your influence, and not mine, which is
important in this matter.   You are a permanent resi-
dent, and I a mere bird of passage.   And" — Flaxman's
countenance kindled — "let me just remind you of
this: if you want to strengthen Meynell's cause — if
you want to win him thousands of new adherents — you
have only to launch against him a calumny which is sure
to break down — and will inevitably recoil upon you!"

The two men had risen.   Barron's face, handsome in
feature, save for some thickened lines and the florid
tint of the cheeks, had somehow emptied itself of expression while Flaxman was speaking.

"Your advice is no doubt excellent," he said quietly,
as he buttoned his coat, "but it is hardly practical.   If

there is one anonymous letter, there are probably others. If there are letters — there is sure to be talk — and talk cannot be stopped. And in time everything gets into the newspapers."

Flaxman hesitated a moment. Something warned him not to push matters to extremities — to make no breach with Barron — to keep him in play.

"I admit, of course, if this goes beyond a certain point it may be necessary to go to Meynell — it may be necessary for Meynell to go to his Bishop. But at present, if you *desire* to suppress the thing, you have only to keep your own counsel — and wait. Dawes is a good fellow, and will, I am sure, say nothing. I could, if need be, speak to him myself. I was able to get his boy into a job not long ago."

Barron straightened his shoulders slowly.

"Should I be doing right — should I be doing my duty — in assisting to suppress it — always supposing that it could be suppressed — my convictions being what they are?"

Then — suddenly — it was borne in on Flaxman that in the whole interview there had been no genuine desire whatever on Barron's part for advice and consultation. He had come determined on a certain course, and the object of the visit had been, in truth, merely to convey to one of Meynell's supporters a hint of the coming attack, and some intimation of its strength. The visit had been in fact a threat — a move in Barron's game.

"That, of course, is a question which I cannot presume

to decide," said Flaxman, with cold politeness. His manner changed instantly. Peremptorily dismissing the subject, he became, on the spot, the mere suave and courteous host of an interesting house; he pointed out the pictures and the view, and led the way to the hall.

As he took leave, Barron stiffly intimated that he should not himself be able to attend Mrs. Flaxman's party that evening; but his daughter and sons hoped to have the pleasure of obeying her invitation.

"Delighted to see them," said Flaxman, standing in the doorway, with his hands in his pockets. "Do you know Edward Norham?"

"I have never met him."

"A splendid fellow — likely I think to be the head of the Ministry before the year's out. My wife was determined to bring him and Meynell together. He seems to have the traditional interest in theology without which no English premier is complete."

Pursued by this parting shot, Barron retired, and Flaxman went back thoughtfully to his wife's sitting-room. Should he tell her? Certainly. Her ready wits and quick brain were indispensable in the battle that might be coming. Now that he was relieved from Barron's bodily presence, he was by no means inclined to pooh-pooh the communication which had been made to him.

As he approached his wife's door he heard voices. Catharine! He remembered that she was to lunch and spend the day with Rose. Now what to do! Devoted as he was to his sister-in-law, he was scarcely inclined to trust her with the incident of the morning.

But as soon as he opened the door, Rose ran upon him, drew him in and closed it. Catharine was sitting on the sofa — with a pale, kindled look — a letter in her hand.

"Catharine has had an abominable letter, Hugh! — the most scandalous thing!"

Flaxman took it from Catharine's hana, looked it through, and turned it over. The same script, a little differently disguised, and practically the same letter, as that which had been shown him in the library! But it began with a reference to the part which Mrs. Elsmere and her daughter had played in the terrible accident of the preceding week, which showed that the rogue responsible for it was at least a rogue possessed of some local and personal information.

Flaxman laid it down, and looked at his sister-in-law. "Well?"

Catharine met his eyes with the clear intensity of her own.

"Isn't it hard to understand how anybody can do such a thing as that?" she said, with her patient sigh — the sigh of an angel grieving over the perversity of men.

Flaxman dropped on the sofa beside her.

"You feel with me, that it is a mere clumsy attempt to injure Meynell, in the interests of the campaign against him?" he asked her, eagerly.

"I don't know about that," said Catharine slowly —

a shining sadness in her look. "But I do know that it could only injure those who are trying to fight his errors — if it could be supposed that they had stooped to such weapons!"

"You dear woman!" cried Flaxman, impulsively, and he raised her hand to his lips.   Catharine and Rose looked their astonishment.   Whereupon he gave them the history of the hour he had just passed through.

CHAPTER XII

BUT although what one may call the natural free-masonry of the children of light had come in to protect Catharine from any touch of that greedy credulity which had fastened on Barron; though she and Rose and Hugh Flaxman were at one in their contemptuous repudiation of Barron's reading of the story, the story itself, so far as it concerned Alice Puttenham and Hester, found in all their minds but little resistance.

"It may — it may be true," said Catharine gently. "If so — what she has gone through! Poor, poor thing!"

And as she spoke — her thin fingers clasped on her black dress, the nun-like veil falling about her shoulders, her aspect had the frank simplicity of those who for their Lord's sake have faced the ugly things of life.

"What a shame — what an outrage — that any of us here should know a word about it!" cried Rose, her small foot beating on the floor, the hot colour in her cheek. "How shall we ever be able to face her to-night?"

Flaxman started.

"Miss Puttenham is coming to-night?"

"Certainly. She comes with Mary — who was to pick her up — after dinner."

Flaxman patrolled the room a little, in meditation. Finally he stopped before his wife.

"You must realize, darling, that we may be all walking on the edge of a volcano to-night."

"If only Henry Barron were! — and I might be behind to give the last little *chiquenade!*" cried Rose.

Flaxman devoutly echoed the wish.

"But the point is — are there any more of these letters out? If so, we may hear of others to-night. Then — what to do? Do I make straight for Meynell?"

They pondered it.

"Impossible to leave Meynell in ignorance," said Flaxman — "if the thing spreads Meynell of course would be perfectly justified — in his ward's interests — in denying the whole matter absolutely, true or no. But can he? — with Barron in reserve — using the Sabin woman's tale for his own purposes?"

Catharine's face, a little sternly set, showed the obscure conflict behind.

"He cannot say what is false," she said stiffly. "But he can refuse to answer."

Flaxman looked at her with an expression as confident as her own.

"To protect a woman, my dear Catharine — a man may say anything in the world — almost."

Catharine made no reply, but her quiet face showed she did not agree with him.

"That child Hester!" Rose emerged suddenly from a mental voyage of recollection and conjecture. "Now one understands why Lady Fox-Wilton — stupid woman! — has never seemed to care a rap for her. It must indeed be annoying to have to mother a child so much handsomer than your own."

"I think I am very sorry for Sir Ralph Fox-Wilton," said Catharine, after a moment.

Rose assented.

"Yes! — just an ordinary dull, pig-headed country gentleman confronted with a situation that only occurs in plays to which you don't demean yourself by going! — and obliged to tell and act a string of lies, when lies happen to be just one of the vices you're not inclined to! And then afterward you find yourself let in for living years and years with a bad conscience — hating the cuckoo-child, too, more and more as it grows up. Yes! — I am quite sorry for Sir Ralph!"

"By the way!" — Flaxman looked up — "Do you know I am sure that I saw Miss Fox-Wilton — with Philip Meryon — in Howlett's spinney this morning. I came back from Markborough by a path I had never discovered before — and there, sure enough, they were. They heard me on the path, I think, and vanished most effectively. The wood is very thick. But I am sure it was they — though they were some distance from me."

Rose exclaimed.

"Naughty, *naughty* child! She has been absolutely forbidden to see him, the whole Fox-Wilton family have made themselves into gaolers and spies — and she just outwits them all! Poor Alice Puttenham hovers about her — trying to distract and amuse her — and has no more influence than a fly. And as for the Rector, it would be absurd, if it weren't enraging! Look at all there is on his shoulders just now — the way people appeal to him from all over England to come and speak — or consult — or organize — (I don't want to be controversial, Catharine, darling! — but there it is). And he can't make up his mind to leave Upcote for twenty-four hours till this girl is safely off the scene! He means to take her to Paris himself on Monday. I only hope he has found a proper sort of Gorgon to leave her with!"

Flaxman could not but reflect that the whole relation of Meynell to his ward might well give openings to such a scoundrel like the writer of the anonymous letters, who was certainly acquainted with local affairs. But he did not express this feeling aloud. Meanwhile Catharine, who showed an interest in Hester which surprised both him and Rose, began to question him on the subject of Philip Meryon. Meryon's mother, it seemed, had been an intimate friend of one of Flaxman's sisters, Lady Helen Varley, and Flaxman was well acquainted with the young man's most unsatisfactory record. He drew a picture of the gradual degeneracy of the handsome lad who had been the hope and delight of his warm-hearted, excitable mother; of her deepening disappointment and premature death.

"Helen kept up with him for a time, for his mother's sake, but unluckily he has put himself beyond the pale now, one way and another. It is too disastrous about this pretty child! What on earth does she see in him?"

"Simply a means of escaping from her home," said Rose — "the situation working out! But who knows whether he hasn't got a wife already? Nobody should trust this young man farther than they can see him."

"It musn't — it can't be allowed!" said Catharine, with energy. And, as she spoke, she seemed to feel again the soft bloom of Hester's young cheek against her own, just as when she had drawn the girl to her, in that instinctive caress. The deep maternity in Catharine had never yet found scope enough in the love of one child.

Then, with a still keener sense of the various difficulties rising along Meynell's path, Flaxman and Rose returned to the anxious discussion of Barron's move and how to meet it. Catharine listened, saying little; and it was presently settled that Flaxman should himself call on Dawes, the colliery manager, that afternoon, and should write strongly to Barron, putting on paper the overwhelming arguments, both practical and ethical, in favour of silence — always supposing there were no further developments.

"Tell me" — said Rose presently, when Flaxman had left the sisters alone — "Mary of course knows nothing of that letter?"

Catharine flushed.

"How could she?" She looked almost haughtily at her sister.

Rose murmured an excuse. Would it be possible to keep all knowledge from Mary that there *was* a scandal — of some sort — in circulation, if the thing developed?"

Catharine, holding her head high, thought it would not only be possible, but imperative.

Rose glanced at her uncertainly. Catharine was the only person of whom she had ever been afraid. But at last she took the plunge.

"Catharine! — don't be angry with me — but I think Mary is interested in Richard Meynell."

"Why should I be angry?" said Catharine. She had coloured a little, but she was perfectly composed. With her gray hair, and her plain widow's dress, she threw her sister's charming mondanity into bright relief. But beauty — loftily understood — lay with Catharine.

"It *is* ill luck — his opinions!" cried Rose, laying her hand upon her sister's.

"Opinions are not 'luck,' " said Catharine, with a rather cold smile.

"You mean we are responsible for them? Perhaps we are, if we are responsible for anything — which I sometimes doubt. But you like him — personally?" The tone was almost pleading.

"I think he is a good man."

"And if — if — they do fall in love — what are we all to do?"

Rose looked half whimsically — half entreatingly at her sister.

"Wait till the case arises," said Catharine, rather

sharply. "And please don't interfere. You are too fond of match-making, Rose!"

"I am — I just ache to be at it, all the time. But I wouldn't do anything that would be a grief to you."

Catharine was silent a moment. Then she said in a tone that went to the listener's heart:

"Whatever happened — will be God's will."

She sat motionless, her eyes drooped, her features a little drawn and pale; her thoughts — Rose knew it — in the past.

Flaxman came back from his interview with Dawes, reporting that nothing could have been in better taste or feeling than Dawes's view of the matter. As far as the Rector was concerned — and he had told Mr. Barron so — the story was ridiculous, the mere blunder of a crazy woman; and, for the rest, what had they to do in Upcote with ferreting into other people's private affairs? He had locked up the letter in case it might some time be necessary to hand it to the police, and didn't intend himself to say a word to anybody. If the thing went any further, why of course the Rector must be informed. Otherwise silence was best. He had given a piece of his mind to Mr. Barron and "didn't want to be mixed up in any such business." "As far as I'm concerned, Mr. Flaxman, I'm fighting for the Church and her Creeds — I'm not out for backbiting!"

"Nice man!" — said Rose, with enthusiasm —"Why didn't I ask him to-night!"

"But"— resumed Flaxman —"he warned me that if any letter of the kind got into the hands of a certain Miss Nairn in the village there might be trouble."

"Miss Nairn? — Miss Nairn?" The sisters looked at each other. "Oh, I know — the lady in black we saw in church the day the revolution began — a strange little shrivelled spinster-thing who lives in that house by the post-office. She quarrelled mortally with the Rector last year, because she ill-treated a little servant girl of hers, and the Rector remonstrated."

"Well, she's one of the 'aggrieved.'"

"They seem to be an odd crew! There's the old sea-captain that lives in that queer house with the single yew tree and the boarded-up window on the edge of the Heath. He's one of them. He used to come to church about once a quarter and wrote the Rector interminable letters on the meaning of Ezekiel. Then there's the publican — East — who nearly lost his license last year — he always put it down to the Rector and vowed he'd be even with him. I must say, the church in Upcote seems rather put to it for defenders!"

"In Upcote," corrected Flaxman. "That's because of Meynell's personal hold. Plenty of 'em — quite immaculate—elsewhere. However, Dawes is a perfectly decent, honest man, and grieved to the heart by the Rector's performances."

Catharine had waited silently to hear this remark, and then went away to write a letter.

"Poor darling! Will she go and call on Dawes — for

sympathy?" said Flaxman, mischievously to his wife
as the door closed.

"Sympathy?" Rose's face grew soft. "It's much as
it was with Robert.   It ought to be so simple — and it
is so mixed!   Nature of course *ought* to have endowed all
unbelievers with the proper horns and tail.   And there
they go — stealing your heart away! — and your daughter's."

The Flaxmans and Catharine — who spent the day with
her sister, before the evening party — were more and
more conscious of oppression as the hours went on; as
though some moral thunder hung in the air.

Flaxman asked himself again and again — "Ought I
to go to Meynell at once?" and could not satisfy himself
with any answer; while he, his wife, and his sister-in-
law, being persons of delicacy, were all ashamed of finding
themselves the possessors, against their will, of facts —
supposing they were facts — to which they had no right.
Meynell's ignorance — Alice Puttenham's ignorance — of
their knowledge, tormented their consciences.   And it
added to their discomfort that they shared their knowledge with such a person as Henry Barron.   However,
there was no help for it.

A mild autumn day drew to its close, with a lingering
gold in the west and a rising moon.   The charming old
house, with its faded furniture, and its out-at-elbows
charm, was lit up softly, with lamps that made a dim but
friendly shining in its wide spaces.   It had never belonged

to rich people, but always to people of taste. It boasted no Gainsboroughs or Romneys; but there were lesser men of the date, possessed of pretty talents of their own, painters and pastellists, who had tried their hands on the family, of whom they had probably been the personal friends. The originals of the portraits on the walls were known neither to history nor scandal; but their good, modest faces, their brave red or blue coats, their white gowns, and drooping feathers looked winningly out from the soft shadows of the rooms. At Maudeley, Rose wore her simplest dresses, and was astonished at the lightness of the household expenses. The house indeed had never known display, or any other luxury than space; and to live in it was to accept its tradition.

The week-enders arrived at tea-time; Mr. Norham with a secretary and a valet, much preoccupied, and chewing the fag-end of certain Cabinet deliberations in the morning; Flaxman's charming sister, Lady Helen Varley, and her husband; his elder brother, Lord Wanless, unmarried, an expert on armour, slightly eccentric, but still, in the eyes of all intriguing mothers, and to his own annoyance, more than desirable as a husband owing to the Wanless collieries and a few other trifles of the same kind; the Bishop of Markborough; Canon France and his sister; a young poet whose very delicate muse had lodged itself oddly in the frame of an athlete; a high official in the Local Government Board, Mr. Spearman, whom Rose regarded with distrust as likely to lead Hugh into too much talk about workhouses; Lady Helen's two girls just

out, as dainty and well-dressed, as gayly and innocently
sure of themselves and their place in life as the "classes"
at their best know how to produce; and two or three
youths, bound for Oxford by the end of the week, samples,
these last, of a somewhat new type in that old University
— combining the dash, family, and insolence of the old
"tuft" or Bullingdon man, with an amazing aptitude
for the classics, rare indeed among the "tufts" of old.
Two out of the three had captured almost every distinction that Oxford offers; and all three had been either
gated for lengthy periods or "sent down," or otherwise
trounced by an angry college, puzzled by the queer connection between Irelands and Hertfords on the one hand
and tipsy frolics on the other.

Meynell appeared for dinner — somewhat late. It was
only with great difficulty that the Flaxmans had prevailed on him to come, for the purpose of meeting Mr.
Norham. But the party within the church which, foreseeing a Modernist defeat in the church courts, was
appealing to Parliament to take action, was strengthening every week; Meynell's Saturday articles in the *Modernist*, the paper founded by the Reformers' League,
were already providing these parliamentarians with a
policy and inspiration; and if the Movement were to go
on swelling during the winter, the government might have
to take very serious cognizance of it during the spring.
Mr. Norham therefore had expressed a wish for some
conversation with the Modernist leader, who happened
to be Rector of Upcote; and Meynell, who had by now cut

himself adrift from all social engagements, had with difficulty saved an evening.

As far as Norham was concerned Meynell would have greatly preferred to take the Home Secretary for a Sunday walk on the Chase; but he had begun to love the Flaxmans, and could not make up his mind to say No to them. Moreover, was it not more than probable that he would meet at Maudeley "one simple girl," of whom he did not dare in these strenuous days to let himself think too much?

So that Rose, as she surveyed her dinner table, could feel that she was maintaining the wide social traditions of England, by the mingling of as many contraries as possible.   But the oil and vinegar were after all cunningly mixed, and the dinner went well.   The Bishop was separated from Meynell by the length of the table, and Norham was carefully protected from Mr. Spearman, in his eyes a prince of bores, who was always bothering the Home Office.

The Bishop, wno was seated beside Rose at one end of the table, noticed the black patch on Meynell's temple, and inquired its origin.   Rose gave him a graphic account both of the accident and the riot.   The Bishop raised his eyebrows.

"How does he contrive to live the two lives?" he said in a tone slightly acid.   "If he continues to lead this Movement, he will have to give up fighting mobs and running up and down mines."

"What is going to happen to the Movement? " Rose asked him, with her most sympathetic smile. Socially and in her own house she was divinely all things to all men. But the Bishop was rather suspicious of her.

"What can happen to it but defeat? The only other alternative is the break-up of the Church. And for that, thank God, they are not strong enough."

"And no compromise is possible?"

"None. In three months Meynell and all his friends will have ceased to belong to the English Church. It is very lamentable. I am particularly sorry for Meynell himself — who is one of the best of men."

Rose felt her colour rising. She longed to ask —"But supposing *England* has something to say? — suppose she chooses to transform her National Church? Hasn't she the right and the power?"

But her instincts as hostess stifled her pugnacity. And the little Bishop looked so worn and fragile that she had no heart for anything but cosseting him. At the same time she noticed — as she had done before on other occasions — the curious absence of any ferocity, any smell of brimstone, in the air! How different from Robert's day! Then the presumption underlying all controversy was of an offended authority ranged against an apologetic rebellion. A tone of moral condemnation on the one side, a touch of casuistry on the other, confused the issues. And now — behind and around the combatants — the clash of equal hosts! — over ground strewn with dead assumptions. The conflict might be no less strenuous; nay! from a series of isolated struggles it had developed into a world-wide battle; but the bitterness between man and man was less.

Yes! — for the nobler spirits — the leaders and generals of each army. But what of the rank and file? And at the thought of Barron she laughed at herself for supposing that religious rancour and religious slander had died out of the world!

"Can we have some talk somewhere?" said Norham languidly, in Meynell's ear, as the gentlemen left the dining-room.

"I think Mrs. Flaxman will have arranged something," said Meynell, with a smile — detecting the weariness of the political Atlas.

And indeed Rose had all her dispositions made. They found her in the drawing-room, amid a bevy of bright gowns and comely faces, illumined by the cheerful light of a big wood fire — a circle of shimmering stuffs and gems, the blaze sparkling on the pointed slippers, the white necks and glossy hair of the girls, and on the diamonds of their mothers.

But Rose, the centre of the circle, sprang up at once, at sight of her two *gros bonnets*.

"The green drawing-room!" she murmured in Meynell's ear, and tripped on before them, while the incoming crowd of gentlemen, mingling with the ladies, served to mask the movement.

Not, however, before the Bishop had perceived the

withdrawal of the politician and the heretic. He saw that Canon France, who followed him, had also an eye to the retreating figures.

"I trust we too shall have our audience!" said the Bishop, ironically.

Canon France shrugged his shoulders, smiling.

Then his small shrewd eyes scanned the Bishop intently. Nothing in that delicate face beyond the sentiments proper to the stituation? — the public situation? As to the personal emotion involved, that, the Canon knew, was for the time almost exhausted. The Bishop had suffered much during the preceding months — in his affections, his fatherly feeling toward his clergy, in his sense of the affront offered to Christ's seamless vesture of the Church. But now, France thought, pain had been largely deadened by the mere dramatic interest of the prospect ahead, by the anodyne of an immense correspondence, and of a vast increase in the business of the day, caused by the various actions pending.

Nothing else — new and disturbing — in the Bishop's mind? He moved on, chatting and jesting with the young girls who gathered round him. He was evidently a favourite with them, and with all nice women. Finally he sank into an armchair beside Lady Helen Varley, exchanging Mrs. Flaxman's cossetting for hers. His small figure was almost lost in the armchair. The firelight danced on his slender stockinged legs, on his episcopal shoe buckles, on the cross which adorned his episcopal breast, and then on the gleaming snow of his hair, above his blue eyes with their slight unearthliness, so large and flower-like in his small white face. He seemed very much at ease — throwing off all burdens.

No! — the Slander which had begun to fly through the diocese, like an arrow by night, had not yet touched the Bishop.

Nor Meynell himself?

Yet France was certain that Barron had not been idle, that he had not let it drop. "I advised him to let it drop"— he said uneasily to himself — "that was all I could do."

Then he looked round him, at the faces of the women present. He scarcely knew any of them. Was she among them — the lady of Barron's tale? He thought of the story as he might have thought of the plot of a novel. When medieval charters were not to be had, it made an interesting subject of speculation. And Barron could not have confided it to any one in the diocese, so discreet — so absolutely discreet — as he.

"I gather this Movement of yours is rapidly becoming formidable?" said Norham to his companion.

He spoke with the affectation of interest that all politicians in office must learn. But there was no heart in it, and Meynell wondered why the great man had desired to speak with him at all.

He replied that the growth of the Movement was certainly a startling fact.

"It is now clear that we must ultimately go to Parlia-

ment.   The immediate result in the Church courts is
of course not in doubt.   But our hope lies in such demonstrations in the country as may induce Parliament"—
he paused, laying a quiet emphasis on each word — "to
reconsider — and resettle — the conditions of membership and office in the English Church."

"Good heavens!" cried Norham, throwing up his
hand — "What a prospect! If that business once gets
into the House of Commons, it'll have everything else
out."

"Yes.   It's big enough to ask for time — and take it."

Norham suppressed a slight yawn as he turned in his
chair.

"The House of Commons, alas! — never shows to advantage in an ecclesiastical debate.   You'd think it was
in the condition of Sydney Smith with a cold — not
sure whether there were nine Articles and Thirty-Nine
Muses — or the other way on!"

Meynell looked at the Secretary of State in silence —
his eyes twinkling.   He had heard from various friends
of this touch of insolence in Norham.   He awaited its
disappearance.

Edward Norham was a man still young; under forty
indeed, though marked prematurely by hard work and hard
fighting.   His black hair had receded on the temples,
and was obviously thinning on the crown of the head;
he wore spectacles, and his shoulders had taken the stoop
of office work.   But the eyes behind the spectacles lost
nothing that they desired to see; and the general impres-

sion was one of bull-dog strength, which could be impertinent and aggressive, and could also masque itself in a good humour and charm by no means insincere. In his political career, he was on the eve of great things; and he would owe them mainly to a power of work, supreme even in these hard-driven days. This power of work enabled him to glean in many fields, and keep his eye on many chances that his colleagues perforce neglected. The Modernist Movement was one of these chances. For years he had foreseen great changes ahead in the relations of Church and State, and this group of men seemed to be forcing the pace.

Suddenly, as his eyes perused the strong humanity of the face beside him, Norham changed his manner. He sat up and put down the paper-knife he had been teasing. As he did so there was a little crash at his elbow and something rolled on the floor.

"What's that?"

"No harm done," said Meynell, stooping — "one of our host's Greek coins. What a beauty!" He picked up the little case and the coin which had rolled out of it — a gold coin of Velia, with a head of Athene — one of the great prizes of the collector.

Norham took it with eagerness. He was a Cambridge man, and a fine scholar, and such things delighted him.

"I didn't know Flaxman cared for these things."

"He inherited them," said Meynell, pointing to the open cabinet on the table. "But he loves them too. Mrs. Flaxman always has them put out on great occasions.

It seems to me they ought to have a watcher! They are quite priceless, I believe. Such things are soon lost."

"Oh! — they are safe enough here," said Norham, returning the coin to its place, with another loving look at it. Then, with an effort, he pulled himself together, and with great rapidity began to question his companion as to the details and progress of the Movement. All the facts up to date, the number of Reformers enrolled since the foundation of the League, the League's finances, the astonishing growth of its petition to Parliament, the progress of the Movement in the Universities, among the ardent and intellectual youth of the day, its spread from week to week among the clergy: these things came out steadily and clearly in Meynell's replies.

"The League was started in July — it is now October. We have fifty thousand enrolled members, all communicants in Modernist churches. Meetings and demonstrations are being arranged at this moment all over England; and in January or February there will be a formal inauguration of the new Liturgy in Dunchester Cathedral."

"Heavens!" said Norham, dropping all signs of languor. "Dunchester will venture it?"

Meynell made a sign of assent.

"It is of course possible that the episcopal proceedings against the Bishop, which, as you see, have just begun, may have been brought to a close, and that the Cathedral may be no longer at our disposal, but ——"

"The Dean, surely, has power to close it!"

"The Dean has come over to us, and the majority of the Canons."

Norham threw back his head with a laugh of amazement.

"The first time in history that a Dean has been of the same opinion as his Bishop! Upon my word, the government has been badly informed or I have not kept up. I had no idea — simply no idea — that things had gone so far. Markborough of course gives us very different accounts — he and the Bishops acting with him."

"A great deal is going on which our Bishop here is quite unaware of."

"You can substantiate what you have been saying?"

"I will send you papers to-morrow morning. But of course" — added Meynell, after a pause — "a great many of us will be out of our berths, in a few months, temporarily at least. It will rest with Parliament whether we remain so!"

"The Non-Jurors of the twentieth century!" murmured Norham, with a half-sceptical intonation.

"Ah, but this *is* the twentieth century!"— said Meynell smiling. "And in our belief the *dénouement* will be different."

"What will you do — you clergy — when you are deprived?"

"In the first place, it will take a long time to deprive us — and so long as there are any of us left in our livings, each will come to the help of the other."

"But you yourself?"

"I have already made arrangements for a big barn in the village" — said Meynell, smiling — "a great tithe-barn of the fifteenth century, a magnificent old place, with a forest of wooden arches, and a vault like a church. The village will worship there for a while. We shall make it beautiful!"

Norham was silent for a moment. He was stupefied by the energy, the passion of religious hope in the face beside him. Then the critical temper in him conquered his emotion, and he said, not without sarcasm:

"This is all very surprising — very interesting — but what are the *ideas* behind you? A thing like this cannot live without ideas — and I confess I have always thought the ideas of Liberal Christianity a rather beggarly set-out — excuse the phrase!"

"There is nothing to excuse! — the phrase fits. 'A reduced Christianity' — as opposed to a 'full Christianity'— that is the description lately given, I think, by a divinity professor. I don't quarrel with it at all. Who can care for a 'reduced' anything! But a *transformed* Christianity — that is another matter."

"Why 'Christianity' at all?"

Meynell looked at him in a smiling silence. He — the man of religion — was unwilling in these surroundings to play the prophet, to plunge into the central stream of argument. But Norham, the outsider and dilettante, was conscious of a kindled mind.

"That is the question to which it always seems to me there is no answer," he said easily, leaning back in his chair. "You think you can take what you like of a great historical religion and leave the rest — that you can fall back on its pre-suppositions and build it anew. But the pre-suppositions themselves are all crumbling. 'God'—'soul,' 'free-will,' 'immortality'—even human identity — is there one of the old fundamental notions that still stands, unchallenged? What are we in the eyes of modern psychology — but a world of automata — dancing to stimuli from outside? What has become of conscience — of the moral law — of Kant's imperative — in the minds of writers like these?"

He pointed to two recent novels lying on the table, both of them brilliant glorifications of sordid forms of adultery.

Meynell's look fired.

"Ah! — but let us distinguish. *We* are not anarchists — as those men are. Our claim is precisely that we are, and desire to remain, a part of a *Society* — a definite community with definite laws — of a National Church — of the nation, that is, in its spiritual aspect. The question for which we are campaigning is as to the terms of membership in that society. But terms and conditions there must always be. The 'wild living intellect of man' must accept conditions in the Church, as *we* conceive it, no less than in the Church as Newman conceived it."

Norham shrugged his shoulders.

"Then why all this bother?"

"Because the conditions must be adjusted from time to time! Otherwise the church suffers and souls are lost

— wantonly, without reason.   But there is no church —
no religion — without some venture, some leap of faith!
If you can't make any leap at all — any venture — then
you remain outside — and you think yourself, perhaps,
entitled to run amuck — as these men do!"   He pointed
to the books.   "But *we* make the venture! — *we* accept
the great hypothesis — of faith."

The sound of voices came dimly to them from the
farther rooms.   Norham pointed toward them.

"What difference then between you — and your
Bishop?"

"Simply that in his case — as *we* say — the hypothesis of faith is weighted with a vast mass of stubborn
matter that it was never meant to carry — bad history,
bad criticism, an out-grown philosophy.   To make
it carry it — in our belief — you have to fly in the face
of that gradual education of the world — education of
the mind, education of the conscience — which is the
chief mark of God in the world.   But the hypothesis of
Faith, itself, remains — take it at its lowest — as rational,
as defensible, as legitimate as any other!"

"What do you mean by it?   God — conscience —
responsibility?"

"Those are the big words!" said Meynell, smiling
— "and of course the true ones.   But what the saint means
by it, I suppose, in the first instance, is that there is in
man something mysterious, superhuman — a Life in
life — which can be indefinitely strengthened, enlightened,
purified, till it reveal to him the secret of the world, till

it 'toss him' to the 'breast' of God!— or again, can be weakened, lost, destroyed, till he relapses into the animal. Believe it, we say! Live by it! — make the venture. *Verificatur vivendo!*"

Again the conversation paused. From the distance once more came the merry clamour of the farther drawing-room. A din of young folk, chaffing and teasing each other — a girl's defiant voice above it —·outbursts of laughter. Norham, who had in him a touch of dramatic imagination, enjoyed the contrast between the gay crowd in the distance and this quiet room where he sat face to face with a visionary — surely altogether remote from the marrying, money-making, sensuous world. Yet after all the League was a big, practical, organized fact.

"What you have expressed — very finely, if I may say so — is of course the mystical creed," he replied at last, with suave politeness. "But why call it Christianity?"

As he spoke, he was conscious of a certain pride in himself. He felt complacently that he understood Meynell and appreciated him; and that hardly any of his colleagues would, or could have done so.

"Why call it Christianity?" he repeated.

"Because Christianity *is* this creed! — 'embodied in a tale.' And mankind must have tales and symbols."

"And the life of Christ is your symbol?"

"More! — it is our Sacrament — the supreme Sacrament — to which all other symbols of the same kind lead — in which they are summed up."

"And that is why you make so much of the Eucharist?"

"It is — to us — just as full of mystical meaning, just as much the meeting-place of God and man, as to the Catholic — Roman or Anglican."

"Strange that there should be so many of you!" said Norham, after a moment, with an incredulous smile.

"Yes — that has been the discovery of the last six months. But we might all have guessed it. The fuel has been long laid — now comes the kindling, and the blaze!"

There was a pause. Then Norham said abruptly —

"Now what is it you want of Parliament?"

The two men plunged into a discussion, in which the politician became presently aware that the parish priest, the visionary, possessed a surprising amount of practical and statesman-like ability.

Meanwhile — a room or two away — in the great bare drawing-room, with its faded tapestries, and its warm mixture of lamplight and firelight, the evening guests had been arriving. Rose stood at the door of the drawing-room, receiving, her husband beside her, Catharine a little way behind.

"Oh!" cried Rose suddenly, under her breath, only heard by Hugh — a little sound of perturbation.

Outside, in the hall, hardly lit at intervals by oil-lamps, a group could be seen advancing; in front Alice Puttenham and Mary, and behind, the Fox-Wilton party,

Hester's golden head and challenging gait drawing all eyes as she passed along.

But it was on Alice Puttenham that Rose's gaze was fixed. She came dreamily forward; and Rose saw her marked out, by the lovely oval of the face, its whiteness, its melancholy, from all the moving shapes around her. She wore a dress of black gauze over white; a little scarf of old lace lay on her shoulders; her still abundant hair was rolled back from her high brow and sad eyes. She looked very small and childish — as frail as thistle-down.

And behind her, Hester's stormy beauty! Rose gave a little gulp. Then she found herself pressing a cold hand, and was conscious of sudden relief. Miss Puttenham's shy composure was unchanged. She could not have looked so — she could not surely have confronted such a gathering of neighbours and strangers, if —

No, no! The Slander — Rose, in her turn, saw it under an image, as though a dark night-bird hovered over Upcote — had not yet descended on this gentle head. With eager kindness, Hugh came forward — and Catharine. They found her a place by the fire, where presently the glow seemed to make its way to her pale cheeks, and she sat silent and amused, watching the triumph of Hester.

For Hester was no sooner in the room than, resenting perhaps the decidedly cool reception that Mrs. Flaxman had given her, she at once set to work to extinguish all the other young women there. And she had very soon succeeded. The Oxford youths, Lord Wanless, the sons of two or three neighbouring squires, they were all presently gathered about her, as thick as bees on honeycomb, recognizing in her instantly one of those beings endowed from their cradle with a double portion of sex-magic, who leave such a wild track behind them in the world.

By her chair stood poor Stephen Barron, absorbed in her every look and tone. Occasionally she threw him a word — Rose thought for pure mischief; and his whole face would light up.

In the centre of the circle round Hester stood one of the Oxford lads, a magnificent fellow, radiating health and gayety, who was trying to wear her down in one of the word-games of the day. They fought hard and breathlessly, everybody listening partly for the amusement of the game, partly for the pleasure of watching the good looks of the young creatures playing it. At last the man turned on his heel with a cry of victory.

"Beaten! — beaten! — by a hair. But you're wonderful, Miss Fox-Wilton. I never found anybody near so good as you at it before, except a man I met once at Newmarket — Philip Meryon — do you know him? Never saw a fellow so good at games. But an awfully queer fish!"

It seemed to the morbid sensitiveness of Rose that there was an instantaneous and a thrilling silence. Hester tossed her head; her colour, after the first start, ebbed away; she grew pale.

312 THE CASE OF RICHARD MEYNELL

"Yes, I do know him. Why is he a queer fish? You only say that because he beat you!"

The young man gave a half-laugh, and looked at his friends. Then he changed the subject. But Hester got up impatiently from her seat, and would not play any more. Rose caught the sudden intentness with which Alice Puttenham's eyes pursued her.

Stephen Barron came to the help of his hostess, and started more games. Rose was grateful to him — and quite intolerably sorry for him.

"But why was I obliged to shake hands with the other brother?" she thought rebelliously, as she watched the disagreeable face of Maurice Barron, who had been standing in the circle not far from Hester. He had a look of bad company which displeased her; and she resented what seemed to her an inclination to stare at the pretty women — especially at Hester, and Miss Puttenham. Heavens! — if that odious father had betrayed anything to such a son! Surely, surely it was inconceivable!

The party was beginning to thin when Meynell, impatient to be quit of his Cabinet Minister that he might find Mary Elsmere before it was too late, hurried from the green drawing-room, in the wake of Mr. Norham, and stumbled against a young man, who in the very imperfect illumination had not perceived the second figure behind the Home Secretary.

"Hullo!" said Meynell brusquely, stepping back. "How do you do? Is Stephen here?"

Maurice Barron answered in the affirmative — and

added, as though from the need to say something, no matter what:

"I hear there are some coins to be seen in there?"

"There are."

Meynell passed on, his countenance showing a sternness, a contempt even, that was rare with him. He and Norham passed through the next drawing-room, and met various acquaintances at the farther door. Maurice Barron stood watching them. The persons invading the room had come intending to see the coins. But meeting the Home Secretary they turned back with him, and Meynell followed them, eager to disengage himself from them. At the door some impulse made him turn and look back. He saw Maurice Barron disappearing into the green drawing-room.

The night was soft and warm. Catharine and Mary had come prepared to walk home, Catharine eagerly resuming, now that her health allowed it, the Spartan habits of their normal life. Flaxman was drawn by the beauty of the moonlight and the park to offer to escort them to the lower lodge. Hester declared that she too would walk, and carelessly accepted Stephen's escort. Meynell stepped out from the house with them, and in the natural sequence of things he found himself with Mary.

Flaxman and Catharine, who led the way, hardly spoke to each other. They walked, pensive and depressed. Each knew what the other was thinking of, and each felt that nothing was to be gained for the moment by any fresh talk about it. Just behind them they could hear Hester laughing and sparring with Stephen; and when Catharine looked back she could see Meynell and Mary far away, in the distance of the avenue they were following.

The great lime-trees on either side threw long shadows on grass covered with the fresh fallen leaf, which gleamed, a pale orange, through the dusk. The sky was dappled with white cloud, and the lime-boughs overhead broke it into patterns of delight. The sharp scent of the fallen leaves was in the air; and the night for all its mildness prophesied winter. Meynell seemed to himself to be moving on enchanted ground, beneath enchanted trees. The tension of his long talk with Norham, the cares of his leadership — the voices of a natural ambition, dropped away. Mary in a blue cloak, a white scarf wound about her head, summed up for him the pure beauty of nature and the night. For the first time he did not attempt to check the thrill in his veins; he began to hope. It was impossible to ignore the change in Mrs. Elsmere's attitude toward him. He had no idea what had caused it; but he felt it. And he realized also that through unseen and inexplicable gradations Mary had come mysteriously near to him. He dared not have spoken a word of love to her; but such feeling as theirs, however restrained, penetrates speech and gesture, and irresistibly makes all things new.

They spoke of the most trivial matters, and hardly

noticed what they said.   He all the time was thinking: "Beyond this tumult there will be rest some day — then I may speak.   We could live hardly and simply — neither of us wants luxury.   But *now* it would be unjust — it would bring too great a burden on her — and her poor mother.   I must wait!   But we shall see each other — we shall understand each other!"

Meanwhile she, on her side, would perhaps have given the world to share the struggle from which he debarred her.

Nevertheless, for both, it was an hour of happiness and hope.

CHAPTER XIII

"SO I see your name this morning, Stephen, on their list."

Henry Barron held up a page of the *Times* and pointed to its first column.

"I sent it in some time ago."

"And pray what does your parish think of it?"

"They won't support me."

"Thank God!"

Barron rose majestically to his feet, and from the rug surveyed his thin, fair-haired son. Stephen had just ridden over from his own tiny vicarage, twelve miles away, to settle some business connected with a family legacy with his father. Since the outbreak of the Reform Movement there had been frequent disputes between the father and son, if aggressive attack on the one side and silent endurance on the other make a dispute. Barron scorned his eldest son, as a faddist and a dreamer; while Stephen could never remember the time when his father had not seemed to him the living embodiment of prejudice, obstinacy, and caprice. He had always reckoned it indeed the crowning proof of Meynell's unworldly optimism that, at the moment of his father's accession to the White House estate, there should have been a passing friendship between him and the Rector.   Yet whenever thoughts of this kind presented themselves explicitly to Stephen he tried to suppress them.   His life, often, was a constant struggle between a genuine and irrepressible dislike of his father and a sore sense that no Christian priest could permit himself such a feeling.

He made no reply to his father's interjection.   But Barron knew very well that his son's self-control was no indication of lack of will; quite the contrary; and the father was conscious of a growing exasperation as he watched the patient compression of the young mouth. He wanted somehow to convict and crush Stephen; and he believed that he held the means thereto in his hand.   He had not been sure before Stephen arrived whether he should reveal the situation or not.   But the temptation was too great.   That the son's mind and soul should finally have escaped his father, "like a bird out of the snare of the fowler," was the unforgivable offence.   What a gentle, malleable fellow he had seemed in his school and college days! — how amenable to the father's spiritual tyranny!   It was Barron's constant excuse to himself for his own rancorous feeling — that Meynell had robbed him of his son.

"You probably think it strange" — he resumed harshly — "that I should rejoice in what of course is your misfortune — that your people reject you; but there are higher interests than those of personal affection concerned in this business.   We who are defending her must think first of the Church!"

"Naturally," said Stephen.

His father looked at him in silence for a moment, at the mild pliant figure, the downcast eyes.

"There is, however, one thing for which I have cause — we all have cause — to be grateful to Meynell," he said, with emphasis.

Stephen looked up.

"I understand he refused to sanction your engagement to Hester Fox-Wilton."

The young man flushed.

"It would be better, I think, father, if we are to talk over these matters quietly — which I understood is the reason you asked me to come here to-day — that you should avoid a tone toward myself and my affairs which can only make frank conversation difficult or impossible between us."

"I have no desire to be offensive," said Barron, checking himself with difficulty, "and I have only your good in view, though you may not believe it. My reason for approving Meynell in the matter is that he was aware — and you were not aware" — he fell into the slow phrasing he always affected on important occasions — "of facts bearing vitally on your proposal; and that in the light of them he acted as any honest man was bound to act."

"What do you mean!" cried Stephen, springing to his feet.

"I mean" — the answer was increasingly deliberate — "that Hester Fox-Wilton — it is very painful to have to go into these things, but it is necessary, I regret to say —

is not a Fox-Wilton at all — and has no right whatever to her name!"

Stephen walked up to the speaker.

"Take care, father! This is a question of a *girl* — an unprotected girl! What right have you to say such an abominable thing!"

He stood panting and white, in front of his father.

"The right of truth!" said Barron. "It happens to be true."

"Your grounds?"

"The confession of the woman who nursed her mother — who was *not* Lady Fox-Wilton."

Barron had now assumed the habitual attitude — thumbs in his pockets, legs slightly apart — that Stephen had associated from his childhood with the long bullying, secular and religious, that Barron's family owed to Barron's temperament.

In the pause, Stephen's quick breathing could be heard.

"Who was she?"

The son's tone had caught the father's sharpness.

"Well, my dear Stephen, I am not sure that I shall tell you while you look at me in that fashion! Believe me — it is not my fault, but my misfortune, that I happen to be acquainted with this very disagreeable secret. And I have one thing to say — you must give me your promise that you will regard any communication from me as entirely confidential, before I say another word."

Stephen walked away to the window and came back. "Very well. I promise."

"Sit down. It is a long story."

The son obeyed mechanically, his frowning eyes fixed upon his father. Barron at once plunged into an account of his interview with Judith Sabin, omitting only those portions of it which connected the story with Meynell. It was evident, presently, that Stephen — to the dawning triumph of his father — listened with an increasingly troubled mind. And indeed, at the first whisper of the story, there had flashed through the young man's memory the vision of Meynell arguing and expostulating on that July afternoon, when he, Stephen, had spoken so confidingly, so unsuspectingly of his love for Hester. He recalled his own amazement, his sense of shock and strangeness. What Meynell said on that occasion seemed to have so little relation to what Meynell habitually was. Meynell, for whom love, in its spiritual aspect, was the salt and significance of life, the foundation of all wisdom — Meynell on that occasion had seemed to make comparatively nothing of love! — to deny its simplest rights — to put it despotically out of count. Stephen, as he had long recognized, had been overborne and silenced by Meynell's personality rather than by Meynell's arguments — by the disabling force mainly of his own devotion to the man who bade him wait and renounce. But in his heart he had never quite forgiven, or understood; and for all the subsequent trouble about Hester, all his own jealousy and pain, he had not been able to prevent himself from blaming Meynell. And now — now! — if this story were true — he began to understand. Poor child — poor mother! With the marriage of the child, must come — he felt the logic of it — the confession of the mother. A woman like Alice Puttenham, a man like Meynell, were not likely to give Hester to her lover without telling that lover what he had a right to know. Small blame to them if they were not prepared to bring about that crisis prematurely, while Hester was still so young! It must be faced — but not, *not* till it must!

Yes, he understood. A rush of warm and pitiful love filled his heart; while his intelligence dismally accepted and endorsed the story his father was telling with that heavy tragic touch which the son instinctively hated as insincere and theatrical.

"Now then, perhaps," — Barron wound up — "you will realize why it is I feel Meynell has acted considerately, and as any true friend of yours was bound to act. He knew — and you were ignorant. Such a marriage could not have been for your happiness, and he rightly interposed."

"What difference does it make to Hester herself," cried Stephen hotly — "supposing the thing is true? I admit — it may be true," and as he spoke a host of small confirmations came thronging into his unwilling mind. "But in any case ——"

He walked up to his father again.

"What have you done about it, father?" he said, sharply. "I suppose you went to Meynell at once."

Barron smiled, with a lift of the eyebrows.   He knocked off the end of his cigarette, and paused.

"Of course you have seen Meynell?" Stephen repeated.

"No, I haven't."

"I should have thought that was your first duty."

"It was not easy to decide what my duty was," said Barron, with the same emphasis, "not at all easy."

"What do you mean, father?   There seems to be something more behind.   If there is, considering my feeling for Hester, it seems to me that having told me so much you are bound to tell me *all* you know.   Remember — this story concerns the girl I love!"

Passion and pain spoke in the young man's voice. His father looked at him with an involuntary sympathy.

"I know.   I am very sorry for you.   But it concerns other people also."

"What is known of the father?" said Stephen abruptly.

"Ah, that is the point!" said Barron, making an abstracted face.

"It is a question to which I am surely entitled to have an answer!"

"I am not sure that I can give it you.   I can tell you of course what the view of Judith Sabin was — what the facts seem to point to.   But — in any case, whether I believe Judith Sabin or no, I should not have said a word to you on the subject but for the circumstance that — unfortunately — there are other people in the case."

Whereupon — watching his son carefully — Barron repeated the story that he had already given to Flaxman.

The effect upon Meynell's young disciple and worshipper may be imagined. He grew deadly pale, and then red; choked with indignant scorn; and could scarcely bring himself to listen at all, after he had once gathered the real gist of what his father was saying.

Yet, by this time, the story was much better worth listening to than it had been when Barron had first presented it to Flaxman. By dint of much brooding, and under the influence of an angry obstinacy which must have its prey, Barron had made it a good deal more plausible than it had been to begin with, and would no doubt make it more plausible still. He had brought in by now a variety of small local observations bearing on the relations between the three figures in the drama — Hester, Alice Puttenham, Meynell — which Stephen must and did often recognize as true and telling. It was true that there was much friction and difference between Hester and the Fox-Wilton family; that Alice Puttenham's position and personality had always teased the curiosity of the neighbourhood; that the terms of Sir Ralph's will were perplexing; and that Meynell was Hester's guardian in a special sense, a fact for which there was no obvious explanation. It was true also that there emerged at times a singular likeness in Hester's beauty — a likeness of expression and gesture — to the blunt and powerful aspect of the Rector. . . .

And yet! Did his father believe, for a moment, the preposterous things he was saying? The young man sharpened his wits as far as possible for Hester's and his friend's sake, and came presently to the conclusion that it was one of those violent, intermittent half-beliefs which, in the service of hatred and party spirit, can be just as effective and dangerous as any other. And when the circumstantial argument passed presently into the psychological — even the theological— this became the more evident.

For in order to explain to himself and others how Meynell could possibly have behaved in a fashion so villainous, Barron had invented by now a whole psychological sequence. He was prepared to show in detail how the thing had probably evolved; to trace the processes of Meynell's mind. The sin once sinned, what more natural than Meynell's proceeding? Marriage would not have mended the disgrace, or averted the practical consequences of the intrigue. He certainly could not have kept his living had the facts been known. On the one hand his poverty — his brothers to educate, — his benefice to be saved. On the other, the natural desire of the Fox-Wiltons and of Alice Puttenham to conceal everything that had occurred. The sophistries of love would come in — repentance — the desire to make a fresh start — to protect the woman he had sacrificed.

And all that might have availed him against sin and temptation — a steadfast Christian faith — was already deserting him; must have been already undermined. What was there to wonder at? — what was there incredible in the story? The human heart was corrupt and desperately wicked; and nothing stood between any man, however apparently holy, and moral catastrophe but the grace of God.

Stephen bore the long, incredible harangue, as best he could, for Meynell's sake. He sat with his face turned away from his father, his hand closing and unclosing on his knee, his nerves quivering under the exasperation of his father's monstrous premises, and still more monstrous deductions. At the end he faced round abruptly.

"I do not wish to offend you, father, but I had better say at once that I do not accept, for a single instant, your arguments or your conclusion. I am positive that the facts, whatever they may be, are *not* what you suppose them to be! I say that to begin with. But now the question is, what to do. You say there are anonymous letters about. That decides it. It is clear that you must go to Meynell at once! And if you do not, I must."

Barron's look flashed.

"You gave me your promise" — he said imperiously — "before I told you this story — that you would not communicate it without my permission. I withhold the permission."

"Then you must go yourself," said the young man vehemently — "You must!"

"I am not altogether unwilling to go," said Barron slowly. "But I shall choose my own time."

And as he raised his cold eyes upon his son it pleased his spirit of intrigue, and of domination through intrigue, that he had already received a letter from Flaxman giving precisely opposite advice, and did not intend to tell Stephen anything about it. Stephen's impulsive candour, however, appealed to him much more than Flaxman's reticence. It would indeed be physically and morally impossible for him — anonymous letters or no — to lock the scandal much longer within his own breast. It had become a living and burning thing, like some wild creature straining at a leash.

A little while later Stephen found himself alone. He believed himself to have got an undertaking from his father that Meynell should be communicated with promptly — perhaps that very evening. But the terms of the promise were not very clear; and the young man's mind was full of a seething wrath and unhappiness. If the story were true, so far as Hester and her unacknowledged mother were concerned — and, as we have seen, there was that in his long and intimate knowledge of Hester's situation which, as he listened, had suddenly fused and flashed in a most unwilling conviction — then, what dire, what pitiful need, on their part, of protection and of help! If indeed any friendly consideration for him, Stephen, had entered into Meynell's conduct, the young man angrily resented the fact.

He paced up and down the library for a time, divided thus between a fierce contempt for Meynell's slanderers and a passionate pity for Hester.

His father had gone to Markborough. Theresa was, he believed, in the garden giving orders. Presently the

clock on the bookcase struck three, and Stephen awoke
with a start to the engagements of the day.

He was in the act of opening the library door when he
suddenly remembered — Maurice!

He blamed himself for not having remembered earlier
that Maurice was at home — for not having asked his
father about him. He went to look for him, could not
find him in any of the sitting-rooms, and finally mounted
to the second-floor bedroom which had always been his
brother's.

"Maurice!" He knocked. No answer. But there
was a hurried movement inside, and something that
sounded like the opening of a drawer.

He called again, and tried the door. It was locked.
But after further shuffling inside, as though some one
were handling papers, it was thrown open.

"Well, Maurice, I hope I haven't disturbed you in
anything very important. I thought I must come and
have a look at you. Are you all right?"

"Come in, old fellow," said Maurice with affected
warmth — "I was only writing a few letters. No room
for anybody downstairs but the pater and Theresa, so
I have to retreat up here."

"And lock yourself in?" said Stephen, laughing.
"Any secrets going?" And as he took a seat on the
edge of the bed, while Maurice returned to his chair, he
could not prevent himself from looking with a certain
keen scrutiny both at the room and his younger brother.

He and Maurice had never been friends. There was a gap of nearly ten years between them, and certain radical and profound differences of temperament. And these differences nature had expressed, with an entire absence of subtlety, in their physique — in the slender fairness and wholesomeness of Stephen, as contrasted with the sallowness, the stoop, the thin black hair, the furtive, excitable look of Maurice.

"Getting on well 'with your new work?" he asked, as he took unwilling note of the half-consumed brandy and soda on the table, of the saucer of cigarette ends beside it, and the general untidiness and stuffiness of the room.

"Not bad," said Maurice, resuming his cigarette.

"What is it?"

"An agency — one of these new phonographs — Yankee of course. I manage the office. A lot of cads — but I make 'em sit up."

And he launched into boasting of his success in the business — the orders he had secured, the economies he had brought about in the office. Stephen found himself wondering meanwhile what kind of a business it could be that entrusted its affairs to Maurice. But he betrayed no scepticism, and the two talked in more or less brotherly fashion for a few minutes, till Stephen, with a look at his watch, declared that he must find his horse and go.

"I thought you were only coming for the week-end," he said as he moved toward the door.

"I got seedy — and took a week off. Besides, I found pater in such a stew."

Stephen hesitated.

"About the Rector?"

Maurice nodded.

"Pater is in an awful way about it. I've been trying to cheer him up. Meynell will be turned out, of course."

"Probably," said Stephen gravely. "So shall I."

"What'll you do?"

"Become a preacher somewhere — under Meynell."

The younger brother looked with a sort of inquisitive grin at the elder.

"You're ready to put your money on him to that extent? Well, all I know is, father's dead set against him — and I've no use for him — never had!"

"That's because you didn't know him," said Stephen briefly. "What did you ever have against him?"

He looked sharply at his brother. The disagreeable idea crossed his mind that his father, whose weakness for Maurice he well knew, might have told the story to the lad.

Maurice laughed, and pulled his scanty moustache as he turned away.

"Oh! I don't know — we never hit it off. My fault, of course. Ta, ta."

As Stephen rode away he was haunted for a few minutes by some disagreeable reminiscences of a school holiday when Maurice had been discovered drunk in one

of the public-houses of the village by the Rector, who
had firmly dug him out and walked him home. But
this and other recollections, not dissimilar, soon passed
away, under the steady assault of thoughts far more
compelling. . . .

He took the bridle-path through Maudeley, and was
presently aware, in a clearing of the wood, of the figure
of Meynell in front of him.

The Rector was walking in haste, without his dogs.
He was therefore out on business, which indeed was
implied by the energy of his whole movement.

He looked round, frowning as Stephen overtook
him.

"Is that you, Stephen? Are you going home?"

"Yes. And you?"

Meynell did not immediately reply. The autumn
wood, a splendour of gold and orange leaf overhead, of
red-brown leaf below, with passages here and there
where the sun struck through the beech trees, of purest
lemon-yellow, or intensest green, breathed and murmured round them. A light wind sang in the tree-tops,
and every now and then the plain broke in — purple
through the gold; with its dim colliery chimneys, its
wreaths of smoke, and its paler patches which stood for
farms and villages.

Meynell walked by the horse in silence for a while,
till, suddenly wiping a hot brow, he turned and looked
at Stephen.

"I think I shall have to tell you, Stephen, where I am going, and why," he said, eying the young man with a deprecating look, almost a look of remorse.

Stephen stared at him in silence.

"Flaxman walked home with me last night — came into the Rectory, and told me that — yesterday — he saw Meryon and Hester together — in Howlett's wood — as you know, a lonely place where nobody goes. It was a great blow to me. I had every reason to believe him safely out of the neighbourhood. All his servants have clearly been instructed to lie — and Hester! — well, I won't trust myself to say what I think of her conduct! I went up this morning to see her — found the whole household in confusion! Nobody knew where Hester was. She had gone out immediately after breakfast, with the maid who is supposed to be always with her. Then suddenly — about an hour later — one of the boys appeared, having seen this woman at the station — and no Hester. The woman, taken by surprise — young Fox-Wilton just had a few words with her as the train was moving off — confessed she was going into Markborough to meet Hester and come back with her. She didn't know where Miss Hester was. She had left her in the village, and was to meet her at a shop in Markborough. After that, things began to come out. The butler told tales. The maid is clearly an unprincipled hussy, and has probably been in Meryon's pay all the time ——"

"Where is Hester? — where are you going to?" cried

Stephen in impatient misery, slipping from his horse, as
he spoke, to walk beside the Rector.

"In my belief she is at Sandford Abbey."

"At Sandford!" cried the young man under his breath.
"Visit that scoundrel in his own house!"

"It appears she has once or twice declared that, in
spite of us all, she would go and see his house and his
pictures. In my belief, she has done it this morning.
It is her last chance. We go to Paris to-morrow. However, we shall soon know."

The Rector pushed on at redoubled speed. Stephen
kept up with him, his lips twitching.

"Why did you separate us?" he broke out at last, in
a low, bitter voice.

And yet he knew why — or suspected! But the inner
smart was so great he could not help the reproach.

"I tried to act for the best," said Meynell, after a
moment, his eyes on the ground.

Stephen watched his friend uncertainly. Again and
again he was on the point of crying out —

"Tell me the truth about Hester!" — on the point
also of warning and informing the man beside him.
But he had promised his father. He held his tongue
with difficulty.

When they reached the spot where Stephen's path
diverged from that which led by a small bridge across
the famous trout-stream to Sandford Abbey, Stephen
suddenly halted.

"Why shouldn't I come too? I'll wait at the lodge.

She might like to ride home.   She can sit anything —
with any saddle.   I taught her."

"Well — perhaps," said Meynell dubiously.   And
they went on together.

Presently Sandford Abbey emerged above the road,
on a rising ground — a melancholy, dilapidated pile;
and they struck into a long and neglected evergreen
avenue leading up to it.   At the end of the avenue
there was an enclosure and a lodge, with some iron gates.
A man saw them, and came out to the gate.

"Sir Philip's gone abroad, sir," he said, affably, when
he saw them.   "Shall I take your card?"

"Thank you.   I prefer to leave it at the house," said
Meynell shortly, motioning to him to open the gate.
The man hesitated, then obeyed.   The Rector went up
the drive, while Stephen turned back a little along the
road, letting his horse pasture on its grassy fringe.   The
lodge keeper — sulky and puzzled — watched him a few
moments and then went back into the house.

The Rector paused to reconnoitre as he came in sight
of the house.   It was a strange, desolate, yet most romantic spot.   Although, seen from the road and the stream,
it seemed to stand on an eminence, it was really at the
bottom of a hill which encircled it on three sides, and what
with its own dilapidation, its broken fences and gates,
the trees which crowded about it, and the large green-
grown pond in front of it, it produced a dank and sinister
impression.   The centre of the building, which had evi-

dently been rebuilt about 1700, to judge from its rose-red
brick, its French classical lunettes, its pedimented doors
and windows, and its fine *perron*, was clearly the inhabited portion of the building. The two wings of
much earlier date, remains of the old Abbey, were falling
into ruin. In front of one a garage had evidently been
recently made, and a motor was standing at its door. To
the left of the approaching spectator was a small deserted
church, of the same date as the central portion of the
Abbey, with twin busts of William and Mary still inhabit-
ing a niche above the classical entrance, and marking
the triumph of the Protestant Succession over the crumbling buildings of the earlier faith. The windows of the
church were boarded up and a few tottering tombstones
surrounded it.

No sign of human habitation appeared as the Rector
walked up to the door. A bright sunshine played on the
crumbling brick, the small-paned windows, the touches
of gilding in the railings of the *perron;* and on the slimy
pond a few ducks moved to and fro, in front of a grass-
grown sun-dial. Meynell walked up to the door, and
rang.

The sound of the bell echoed through the house
behind, but, for a while, no one came. One of the
lunette windows under the roof opened overhead; and
after another pause the door was slowly opened a few
inches by a man in a slovenly footman's jacket.

"Very sorry, sir, but Sir Philip is not at home."

"When did he leave?"

"The end of last week, sir," said the man, with a jaunty air.

"That, I think, is not so," said Meynell, sternly. "I shall not trouble you to take my card."

The youth's expression changed. He stood silent and sheepish, while Meynell considered a moment, on the steps.

Suddenly a sound of voices from a distance became audible through the grudgingly opened door. It appeared to come from the back of the house. The man looked behind him, his mouth twitching with repressed laughter. Meynell ran down the steps and turned to the left, where a door led through a curtain-wall to the garden. Meanwhile the house door was hastily banged behind him.

"Uncle Richard!"

Behind the house Meynell came upon the persons he sought. In an overgrown formal garden, full of sun, he perceived an old stone bench, under an overhanging yew. Upon it sat Hester, bareheaded, the golden masses of her hair shining against the blackness of the tree. Roddy mounted guard beside her, his nose upon her lap; and on a garden chair in front of her lounged Philip Meryon, smoking and chatting. At sight of Meynell they both sprang to their feet. Roddy first growled, and then, as soon as he recognized Meynell, wagged his tail. Philip, with a swaying step, advanced toward the newcomer, cigar in hand.

"How do you do, Richard! It is not often you honour me with a visit."

For a moment Meynell looked from one to the other in silence.

And they, whether they would or no, could not but feel the power of the rugged figure in the short clerical coat and wide-awake, and of the searching look with which he regarded them. Hester nervously began to put on her hat. Philip threw away his cigar, and braced himself angrily.

"Your mother has been anxious about you, Hester," said Meynell, at last. "And I have come to bring you home."

Then turning to Meryon he said — "With you, Philip, I will reckon later on. The lies you have instructed your servants to tell are a sufficient indication that you are ashamed of your behaviour. This young lady is under age. Her mother and I, who are her lawful guardians, forbid her acquaintance with you."

"By what authority, I should like to know?" said Philip sneeringly. "Hester is not a child — nor am I."

"All that we will discuss when we meet," said the Rector. "I propose to call upon you to-morrow."

"This time you may really find me fled," laughed Philip, insolently. But he had turned white.

Meynell made no reply. He went to Hester, and lifting the girl's silk cape, which had fallen off, he put it round her shoulders. He felt them trembling. But she looked at him fiercely, put him aside, and ran to Meryon.

"Good-bye, Philip, good-bye! — it won't be for long!" And she held out her two hands — pleadingly. Meryon took them, and they stared at each other — while the Rector was conscious of a flash of dismay.

What if there was now more in the business than mere mischief and wantonness? Hester was surprisingly lovely, with this touching, tremulous look, so new, and, to the Rector, so intolerable!

"I must ask you to come at once," he said, walking up to her, and the girl, with compressed lips, dropped Meryon's hands and obeyed.

Meryon walked beside them to the garden door, very pale, and breathing quick.

"You can't separate us" — he said to Meynell — "though of course you'll try. Hester, don't believe anything he tells you — till I confirm it."

"Not I!" she said proudly.

Meynell led her through the door, and then turning peremptorily desired Meryon not to follow them. Philip hesitated, and yielded. He stood in the doorway, his hands in his pockets, watching them, a splendid figure, with his melodramatic good looks and vivid colour.

CHAPTER XIV

HESTER and Meynell walked down the avenue, side by side. Behind them, the lunette window under the roof opened again, and a woman's face, framed in black, touzled hair, looked out, grinned and disappeared.

Hester carried her head high, a scornful defiance breathing from the flushed cheeks and tightened lips. Meynell made no attempt at conversation, till just as they were nearing the lodge he said — "We shall find Stephen a little farther on. He was riding, and thought you might like his horse to give you a lift home."

"Oh, a *plot!*" — cried Hester, raising her chin still higher — "and Stephen in it too! Well, really I shouldn't have thought it was worth anybody's while to spy upon my very insignificant proceedings like this. What does it matter to him, or you, or any one else what I do?"

She turned her beautiful eyes — tragically wide and haughty — upon her companion. There was absurdity in her pose, and yet, as Meynell uncomfortably recognized, a new touch of something passionate and real.

The Rector made no reply, for they were at the turn of the road and behind it Stephen and his horse were to be seen waiting.

Stephen came to meet them, the bridle over his arm. "Hester, wouldn't you like my horse? It is a long way home. I can send for it later."

She looked proudly from one to the other. Her colour had suddenly faded, and from the pallor, the firm, yet delicate, lines of the features emerged with unusual emphasis.

"I think you had better accept," said Meynell gently. As he looked at her, he wondered whether she might not faint on their hands with anger and excitement. But she controlled herself, and as Stephen brought the brown mare alongside, and held out his hand, she put her foot in it, and he swung her to the saddle.

"I don't want both of you," she said, passionately. "One warder is enough!"

"Hester!" cried Stephen, reproachfully. Then he added, trying to smile, "I am going into Markborough. Any commission?"

Hester disdained to answer. She gathered up the reins and set the horse in motion. Stephen's way lay with them for a hundred yards. He tried to make a little indifferent conversation, but neither Meynell nor Hester replied. Where the lane they had been following joined the Markborough road, he paused to take his leave of them, and as he did so he saw his two companions brought together, as it were, into one picture by the overcircling shade of the autumnal trees which hung over the road; and he suddenly perceived as he had never yet done the strange likeness between them. Perplexity,

love — despairing and jealous love — a passionate cham-
pionship of the beauty that was being outraged and in-
sulted by the common talk and speculation of indifferent
and unfriendly mouths; an earnest desire to know the
truth, and the whole truth, that he might the better prove
his love, and protect his friend; and a dismal certainty
through it all that Hester had been finally snatched from
him — these conflicting feelings very nearly overpowered
him.   It was all he could do to take a calm farewell of
them.   Hester's eyes under their fierce brows followed
him along the road.

Meanwhile she and Meynell turned into a bridle-path
through the woods.   Hester sat erect, her slender body
adjusting itself with unconscious grace to the quiet
movements of the horse, which Meynell was leading.
Overhead the October day was beginning to darken, and
the yellow leaves shaken by occasional gusts were drifting mistily down on Hester's hair and dress, and on the
glossy flanks of the mare.

At last Meynell looked up.   There was intense feeling
in his face — a deep and troubled tenderness.

"Hester! — is there no way in which I can convince
you that if you go on as you have been doing — deceiving
your best friends — and letting this man persuade you
into secret meetings — you will bring disgrace on yourself, and sorrow on us?   A few more escapades like
to-day, and we might not be able to save you from
disgrace."

He looked at her searchingly.

"I am going to choose for myself!" said Hester after a moment, in a low, resolute voice; "I am not going to sacrifice my life to anybody."

"You *will* sacrifice it if you go on flirting with this man — if you will not believe me — who am his kinsman and have no interest whatever in blackening his character — when I tell you that he is a bad man, corrupted by low living and self-indulgence, with whom no girl should trust herself. The action you have taken to-day, your deliberate defiance of us all, make it necessary that I should speak in even plainer terms to you than I have done yet; that I should warn you as strongly as I can that by allowing this man to make love to you — perhaps to propose a runaway match to you — how do I know what villainy he may have been equal to? — you are running risks of utter disaster and disgrace."

"Perhaps. That is my affair."

The girl's voice shook with excitement.

"No! — it is not your affair only. No man liveth to himself, and no man dieth to himself! It is the affair of all those who love you — of your family — of your poor Aunt Alice, who cannot sleep for grieving ——"

Hester raised her free hand, and angrily pushed back the masses of fair hair that were failing about her face.

"What is the good of talking about 'love,' Uncle Richard?" She spoke with a passionate impatience — "You know very well that *nobody* at home loves me. Why should we all be hypocrites? I have got, I tell you, to look after *myself*, to plan my life for myself!

My mother can't help it if she doesn't love me. I don't complain; but I do think it a shame you should say she does, when you know — know — *know* — she doesn't! My sisters and brothers just dislike me — that's all there is in that! All my life I've known it — I've felt it. Why, when I was a baby they never played with me — they never made a pet of me — they wouldn't have me in their games. My father positively disliked me. Whenever the nurse brought me downstairs — he used to call to her to take me up again. Oh, how tired I got of the nursery! — I hated it — I hated nurse — I hated all the old toys — for I never had any new ones. Do you remember" — she turned on him — "that day when I set fire to all the clean clothes — that were airing before the fire?"

"Perfectly!" said the Rector, with an involuntary smile that relaxed the pale gravity of his face.

"I did it because I hadn't been downstairs for three nights. I might have been dead for all anybody cared. Then I was determined they should care — and I got hold of the matches. I thought the clothes would burn first — and then my starched frock would catch fire — and then — everybody would be sorry for me at last. But unfortunately I got frightened, and ran up the passage screaming — silly little fool! That might have made an end of it — once for all —— "

Meynell interrupted —

"And after it," he said, looking her in the eyes — "when the fuss was over — I remember seeing you in

Aunt Alsie's arms. Have you forgotten how she cried over you, and defended you — and begged you off? You were ill with terror and excitement; she took you off to the cottage, and nursed you till you were well again, and it had all blown over; as she did again and again afterward. Have you forgotten *that* — when you say that no one loved you?"

He turned upon her with that bright penetrating look, with its touch of accusing sarcasm, which had so often given him the mastery over erring souls. For Meynell had the pastoral gift almost in perfection; the courage, the ethical self-confidence and the instinctive tenderness which belong to it. The certitudes of his mind were all ethical; and in this region he might have said with Newman that "a thousand difficulties cannot make one doubt."

Hester had often yielded to this power of his in the past, and it was evident that she trembled under it now. To hide it she turned upon him with fresh anger.

"No, I haven't forgotten it! — and I'm *not* an ungrateful fiend — though of course you think it. But Aunt Alsie's like all the others now. She — she's turned against me!" There was a break in the girl's voice that she tried in vain to hide.

"It isn't true, Hester! I think you know it isn't true."

"It *is* true! She has secrets from me, and when I ask her to trust me — then she treats me like a child — and shakes me off as if I were just a stranger. If she holds me at arm's-length, I am not going to tell her all *my* affairs!"

The rounded bosom under the little black mantle rose and fell tumultuously, and angry tears shone in the brown eyes. Meynell had raised his head with a sudden movement, and regarded her intently.

"What secrets?"

"I found her — one day — with a picture — she was crying over. It — it was some one she had been in love with — I am certain it was — a handsome, dark man. And I *begged* her to tell me — and she just got up and went away. So then I took my own line!"

Hester furiously dashed away the tears she had not been able to stop.

Meynell's look changed. His voice grew strangely pitiful and soft.

"Dear Hester — if you knew — you couldn't be unkind to Aunt Alice."

"Why shouldn't I know? Why am I treated like a baby?"

"There are some things too bitter to tell," — he said gravely — "some griefs we have no right to meddle with. But we can heal them — or make them worse. You" — his kind eyes scourged her again — "have been making everything worse for Aunt Alsie for a long time past."

Hester shrugged her shoulders passionately, as though to repel the charge, but she said nothing. They moved on in silence for a little. In Meynell's mind there reigned a medley of feelings — tragic recollections, moral ques-

tionings, which time had never silenced, perplexity as to
the present and the future, and with it all, the liveliest
and sorest pity for the young, childish, violent creature
beside him. It was not for those who, with whatever
motives, had contributed to bring her to that state and
temper, to strike any note of harshness.

Presently, as they neared the end of the woody path,
he looked up again. He saw her sitting sullenly on the
gently moving horse, a vision of beauty at bay. The
sight determined him toward frankness.

"Hester! — I have told you that if you go on flirting
with Philip Meryon you run the risk of disgrace and
misery, because he has no conscience and no scruples, and
you are ignorant and inexperienced, and have no idea of
the fire you are playing with. But I think I had better
go farther. I am going to say what you force me to say
to you — young as you are. My strong belief is that
Philip Meryon is either married already, or so entangled
that he has no right to ask any decent woman to marry
him. I have suspected it a long time. Now you force
me to prove it."

Hester turned her head away.

"He told me I wasn't to believe what you said about
him!" she said in her most obstinate voice.

"Very well. Then I must set at once about proving
it. The reasons which make me believe it are not for
your ears." Then his tone changed — "Hester! — my
child! — you can't be in love with that fellow — that
false, common fellow! — you can't!"

Hester tightened her lips and would not answer. A rush of distress came over Meynell as he thought of her movement toward Philip in the garden. He gently resumed:

"Any day now might bring the true lover, Hester! — the man who would comfort you for all the past, and show you what joy really means. Be patient, dear Hester — be patient! If you wanted to punish us for not making you happy enough, well, you have done it! But don't plunge us all into despair — and take a little thought for your old guardian, who seems to have the world on his shoulders, and yet can't sleep at nights, for worriting about his ward, who won't believe a word he says, and sets all his wishes at defiance."

His manner expressed a playful and reproachful affection. Their eyes met. Hester tried hard to maintain her antagonism, and he was well aware that he was but imperfectly able to gauge the conflict of forces in her mind. He resumed his pleading with her — tenderly — urgently. And at last she gave way, at least apparently. She allowed him to lay a friendly hand on hers that held the reins, and she said with a long bitter breath:

"Oh, I know I'm a little beast!"

"My old-fashioned ideas don't allow me to apply that epithet to young women! But if you'll say 'I want to be friends, Uncle Richard, and I won't deceive you any more,' why, then, you'll make an old fellow happy! Will you?"

Slowly she let her cold fingers slip into his warm, protecting palm as he smiled upon her. She yielded to the dignity and charm of Meynell's character as she had done a thousand times before; but in the proud, unhappy look she bent upon him there were new and disquieting things — prophecies of the coming womanhood, not to be unravelled. Meynell pressed her hand, and put it back upon the reins with a sigh he could not restrain.

He began to talk with a forced cheerfulness of their coming journey — of the French *milieu* to which she was going. Hester answered in monosyllables, every now and then — he thought — choking back a sob. And again and again the discouraging thought struck through him — "Has this fellow touched her heart?" — so strong was the impression of an emerging soul and a developing personality.

Suddenly through the dispersing trees a light figure came hurriedly toward them. It was Alice Puttenham.

She was pale and weary, and when she saw Hester, with Meynell beside her, she gave a little cry. But Meynell, standing behind Hester, put his finger on his lips, and she controlled herself. Hester greeted her without any sign of emotion; and the three went homeward along the misty ways of the park. The sun had been swallowed up by rising fog; all colour had been sucked out of the leaves and the heather, even from the golden glades of fern. Only Hester's hair, and her white dress as she passed along, uplifted, made of her a kind of luminous wraith, and beside her, like the supports of an altar-piece, moved the two pensive figures of Meynell and Alice.

From a covert of thorn in the park, a youth who had

retreated into its shelter on their approach watched them
with malicious eyes.   Another man was with him — a
sheepish, red-faced person, who peered curiously at the
little procession as it passed about a hundred yards
away.

"Quite a family party!" said Maurice Barron with a
laugh.

In the late evening Meynell returned to the Rectory
a wearied man, but with hours of occupation and correspondence still before him.   He had left Hester with
Alice Puttenham, in a state which Meynell interpreted
as at once alarming and hopeful; alarming because it
suggested that there might be an element of passion in
what had seemed to be a mere escapade dictated by
vanity and temper; and hopeful because of the emotion
the girl had once or twice betrayed, for the first time in
the experience of any one connected with her.   When
they entered Alice Puttenham's drawing-room, for instance — for Hester had stipulated she was not to be
taken home — Alice had thrown her arms round her, and
Hester had broken suddenly into crying, a thing unheard
of.   Meynell of course had hastily disappeared.

Since then the parish had taken its toll.   Visits to two
or three sick people had been paid.   The Rector had
looked in at the schools, where a children's evening was
going on, and had told the story of Aladdin with riotous
success; he had taken off his coat to help in putting up
decorations for an entertainment in the little Wesleyan

meeting-house of corrugated iron; the parish nurse had waylaid him with reports, and he had dashed into the back parlour of a small embarrassed tradesman, in mortal fear of collapse and bankruptcy, with the offer of a loan, sternly conditional upon facing the facts, and getting in an auditor. Lady Fox-Wilton of course had been seen, and the clamour of her most unattractive offspring allayed as much as possible. And now, emerging from this tangle of personal claims and small interests, in the silence and freedom of the night hours, Meynell was free to give himself once more to the intellectual and spiritual passion of the Reform Movement. His table was piled with unopened letters; on his desk lay a half-written article, and two or three foreign books, the latest products of the Modernist Movement abroad. His crowded be-littered room smiled upon him, as he shut its door upon the outer world. For within it, he lived more truly, more vividly, than anywhere else; and all the more since its threadbare carpet had been trodden by Mary Elsmere.

Yet as he settled himself by the fire with his pipe and his letters for half an hour's ease before going to his desk, his thoughts were still full of Hester. The incurable optimism, the ready faith where his affections were concerned, which were such strong notes of his character, was busy persuading him that all would be well. At last, between them, they had made an impression on the poor child; and as for Philip, he should be dealt with this time with a proper disregard of either his own or his

servants' lying. Hester was now to spend some months
with a charming and cultivated French family. Plenty
of occupation, plenty of amusement, plenty of appeal to
her intelligence. Then, perhaps, travel for a couple of
years, with Aunt Alice — as much separation as possible,
anyway, from the Northleigh family and house. Alice
was not rich, but she could manage as much as that, if
he advised it, and he would advise it. Then with her
twenty-first year, if Stephen or any other wooer were to
the fore, the crisis must be faced, and the child must
know! and it would be a cold-blooded lover that would
weigh her story against her face.

Comfort himself as he would, however, dream as he
would, Meynell's conscience was always sore for Hester.
Had they done right? — or hideously wrong? Had not all
their devices been a mere trifling with nature — a mere
attempt to "bind the courses of Orion," with the inevitable result in Hester's unhappy childhood and perverse
youth?

The Rector as he pulled at his pipe could still feel the
fluttering of her slender hand in his. The recollection
stirred in him again all the intolerable pity, the tragic
horror of the past. Poor, poor little girl. But she should
be happy yet, "with rings on her fingers," and everything
proper!

Then from this fatherly and tender preoccupation he
passed into a more intimate and poignant dreaming.
Mary! — in the moonlight, under the autumn trees, was
the vision that held him; varied sometimes by the dream

of her in that very room, sitting ghostly in the chair beside him, her lovely eyes wandering over its confusion of books and papers. He thought of her exquisite neatness of dress and delicacy of movement, and smiled happily to himself. "How she must have wanted to tidy up!" And he dared to think of a day when she would come and take possession of him altogether — books, body and soul, and gently order his life. . . .

"Why, you rascals!" — he said, jealously, to the dogs — "she fed you — I know she did — she patted and pampered you, eh, didn't she? She likes dogs — you may thank your lucky stars she does!"

But they only raised their eager heads, and turned their loving eyes upon him, prepared to let loose pandemonium as soon as he showed signs of moving.

"Well, you don't expect me to take you out for a walk at ten o'clock at night, do you? — idiots!" he hurled at them reprovingly; and after another moment of bright-eyed interrogation, disappointment descended, and down went their noses on their paws again.

His trust in the tender steadfastness of Mary's character made itself powerfully felt in these solitary moments. She knew that while these strenuous days were on he could allow himself no personal aims. But the growing knowledge that he was approved by a soul so pure and so devout had both strung up all his powers and calmed the fevers of battle. He loved his cause the more because it was ever more clear to him that she passionately loved it too. And sensitive and depressed as he often was — the penalty of the optimist — her faith in him had doubled his faith in himself.

There was a singular pleasure also in the link his love for her had forged between himself and Elsmere — the dead leader of an earlier generation. "Latitudinarianism is coming in upon us like a flood!" — cried the *Church Times*, wringing its hands. In other words, thought Meynell, "a New Learning is at last penetrating the minds and consciences of men — in the Church, no less than out of it." And Elsmere had been one of its martyrs. Meynell thought with emotion of the emaciated form he had last seen in the thronged hall of the New Brotherhood. "*Our* venture is possible — because *you* suffered," he would say to himself, addressing not so much Elsmere, as Elsmere's generation, remembering its struggles, its thwarted hopes, and starved lives.

And Elsmere's wife? — that rigid, pathetic figure, who, before he knew her in the flesh, had been to him, through the reports of many friends, a kind of legendary presence — the embodiment of the Old Faith. Meynell only knew that as far as he was concerned something had happened — something which he could not define. She was no longer his enemy; and he blessed her humbly in his heart. He thought also, with a curious thankfulness, of her strong and immovable convictions. Each thinking mind, as it were, carries within it its own Pageant of the Universe, and lights the show with its own passion. Not to quench the existing light in any human breast — but to kindle and quicken where no light is: to bring forever new lamp-bearers into the Lampadephoria of life, and marshal them there in their places, on equal terms with the old, neither excluded, nor excluding: this, surely this was the ideal of Modernism.

Elsmere's widow might never admit his own claim to equal rights within the Christian society. What matter! It seemed to him that in some mysterious way she had now recognized the spiritual necessity laid upon him to fight for that claim; had admitted him, so to speak, to the rights of a belligerent. And that had made all the difference.

He did not know how it had happened. But he was strangely certain that it had happened.

But soon the short interval of rest and dream he had allowed himself was over. He turned to his writing-table.

What a medley of letters! Here was one from a clergyman in the Midlands:

"We introduced the new Liturgy last Sunday, and I cannot describe the emotion, the stirring of all the dead-bones it has brought about. There has been of course a secession; but the church at Patten End amply provides for the seceders, and among our own people one seems to realize at last something of what the simplicity and sincerity of the first Christian feeling must have been! No 'allowances' to make for scandalous mistranslations and misquotations — no foolish legends, or unedifying tales of barbarous people — no cursing psalms — no old Semitic nonsense about God resting on the seventh day, delivered in the solemn sing-song which makes it not only nonsense but hypocrisy. . . .

"I have held both a marriage and a funeral this week under the new service-book. I think that all persons accustomed to think of what they are saying felt the strangest delight and relief in the disappearance of the old marriage service. It was like the dropping of a weight to which our shoulders had become so accustomed that we hardly realized it till it was gone. Instead of pompous and futile absurdity — as in the existing exhortation, and homily — beautiful and fitting quotation from the unused treasures of the Bible. Instead of the brutal speech, the crudely physical outlook of an earlier day, the just reticence and nobler perceptions of our own, combined with perfectly plain and tender statement as to the founding of the home and the family. Instead of besmirching bits of primitive and ugly legend like the solemn introduction of Adam's rib into the prayers, a few new prayers of great beauty — some day you must tell me who wrote them, for I suppose you know? (and, by the way, why should we not write as good prayers, to-day, as in any age of the Christian Church?). Instead of the old 'obey,' for the woman, which has had such a definitely debasing effect, as I believe, on the position of women, especially in the working classes — a formula, only slightly altered, but the same for the man and the woman. . . .

"In short, a seemly, and beautiful, and moving thing, instead of a ceremony which in spite of its few fine, even majestic, elements, had become an offence and a scandal. All the fine elements have been kept, and only the scandal amended. Why was it not done long ago?

"Then as to the burial service. The Corinthian chapter stripped of its arguments which are dead, and confined to its cries of poetry and faith which are immortal, made a new and thrilling impression. I confess I thought I should have broken my heart over the omission of 'I know that my Redeemer liveth' — and yet now that it is gone, there is a sense of moral exhilaration in having let it go! One knew all the time that whoever wrote the poem of Job neither said what he was made to say in the famous passage, nor meant what he was supposed to mean. One was perfectly aware, from one's Oxford days, as the choir chanted the great words, that they were a flagrant mistranslation of a corrupt and probably interpolated passage. And yet the glory of Handel's music, the glamour of association overcame one. But now that it is cut ruthlessly away from those moments in life when man can least afford any make-believe with himself or his fellows — now that music alone declaims and fathers it — there is the strangest relief! One feels, as I have said, the joy that comes from something difficult and righteous *done* — in spite of everything!

"I could go on for hours telling you these very simple and obvious things which must be so familiar to you. To me the amazement of this Movement is that it has taken so long to come. We have groaned under the oppression of what we have now thrown off, so long and so hopelessly; the Revision that the High Churchmen made such a bother about a few years ago came to so little; that now, to see this thing spreading like a great spring-tide over the face of England is marvellous indeed! And when one knows what it means — no mere liturgical change, no mere lopping off here and changing there, but a transformation of the root ideas of Christianity; a transference of its whole proof and evidence from the outward to the inward field, and therewith the uprush of a certainty and joy unknown to our modern life; one can but bow one's head, as those that hear mysterious voices on the wind.

"For so into the temple of man's spirit, age by age, comes the renewing Master of man's life — and makes His tabernacle with man.   'Lift up your heads, O ye gates, and be ye lift up, ye everlasting doors, And the King of Glory shall come in.'"

. Meynell bowed his head upon his hands.   The pulse of hope and passion in the letter was almost overpowering.   It came, he knew, from an elderly man, broken by many troubles, and tormented by arthritis, yet a true saint, and at times a great preacher.

The next letter he opened came from a priest in the diocese of Aix. . . .

"The effect of the various encyclicals and of the ill-advised attempt to make both clergy and laity sign the Modernist decrees has had a prodigious effect all over France — precisely in the opposite sense to that desired by Pius X.   The spread of the Movement is really amazing.   Fifteen years ago I remember hearing a French critic say — Edmond Scherer, I think, the successor of Sainte Beuve — 'The Catholics have not a single intellectual of any eminence — and it is a misfortune for *us*, the liberals.   We have nothing to fight — we seem to be beating the air.'

"Scherer could not have said this to-day.   There are Catholics everywhere — in the University, the Ecole Normale, the front ranks of literature.   But with few

exceptions *they are all Modernist;* they have thrown over-
board the whole *fatras* of legend and tradition.   Christianity has become to them a symbolical and spiritual
religion; not only personally important and efficacious,
but of enormous significance from the national point of
view.   But as you know, *we* do not at present aspire to
outward or ceremonial changes.   We are quite content
to leaven the meal from within; to uphold the absolute
right and necessity of the two languages in Christianity
— the popular and the scientific, the mythological and
the mystical.   If the Pope could have his way, Catholicism would soon be at an end — except as a peasant-
cult — in the Latin countries.   But, thank God, he will
not have his way.   One hears of a Modernist free-
masonry among the Italian clergy — of a secret press —
an enthusiasm, like that of the Carboneria in the forties.
So the spirit of the Most High blows among the dead clods
of the world — and, in a moment the harvest is there!"

Meynell let the paper drop.   He began to write, and
he wrote without stopping with great ease and inspiration
for nearly two hours.   Then as midnight struck, he put
down his pen, and gazed into the dying fire.   He felt as
Wordsworth's skater felt on Esthwaite, when, at a sudden
pause, the mountains and cliffs seemed to whirl past him
in a vast headlong procession.   So it was in Meynell's
mind with thoughts and ideas.   Gradually they calmed
and slackened, till at last they passed into an abstraction
and ecstasy of prayer.

When he rose, the night had grown very cold.   He
hurriedly put his papers in order, before going to bed,

and as he did so, he perceived two unopened letters which had been overlooked.

One was from Hugh Flaxman, communicating the news of the loss of two valuable gold coins from the collection exhibited at the party. "We are all in tribulation. I wonder whether you can remember seeing them when you were talking there with Norham? One was a gold stater of Velia with a head of Athene." . . .

The other letter was addressed in Henry Barron's handwriting. Meynell looked at it in some surprise as he opened it, for there had been no communication between him and the White House for a long time

"I should be glad if you could make it convenient to see me to-morrow morning. I wish to speak with you on a personal matter of some importance — of which I do not think you should remain in ignorance. Will it suit you if I come at eleven?"

Meynell stood motionless. But the mind reacted in a flash. He thought —

"*Now* I shall know what she told him in those two hours!"

CHAPTER XV

THE Rector will be back, sir, direckly. I was to tell you so pertickler. They had 'im out to a man in the Row, who's been drinkin' days, and was goin' on shockin' — his wife was afraid to stop in the house. But he won't be long, sir."

And Anne, very stiff and on her dignity, relieved one of the two armchairs of its habitual burden of books, gave it a dusting with her apron, and offered it to the visitor. It was evident that she regarded his presence with entire disfavour, but was prepared to treat him with prudence for the master's sake. Her devotion to Meynell had made her shrewd; she perfectly understood who were his enemies, and who his friends.

Barron, with a sharp sense of annoyance that he should be kept waiting, merely because a drunken miner happened to be beating his wife, coldly accepted her civilities, and took up a copy of the *Times* which was lying on the table. But when Anne had retired, he dropped the newspaper, and began with a rather ugly curiosity to examine the room. He walked round the walls, looking at the books, raising his eyebrows at the rows of paperbound German volumes, and peering closely into the titles of the English ones. Then his attention was caught by a wall-map, in which a number of small flags attached to pins were sticking. It was an outline map of England, apparently sketched by Meynell himself, as the notes and letterings were in his handwriting. It was labelled "Branches of the Reform League." All over England the little flags bristled, thicker here, and thinner there, but making a goodly show on the whole. Barron's face lengthened as he pondered the map.

Then he passed by the laden writing-table. On it lay an open copy of the *Modernist*, with a half-written "leader" of Meynell's between the sheets.   Beside it was a copy of Thomas à Kempis, and Father Tyrrell's posthumous book, in which a great soul, like a breaking wave, had foamed itself away; a volume of Sanday, another of Harnack, into the open cover of which the Rector had apparently just pinned an extract from a Church paper. Barron involuntarily stooped to read it.   It ran:

"This is no time for giving up the Athanasian Creed. The moment when the sewage of continental unbelief is pouring into England is not the moment for banishing to a museum a screen that was erected to guard the sanctuary."

Beneath it, in Meynell's writing:

"A gem, not to be lost! The muddle of the metaphor, the corruption of the style, everything is symbolic. In a preceding paragraph the writer makes an attack on

Harnack, who is described as 'notorious for opposing' the doctrines of the Virgin Birth and the Resurrection. That history has a right to its say on so-called historical events never seems to have occurred to this gentleman; still less that there is a mystical and sacred element in all truth, all the advancing knowledge of mankind, including historical knowledge, and that therefore his responsibility, his moral and spiritual risk even, in disbelieving Harnack, is probably infinitely greater than Harnack's in dealing historically with the Birth Stories.

"The fact is the whole onus is now on the orthodox side. It is not we that are on our defence; but they."

Barron raised himself with a flushed cheek, and a stiffened mouth. Meynell's note had removed his last scruples. It was necessary to deal drastically with a clergyman who could write such things.

A step outside. The sleeping dogs on the doorstep sprang up and noisily greeted their master. Meynell shut them out, to their great disgust, and came hurriedly toward the study.

Barron, as he saw him in the doorway, drew back with an exclamation. The Rector's dress and hair were dishevelled and awry, and his face — pale, drawn, and damp with perspiration — showed that he had just come through a personal struggle.

"Sorry to have kept you waiting, Mr. Barron. But that fellow, Pinches — you remember? — the new blacksmith — has been drinking for nearly a week, and went quite mad this morning. We just prevented him from

killing his wife, but it was a tough business.   I'll go and
wash and change my coat, if you will allow me."

So he went away, and Barron had a few more minutes
in which to meditate on the room and its owner.   When
at last Meynell came back, and settled himself in the
chair opposite to his visitor, with a quiet "Now I am
quite at your service," Barron found himself overtaken
with a curious and unwelcome hesitation.   The signs —
a slightly strained look, a quickened breathing — that
Meynell still bore upon him of a physical wrestle, combined perhaps with a moral victory, suddenly seemed,
even in Barron's own eyes, to dwarf what he had to say —
to make a poor mean thing out of his story.   And Meynell's shining eyes, divided between close attention to the
man before him and some recent and disturbing recollections in which Barron had no share, reinforced the
impression.

But he recaptured himself quickly.   After all, it was
at once a charitable and a high-judicial part that he had
come to play.   He gathered his dignity about him, resenting the momentary disturbance of it.

"I am come to-day, Mr. Meynell, on a very unpleasant
errand."

The formal "Mr." marked the complete breach in their
once friendly relations.   Meynell made a slight inclination.

"Then I hope you will tell it me as quickly as may
be.   Does it concern yourself, or me?   Maurice, I hope,
is doing well?"

Barron winced.   It seemed to him an offence on the

Rector's part that Meynell's tone should subtly though quite innocently remind him of days when he had been thankful to accept a strong man's help in dealing with the escapades of a vicious lad.

"He is doing excellently, thank you — except that his health is not all I could wish. My business to-day," he continued, slowly — "concerns a woman, formerly of this village, whom I happened by a strange accident to see just after her return to it ——"

"You are speaking of Judith Sabin?" interrupted Meynell.

"I am. You were of course aware that I had seen her?"

"Naturally — from the inquest. Well?"

The quiet, interrogative tone seemed to Barron an impertinence. With a suddenly heightened colour he struck straight — violently — for the heart of the thing.

"She told me a lamentable story — and she was led to tell it me by seeing — and identifying — yourself — as you were standing with a lady in the road outside the cottage."

"Identifying me?" repeated Meynell, with a slight accent of astonishment. "That I think is hardly possible. For Judith Sabin had never seen me."

"You were not perhaps aware of it — but she had seen you."

Meynell shook his head.

"She was mistaken — or you are. However, that

doesn't matter.   I gather you wish to consult me about
something that Judith Sabin communicated to you?"

"I do.   But the story she told me turns very closely
on her identification of yourself; and therefore it does
matter," said Barron, with emphasis.

A puzzled look passed again over Meynell's face.
But he said nothing.   His attitude, coldly expectant,
demanded the story.

Barron told it — once more.   He repeated Judith
Sabin's narrative in the straightened, rearranged form
he had now given to it, postponing, however, any further
mention of Meynell's relation to it till a last dramatic
moment.

He did not find his task so easy on this occasion.
There was something in the personality of the man sitting opposite to him which seemed to make a narrative
that had passed muster elsewhere sound here a mere
vulgar impertinence, the wanton intrusion of a common
man on things sacredly and justly covered from sight.

He laboured through it, however, while Meynell sat
with bent head, looking at the floor, making no sign
whatever.   And at last the speaker arrived at the
incident of the Grenoble visitor.

"I naturally find this a very disagreeable task," he
said, pausing a moment.   He got, however, no help from
Meynell, who was dumb; and he presently resumed —
"Judith Sabin saw the gentleman who came distinctly.
She felt perfectly certain in her own mind as to his
relation to Miss Puttenham and the child; and she

was certain also, when she saw you and Miss Puttenham
standing in the road, while I was with her that —"

Meynell looked up, slightly frowning, awaiting the
conclusion of the sentence —

— "that she saw — the same man again!"

Barron's naturally ruddy colour had faded a little;
his eyes blinked. He drew his coat forward over his
knee, and put it back again nervously.

Meynell's face was at first blank, or bewildered. Then
a light of understanding shot through it. He fell back
in his chair with an odd smile.

"So *that* — is what you have in your mind?"

Barron coughed a little. He was angrily conscious of
an anxiety and misgiving he had not expected. He made
all the greater effort to recover what seemed to him the
proper tone.

"It is all most sad — most lamentable. But I had,
you perceive, the positive statement of a woman who
should have known the facts first-hand, if any one did.
Owing to her physical state, it was impossible to cross-
examine her, and her sudden death made it impossible
to refer her to you. I had to consider what I should
do ——"

"Why should you have done anything —" said Meynell dryly, raising his eyes — "but forget as quickly as
possible a story you had no means of verifying, and which
bore its absurdity on the face of it?"

Barron allowed himself a slight and melancholy smile.

"I admit of course — at once — that I could not

verify it. As to its *prima facie* absurdity, I desire to say nothing offensive to you, but there have been many curious circumstances connected with your relation to the Fox-Wilton family which have given rise before now to gossip in this neighbourhood. I could not but perceive that the story told me threw light upon them. The remarkable language of Sir Ralph's will, the position of Miss Hester in the Fox-Wilton family, your relation to her — and to — to Miss Puttenham."

Meynell's composure became a matter of some difficulty, but he maintained it.

"What was there abnormal — or suspicious — in any of these circumstances?" he asked, his eyes fixed intently on his visitor.

"I see no purpose to be gained by going into them on this occasion," said Barron, with all the dignity he could bring to bear. "For the unfortunate thing is — the thing which obliged me whether I would or no — and you will see from the dates that I have hesitated a long time — to bring Judith Sabin's statement to your notice — is that she seems to have talked to some one else in the neighbourhood before she died, besides myself. Her son declares that she saw no one. I have questioned him; of course without revealing my object. But she must have done so. And whoever it was has begun to write anonymous letters — repeating the story — in full detail — *with* the identification — that I have just given you."

"Anonymous letters?" repeated Meynell, raising himself sharply. "To whom?"

"Dawes, the colliery manager, received the first."

"To whom did he communicate it?"

"To myself — and by his wish, and in the spirit of entire friendliness to you, I consulted your friend and supporter, Mr. Flaxman."

Meynell raised his eyebrows.

"Flaxman? You thought yourself justified?"

"It was surely better to take so difficult a matter to a friend of yours, rather than to an enemy."

Meynell smiled — but not agreeably.

"Any one else?"

"I have heard this morning on my way here that Miss Nairn has received a copy."

"Miss Nairn? That means the village."

"She is a gossiping woman," said Barron.

Meynell pondered. He got up and began to pace the room — coming presently to an abrupt pause in front of his visitor.

"This story then is now all over the village — will soon be all over the diocese. Now — what was your object in yourself bringing it to me?"

"I thought it right to inform you — to give you warning — perhaps also to suggest to you that a retreat from your present position —— "

"I see — you thought it a means of bringing pressure to bear upon me? — you propose, in short, that I should throw up the sponge, and resign my living?"

"Unless, of course, you can vindicate yourself publicly."

Barron to his annoyance could not keep his hand which

held a glove from shaking a little. The wrestle between their personalities was rapidly growing in intensity.

"Unless I bring an action, you mean — against any one spreading the story? No — I shall not bring an action — I shall *not* bring an action!" Meynell repeated, with emphasis.

"In that case — I suggest — it might be better to meet the wishes of your Bishop, and so avoid further publicity."

"By resigning my living?"

"Precisely. The scandal would then drop of itself. For Miss Puttenham's sake alone you must, I think, desire to stop its development."

Meynell flushed hotly. He took another turn up the room — while Barron sat silent, looking straight before him.

"I shall not take action" — Meynell resumed — "and I shall not dream of retreating from my position here. Judith Sabin's story is untrue. She did not see me at Grenoble and I am not the father of Hester Fox-Wilton. As to anything else, I am not at liberty to discuss other people's affairs, and I shall not answer any questions whatever on the subject."

The two men surveyed each other.

"Your Bishop could surely demand your confidence," said Barron coldly.

"If he does, it will be for me to consider."

A silence. Barron looked round for his stick. Meynell stood motionless, his hands in his baggy pockets, his eyes on Barron. Lightings of thought and will seemed to pass through his face. As Barron rose, he began to speak.

"I have no doubt you think yourself justified in taking the line you clearly do take in this matter. I can hardly imagine that you really believe the story you say you got from Judith Sabin — which you took to Flaxman — and have, I suppose, discussed with Dawes. I am convinced — forgive me if I speak plainly — that you cannot and do not believe anything so preposterous — or at any rate you would not believe it in other circumstances. As it is, you take it up as a weapon. You think, no doubt, that everything is fair in controversy as in war. Of course the thing has been done again and again. If you cannot defeat a man in fair fight, the next best thing is to blacken his character. We see that everywhere — in politics — in the church — in private life. This story *may* serve you; I don't think it will ultimately, but it may serve you for a time. All I can say is, I would rather be the man to suffer from it than the man to gain from it!"

Barron took up his hat. "I cannot be surprised that you receive me in this manner," he said, with all the steadiness he could muster. "But as you cannot deal with this very serious report in the ordinary way, either by process of law, or by frank explanation to your friends ——"

"My 'friends'!" interjected Meynell.

"— Let me urge you at least to explain matters to

your diocesan.   You cannot distrust either the Bishop's discretion, or his good will.   If he were satisfied, we no doubt should be the same."

Meynell shook his head.

"Not if I know anything of the *odium theologicum!* Besides, the Miss Nairns of this world pay small attention to bishops.   By the way — I forgot to ask — you can tell me nothing on the subject of the writer of the anonymous letters? — you have not identified him?"

"Not in the least.   We are all at sea." ,

"You don't happen to have one about you?"

Barron hesitated and fumbled, and at last produced from his breast-pocket the letter to Dawes, which he had again borrowed from its owner that morning.   Meynell put it into a drawer of his writing-table without looking at it.

The two men moved toward the door.

"As to any appeal to you on behalf of a delicate and helpless lady —" said Meynell, betraying emotion for the first time — "that I suppose is useless.   But when one remembers her deeds of kindness in this village, her quiet and irreproachable life amongst us all these years, one would have thought that any one bearing the Christian name would have come to me as the Rector of this village on one errand only — to consult how best to protect her from the spread of a cruel and preposterous story!   You — I gather — propose to make use of it in the interests of your own Church party."

Barron straightened himself, resenting at once what seemed to him the intrusion of the pastoral note.

"I am heartily sorry for her" — he said coldly. "Naturally it is the women who suffer in these things. But of course you are right — though you put the matter from your own point of view — in assuming that I regard this as no ordinary scandal. I am not at liberty to treat it as such. The honour concerned — is the honour of the Church. To show the intimate connection of creed and life may be a painful — it is also an imperative duty!"

He threw back his head with a passion which, as Meynell clearly recognized, was not without its touch of dignity.

Meynell stepped back.

"We have talked enough, I think. You will of course take the course that seems to you best, and I shall take mine. I bid you good day."

From the study window Meynell watched the disappearing figure of his adversary. The day was wet, and the funereal garden outside was dank with rain. The half-dead trees had shed such leaves as they had been able to put forth, and behind them was a ragged sky of scudding cloud.

In Meynell's soul there was a dull sense of catastrophe. In Barron's presence he had borne himself as a wronged man should; but he knew very well that a sinister thing had happened, and that for him, perhaps, to-morrow might never be as yesterday.

ᛁ What was passing in the village at that moment? His quick visualizing power showed him the groups in the various bar parlours, discussing the Scandal, dividing it up into succulent morsels, serving it up with every variety of personal comment, idle or malicious; amplyfying, exaggerating, completing. He saw the neat and plausible spinster from whose cruel hands he had rescued a little dumb, wild-eyed child, reduced by ill-treatment to skin and bone — he saw her gloating over the anonymous letter, putting two and two maliciously together, whispering here, denouncing there. He seemed to be actually present in the most disreputable publichouse of the village, a house he had all but succeeded in closing at the preceding licensing sessions. How natural, human, inevitable, would be the coarse, venomous talk — the inferences — the gibes!

There would be good men and true of course, his personal friends in the village, the members of his Parish Council, who would suffer, and stand firm. The postponed meeting of the Council, for the acceptance of the new Liturgy, was to be held the day after his return from Paris. To them he would speak — so far as he could; yes, to them he would speak! Then his thought spread to the diocese. Charges of this kind spread with extraordinary rapidity. Whoever was writing the anonymous letters had probably not confined himself to two or three. Meynell prepared himself for the discovery of the much wider diffusion.

He moved back to his writing-table, and took the

letter from the drawer.   Its ingenuity, its knowledge of local circumstance, astonished him as he read.   He had expected something of a vulgarer and rougher type. The handwriting was clearly disguised, and there was a certain amount of intermittent bad spelling, which might very easily be a disguise also.   But whoever wrote it was acquainted with the Fox-Wilton family, with their habits and his own, as well as with the terms of Sir Ralph's will, so far as — mainly he believed through the careless talk of the elder Fox-Wilton girls — it had become a source of gossip in the village.   The writer of it could not be far away.   Was it a man or a woman?   Meynell examined the handwriting carefully.   He had a vague impression that he had seen something like it before, but could not remember where or in what connection.

He put it back in his drawer, and as he did so his eyes fell upon his half-written article for the *Modernist* and on the piles of correspondence beside it.   A sense of bitter helplessness overcame him, a pang not for himself so much as for his cause.   He realized the in-evitable effect of the story in the diocese, weighted, as it would be, with all the colourable and suspicious cir-cumstances that could undoubtedly be adduced in sup-port of it; its effect also beyond the diocese, through the Movement of which he was the life and guiding spirit; through England — where his name was rapidly becom-ing a battle-cry.

And what could he do to meet it?   Almost nothing! The story indeed as a whole could be sharply and categorically denied, because it involved a fundamental falsehood. He was not the father of Hester Fox-Wilton.

But simple denial was all that was open to him. He could neither explain, nor could he challenge inquiry. His mouth was shut. He had made no formal vow of secrecy to any one. He was free to confide in whom he would. But all that was tender, pitiful, chivalrous in his soul stood up and promised for him, as he stood looking out into the October rain, that for no personal — yes! — and for no public advantage — would he trifle with what he had regarded for eighteen years as a trust, laid upon him by the dying words of a man he had loved, and enforced more and more sharply with time by the constant appeal of a woman's life — its dumb pain, the paradox of its frail strength, its shrinking courage. That life had depended upon him during the worst crisis of its fate as its spiritual guide. He had toward Alice Puttenham the feeling of the "director," as the saints have understood it; and toward her story something of the responsiblity of a priest toward a confession. To reveal it in his own interest was simply impossible. If the Movement rejected him — it must reject him.

"Not so will I fight for thee, my God! — not so!" he said to himself in great anguish of mind.

It was true indeed that at some future time Alice Puttenham's poor secret must be told — to a specified person, with her consent, and by the express direction of that honest, blundering man, her brother-in-law, whose life, sorely against his will, had been burdened with it.

But the indiscriminate admission of the truth, after the lapse of years, would, he believed, simply bring back the old despair, and paralyze what had always been a frail vitality. And as to Hester, the sudden divulgence of it might easily upset the unstable balance in her of mind and nerve and drive her at once into some madness. He *must* protect them, if he could.

Could he? He pondered it.

At any moment one of these letters might reach Alice. What if this had already happened? Supposing it had, he might not be able to prevent her from doing what would place the part played toward her by himself in its true light. She would probably insist upon his taking legal action, and allowing her to make her statement in court.

The thought of this was so odious to him that he promptly put it from him. He should assume that she knew nothing; though as a practical man he was well aware that she could not long remain ignorant; certainly not if she continued to live in Upcote. Then, it was a question probably of days or hours. Her presence in the cottage, when once the village was in full possession of the slander, would be a perpetual provocation. One way or another the truth must penetrate to her.

An idea occurred to him. Paris! So far he had insisted on going himself with Hester to Paris because of his haunting feeling of responsibility toward the girl, and his resolve to see with his own eyes the household in which he was placing her. But suppose he made excuses? The burden of work upon him was excuse enough for any man. Suppose he sent Alice in his stead, and so contrived as to keep her in or near Paris for a while? Then Edith Fox-Wilton would of course have the forwarding of her sister's correspondence, and might, it seemed to him, take the responsibility of intercepting whatever might inform or alarm her.

Not much prospect of doing so indefinitely! — that he plainly saw. But to gain time was an immense thing; to prevent her from taking at once Quixotic steps. He knew that in health she had never been the same since the episode of Judith's return and death. She seemed suddenly to have faded and drooped, as though poisoned by some constant terror.

He stood lost in thought a little longer by his writing-table. Then his hand felt slowly for a parcel in brown paper that lay there.

He drew it toward him and undid the wrappings. Inside it was a little volume of recent poems of which he had spoken to Mary Elsmere on their moonlit walk through the park. He had promised to lend her his copy, and he meant to have left it at the cottage that afternoon. Now he lingeringly removed the brown paper, and walking to the bookcase, he replaced the volume.

He sat down to write to Alice Puttenham, and to scribble a note to Lady Fox-Wilton asking her to see him as soon as possible. Then Anne forced some luncheon on him, and he had barely finished it when a step outside made itself heard. He looked up and saw Hugh Flaxman.

"Come in!" said the Rector, opening the front door himself. "You are very welcome."

Flaxman grasped — and pressed — the proffered hand, looking at Meynell the while with hesitating interrogation. He guessed from the Rector's face that the errand on which he came had been anticipated.

Meynell led him into the study and shut the door. "I have just had Barron here," he said, turning abruptly, after he had pushed a chair toward his guest. "He told me he had shown one of these precious documents to you." He held up the anonymous letter.

Flaxman took it, glanced it over in silence and returned it.

"I can only forgive him for doing it when I reflect that I may thereby — perhaps — be enabled to be of some little use to you. Barron knows what I think of him, and of the business."

"Oh! for him it is a weapon — like any other. Though to do him justice he might not have used it, but for the other mysterious person in the case — the writer of these letters. You know —" he straightened himself vehemently — "that I can say nothing — except that the story is untrue?"

"And of course I shall ask you nothing. I have spent twenty-four hours in arguing with myself as to whether I should come to you at all. Finally I decided you might blame me if I did not. You may not be aware of the letter to my sister-in-law?"

Meynell's start was evident.

"To Mrs. Elsmere?"

"She brought it to us on Friday, before the party. It was, I think, identical with this letter" — he pointed to the Dawes envelope — "except for a few references to the part Mrs. Elsmere had played in helping the families of those poor fellows who were killed in the cage-accident."

"And Miss Elsmere?" said Meynell in a tone that wavered in spite of himself. He sat with his head bent and his eyes on the floor.

"Knows, of course, nothing whatever about it," said Flaxman hastily. "Now will you give us your orders? A strong denial of the truth of the story, and a refusal to discuss it at all — with any one — that I think is what you wish?"

Meynell assented.

"In the village, I shall deal with it at the Reform meeting on Thursday night." Then he rose. "Are you going to Forkéd Pond?"

"I was on my way there."

"I will go with you. If Mrs. Elsmere is free, I should like to have some conversation with her."

They started together through a dripping world on which the skies had but just ceased to rain. On his way through the park Meynell took off his hat and walked bareheaded through the mist, evidently feeling it a physical relief to let the chill, moist air beat freely on brow and temples. Flaxman could not help watching him occasionally — the forehead with its deep vertical furrow, the rugged face, stamped and lined everywhere by travail of mind and body, and the nobility of the large grizzled head. In the voluminous cloak — of an antiquity against which Anne protested in vain — which was his favourite garb on wet days, he might have been a friar of the early time, bound on a preaching tour. The spiritual, evangelic note in the personality became — so Flaxman thought —ever more conspicuous. And yet he walked to-day in very evident trouble, without, however, allowing to this trouble any spoken expression whatever.

As they neared the Forkéd Pond enclosure, Meynell suddenly paused.

"I had forgotten — I must go first to Sandford — where indeed I am expected."

"Sandford? I trust there is no fresh anxiety?"

"There *is* anxiety," said Meynell briefly.

Flaxman expressed an unfeigned sympathy.

"What is Miss Hester doing to-day?"

"Packing, I hope. She goes to-morrow."

"And you — are going to interview this fellow?" asked Flaxman reluctantly.

"I have done it already — and must now do it again. This time I am going to threaten."

"With anything to go upon?"

"Yes. I hope at last to be able to get some grip on him; though no doubt my chances are not improved since yesterday," said Meynell, with a grim shadow of a smile, "supposing that anybody from Upcote has been gossipping at Sandford.   It does not exactly add to one's moral influence to be regarded as a Pharisaical humbug."

"I wish I could take the business off your shoulders!" said Flaxman, heartily.

Meynell gave him a slight, grateful look.   They walked on briskly to the high road, Flaxman accompanying his friend so far.   There they parted, and Hugh returned slowly to the cottage by the water, Meynell promising to join him there within an hour.

BOOK III

CATHARINE

"Such was my mother's way, learnt from Thee in the school of the heart, where Thou art Master."

CHAPTER XVI

IN THE little drawing-room at Forkéd Pond Catharine and Mary Elsmere were sitting at work. Mary was embroidering a curtain in a flowing Venetian pattern — with a handful of withered leaves lying beside her to which she occasionally matched her silks. Catharine was knitting. Outside the rain was howling through the trees; the windows streamed with it. But within, the bright wood-fire threw a pleasant glow over the simple room, and the figures of the two ladies. Mary's trim jacket and skirt of prune-coloured serge, with its white blouse fitting daintily to throat and wrist, seemed by its neatness to emphasize the rebellious masses and the rare colour of her hair. She knew that her hair was beautiful, and it gave her a pleasure she could not help, though she belonged to that type of Englishwoman, not yet nearly so uncommon as modern newspapers and books would have us believe, who think as little as they can of personal adornment and their own appearance, in the interests of some hidden ideal that "haunts them like a passion; of which even the most innocent vanity seems to make them unworthy."

In these feelings and instincts she was, of course, her mother's daughter. Catharine Elsmere's black dress of some plain woollen stuff could not have been plainer, and she wore the straight collar and cuffs, and — on her nearly white hair — the simple cap of her widowhood. But the spiritual beauty which had always been hers was hers still. One might guess that she, too, knew it; that in her efforts to save persons in sin or suffering she must have known what it was worth to her; what the gift of lovely line and presence is worth to any human being. But if she had been made to feel this — passingly, involuntarily — she had certainly shrunk from feeling it.

Mary put her embroidery away, made up the fire, and sat down on a stool at her mother's feet.

"Darling, how many socks have you knitted since we came here? Enough to stock a shop?"

"On the contrary. I have been very idle," laughed Catharine, putting her knitting away. "How long is it? Four months?" she sighed.

"It *has* done you good? — yes, it has!" Mary looked at her closely.

"Then why don't you let me go back to my work? — tyrant!" said Catharine, stroking the red-gold hair.

"Because the doctor said 'March' — and you sha'n't be allowed to put your feet in London a day earlier," said Mary, laying her head on Catharine's knee. "You needn't grumble. Next week you'll have your fells and your becks — as much Westmoreland as ever you want. Only ten days more here," and this time it was Mary who sighed, deeply, unconsciously.

The face above her changed — unseen by Mary.

"You've liked being here?"

"Yes — very much."

"It's a dear little house, and the woods are beautiful."

"Yes. And — I've made a new friend."

"You like Miss Puttenham so much?"

"More than anybody I have seen for years," said Mary, raising herself and speaking with energy; "but, oh dear, I wish I could do something for her!"

Catharine moved uneasily.

"Do what?"

"Comfort her — help her — make her tell me what's the matter."

"You think she's unhappy?"

Mary propped her chin on her hand, and looked into the fire.

"I wonder whether she's ever had any real joy — a week's — a day's — happiness — in her life?"

She said it musingly but intensely. Catharine did not know how to answer her. All the day long, and a good deal of the night, she had been debating with herself what to do — toward Mary. Mary was no longer a child. She was a woman, of nearly six and twenty, strong in character, and accustomed of late to go with her mother into many of the dark places of London life. The betrayal — which could not be hidden from her — of a young servant girl in their employ, the year before, and the fierce tenderness with which Mary had thrown herself into the saving of the girl and her child, had brought about — Catharine knew it — a great deepening and overshadowing of her youth. Catharine had in some ways regretted it bitterly; for she belonged to that older generation which believed — and were amply justified in believing — that it is well for the young to be ignorant, so long as they can be ignorant, of the ugly and tragic things of sex. It was not that her Mary seemed to her in the smallest degree besmirched by the experience she had passed through; that any bloom had been shaken from the flower. Far from it. It was rather that some touch of careless joy was gone forever from her child's life; and how that may hurt a mother, only those know who have wept in secret hours over the first ebbing of youth in a young face.

So that she received Mary's outburst in silence. For she said to herself that she could have no right to reveal Alice Puttenham's secret, even to Mary. That cruel tongues should at that moment be making free with it burnt like a constant smart in Catharine's mind. Was the poor thing herself aware of it? — could it be kept from her? If not, Mary must know — would know — sooner or later. "But for me to tell her without permission" — thought Catharine firmly — "would not be right — or just. Besides, I know nothing — directly."

As to the other and profounder difficulty involved, Catharine wavered perpetually between two different poles of feeling. The incidents of the preceding weeks had made it plain that her resistance to Meynell's influence with Mary had strangely and suddenly broken

" 'I wonder whether she's ever had any real joy—a week's—
a day's—happiness—in her life?' "

down. Owing to an experience of which she had not yet spoken to Mary, her inner will had given way. She saw with painful clearness what was coming; she was blind to none of the signs of advancing love; and she felt herself powerless. An intimation had been given her — so it seemed to her — to which she submitted. Her submission had cost her tears often, at night, when there was no one to see. And yet it had brought her also a strange happiness — like all such yieldings of soul.

But if she had yielded, if there was in her a reluctant practical certainty that Mary would some day be Meynell's wife, then her conscience, which was that of a woman who had passionately loved her husband, began to ask: "Ought she not to be standing by him in this trouble? If we keep it all from her, and he suffers and perhaps breaks down, when she might have sustained him, will she not reproach us? Should I not have bitterly reproached any one who had kept me from helping Robert in such a case?"

A state of mind, it will be seen, into which there entered not a trace of ordinary calculations. It did not occur to her that Mary might be injured in the world's eyes by publicly linking herself with a man under a cloud. Catharine, whose temptation to "scruple" in the religious sense was constant and tormenting, who recoiled in horror from what to others were the merest venial offences, in this connection asked one thing only. Where Barron had argued that an unbeliever must necessarily have a carnal mind, Catharine had simply assured herself at once by an unfailing instinct that the mind was noble and the temper pure. In those matters she was not to be deceived; she knew.

That being so, and if her own passionate objections to the marriage were to be put aside, then she could only judge for Mary as she would judge for herself. *Not* to love — *not* to comfort — could there be — for love — any greater wound, any greater privation? She shrank, in a kind of terror, from inflicting it on Mary — Mary, unconscious and unknowing.

. . . The soft chatter of the fire, the plashing of the rain, filled the room with the atmosphere of reverie. Catharine's thoughts passed from her obligations toward Mary to grapple anxiously with those she might be under toward Meynell himself. The mere possession of the anonymous letter — and Flaxman had not given her leave to destroy it — weighed upon her conscience. It seemed to her she ought not to possess it; and she had been only half convinced by Flaxman's arguments for delay. She was rapidly coming to the belief that it should have been handed instantly to the Rector.

A step outside.

"Uncle Hugh!" said Mary, springing up. "I'll go and see if there are any scones for tea!" And she vanished into the kitchen, while Catharine admitted her brother-in-law.

"Meynell is to join me here in an hour or so," he said, as he followed her into the little sitting-room. Catharine closed the door, and looked at him anxiously. He lowered his voice.

"Barron called on him this morning — had only just gone when I arrived. Meynell has seen the letter to Dawes. I informed him of the letter to you, and I think he would like to have some talk with you."

Catharine's face showed her relief.

"Oh, I am glad — I am *glad* he knows!" — she said, with emphasis. "We were wrong to delay."

"He told me nothing — and I asked nothing. But, of course, what the situation implies is unfortunately clear enough! — no need to talk of it. He won't and he can't vindicate himself, except by a simple denial. At any ordinary time that would be enough. But now — with all the hot feeling there is on the other subject — and the natural desire to discredit him ——" Flaxman shrugged his shoulders despondently. "Rose's maid — you know the dear old thing she is —— came to her last night, in utter distress about the talk in the village. There was a journalist here, a reporter from one of the papers that have been opposing Meynell most actively ——"

"They are quite right to oppose him," interrupted Catharine quickly. Her face had stiffened.

"Perfectly! But you see the temptation?"

Catharine admitted it. She stood by the window looking out into the rain. And as she did so she became aware of a figure — the slight figure of a woman — walking fast toward the cottage along the narrow grass causeway that ran between the two ponds. On either side of the woman the autumn trees swayed and bent under the rising storm, and every now and then a mist of scudding leaves almost effaced her. She seemed to be breathlessly struggling with the wind as she sped onward, and in her whole aspect there was an indescribable forlornness and terror.

Catharine peered into the rain. . . .

"Hugh!" — She turned swiftly to her brother-in-law — "There is some one coming to see me. Will you go?" — she pointed to the garden door on the farther side of the drawing-room — "and will you take Mary? Go round to the back. You know the old summer-house at the end of the wood-walk. We have often sheltered there from rain. Or there's the keeper's cottage a little farther on. I know Mary wanted to go there this afternoon. Please, dear Hugh!"

He looked at her in astonishment. Then through the large French window he too saw the advancing form. In an instant he had disappeared by the garden door. Catharine went into the hall, opened the door of the kitchen and beckoned to Mary, who was standing there with their little maid. "Don't come back just yet, darling!" she said in her ear — "Get your things on, and go with Uncle Hugh. I want to be alone."

Mary stepped back bewildered, and Catharine shut her in. Then she went back to the hall, just as a bell rang faintly

"Is Mrs. Elsmere ——"

Then as the visitor saw Catharine herself standing in the open doorway, she said with broken breath:

"Can I come in — can I see you?"

Catharine drew her in.

"Dear Miss Puttenham! — how tired you are — and how wet! Let me take the cloak off."

And as she drew off the soaked waterproof, Catharine felt the trembling of the slight frame beneath.

"Come and sit by the fire," she said tenderly.

Alice sank into the chair that was offered her, her eyes fixed on Catharine. Every feature in the delicate oval face was pinched and drawn. The struggle with wild weather had drained the lips and the cheeks of colour, and her brown hair under her serge cap fell limply about her small ears and neck. She was an image not so much of grief as of some unendurable distress.

Catharine began to chafe her hands — but Alice stopped her —

"I am not cold — oh no, I'm not cold. Dear Mrs. Elsmere! You must think it so strange of me to come to you in this way. But I am in trouble — such great trouble — and I don't know what to do. Then I thought I'd come to you. You — you always seem to me so kind — you won't despise — or repulse me — I know you won't!"

Her voice sank to a whisper. Catharine took the two icy hands in her warm grasp.

"Tell me if there is anything I can do to help you."

"I — I want to tell you. You may be angry — because I've been Mary's friend — when I'd no right. I'm not what you think. I — I have a secret — or — I had. And now it's discovered — and I don't know what I shall do — it's so awful — so awful!"

Her head dropped on the chair behind her — and her eyes closed. Catharine, kneeling beside her, bent forward and kissed her.

"Won't you tell me?" she said, gently.

Alice was silent a moment. Then she suddenly opened her eyes — and spoke in a whisper.

"I — I was never married. But Hester Fox-Wilton's — my child!"

The tears came streaming from her eyes. They stood in Catharine's.

"You poor thing!" said Catharine brokenly, and raising one of the cold hands, she pressed it to her lips.

But Alice suddenly raised herself.

"You knew!" — she said — "You knew!" And her eyes, full of fear, stared into Catharine's. Then as Catharine did not speak immediately she went on with growing agitation, "You've heard — what everybody's saying? Oh! I don't know how I can face it. I often thought it would come — some time. And ever since that woman — since Judith — came home — it's been a nightmare. For I felt certain she'd come home because she was angry with us — and that she'd said something — before she died. Then nothing happened — and I've tried to think — lately — it was all right. But last night ——"

She paused for self-control. Catharine was alarmed by her state — by its anguish, its excitement. It required an effort of her whole being before the sufferer could recover voice and breath, before she hurried on, holding Catharine's hands, and looking piteously into her face.

"Last night a woman came to see me — an old servant of mine who's nursed me sometimes — when I've been ill. She loves me — she's good to me. And she came to tell me what people were saying in the village — how there were letters going round, about me — and Hester — how everybody knew — and they were talking in the public-houses. She thought I ought to know — she cried — and wanted me to deny it. And of course I denied it — I was fierce to her — but it's true!"

She paused a moment, her pale lips moving soundlessly, unconsciously.

"I — I'll tell you about that presently. But the awful thing was — she said people were saying — that the Rector — that Mr. Meynell — was Hester's father — and Judith Sabin had told Mr. Barron so before her death. And they declared the Bishop would make him resign — and give up his living. It would be such a scandal, she said — it might even break up the League. And it would ruin Mr. Meynell, so people thought. Of course there were many people who were angry — who didn't believe a word — but this woman who told me was astonished that so many *did* believe. . . . So then I thought all night — what I should do. And this morning I went to Edith, my sister, and told her. And she went into hysterics, and said she always knew I should bring disgrace on them in the end — and her life had been a burden to her for eighteen years — oh! that's what she says to me so often! But the strange thing was she wanted to make me promise I would say nothing — not a word. We were to go abroad, and the thing would die away. And then ——"

She withdrew her hands from Catharine, and rising to her feet she pressed the damp hair back from her face, and began to pace the room — unconsciously — still talking.

"I asked her what was to happen about Richard — about the Rector. I said he must bring an action, and I would give evidence — it must all come out. And then she fell upon me — and said I was an ungrateful wretch. My sin had spoilt her life — and Ralph's. They had done all they could — and now the publicity — if I insisted — would disgrace them all — and ruin the girls' chances of marrying, and I don't know what besides. But if I held my tongue — we could go away for a time — it would be forgotten, and nobody out of Upcote need ever hear of it. People would never believe such a thing of Richard Meynell. Of course he would deny it — and of course his word would be taken. But to bring out the whole story in a law-court ——"

She paused beside Catharine, wringing her hands, gathering up as it were her whole strength to pour it — slowly, deliberately — into the words that followed:

" But I — will run no risk of ruining Richard Meynell!
As for me — what does it matter what happens to me!
And darling Hester! — we could keep it from her — we
would! She and I could live abroad. And I don't see
how it could disgrace Edith and the girls — people would
only say she and Ralph had been very good to me. But
Richard Meynell! — with these trials coming on — and
all the excitement about him — there'll be ever so many
who would be wild to believe it! They won't care how
absurd it is — they'll want to *crush* him! And he — he'll
never say a word for himself — to explain — never! Because
he couldn't without telling all my story. And that — do
you suppose Richard Meynell would ever do *that?* — to
any poor human soul that had trusted him?"

The colour had rushed back into her cheeks; she held
herself erect, transfigured by the emotion that possessed
her. Catharine looked at her in doubt — trouble —
amazement. And then, her pure sense divined something — dimly — of what the full history of this soul
had been; and her heart melted. She put out her hands
and drew the speaker down again into the seat beside her.

"I think you'll have to let him decide that for you.
He's a strong man — and a wise man. He'll judge what's
right. And I ought to warn you that he'll be here probably — very soon. He wanted to see me."

Alice opened her startled eyes.

"About this? To see you? I don't understand."

"I had one of these letters — these wicked letters,"
said Catharine reluctantly.

Alice shrank and trembled. "It's terrible!" — her voice was scarcely to be heard. "Who is it hates me so? — or Richard?"

There was silence a moment. And in the pause the stress and tumult of nature without, the beating of the wind, and the plashing of the rain, seemed to be rushing headlong through the little room. But neither Catharine nor Alice was aware of it, except in so far as it played obscurely on Alice's tortured nerves, fevering and goading them the more. Catharine's gaze was bent on her companion; her mind was full of projects of help, which were also prayers; moments in that ceaseless dialogue with a Greater than itself, which makes the life of the Christian. And it was as though, by some secret influence, her prayers worked on Alice; for presently she turned in order that she might look straight into the face beside her.

"I'd like to tell you" — she said faintly — "oh — I'd like to tell you!"

"Tell me anything you will."

"It was when I was so young — just eighteen — like Hester. Oh! but you don't know about Neville — no one does now. People seem all to have forgotten him. But he came into his property here — the Abbey — the old Abbey — just when I was growing up. I saw him here first — but only once or twice. Then we met in Scotland. I was staying at a house near his shooting. And we fell in love. Oh, I knew he was married! — I can never say that I didn't know, even at the beginning. But his wife was so cruel to him — he was very, very unhappy.

She couldn't understand him — or make allowances for him — she despised him, and wouldn't live with him. He was miserable — and so was I. My father and mother were dead! I had to live with Ralph and Edith; and they always made me feel that I was in their way. It wasn't their fault! — I *was* in the way. And then Neville came. He was so handsome, and so clever — so winning and dear — he could do everything. I was staying with some old cousins in Ross-shire, who used to ask me now and then. There were no young people in the house. My cousins were quite kind to me, but I spent a great deal of time alone — and Neville and I got into a way of meeting — in lonely places — on the moors. No one found out. He taught me everything I ever knew, almost. He gave me books — and read to me. He was sorry for me — and at last — he loved me! And we never looked ahead. Then — in one week — everything happened together. I had to go home. He talked of going to Sandford, and implored me still to meet him. And I thought how Ralph and Edith would watch us, and spy upon us, and I implored him never to go to Sandford when I was at Upcote. We must meet at other places. And he agreed. Then the day came for me to go south. I travelled by myself — and he rode twenty miles to a junction station and joined me. Then we travelled all day together."

Her voice failed her. She pressed her thin hands together under the onset of memory, and that old conquered anguish which in spite of all the life that had been lived since still smouldered amid the roots of being.

"I may tell you?" she said at last, with a piteous look. Catharine bent over her.

"Anything that will help you. Only remember I don't ask or expect you to say anything."

"I ought" — said Alice miserably — "I ought — because of Mary."

Catharine was silent. She only pressed the hand she held. Alice resumed:

"It was a day that decided all my life. We were so wretched. We thought we could never meet again — it seemed as though we were both — with every station we passed — coming nearer to something like death — something worse than death. Then — before we got to Euston — I couldn't bear it — I — I gave way. We sent a telegram from Euston to Edith that I was going to stay with a school friend in Cornwall — and that night we crossed to Paris ——"

She covered her face with her hands a moment; then went on more calmly:

"You'll guess all the rest. I was a fortnight with him in Paris. Then I went home. In a few weeks Edith guessed — and so did Judith Sabin, who was Edith's maid. Edith made me tell her everything. She and Ralph were nearly beside themselves. They were very strict in those days; Ralph was a great Evangelical, and used to speak at the May meetings. All his party looked up to him so — and consulted him. It was a fearful blow to him. But

Edith thought of what to do — and she made him agree. We went abroad, she and I — with Judith.   It was given out that Edith was delicate, and must have a year away. We stopped about in little mountain places — and Hester was born at Grenoble.   And then for the last and only time, they let Neville come to see me ——"

Her voice sank.   She could only go on in a whisper.

"Three weeks later he was drowned on the Donegal coast.   It was called an accident — but it wasn't.   He had hoped and hoped to get his wife to divorce him — and make amends.   And when Mrs. Flood's — his wife's — final letter came — she was a Catholic and nothing would induce her — he just took his boat out in a storm, and never came back ——"

The story lost itself in a long sobbing sigh that came from the depths of life.   When she spoke again it was with more strength:

"But he had written the night before to Richard — Richard Meynell.   You know he was the Rector's uncle, though he was only seven years older?   I had never seen Richard then.   But I had often heard of him from Neville. Neville had taken a great fancy to him a year or two before, when Richard was still at college, and Neville was in the Guards.   They used to talk of religion and philosophy.   Neville was a great reader always — and they became great friends.   So on his last night he wrote to Richard, telling him everything, and asking him to be kind to me — and Hester.   And Richard— who had just been appointed to the living here — came out to the Riviera, and brought me the letter — and the little book that was in his pocket — when they found him. So you see . . ."

She spoke with fluttering colour and voice, as though to find words at all were a matter of infinite difficulty:

"You see that was how Richard came to take an interest in us — in Hester and me — how he came to be the friend too of Ralph and Edith. Poor Ralph! — Ralph was often hard to me, but he meant kindly — he would never have got through at all but for Richard. If Richard was away for a week, he used to fret. That was eighteen years ago — and I too should never have had any peace — any comfort in life again — but for Richard. He found somebody to live with me abroad for those first years, and then, when I came back to Upcote, he made Ralph and Edith consent to my living in that little house by myself — with my chaperon. He would have preferred — indeed he urged it — that I should go on living abroad. But there was Hester! — and I knew by that time that none of them had the least bit of love for her! — she was a burden to them all. I couldn't leave her to them — I *couldn't!* . . . Oh! they were terrible, those years!" And again she caught Catharine's hands and held them tight. "You see, I was so young — not much over twenty — and nobody suspected anything. Nobody in the world knew anything — except Judith Sabin, who was in America, and *she* never knew who Hester's father was — and my own people — and Richard! Richard taught me how to bear it — oh! not in words —

for he never preached to me — but by his life. I couldn't
have lived at all — but for him. And now you see —
you see — how I am paying him back!"

And again, as the rush of emotion came upon her, she
threw herself into a wild pleading, as though the gray-
haired woman beside her were thwarting and opposing
her.

"How can I let my story — my wretched story —
ruin his life — and all his work? I can't — I can't! I
came to you because you won't look at it as Edith does.
You'll think of what's right — right to others. Last
night I thought one must die of — misery. I suppose
people would call it shame. It seemed to me I heard
what they were all saying in the village — how they were
gloating over it — after all these years. It seemed to
strip one of all self-respect — all decency. And to-day I
don't care about that! I care only that Richard shouldn't
suffer because of what he did for me — and because of
me. Oh! do help me, do advise me! Your look — your
manner — have often made me want to come and tell
you" — her voice was broken now with stifled sobs —
"like a child — a child. Dear Mrs. Elsmere! — what
ought I to do?"

And she raised imploring eyes to the face beside her,
so finely worn with living and with human service.

"You must think first of Hester," said Catharine,
with gentle steadiness, putting her arm round the bent
shoulders. "I am sure the Rector would tell you that.
She is your first — your sacredest duty."

Alice Puttenham shivered as though something in Catharine's tender voice reproached her.

"Oh, I know — my poor Hester! My life has set hers all wrong. Wouldn't it have been better to face it all from the beginning — to tell the truth — wouldn't it?" She asked it piteously.

"It might have been. But the other way was chosen; and now to undo it — publicly — affects not you only, but Hester. It mayn't be possible — it mayn't be right."

"I must! — I must!" said Alice impetuously, and rising to her feet she began to pace the room again with wild steps, her hands behind her, her slender form drawn tensely to its height.

At that moment Catharine became aware of some one standing in the porch just beyond the drawing-room of the tiny cottage.

"This may be Mr. Meynell." She rose to admit him.

Alice stood expectant. Her outward agitation disappeared. Some murmured conversation passed between the two persons in the little hall. Then Catharine came in again, followed by Meynell, who closed the door, and stood looking sadly at the pale woman confronting him.

"So they haven't spared even you?" he said at last, in a voice bitterly subdued. "But don't be too unhappy. It wants courage and wisdom on our part. But it will all pass away."

He quietly pushed a chair toward Alice, and then took off his dripping cloak, carried it into the passage outside, and returned.

"Don't go, Mrs. Elsmere," he said, as he perceived Catharine's uncertainty. "Stay and help us, if you will."

Catharine submitted. She took her accustomed seat by the fire; Alice, or the ghost of Alice, sat opposite to her, in Mary's chair, surrounded by Mary's embroidery things; and Meynell was between them.

He looked from one to the other, and there was something in his aspect which restrained Alice's agitation, and answered at once to some high expectation in Catharine.

"I know, Mrs. Elsmere, that you have received one of the anonymous letters that are being circulated in this neighbourhood, and I presume also — from what I see — that Miss Puttenham has given you her confidence. We must think calmly what is best to do. Now — the first person who must be in all our minds — is Hester."

He bent forward, looking into Alice's face, without visible emotion; rather with the air of peremptory common sense which had so often helped her through the difficulties of her life.

She sat drooping, her head on her hand, making no sign.

"Let us remember these facts," he resumed. "Hester is in a critical state of life and mind. She imagines herself to be in love with my cousin Philip Meryon, a worthless man, without an ounce of conscience where women are concerned, who, in my strong belief, is already married under the ambiguities of Scotch law, though his wife, if she is his wife, left him some years ago, detests him, and has never been acknowledged. I have convinced him at last — this morning — that I mean to bring this home to him. But that does not dispose of the thing — finally. Hester is in danger — in danger from herself. She is at war with her family — with the world. She believes nobody loves her — that she is and always has been a pariah at home — and with her temperament she is in a mood for desperate things. Tell her now that she is illegitimate — let your sister Edith go talking to her about 'disgrace' — and there is no saying what will happen. She will say — and think — that she has no responsibilities, and may do what she pleases. There is no saying what she might do. We might have a tragedy that none of us could prevent."

Alice lifted her head.

"I could go away with her," she said, imploringly. "I could watch over her day and night. But let me put this thing straight now publicly. Indeed — indeed, it is time."

"You mean you wish to bring an action? In that case you would have to return to give evidence."

"Yes — for a short time. But that could be managed. She should never see the English papers — I could promise that."

"And what is to prevent Philip Meryon telling her? At present he is entirely ignorant of her parentage. I have convinced myself of that this morning. He has no dealings with the people here, nor they with him. What has been happening here has not reached him. And he is

really off to-night. We must, of course, always take the
risk of his knowing, and of his telling her.   A libel action
would convert that risk into a certainty.   Would it not
simply forward whatever designs he may have on her —
for I do not believe for a moment he will abandon them —
it will be a duel, rather, between him and us — would
it not actually forward his designs — to tell her?"

Alice did not reply.   She sat wringing her delicate
hands in a silent desperation; while Catharine opposite
was lost in the bewilderment of the situation — the
insistence of the woman, the refusal of the man.

"My advice is this" — continued Meynell, still addressing Alice —"that you should take her to Paris to-
morrow in my stead, and should stay near her for some
months.   Lady Fox-Wilton — whom I have just seen —
she overtook me driving on the Markborough road half
an hour ago, and we had some conversation — talks of
taking a house at Tours for a year — an excellent thing
— for them all.   We don't want her on the spot any
longer — we don't want any of them !" said the Rector, dismissing the Fox-Wilton family with an emphatic
gesture which probably represented what he had gone
through in the interview with Edith. . . .   "In that
way the thing will soon die down.   There will be nobody
here — nobody within reach — for the scoundrel who is
writing these letters to attack — except, of course, myself
— and I shall know how to deal with it.   He will probably tire of the amusement.   Other people will be ashamed
of having read the letters and believed them.   I even

dare to hope that Mr. Barron — in time — may be ashamed."

Alice looked at him in tremulous despair.

"Nobody to attack!" she said — "nobody to attack! And you, Richard — *you?*"

A dry smile flickered on his face.

"Leave that to me — I assure you you may leave it to me."

"Richard!" said Alice imploringly — "just think. I know what you say is very important — very true. But for me personally" — she looked round the room with wandering eyes; then found a sudden passionate gesture, pressing back the hair from her brow with both hands — "for me personally — to tell the truth — to face the truth — would be relief — infinite relief! It would kill the fear in which I have lived all these years — kill it forever. It would be better for all of us if we had told the truth — from the beginning. And as for Hester — she must know — you say yourself she must know before long — when she is of age — when she marries ——"

Meynell's face took an unconscious hardness.

"Forgive me! — the matter must be left to me. The only person who could reasonably take legal action would be myself — and I shall not take it. I beg you, be advised by me." He bent forward again. "My dear friend!" — and now he spoke with emotion — "in your generous consideration for me you do not know what you are proposing — what an action in the courts would mean, especially at this moment. Think of the party spirit that would be brought into it — the venom — the prejudice — the base insinuations. No! — believe me — that is out of the question — for your sake — and Hester's."

"And your work — your influence?"

"If they suffer — they must suffer. But do not imagine that I shall not defend myself — and you — you above all — from calumny and lies. Of course I shall — in my own way."

There was silence — a dismal silence. At the end of it Meynell stretched out his hand to Alice with a smile. She placed her own in it, slowly, with a look which filled Catharine's eyes once more with tears.

"Trust me!" said Meynell, as he pressed the hand. "Indeed you may." Then he turned to Catharine Elsmere —

"I think Mrs. Elsmere is with me — that she approves?"

"With one reservation." The words came gravely, after a moment's doubt.

His eyes asked her to be frank.

"I think it would be possible — I think it would be just — if Miss Puttenham were to empower you to go to your Bishop. He too has rights!" said Catharine, her clear skin reddening.

Meynell paused: then spoke with hesitation.

"Yes — that I possibly might do — if you permit me?" He turned again to Alice.

"Go to him — go to him at once!" she said with a sob she could not repress.

Another silence. Then Meynell walked to the window and looked at the weather.

"It is not raining so fast," he said in his cheerful voice. "Oughtn't you to be going home — getting ready and arranging with Hester? It's an awful business going abroad."

Alice rose silently. Catharine went into the kitchen to fetch the waterproof which had been drying.

Alice and Meynell were left alone.

She looked up.

"It is so hard to be hated!" she said passionately — "to see you hated. It seems to burn one's heart — the coarse and horrible things that are being said ——"

He frowned and fidgeted — till the thought within forced its way:

"Christ was hated. Yet directly the least touch of it comes to us, we rebel — we cry out against God."

"It is because we are so weak — we are not Christ!" She covered her face with her hands.

"No — but we are his followers — if the Life that was in him is in us too. *'Life that in me has rest — as I — Undying Life — have power in Thee!'*" He fell — murmuring — into lines that had evidently been in his thoughts, smiling upon her.

Then Catharine returned. Alice was warmly wrapped up, and Catharine took her to the door, leaving Meynell in the sitting-room.

"We will come and help you this evening — Mary and I," she said tenderly, as they stood together in the little passage.

"Mary?" Alice looked at her in a trembling uncertainty.

"Mary — of course."

Alice thought a moment, and then said with a low intensity, a force to which Catharine had no clue — "I want you — to tell her — the whole story. Will you?"

Catharine kissed her cheek in silence, and they parted.

Catharine went slowly back to the little sitting-room. Meynell was standing abstracted before the fire, his hands clasped in front of him, his head bent. Catharine approached him — drawing quick breath.

"Mr. Meynell — what shall I do — what do you wish me to do or say — with regard to my daughter?"

He turned — pale with amazement.

And so began what one may call — perhaps — the most romantic action of a noble life!

CHAPTER XVII

WHEN Catharine returned to the little sitting-room, in which the darkness of a rainy October evening was already declaring itself, she came shaken by many emotions in which only one thing was clear — that the man before her was a good man in distress, and that her daughter loved him.

If she had been of the true bigot stuff she would have seen in the threatened scandal a means of freeing Mary from an undesirable attachment. But just as in her married life, her heart had not been able to stand against her husband while her mind condemned him, so now. While in theory, and toward people with whom she never came in contact, she had grown even more bitter and in-transigent since Robert's death than she had been in her youth, she had all the time been living the daily life of service and compassion which — unknown to herself — had been the real saving and determining force. Im-pulses of love, impulses of sacrifice toward the miserable, the vile, and the helpless — day by day she had felt them, day by day she had obeyed them. And thus all the arteries, so to speak, of the spiritual life had remained soft and pliant — that life itself in her was still young. It was there in truth that her Christianity lay; while she imagined it to lie in the assent to certain historical and dogmatic statements. And so strong was this inward and vital faith — so strengthened in fact by mere living — that when she was faced with this second crisis in her life, brought actually to close grips with it, that faith, against all that might have been expected, carried her through the difficult place with even greater sureness than at first. She suffered indeed. It seemed to her all through that she was endangering Mary, and condoning a betrayal of her Lord. And yet she could not act upon this belief. She must needs act — with pain often, and yet with mysterious moments of certainty and joy, on quite another faith, the faith which has expressed itself in the perennial cry of Christianity: "Little children, love one another!" And therein lay the difference between her and Barron.

It was therefore in this mixed — and yet single — mood that she came back to Meynell, and asked him — quietly — the strange question: "What shall I do — what do you wish me to do or say — with regard to my daughter?"

Meynell could not for a moment believe that he had heard aright. He stared at her in bewilderment, at first pale, and then in a sudden heat and vivacity of colour.

"I — I hardly understand you, Mrs. Elsmere."

They stood facing each other in silence.

"Surely we need not inform her," he said, at last, in a low voice.

"Only that a wicked and untrue story has been circulated — that you cannot, for good reasons, involving

THE CASE OF RICHARD MEYNELL

other persons, prosecute those responsible for it in the usual way. And if she comes across any signs of it, or its effects, she is to trust your wisdom in dealing with it — and not to be troubled — is not that what you would like me to say?"

"That is indeed what I should like you to say." He raised his eyes to her gravely.

"Or — will you say it yourself?"

He started.

"Mrs. Elsmere!" — he spoke with quick emotion — "You are wonderfully good to me." He scanned her with an unsteady face — then made an agitated step toward her. "It almost makes me think — you permit me ——"

"No — no," said Catharine, hurriedly, drawing back. "But if you would like to speak to Mary — she will be here directly."

"No!" — he said, after a moment, recovering his composure — "I couldn't! But — will you?"

"If you wish it." Then she added, "She will of course never ask a question; it will be her business to know nothing of the matter — in itself. But she will be able to show you her confidence, and to feel that we have treated her as a woman — not a child."

Meynell drew a deep breath. He took Catharine's hand and pressed it. She felt with a thrill — which was half bitterness — that it was already a son's look he turned upon her.

"You — you have guessed me?" he said, almost inaudibly.

"I see there is a great friendship between you."

"*Friendship!*"   Then he restrained himself sharply. "But I ought not to speak of it — to intrude myself and my affairs on her notice at all at this moment.   .   .   . " He looked at his companion almost sternly.   "Is it not clear that I ought not?   I meant to have brought her a book to-day.   I have not brought it.   I have been even glad — thankful — to think you were going away, although ——" But again he checked the personal note. "The truth is I could not endure that through me — through anything connected with me — she might be driven upon facts and sorrows — ugly facts that would distress her, and sorrows for which she is too young.   It seemed to me indeed I might not be able to help it.   But at the same time it was clear to me, to-day, that at such a time — feeling as I do — I ought not in the smallest degree to presume upon her — and your — kindness to me.   Above all" — his voice shook — "I could not come forward — I could not speak to her — as at another time I might have spoken.   I could not run the smallest risk — of her name being coupled with mine — when my character was being seriously called in question.   It would not have been right for her; it would not have been seemly for myself.   So what was there — but silence?   And yet I felt — that through this silence — we should somehow trust each other!"

He paused a moment, looking down upon his companion.   Catharine was sitting by the fire near a small table on which her elbow rested, her face propped on her

hand.   There was something in the ascetic refinement, the
grave sweetness of her aspect, that played upon him with
a tonic and consoling force.   He remembered the frozen
reception she had given him at their first meeting; and
the melting of her heart toward him seemed a wonderful
thing.   And then came the delicious thought — "Would
she so treat him, unless Mary — *Mary!* ——"

But, at the same time, there was in him the mind of
the practical man, which plainly and energetically disapproved her.   And presently he tried, with much difficulty, to tell her so, to impress upon her — upon her,
Mary's mother — that Mary must not be allowed to hold
any communication with him, to show any kindness
toward him, till this cloud had wholly cleared away,
and the sky was clear again.   He became almost angry
as he urged this; so excited, indeed, and incoherent that
a charming smile stole into Catharine's gray eyes.

"I understand quite what you feel," she said as she
rose, "and why you feel it.   But I am not bound to
follow your advice — or to agree with you — am I?"

"Yes, I think you are," he said stoutly.

Then a shadow fell over her face.

"I suppose I am doing a strange thing" — her manner
faltered a little — "but it seems to me right — I have
been *led* — else why was it so plain?"

She raised her clear eyes, and he understood that she
spoke of those "hints" and "voices" of the soul that play
so large a part in the more mystical Christian experience.
She hurried on:

"When two people — two people like you and Mary — feel such a deep interest in each other — surely it is God's sign." Then, suddenly, the tears shone. "Oh, Mr. Meynell! — trial brings us nearer to our Saviour. Perhaps — through it — you and Mary — will find Him!"

He saw that she was trembling from head to foot; and his own emotion was great.

He took her hand again, and held it in both his own.

"Do you imagine," he said huskily "that you and I are very far apart?"

And again the tenderness of his manner was a son's tenderness.

She shook her head, but she could not speak. She gently withdrew her hand, and turned aside to gather up some letters on the table.

A sound of footsteps could be heard outside. Catharine moved to the window.

"It is Mary," she said quietly. "Will you wait a little while I meet her?" And without giving him time to reply, she left the room.

He walked up and down, not without some humorous bewilderment in spite of his emotion. The saints, it seemed, are persons of determination! But, after a minute, he thought of nothing, realized nothing, save that Mary was in the little house again, and that one of those low voices he could just hear, as a murmur in the distance, through the thin walls of the cottage, was hers.

The door opened softly, and she came in. Though she had taken off her hat, she still wore her blue cloak of Irish frieze, which fell round her slender figure in long folds. Her face was rosy with rain and wind; the same wind and rain which had stamped such a gray fatigue on Alice Puttenham's cheeks. Amid the dusk, the fire-light touched her hair and her ungloved hand. She was a vision of youth and soft life; and her composure, her slight, shy smile, would alone have made her beautiful.

Their hands met as she gently greeted him. But there was that in his look which disturbed her gentleness — which deepened her colour. She hurried to speak.

"I am so glad that mother made you stay — just that I might tell you." Then her breath began to hasten. "Mother says you are — or may be — unjustly attacked — that you don't think it right to defend yourself publicly — and those who follow you, and admire you, may be hurt and troubled. I wanted to say — and mother approves — that whoever is hurt and troubled, I can never be — except for you. Besides, I shall know and ask nothing. You may be sure of that. And people will not dare to speak to me."

She stood proudly erect.

Meynell was silent for a moment. Then, by a sudden movement, he stooped and kissed a fold of her cloak. She drew back with a little stifled cry, putting out her hands, which he caught. He kissed them both, dropped them, and walked away from her.

When he returned it was with another aspect.

"Don't let's make too much of this trouble. It may all die away — or it may be a hard fight. But whatever happens, you are going to Westmoreland immediately. That is my great comfort."

"Is it?" She laughed unsteadily.

He too smiled. There was intoxication he could not resist — in her presence — and in what it implied.

"It is the best possible thing that could be done. Then — whatever happens — I shall not be compromising my friends. For a while — there must be no communication between them and me."

"Oh, yes!" she said, involuntarily clasping her hands. "Friends may write."

"May they?" He thought it over, with a furrowed brow, then raised it, clear. "What shall they write about?"

An exquisite joyousness trembled in her look.

"Leave it to them!"

Then, as she once more perceived the anxiety and despondency in him, the brightness clouded; pity possessed her: "Tell me what you are preaching — and writing."

"*If* I preach — *if* I write. And what will you tell me?"

"'How the water comes down at Lodore,'" she said gayly. "What the mountains look like, and how many rainy days there are in a week."

"Excellent! I perceive you mean to libel the country I love!"

"You can always come and see!" she said, with a shy courage.

He shook his head.

"No. My Westmoreland holiday is given up."

"Because of the Movement?"

And sitting down by the fire, still with that same look of suppressed and tremulous joy, she began to question him about the meetings and engagements ahead. But he would not be drawn into any talk about them. It was no doubt quite possible — though not, he thought, probable — that he might soon be ostracized from them all. But upon this he would not dwell, and though her understanding of the whole position was far too vague to warn her from these questions, she soon perceived that he was unwilling to answer them as usual. Silence indeed fell between them; but it was a silence of emotion. She had thrown off her cloak, and sat looking down, in the light of the fire; she knew that he observed her, and the colour on her cheek was due to something more than the flame at her feet. As they realized each other's nearness indeed, in the quiet of the dim room, it was with a magic sense of transformation. Outside the autumn storm was still beating — symbol of the moral storm which threatened them. Yet within were trust and passionate gratitude and tender hope, intertwined, all of them, with the sacred impulse of the woman toward the man, and of the man toward the woman. Each moment as it passed built up one of those watersheds of life from which henceforward the rivers flow broadening to undreamt-of seas.

When Catharine returned, Meynell was hat in hand for departure. There was no more expression of feeling

or reference to grave affairs. They stood a few moments
chatting about ordinary things. Incidentally Hugh
Flaxman's loss of the two gold coins was mentioned.
Meynell inquired when they were first missed.

"That very evening," said Mary. "Rose always puts
them away herself. She missed the two little cases at once.
One was a coin of Velia, with a head of Athene ——"

"I remember it perfectly," said Meynell. "It dropped
on the floor when I was talking to Norham — and I picked
it up — with another, if I remember right — a Hermes!"

Mary replied that the Hermes too was missing — that
both were exceedingly rare; and that in the spring a buyer
for the Louvre had offered Hugh four hundred pounds for
the two.

"They feel most unhappy and uncomfortable about it.
None of the servants seems to have gone into that room
during the party. Rose put all the coins on the table
herself. She remembers saying good-bye to Canon France
and his sister in the drawing-room — and two or three
others — and immediately afterward she went into the
green drawing-room to lock up the coins. There were
two missing."

"She doesn't remember who had been in the room?"

"She vaguely remembers seeing two or three people
go in and out — the Bishop! — Canon Dornal!"

They both laughed. Then Meynell's face set sharply.
A sudden recollection shot through his mind. He beheld
the figure of a sallow, dark-haired young man slipping —
alone — through the doorway of the green drawing-room.

And this image in the mind touched and fired others, like a spark running through dead leaves. . . .

When he had gone, Catharine turned to Mary, and Mary, running, wound her arms close round her mother, and lay her head on Catharine's breast.

"You angel! — you darling!" she said, and raising her mother's hand she kissed it passionately.

Catharine's eyes filled with tears, and her heart with mingled joy and revolt. Then, quickly, she asked herself as she stood there in her child's embrace whether she should speak of a certain event — certain experience — which had, in truth, though Mary knew nothing of it, vitally affected both their lives.

But she could not bring herself to speak of it.

So that Mary never knew to what, in truth, she owed the painful breaking down of an opposition and a hostility which might in time have poisoned all their relations to each other.

But when Mary had gone away to change her damp clothes, the visionary experience of which Catharine could not tell came back upon her; and again she felt the thrill — the touch of bodiless ecstasy.

It had been in the early morning, when all such things befall. For then the mind is not yet recaptured by life and no longer held by sleep. There is in it a pure expectancy, open to strange influences: influences from memory and the under-soul. It visualizes easily, and dream and fact are one.

In this state Catharine woke on a September morning and felt beside her a presence that held her breathless. The half-remembered images and thoughts of sleep pursued her — became what we call "real."

"Robert!" she said, aloud — very low.

And without voice, it seemed to her that some one replied. A dialogue began into which she threw her soul. Of her body, she was not conscious; and yet the little room, its white ceiling, its open windows, and the dancing shadows of the autumn leaves were all present to her. She poured out the sorrow, the anxiety — about Mary — that pressed so heavy on her heart, and the tender voice answered, now consoling, now rebuking.

"And we forbade him, because he followed not us . . . Forbid him not — *forbid him not!*" — seemed to go echoing through the quiet air.

The words sank deep into her sense — she heard herself sobbing — and the unearthly presence came nearer — though still always remote, intangible — with the same baffling distance between itself and her. . . .

The psychology of it was plain. It was the upthrust into consciousness of the mingled ideas and passions on which her life was founded, piercing through the intellectualism of her dogmatic belief. But though she would have patiently accepted any scientific explanation, she believed in her heart that Robert had spoken to her, bidding her renounce her repugnance to Mary's friendship with Meynell — to Mary's love for Meynell.

She came down the morning after with a strange, dull

sense of change and disaster. But the currents of her
mind and will had set firmly in a fresh direction. It was
almost mechanically — under a strong sense of guidance
— that she had made her hesitating proposal to Mary
to go with her to the Upcote meeting. Mary's look of
utter astonishment had sent new waves of disturbance
and compunction through the mother's mind.

But if these things could not be told — even to Mary
— there were other revelations to make.

When the lamp had been brought in, and the darkness
outside shut out, Catharine laid her hand on Mary's,
and told the story of Alice Puttenham.

Mary heard it in silence, growing very pale. Then,
with another embrace of her mother, she went away upstairs, only pausing at the door of the sitting-room to
ask when they should start for the cottage.

Upstairs Mary sat for long in the dark, thinking. . .
Through her uncurtained windows she watched the obscure dying away of the storm, the calming of the trees,
and the gradual clearing of the night sky. Between the
upfurling clouds the stars began to show; tumult passed
into a great tranquillity; and a breath of frost began
to steal through the woods, and over the water. . . .

Catharine too passed an hour of reflection — and of
yearning over the unhappy. Naturally, to Mary, her
lips had been sealed on that deepest secret of all, which
she had divined for a moment in Alice. She had clearly
perceived what was or had been the weakness of the

woman, together with the loyal unconsciousness and in-
tegrity of the man.   And having perceived it, not only
pity but the strain in Catharine of plain simplicity and
common sense bade her bury and ignore it henceforward.
It was what Alice's true mind must desire; and it was the
only way to help her. She began however to understand what might be the full meaning of Alice's last in-
junction — and her eyes grew wet.

Mother and daughter started about eight o'clock for
the cottage. They had a lantern with them, but they
hardly needed it, for through the tranquillized air a new
moon shone palely, and the frost made way. Catharine
walked rejoicing apparently in renewed strength and
recovered powers of exertion. Some mining, crippling
influence seemed to have been removed from her since
her dream. And yet, even at this time, she was not
without premonitions — physical premonitions — as to
the future — faint signal-voices that the obscure life of
the body can often communicate to the spirit.
   They found the cottage all in light and movement.
Servants were flying about; boxes were in the hall; Hester
had come over to spend the night at the cottage that she
and "Aunt Alice" might start by an early train.
   Alice came out to meet her visitors in the little hall.
Catharine slipped into the drawing-room.   Alice and
Mary held each other enwrapped in one of those moments
of life that have no outward expression but dimmed eyes
and fluttering breath.

"Is it all done? Can't I help?" said Mary at last, scarcely knowing what she said, as Alice released her.

"No, dear, it's all done — except our books. Come up with me while I pack them."

And they vanished upstairs, hand in hand.

Meanwhile Hester in her most reckless mood was alternately flouting and caressing Catharine Elsmere. She was not in the least afraid of Catharine, and it was that perhaps which had originally drawn Catharine's heart to her. Elsmere's widow was accustomed to feel herself avoided by young people who discussed a wild literature, and appeared to be without awe toward God, or reverence toward man. Yet all the time, through her often bewildered reprobation of them, she hungered for their affection, and knew that she carried in herself treasures of love to give — though no doubt, on terms.

But Hester had always divined these treasures, and was, besides, as a rule, far too arrogant and self-centred to restrain herself in anything she wished to say or do for fear of hurting or shocking her elders.

At this moment she had declared herself tired out with packing, and was lounging in an armchair in the little drawing-room. A Japanese dressing-gown of some pale pink stuff sprayed with almond blossom floated about her, disclosing a skimpy silk petticoat and a slender foot from which she had kicked its shoe. Her pearly arms and neck were almost bare; her hair tumbled on her shoulders; her eyes shone with excitement provoked by a dozen hidden and conflicting thoughts. In her beauty, her

ardent and provocative youth, she seemed to be bursting
out of the little room, with its artistic restraint of colour
and furnishing.

"Don't please do any more fussing," she said imploringly to Catharine. "It's all done — only Aunt Alice
thinks it's never done. Do sit down and talk."

And she put out an impatient hand, and drew the
stately Catharine toward a chair beside her.

"You ought to be in bed," said Catharine, retaining
her hand. The girl's ignorance of all that others knew
affected her strangely — produced a great softness and
compunction.

"I shouldn't sleep. I wonder when I shall get a decent
amount of sleep again!" said Hester, pressing back the
hair from her cheeks. Then she turned sharply on her
visitor:

"Of course you know, Mrs. Elsmere, that I am simply
being sent away — in disgrace."

"I know" — Catharine smiled, though her tone was
grave — "that those who love you think there ought to
be a change."

"That's a nice way of putting it — a real gentlemanly
way," said Hester, swaying backward and forward, her
hands round her knees. "But all the same it's true.
They're sending me away because they don't know what
I'll do next. They think I'll do something abominable."

The girl's eyes sparkled.

"Why will you give your guardians this anxiety?"
asked Catharine, not without severity. "They are never

at rest about you. My dear — they only wish your good."

Hester laughed. She threw out a careless hand and laid it on Catharine's knee.

"Isn't it odd, Mrs. Elsmere, that you don't know anything about me, though — you won't mind, will you? — though you're so kind to me, and I do like you so. But you can't know anything, can you, about girls — like me?"

And looking up from where she lay deep in the arm-chair, she turned half-mocking eyes on her companion.

"I don't know — perhaps — about girls like you," said Catharine, smiling, and shyly touching the hand on her knee. "But I live half my life — with girls."

"Oh — poor girls? Girls in factories — girls that wear fringes, and sham pearl beads, and six ostrich feathers in their hats on Sundays? No, I don't think I'm like them. If I were they, I shouldn't care about feathers or the sham pearls. I should be more likely to try and steal some real ones! No, but I mean really girls like me — rich girls, though of course I'm not rich — but you understand? Do you know any girls who gamble and paint — their faces I mean — and let men lend them money, and pay for their dresses?"

Hester sat up defiantly, looking at her companion.

"No, I don't know any of that kind," said Catharine quietly. "I'm old-fashioned, you see — they wouldn't want to know me."

Hester's mouth twitched.

"Well, I'm not that kind exactly! I don't paint because — well, I suppose I needn't! And I don't play for money, because I've nobody to play with. As for letting men lend you money ——"

"That you would never disgrace yourself by doing!" said Catharine sharply.

Hester's look was enigmatic.

"Well, I never did it. But I knew a girl in London — very pretty — and as mad as you like. She was an orphan and her relatives didn't care twopence about her. She got into debt, and a horrid old man offered to lend her a couple of hundred pounds if she'd give him a kiss. She said no, and then she told an older woman who was supposed to look after her. And what do you suppose she said?"

Catharine was silent.

"'Well, you *are* a little fool!' That was all she got for her pains. Men are villains — *I* think! But they're exciting!" And Hester clasped her hands behind her head, and looked at the ceiling, smiling to herself, while the dressing-gown sleeves fell back from her rounded arms.

Catharine frowned. She suddenly rose, and kneeling down by Hester's chair, she took the girl in her arms.

"Hester, dear! — if you want a friend — whenever you want a friend — come to me! If you are ever in trouble send for me. I would always come — always!"

She felt the flutter of the girl's heart as she enfolded her. Then Hester lightly freed herself, though her voice shook —

"You're the kindest person, Mrs. Elsmere — you're awfully, awfully, kind. But I'm going to have a jolly good time in Paris. I shall read all kinds of things — I shall go to the theatre — I shall enjoy myself famously."

"And you'll have Aunt Alice all to yourself."

Hester was silent. The lovely corners of her mouth stiffened.

"You must be very good to her, Hester," said Catharine, with entreaty in her voice. "She's not well — and very tired."

"Why doesn't she *trust* me?" said Hester, almost between her teeth.

"What do you mean?'

After a hesitating pause, the girl broke out with the story of the miniature.

"How can I love her when she won't trust me?" she cried again, with stormy breath.

Catharine's heart melted within her.

"But you *must* love her, Hester! Why, she has watched over you all your life. Can't you see — that she's had trouble — and she's not strong!"

And she looked down with emotion on the girl thus blindly marching to a veiled future, unable, by no fault of her own, to distinguish her lovers from her foes. Had a lie, ever yet, in human history, justified itself? So this pure moralist! — to whom morals had come, silently, easily, irresistibly, as the sun slips into the sky.

"Oh, I'll look after her," said Hester shortly; "why, of course I will. I'm very glad she's going to Paris —

it'll be good for her.   And as for you" — she bent forward like a queen, and lightly kissed Catharine on the cheek — "I daresay I'll remember what you've said — you're a great, great dear!   It was luck for Mary to have got you for a mother.   But I'm all right — I'm all right!"

When the Elsmeres were gone, Hester still sat on alone in the drawing-room.   The lamp had burnt dim, and the little room was cold.

Presently she slipped her hand into the white bodice she wore.   A letter lay there, and her fingers caressed it. "I don't know whether I love him or not — perhaps I do, and perhaps I don't.   I don't know whether I believe Uncle Richard — or this letter.   But — I'm going to find out!   I'm not going to be stopped from finding out."

And as she lay there, she was conscious of bonds she was half determined to escape, half willing to bear; of a fluttering excitement and dread.   Step by step, and with a childish bravado, she had come within the influences of sex; and her fate was upon her.

CHAPTER XVIII

MEANWHILE, amid this sensitive intermingling of the thoughts and feelings of women, there arose the sudden tumult and scandal of the new elements which had thrust themselves into what was already known to the religious world throughout England as "the Meynell case." During November and December that case came to include two wholly different things: the ecclesiastical suit in the Court of Arches, which, owing to a series of delays and to the illness of the Dean of the Court, was not to be heard in all probability before February, and the personal charges brought against the incumbent of Upcote Minor.

These fresh charges were formally launched by Henry Barron, the chief promoter also, as we know, of the ecclesiastical suit, in a letter written by him to Bishop Craye, on the very night when Alice Puttenham revealed her secret to Catharine Elsmere. But before we trace the effect of the letter, let us look for a moment at the general position of the Movement when this second phase of Meynell's connection with it began.

At that time the pending suits against the Modernist leaders — for there were now five instituted by different bishops, as test cases, in different parts of England —

were already the subject of the keenest expectation and debate not only in church circles, but amid sections of the nation which generally trouble themselves very little about clerical or religious disputes. New births of time were felt to be involved in the legal struggle; passionate hopes and equally passionate fears hung upon it. There were old men in quiet country parsonages who, when they read the *Modernist* and followed the accounts of the Movement, were inclined to say to themselves with secret joy and humility that other men were entering into their labours, and the fields were at last whitening to harvest; while others, like Newman of old, had "fierce thoughts toward the Liberals," talked and spoke of Meynell and the whole band of Modernist clergy as traitors with whom no parley could be kept, and were ready to break up the Church at twenty-four hours' notice rather than sit down at the same table of the Lord with heretics and Socinians.

Between these two groups of men, each equally confident and clear, though by no means equally talkative, there was a middle region that contained many anxious minds and some of the wisest heads in England. If, at the time of Norham's visit to Maudeley, Bishop Craye of Markborough, and many other bishops with him, were still certain that the Movement would be promptly and easily put down, so far at least as its organic effect on the Church of England was concerned, yet, as November and December wore on, anxieties deepened, and confidence began to waver. The passion of the Movement was beginning to run through England, as it seemed to many, like the flame of an explosion through a dusty mine. What amazed and terrified the bishops was the revelation of pent-up energies, rebellions, ideals, not only among their own flocks, but in quarters, and among men and women, hitherto ruled out of religious affairs by general consent. They pondered the crowds which had begun to throng the Modernist churches, the extraordinary growth of the Modernist press, and the figures reported day by day as to the petition to be presented to Parliament in February. There was no orthodox person in authority who was not still determined on an unconditional victory; but it was admitted that the skies were darkening.

The effect of the Movement on the Dissenters — on that half of religious England which stands outside the National Church, where "grace" takes the place of authority, and bishops are held to be superfluities incompatible with the pure milk of the Word — was in many respects remarkable. The majority of the Wesleyan Methodists had thrown themselves strongly on to the side of the orthodox party in the Church; but among the Congregationalists and Presbyterians there was visible a great ferment of opinion and a great cleavage of sympathy; while, among the Primitive Methodists, a body founded on the straitest tenets of Bible worship, yet interwoven, none the less, with the working class life of England and Wales, and bringing day by day the majesty and power of religion to bear upon the acts and consciences of plain, poor, struggling men, there was visible a strong and definite current of acquiescence in Modernist ideas, which was inexplicable, till one came to know that among Meynell's friends at Upcote there were two or three Primitive local preachers who had caught fire from him, were now active members of his Church Council, and ardent though persecuted missionaries to their own body.

Meanwhile the Unitarians — small and gallant band! — were like persons standing on tiptoe before an opening glory. In their isolated and often mistaken struggle they had felt themselves for generations stricken with chill and barrenness; their blood now began to feel the glow of new kinships, the passion of large horizons. So, along the banks of some slender and much hindered stream, there come blown from the nearing sea prophetic scents and murmurs, and one may dream that the pent water knows at last the whence and whither of its life.

But the strangest spectacle of all perhaps was presented by the orthodox camp. For, in proportion as the Modernist attack developed, was the revival of faith among those hostile to it, or unready for it. For the first time in their lives, religion became interesting — thrilling even — to thousands of persons for whom it had long lost all real savour. Fierce question and answer, the hot cut and thrust of argument, the passion of honest fight on equal terms — without these things, surely, there has been no religious epoch, of any importance, in

man's history. English orthodoxy was at last vitally
attacked; and it began to show a new life, and express
itself in a new language. These were times when men
on all sides felt that stretching and straining of faculty
which ushers in the days of spiritual or poetic creation;
times when the most confident Modernist of them all
knew well that he, no more than any one else, could
make any guess worth having as to the ultimate future.

Of all this rapid and amazing development the personality and the writings of Richard Meynell had in
few months become the chief popular symbol. There
were some who thought that he was likely to take much
the same place in the Modernist Movement of the twentieth century as Newman had taken in the Oxford
Movement of the nineteenth; and men were beginning
to look for the weekly article in the *Modernist* with the
same emotion of a passionate hero-worship on the one
hand, and of angry repulsion on the other, with which
the Oxford of the thirties had been wont to look for each
succeeding "Tract," or for Newman's weekly sermon
at St. Mary's. To Newman's high subtleties of brain,
to Newman's magic of style, Richard Meynell could not
pretend. But he had two advantages over the great
leader of the past: he was the disciple of a new learning which was inaccessible to Newman; and he was on
fire with social compassions and enthusiasms to which
Newman, the great Newman, was always pathetically
a stranger. In these two respects Meynell was the
representative of his own generation; while the influences

flowing from his personal character and life were such that thousands who had never seen him loved and trusted him wholly. Men who had again and again watched great causes break down for want of the incommunicable something which humanity exacts from its leaders felt with a quiet and confident gladness that in Meynell they had got the man they wanted, the efficacious, indispensable man.

And now — suddenly — incredible things began to be said. It was actually maintained that the leader round whom such feelings had gathered had been, since his ordination, the betrayer of a young and innocent girl, belonging to a well-known family; that although it had been in his power for twenty years to marry the lady he had wronged, he had never attempted to do so, but had rather, during all that time, actively connived at the fraud by which his illegitimate child had passed as the daughter of Sir Ralph Fox-Wilton; while over the whole period he had kept up relations — and who knew of what character? — with the child's mother, an inhabitant of the very village where he himself was Rector.

Presently — it was added that Mr. Henry Barron, of Upcote Minor, one of the prosecutors in the ecclesiastical suit, had obtained unexpected and startling confirmation of these extraordinary facts from the confession of a woman who had been present at the birth of the child and had identified the Rector of Upcote as the father. Then, very soon, paragraphs of a veiled sort began to appear in some of the less responsible newspapers. The circulation of the anonymous letters began to be known; and the reader of a Modernist essay at an Oxford meeting caused universal consternation by telling an indiscreet friend, who presently spread it abroad, that Barron had already written to the Bishop of Markborough, placing in his hands a mass of supporting evidence relating to "this most lamentable business."

At first Meynell's friends throughout the country regarded these rumours as a mere device of the evil one. Similar things they said, and with truth, are constantly charged against heretics who cannot be put down. Slander is the first weapon of religious hatred. Meynell, they triumphantly answered, will put the anonymous letters in the hands of the police, and proceed against Henry Barron. And they who have taken up such a weapon shall but perish by it themselves the sooner.

But the weeks passed on. Not only were no proceedings taken, or, apparently, in prospect, by Meynell against his accusers; not only did the anonymous letters reappear from time to time, untracked and unpunished, but reports of a meeting held at Upcote itself began to spread — a meeting where Meynell had been definitely and publicly challenged by Barron to take action for the vindication of his character, and had definitely and publicly refused.

The world of a narrow and embittered orthodoxy began to breathe again; and there was black depression in the Modernist camp.

Let us, however, go back a little.

Barron's letter to the Bishop was the first shot in the direct and responsible attack. It consisted of six or seven closely written sheets, and agreed in substance with four or five others from the same hand, addressed at the same moment to the chief heads of the Orthodox party.

The Bishop received it at breakfast, just after he had concluded a hot political argument with his little granddaughter Barbara.

"All Tories are wicked," said Barbara, who had a Radical father, "except grandpapa, and he, mummy says, is weally a Riberal."

With which she had leaped into the arms of her nurse, and was carried off gurgling, while the Bishop threatened her from afar.

Then, with a sigh of impatience, as he recognized the signature on the envelope, he resigned himself to Barron's letter. When he had done it, sitting by the table in his library, he threw it from him with indignation, called for his coat, and hurried across his garden to the Cathedral for matins. After service, as with a troubled countenance he was emerging from the transept door, he saw Dornal in the Close and beckoned to him.

"Come into the library for ten minutes. I very much want to speak to you."

The Bishop led the way, and as soon as the door was shut he turned eagerly on his companion:

"Do you know anything of these abominable stories that are being spread about Richard Meynell?"

Dornal looked at him sadly.

"They are all over Markborough — and there is actually a copy of one of the anonymous letters — with dashes for the names — in the *Post* to-day?"

"I never hear these things!" said the Bishop, with an impatience which was meant, half for a scandal-mongering world, and half for himself. "But Barron has written me a perfectly incredible letter to-day. He seems to be the head and front of the whole business. I don't like Barron, and I don't like his letters!"

And throwing one slender leg over the other, while the tips of his long fingers met in a characteristic gesture, the little Bishop stared into the fire before him with an expression of mingled trouble and disgust.

Dornal, clearly, was no less unhappy. Drawing his chair close to the Bishop's he described the manner in which the story had reached himself. When he came to the curious facts concerning the diffusion and variety of the anonymous letters, the Bishop interrupted him:

"And Barron tells me he knows nothing of these letters!"

"So I hear also."

"But, my dear Dornal, if he doesn't, it makes the thing inexplicable! Here we have a woman who comes home dying, and sees one person only — Henry Barron — to whom she tells her story."

The Bishop went through the points of Barron's narrative, and concluded:

"Then, on the top of this, after her death — her son denying all knowledge of his mother's history — comes this crop of extraordinary letters, showing, you tell me, an intimate acquaintance with the neighbourhood and the parties concerned. And yet Barron — the only person Mrs. Sabin saw — knows nothing of them! They are a mystery to him. But, my dear Dornal, how *can* they be?" The Bishop faced round with energy on his companion. "He must at least have talked incautiously before some one!"

Dornal agreed, but could put forward no suggestion of his own. He sat drooping by the Bishop's fire, his aspect expressing the deep distress he did not shape in words. That very distress, however, was what made his company so congenial to the much perturbed Bishop, who felt, moreover, a warmer affection for Dornal than for any other member of his Chapter.

The Bishop resumed:

"Meanwhile, not a word from Meynell himself! That I confess wounds me." He sighed. "However, I suppose he regards our old confidential relations as broken off. To me — until the law has spoken — he is always one of my 'clergy' " — the Bishop's voice showed emotion — "and he would get my fatherly help just as freely as ever, if he chose to ask for it. But I don't know whether to send for him. I don't think I can send for him. The fact is — one feels the whole thing an outrage!"

Dornal looked up.

"That's the word!" he said gratefully. Then he added — hesitating — "I ought perhaps to tell you that I have written to Meynell — I wrote when the first report of the thing reached me. And I am sure that he can have no possible objection to my showing you his reply!" He put his hand into his pocket.

"By all means, my dear Dornal!" cried the Bishop with a brightening countenance. "We are both his friends, in spite of all that has happened and may happen. By all means, show me the letter."

Dornal handed it over. It ran as follows:

"MY DEAR DORNAL: It was like you to write to me, and with such kindness and delicacy. But even to you I can only say what I say to other questioners of a very different sort. The story to which you refer is untrue. But owing to peculiar circumstances it is impossible for me to defend myself in the ordinary way, and my lips are sealed with regard to it. I stand upon my character as known to my neighbours and the diocese for nearly twenty years. If that is not enough, I cannot help it.

"Thank you always for the goodness and gentleness of your letter. I wish with all my heart I could give you more satisfaction."

The two men looked at each other, the same conjectures passing through both minds.

"I hear the Fox-Wiltons and Miss Puttenham have all gone abroad," said the Bishop thoughtfully. "Poor things! I begin to see a glimmer. It seems to me that Meynell has been the repository of some story he feels

he cannot honourably divulge. And then you tell me
the letters show the handiwork of some one intimately
acquainted with the local circumstances, who seems to
have watched Meynell's daily life. It is of course possible
that he may have been imprudent with regard to this
poor lady. Let us assume that he knew her story and
advised her. He may not have been sufficiently careful.
Further, there is that striking and unfortunate likeness
of which Barron of course makes the most. I noticed
it myself, on an evening when I happened, at Maudeley,
to see that handsome girl and Meynell in the same room.
It is difficult to say in what it consists, but it must occur
to many people who see them together."

There was silence a moment. Then Dornal said:
"How will it all affect the trial?"

"In the Court of Arches? Technically of course —
not at all. But it will make all the difference to the
atmosphere in which it is conducted. One can imagine
how certain persons are already gloating over it — what
use they will make of it — how they will magnify and
embroider everything. And such an odious story! It
is the degradation of a great issue!"

The little Bishop frowned. As he sat there in the
dignity of his great library, so scrupulously refined and
correct in every detail of dress, yet without a touch of
foppery, the gleam of the cross on his breast answering
the silver of the hair and the frank purity of the eyes,
it was evident that he felt a passionate impatience—
half moral, half esthetic — toward these new elements

of the Meynell case. It was the fastidious impatience of a man for whom personal gossip and scandal ranked among the forbidden indulgences of life. "Things, not persons!" had been the time-honoured rule for conversation at the Palace table — persons, that is, of the present day. In those happy persons who had already passed into biography and history, in their peccadilloes no less than their virtues, the Bishop's interest was boundless. The distinction tended to make him a little super- or infra-human; but it enhanced the fragrance and delicacy of his personality.

Dornal was no less free from any stain of mean or scandalous gossip than the Bishop, but his knowledge of the human heart was far deeper, his sympathy far more intimate. It was not only that he scorned the slander, but, hour by hour, he seemed to walk in the same cloud with Meynell.

After some further discussion, the Bishop took up Barron's letter again. "I see there is likely to be a most painful scene at the Church Council meeting — which of course will be also one of their campaign meetings — the day after to-morrow. Barron declares that he means to challenge Meynell publicly to vindicate his character. Can I do anything?"

Dornal did not see anything could be done. The parish was already in open rebellion.

"It is a miserable, miserable business!" said the Bishop unhappily. "How can I get a report of the meeting — from some one else than Barron?"

"Mr. Flaxman is sure to be there?"

"Ah! — get him to write to me?"

"And you, my lord — will send for Meynell?"

"I think" — said the Bishop, with returning soreness — "that as he has neither written to me, nor consulted me, I will wait a little. We must watch — we must watch. Meanwhile, my dear fellow!" — he laid his hand on Dornal's shoulder — "let us think how to stop the talk! It will spoil everything. Those who are fighting with us must understand there are weapons we cannot stoop to use!"

As Dornal left the Palace, on his way past the Cathedral, he met young Fenton, the High Churchman who some months earlier had refused to recognize Meynell after the first Modernist meeting in Markborough. Fenton was walking slowly and reading the local newspaper — the same which contained the anonymous letter. His thin, finely modelled face, which in a few years would resemble the Houdon statue of St. Bruno, expressed an eager excitement that was not unlike jubilation. Dornal was practically certain that he was reading the paragraph that concerned Meynell, and certain also that it gave him pleasure. He hurriedly passed over to the other side of the street, that Fenton might not accost him.

Afterward, he spent the evening, partly in writing urgently in Meynell's defence to certain of his own personal friends in the diocese, and partly in composing an anti-Modernist address, full of a sincere and earnest eloquence, to be delivered the following week at a meeting of the Church party in Cambridge.

Meanwhile Cyril Fenton had also spent the evening in writing. He kept an elaborate journal of his own spiritual state; or rather he had begun to keep it about six months before this date, at the moment when the emergence of the Modernist Movement had detached him from his nascent friendship with Meynell, and had thrown him back, terrified, on a more resolute opposition than ever to the novelties and presumptions of free inquiry. The danger of reading anything, unawares, that might cause him even a moment's uneasiness had led to his gradually cutting himself off entirely from modern newspapers and modern books, in which, indeed, he had never taken any very compelling interest. His table was covered by various English and French editions of the Fathers — of St. Cyprian in particular, for whom he had a cult. On the bare walls of his study were various pictures of saints, a statuette of the Virgin, and another of St. Joseph, both of them feebly elegant in the Munich manner. Through his own fresh youthfulness, once so winning and wholesome, something pinched and cloistered had begun to thrust itself. His natural sweetness of temper was rapidly becoming sinful in his own eyes, his natural love of life also, and its harmless, even its ideal, pleasures.

It was a bitter winter day, and he had not allowed

himself a greatcoat. In consequence he felt depressed
and chilled; yet he could not make up his mind to go to
bed earlier than usual, lest he should be thereby pam-
pering the flesh. He was thoroughly dissatisfied with
his own spiritual condition during the day, and had just
made ample confession thereof in the pages of his diary.
A few entries from that document will show the tone of
a mind morbid for lack of exercise:

"D. came to see me this morning. We discussed war
a good deal. In general, of course, I am opposed to war,
but when I think of this ghastly plague of heresy which
is sweeping away so many souls at the present moment,
I feel sometimes that the only war into which I could enter with spirit would be a civil war. . . . In a great
deal of my talk with D. I posed abominably. I talked
of shooting and yachting as though I knew all about them.
I can't be content that people should think me 'out' of
anything, or a dull fool. It was the same with my talk
to S. about church music. I talked most arrogantly;
and in reality I know hardly anything about it.

"As to my vow of simplicity in food, I must keep my
attention more on the alert. Yet to-day I have not
done so badly; some cold ends of herring at breakfast, and
a morsel of mackerel at lunch are the only things I have
to reproach myself with; the only lapses from the strict
rule of simplicity. But the quantity was deplorable —
no moderation — not even a real attempt at it. Whenever I am disgusted with myself for having eaten too
much at dinner, I constantly fail to draw the proper
inference — that I should eat less at tea. . . .

"I feel that this scandal about poor Meynell is probably providential. It must and will weaken the Modernist party enormously. To thank God for such a thing sounds horrible, but after all, have we any right to be more squeamish than Holy Writ? 'Let God arise and let His enemies be scattered.' The warnings and menaces of what are called the Imprecatory Psalms show us plainly that His enemies must be ours."

He closed his book, and came to shiver over the very inadequate fire which was all he allowed himself. Every shilling that he could put aside was being saved in order to provide his church with a new set of altar furniture. The congregation of the church was indeed fast ebbing away, and his heart was full of bitterness on the subject. But how could a true priest abate any fraction of either his Church principles, or his sound doctrine, to appease persons who were not and could not be judges of what was necessary to their own spiritual health?

As he warmed his thin hands, his bodily discomfort increased his religious despondency. Then, of a sudden, his eyes fell upon the portrait of a child standing on the mantelpiece — his sister's child, aged four. The cloud on the still boyish brow lightened at once.

"Tommy's birthday to-morrow," he said to himself. "Jolly little chap! Must write to him. Here goes!"

And reaching out his hand for his writing-case he wrote eagerly, a letter all fun and baby-talk, and fantastic drawings, in the course of which Tommy grew up, developed moustaches, and became a British Grenadier.

When he had finished it and put it up, he lay back laughing to himself, a different being.

But the gleam was only momentary. A recurring sense of chill and physical oppression dispersed it. Presently he rose heavily, glanced at his open diary, reread the last page with a sigh, and closed it. Then, as it was nearly midnight, he retreated upstairs to his bare and icy bedroom, where half-an-hour's attempt to meditate completed the numbness of body and mind, in which state ultimately he went to bed, though not to sleep.

The meeting of the Church Council of Upcote was held in the Church House of the village a few days after the Bishop's conversation with Canon Dornal. It was an evening long remembered by those who shared in it. The figure of Meynell instinct with a kind of fierce patience; the face rugged as ever, but paler and tenderer in repose, as of one who, mystically sustained, had been passing through deep waters; his speech, sternly repressed, and yet for the understanding ear, enriched by new tones and shades of feeling — on those who believed in him the effect of these slight but significant changes in the man they loved was electrical.

And five-sixths of those present believed in him, loved him, and were hotly indignant at the scandals which had arisen. They were, some of them, the élite of the mining population, men whom he had known and taught from childhood; there were many officials from the surrounding collieries; there was a miners' agent, who was also one of the well-known local preachers of the district; there were half a dozen women — the schoolmistress, the wife of the manager of the coöperative store, and three or four wives of colliers — women to whom other women in childbirth, or the girl who had gone astray, or the motherless child, might appeal without rebuff, who were in fact the Rector's agents in any humanizing effort.

All these persons had come to the meeting eagerly expecting to hear from the Rector's own lips the steps he proposed to take for the putting down of the slanders circulating in the diocese, and the punishment of their authors. In the rear of the Council — who had been themselves elected by the whole parish — there were two or three rows of seats occupied by other inhabitants of the village, who made an audience. In the front row sat the strange spinster, Miss Nairn, a thin, sharp nosed woman of fifty, in rusty black clothes, holding her head high; not far from her the dubious publican who had been Maurice Barron's companion on a certain walk some days before. There too were Hugh and Rose Flaxman. And just as the proceedings were about to begin, Henry Barron opened the heavy door, hat in hand, came in with a firm step, and took a seat at the back, while a thrill of excitement went through the room.

It was an ancient room, near the church, and built like it, of red sandstone. It had been once the tiny grammar school of the village. Meynell had restored and adapted it, keeping still its old features — the low ceiling heavily beamed with oak, and the row of desks inscribed with the scholars' names of three centuries. Against the background of its white walls he stood thrown out in strong relief by the oil lamp on the table in front of him, his eyes travelling over the rows of familiar faces.

He spoke first of the new Liturgy of which copies had been placed on the seats. He reminded them they were all — or nearly all — comrades with him in the great Modernist venture; that they had given him the help of their approval and support at every step, and were now rebels with him against the authorities of the day. He pointed to his approaching trial, and the probability — nay the certainty — of his deprivation. He asked them to be steadfast with him, and he dwelt on the amazing spread of the Movement, the immense responsibility resting upon its first leaders and disciples, and the need for gentleness and charity   The room was hushed in silence.

Next, he proceeded to put the adoption of the new Liturgy to the vote. Suddenly Barron rose from his seat at the back. Meynell paused. The audience looked in suppressed excitement from one to the other.

"I regret," said the Rector, courteously, "that we cannot hear Mr. Barron at this moment. He is not a member of the Church Council. When the proceedings of the Council are over, this will become an open meeting, and Mr. Barron will then of course say what he wishes to say."

Barron hesitated a moment; then sat down.

The revised Liturgy was adopted by twenty-eight votes to two. One of the two dissentients was Dawes, the colliery manager, a sincere and consistent evangelical of the Simeon School, who made a short speech in support of his vote, dwelling in a voice which shook on the troubles coming on the parish.

"We may get another Rector," he said as he sat down. "We shall never get another Richard Meynell." A deep murmur of acquiescence ran through the room.

Meynell rose again from his seat.

"Our business is over. We now become an open meeting. Mr. Barron, I believe, wishes to speak."

The room was, at this point, densely crowded and every face turned toward the tall and portly form rising from the back. In the flickering lamplight it could be seen that the face usually so ruddy and full was blanched by determination and passion.

"My friends and neighbours!" said Barron, "it is with sorrow and grief that I rise to say the few words that I intend to say. On the audacity and illegality of what you have just done I shall say nothing. Argument, I know, would be useless. But *this* I have come to say: You have just been led — misled — into an act of heresy and rebellion by the man who should be your pastor in the Faith, who is responsible to God for your souls. *Why* have you been misled? — *why* do you follow him?" He flung out his hand toward Meynell.

"Because you admire and respect him — because you

believe him a good man — a man of honest and pure life.
And I am here to tell you, or rather to remind you, for
indeed you all know it — that your Rector lies at this
moment under a painful and disgraceful charge; that this
charge has been circulated — in a discreditable way —
a way for which I have no defence and of which I know
nothing — throughout this diocese, and indeed throughout England; that your fair fame, as well as his are concerned; and, nevertheless, he refuses to take the only
steps which can clear his character, and repay you for
the devotion you have shown him! I call upon you,
sir!" — the speaker bent forward, pointing impressively
to the chairman of the meeting and emphasizing every
word — "to take those steps at once! They are open
to you at any moment. Take them against myself!
I have given, I will give, you every opportunity. But
till that is done do not continue, in the face of the congregation you have deceived and led astray, to assume
the tone of hypocritical authority in which you have
just spoken! You have no moral right to any authority
among us; you never had any such right; and in Christian
eyes your infidel teaching has led to its natural results.
At any rate, I trust that now, at last, even these your
friends and dupes will see the absolute necessity, before
many weeks are over, of either *forcing* you to resign your
living, or *forcing* you to take the only means open to
honest men of protecting their character!"

He resumed his seat. The audience sat petrified a
moment. Then Hugh Flaxman sprang to his feet, and

two or three others, the local preacher among them.
But Meynell had also risen.

"Please, Mr. Flaxman — my friends —— !"

He waved a quiet hand toward those who had risen,
and they unwillingly gave way. Then the Rector looked
round the room for a few silent instants. He was very
white, but when he spoke it was with complete composure.

"I expected something of this kind to happen, and
whether it had happened or no I should have spoken
to you on this matter before we separated. I know —
you all know — to what Mr. Barron refers — that he
is speaking of the anonymous letters concerning myself
and others which have been circulated in this neighbourhood. He calls upon me, I understand, to take legal
action with regard both to them and to the reports which
he has himself circulated, by word of mouth, and probably by letter. Now I want you plainly to understand"
— he bent forward, his hands on the table before him,
each word clear and resonant — "that I shall take no
such action! My reasons I shall not give you. I stand
upon my life among you and my character among you
all these years. This only I will say to you, my friends
and my parishioners: The abominable story told in
these letters — the story which Mr. Barron believes, or
tries to make himself believe — is untrue. But I will
say no more than that — to you, or any one else. And
if you are to make legal action on my part a test of
whether you will continue to follow me religiously — to
accept me as your leader, or no — then my friends, we

must part! You must go your way, and I must go mine. There will be still work for me to do; and God knows our hearts — yours and mine."

He paused, looking intently into the lines of blanched faces before him. Then he added:

"You may wish to discuss this matter. I recognize it as natural you should wish to discuss it. But I shall not discuss it with you. I shall withdraw. Mr. Dawes — will you take the chair?"

He beckoned to the colliery manager, who automatically obeyed him. The room broke into a hubbub, men and women pressing round Meynell as he made his way to the door. But he put them aside, gently and cheerfully.

"Decide it for yourselves!" he said with his familiar smile. "It is your right."

And in another moment, the door had opened and shut, and he was gone.

He had no sooner disappeared than a tumultuous scene developed in the Church room.

Beswick, the sub-agent and local preacher, a sandy-haired, spectacled, and powerfully built man, sprang on to the platform, to the right hand of Dawes, and at last secured silence by a passionate speech in defence of Meynell and in denunciation of the men who in order to ruin him ecclesiastically were spreading these vile tales about him "and a poor lady that has done many a good turn to the folk of this village, and nothing said about it too!"

"Don't you, sir" — he said, addressing Barron with a threatening finger — "don't you come here, telling us what to think about the man we've known for twenty years in this parish! The people that don't know Richard Meynell may believe these things if they please — it'll be the worse for them! But we've seen this man comforting and uplifting our old people in their last hours — we've seen him teaching our children — and giving just a kind funny word now an' again to keep a boy or a girl straight — aye, an' he did it too — they knew he had his eye on 'em! We've seen him go down these pits, when only a handful would risk their lives with him, to help them as was perhaps past hope. We've seen him skin himself to the bone that other men might have plenty — we've heard him Sunday after Sunday. We *know* him!" The speaker brought one massive hand down on the other with an emphasis that shook the room. "Don't you go talking to us! If Richard Meynell won't go to law with you and the likes of you, sir, he's got his reasons, and his good ones, I'll be bound. And don't you, my friends" — he turned to the room — "don't you be turned back from this furrow you've begun to plough. You stick to your man! If you don't, you're fools, aye, and ungrateful fools too! You know well enough that Albert Beswick isn't a parson's man! You know that I don't hold with Mr. Meynell in many of his views. There's his views about 'election,' and the like o' that — quite wrong, in my 'umble opinion. But what does that matter? You know that I never

set foot in Upcote Church till three years ago — that
bishops and ceremonies are nought to me — that I
came to God, as many of you did, by the Bible class and
the penitent form. But I declare to you that Richard
Meynell, and the men with him, are *out for a big thing!*
They're out for breaking down barriers and letting in
light. They're out for bringing Christian men together
and letting them worship freely in the old churches that
our fathers built. They're out for giving men and women
new thoughts about God and Christ, and for letting
them put them into new words, if they want to. Well,
I say again, it's *a big thing!* And Satan's out, too,
for stopping it! Don't you make any mistake about it!
This bad business — of these libels that are about —
is one of the obstacles in our race he'll trip us up on, if
he can. Now I put it to you — let us clear it out o'
the way this very night, as far as we're concerned! Let
us send the Rector such a vote of confidence from this
meeting as'll show him fast enough where he stands
in Upcote — aye, and show others too! And as for these
vile letters that are going round — I'd give my right hand
to know the man who wrote them! — and the story that
you, sir" — he pointed again to Barron — "say you
took from poor Judith Sabin when her mind was clouded
and she near her end — why, it's base minds that harbour
base thoughts about their betters! He shall be no
friend of mine — that I know — that spreads these
tales. Friends and neighbours, let us keep our tongues
from them — and our children's tongues! Let us show

that we can trust a man that deserves our trust. Let us stand by a good man that's stood by us; and let us pray God to show the right!"

The greater part of the audience, sincerely moved, rose to their feet and cheered. Barron endeavoured to reply, but was scarcely listened to. The publican East sat twirling his hat in his hands, sarcastic smiles going out and in upon his fat cheeks, his furtive eyes every now and then consulting the tall spinster who sat beside him, grimly immovable, her spectacled eyes fixed apparently on the lamp above the platform.

Flaxman wished to speak, but was deterred by the reflection that as a newcomer in the district he had scarcely a valid right to interfere. He and Rose stayed till the vote of confidence had been passed by a large majority — though not so large as that which had accepted the new Liturgy — after which they drove home rather depressed and ill at ease. For in truth the plague of anonymous letters was rather increasing than abating. Flaxman had had news that day of the arrival of two more among their own country-house acquaintance of the neighbourhood. He sat down, in obedience to a letter from Dornal, to write a doleful report of the meeting to the Bishop.

Meynell received the vote of confidence very calmly, and wrote a short note of thanks to Beswick. Then for some weeks, while the discussion of his case in its various aspects, old and new, ran raging through England, he went about his work as usual, calm in the centre of the whirlwind, though the earth he trod seemed to him very often a strange one. He prepared his defence for the Court of Arches; he wrote for the *Modernist;* and he gave as much mind as he could possibly spare to the unravelling of Philip Meryon's history.

In this matter, however, he made but very slow and disappointing progress. He became more and more convinced, and his solicitor with him, that there had been a Scotch marriage some eighteen months before this date between Meryon and the sister of a farmer in the Lothians, with whom he had come in contact during a fishing tenancy. But what appeared in the course of investigation was that the woman concerned and all her kindred were now just as anxious — aided by the ambiguities of the Scotch marriage law — to cover up and conceal the affair as was Meryon himself. She could not be got to put forward any claim; her family would say nothing; and the few witnesses hitherto available were tending to disappear. No doubt Philip was at work corrupting them; and the supposed wife was evidently quite willing, if not eager, to abet him.

Every week he heard from Mary, letters which, written within bounds fully understood by them both and never transgressed, revealed to him the tremulous tenderness and purity of the heart he knew — though he would not confess it to himself — he had conquered. These letters became to him the stay of life, the manna which fed him, the water of healing and strength. It was evident that, according to his wish, she did not know and was determined not to know the details of his struggle; and nothing helped him more than the absolute trust of her ignorance.

He heard also constantly from Alice Puttenham. She, too, poor soul — but how differently! — was protecting herself as best she could from an odious knowledge.

"Edith writes to me, full of terrible things that are being said in England; but as I can do nothing, and must do nothing according to you, I do not read her letters. She sends me a local newspaper sometimes, scored with her marks and signs that are like shrieks of horror, and I put it in the fire. What I suffer I will keep to myself. Perhaps the worst part of every day comes when I take Hester out and amuse her in this gay Paris. She is so passionately vital herself, and one dreads to fail her in spirits or buoyancy.

"She is very well and wonderfully beautiful; at present she is having lessons in dancing and elocution, and turning the heads of her teachers. It is amusing — or would be amusing, to any one else than me — to see how the quiet family she is with clucks after her in perpetual anxiety, and how cavalierly she treats them. I think she is fairly happy; she never mentions Meryon's name; but I often have a strange sense that she is looking for some one — expects some one. When we turn into a new street, or a new alley of the Bois, I have sometimes seemed to catch a wild *listening* in her face. I live only for her — and I cannot feel that it matters to her in the least whether I do or not. Perhaps, some day. Meanwhile you may be sure I think of nothing else. She knows nothing of what is going on in England — and she says she adores Paris."

One night in December Meynell came in late from a carpentering class of village boys. The usual pile of letters and books awaited him, and he began upon them reluctantly. As he read them, and put them aside, one by one, his face gradually changed and darkened. He recalled a saying of Amiel's about the French word "consideration" — what it means to a man to have enjoyed unvarying and growing "consideration" from his world; and then, suddenly, to be threatened with the loss of it. Life and consciousness drop, all in a moment, to a lower and a meaner plane.

Finally, he lit on a letter from one of his colleagues on the Central Modernist Committee. For some months it had been a settled thing that Meynell should preach the sermon in Dunchester Cathedral on the great occasion in January when the new Liturgy of the Reform was to be inaugurated with all possible solemnity in one of England's most famous churches.

His correspondent wrote to suggest that after all the sermon would be more fitly entrusted to the Modernist Bishop of Dunchester himself. "He has worked hard, and risked much for us. I may say that inquiries have been thrown out, and we find he is willing."

No apology — perfunctory regrets — and very little explanation! Meynell understood.

He put the letter away, conscious of a keenly smarting

mind. It was now clear to him that he had made a grave mis-reckoning; humiliating, perhaps irreparable. He had counted, with a certain confident simplicity, on the power of his mere word, backed by his character and reputation, to put the thing down; and they were not strong enough. Barron's influence seemed to him immense and increasing. A proud and sensitive man forced himself to envisage the possibility of an eventual overthrow.

He opened a drawer in order to put away the letter. The drawer was very full, and in the difficulty of getting it out he pulled it too far and its contents fell to the floor. He stooped to pick them up — perceived first the anonymous letter that Barron had handed to him, the letter addressed to Dawes; and then, beneath it, a long envelope deep in dust — labelled "M. B. — Keep for three years." He took up both letter and envelope with no distinct intention. But he opened the anonymous letter, and once more looked searchingly at the handwriting.

Suddenly an idea struck him. With a hasty movement, he lifted the long envelope and broke the seal. Inside was a document headed, "A Confession." And at the foot of it appeared a signature — "Maurice Barron."

Meynell put the two things together — the "confession" and the anonymous letter. Very soon he began to compare word with word and stroke with stroke, gradually penetrating the disguise of the later handwriting. At the end of the process he understood the vague recollection which had disturbed him when he first saw the letter.

He stood motionless a little, expressions chasing each other across his face. Then he locked up both letters, reached a hand for his pipe, called a good night to Anne, who was going upstairs to bed, and with his dogs about him fell into a long meditation, while the night wore on.

CHAPTER XIX

IT WAS in the week before Christmas that Professor
Vetch — the same Professor who had been one of the
Bishop's Commission of Inquiry in Richard Meynell's case — knocked one afternoon at Canon France's
door to ask for a cup of tea. He had come down to give
a lecture to the Church Club which had been recently
started in Markborough in opposition to the Reformers'
Club; but his acceptance of the invitation had been a
good deal determined by his very keen desire to probe
the later extraordinary developments of the Meynell
affair on the spot.

France was in his low-ceiled study, occupied as usual
with drawers full of documents of various kinds; most of
them mediæval deeds and charters which he was calen-
daring for the Cathedral Library. His table and the
floor were littered by them; a stack of the Rolls publica-
tions was on his right hand; a Dugdale's "Monasticon"
lay open at a little distance; and curled upon a newspaper beside it lay a gray kitten. The kitten had that
morning upset an inkstand over three sheets of the
Canon's laborious handwriting. At the time he had
indeed dropped her angrily by the scruff of the neck
into a wastepaper basket to repent of her sins; but here

she was again, and the Canon had patiently rewritten the sheets.

There were not many softnesses in the Canon's life. The kitten was one; of the other perhaps only his sister, nearly as old as himself, who lived with him, was aware. Twenty years before — just after his appointment to the canonry — he had married a young and — in the opinion of his family — flighty wife, who had lived a year and then died. She had passed like a spring flower; and after a year or two all that was remembered about her was that she had chosen the drawing-room paper, which was rather garishly pink, like her own cheeks. In the course of time the paper had become so discoloured and patchy that Miss France was ashamed of it. For years her brother turned a deaf ear to her remarks on the subject. At last he allowed her to repaper the room. But she presently discovered that close to the seat he generally occupied in the drawing-room of an evening there was a large hole in the new paper made by the rubbing and scraping of the Canon's fingers as he sat at tea. Through it the original pink reappeared. More than once Miss France caught her brother looking contentedly at his work of mischief. But she dared not speak of it to him, nor do anything to repair the damage.

As France perceived the identity of the visitor whom his old manservant was showing into the study, a slight shade of annoyance passed over his face. But he received the Professor civilly, cleared a chair of books in order that he might sit down, and gave a vigorous poke to the fire.

The Professor did not wish to appear too inquisitive on the subject of Meynell, and he therefore dallied a little with matters of Biblical criticism. France, however, took no interest whatever in them; and even an adroit description of a paper recently read by the speaker himself at an Oxford meeting failed to kindle a spark. Vetch found himself driven upon the real object of his visit.

He desired to know — understanding that the Canon was an old friend of Henry Barron — where the Meynell affair exactly was.

"Am I an old friend of Henry Barron?" said France slowly.

"He says you are," laughed the Professor. "I happened to go up to town in the same carriage with him a fortnight ago."

"He comes here a good deal — but he never takes my advice," said France.

The Professor inquired what the advice had been.

"To let it alone!" France looked round suddenly at his companion. "I have come to the conclusion," he added dryly, "that Barron is not a person of delicacy."

The Professor, rather taken aback, argued on Barron's behalf. Would it have been seemly or right for a man — a Churchman of Barron's prominence — to keep such a thing to himself at such a critical moment? Surely it had an important bearing on the controversy.

"I see none," said France, a spark of impatience in the small black eyes that shone so vividly above his large hanging cheeks. "Meynell says the story is untrue."

"Ah! but let him prove it!" cried the Professor, his young-old face flushing. "He has made a wanton attack upon the Church; he cannot possibly expect any quarter from us. We are not in the least bound to hold him immaculate — quite the contrary. Men of that impulsive, undisciplined type are, as we all know, very susceptible to woman."

France faced round upon his companion in a slow, contemptuous wonder.

"I see you take your views from the anonymous letters?"

The Professor laughed awkwardly.

"Not necessarily. I understand Barron has direct evidence. Anyway, let Meynell take the usual steps. If he takes them successfully, we shall all rejoice. But his character has been made, so to speak, one of the pieces in the game. We are really not bound to accept it at his own valuation."

"I think you will have to accept it," said France.

There was a pause. The Professor wondered secretly whether France too was beginning to be tarred with the Modernist brush. No!—impossible. For that the Canon was either too indolent or too busy.

At last he said:

"Seriously, I should like to know what you really think."

"It is of no importance what I think. But what suggests itself, of course, is that there is some truth in the story, but that Meynell is not the hero. And he doesn't see his way to clear himself by dishing other people."

"I see." The obstinacy in the smooth voice rasped France. "If so, most unlucky for him! But then let him resign his living, and go quietly into obscurity. He owes it to his own side. For them the whole thing is disaster. He *must* either clear himself or go."

"Oh, give him a little time!" said France sharply, "give him a little time." Then, with a change of tone — "The anonymous letters, of course, are the really interesting things in the case. Perhaps you have a theory about them?"

The Professor shrugged his shoulders.

"None whatever. I have seen three — including that published in the *Post*. I understand about twenty have now been traced; and that they grow increasingly dramatic and detailed. Evidently some clever fellow — who knows a great deal — with a grudge against Meynell?"

"Ye—es," said France, with hesitation.

"You suspect somebody?"

"Not at all.   It is a black business."

Then with one large and powerful hand, France restrained the kitten, who was for deserting his knee, and with the other he drew toward him the folio volume on which he had been engaged when the Professor came in.

Vetch took the hint, said a rather frosty good-bye, and departed.

"A popinjay!" said France to himself when he was

left alone, thinking with annoyance of the Professor's curly hair, of his elegant serge suit, and the gem from Knossos that he wore on the little finger of his left hand. Then he took up a large pipe which lay beside his books, filled it, and hung meditatively over the fire. He was angry with Vetch, and disgusted with himself.

"Why haven't I given Meynell a helping hand? Why did I talk like that to Barron when he first began this business? And why have I let him come here as he has done since — without telling him what I really thought of him?"

He fell for some minutes into an abyss of thought; thought which seemed to range not so much over the circumstances connected with Meynell as over the whole of his own past.

But he emerged from it with a long shake of the head.

"My habits are my habits!" he said to himself with a kind of bitter decision, and laying down his pipe he went back to his papers.

Almost at the same moment the Bishop was interviewing Henry Barron in the little book-lined room beyond the main library, which he kept for the business he most disliked. He never put the distinction into words, but when any member of his clergy was invited to step into the farther room, the person so invited felt depressed.

Barron's substantial presence seemed to fill the little study, as, very much on his defence, he sat *tête-à-tête* with the Bishop. He had recognized from the beginning that nothing of what he had done was really welcome or acceptable to Bishop Craye.   While he, on his side, felt himself a benefactor to the Church in general, and to the Bishop of Markborough in particular, instinctively he knew that the Bishop's taste ungratefully disapproved of him; and the knowledge contributed an extra shade of pomposity to his manner.

He had just given a sketch of the church meeting at Upcote, and of the situation in the village up to date. The Bishop sat absently patting his thin knees, and evidently very much concerned.

"A most unpleasant — a most painful scene.   I confess, Mr. Barron, I think it would have been far better if you had avoided it."

Barron held himself rigidly erect.

"My lord, my one object from the beginning has been to force Meynell into the open.   For his own sake — for the parish's — the situation must be brought to an end, in some way.   The indecency of it at present is intolerable."

"You forget.   The trial is only a few weeks off.   Meynell will certainly be deprived."

"No doubt.   But then there is the Privy Council Appeal.   And even when he is deprived, Meynell does not mean to leave the village.   He has made all his arrangements to stay and defy the judgment.   We *must* prove to him, even if we have to do it with what looks like harshness, that until he clears himself of this business this diocese at least will have none of him!"

"Why, the great majority of the people adore him!" cried the Bishop. "And meanwhile I understand the other poor things are already driven away. They tell me the Fox-Wiltons' house is to let, and Miss Puttenham gone to Paris indefinitely."

Barron slightly shrugged his shoulders. "We are all very sorry for them, my lord. It is indeed a sad business. But we must remember at the same time that all these persons have been in a conspiracy together to impose a falsehood on their neighbours; and that for many years we have been admitting Miss Puttenham to our house and our friendship—to the companionship of our daughters — in complete ignorance of her character."

"Oh, poor thing! poor thing!" said the Bishop hastily. "The thought of her haunts me. She must know what is going on — or a great deal of it — though indeed I hope she doesn't — I hope with all my heart she doesn't! Well, now, Mr. Barron — you have written me long letters — and I trust that you will allow me a little close inquiry into some of these matters."

"The closer the better, my lord."

"You have not as yet come to any opinion whatever as to the authorship of these letters?"

Barron looked troubled.

"I am entirely at a loss," he said, emphatically. "Once or twice I have thought myself on the track. There is that man East, whose license Meynell opposed ——"

"One of the 'aggrieved parishioners'," said the Bishop, raising his hands and eyebrows.

"You regret, my lord, that we should be mixed up with such a person? So do I. But with a whole parish in a conspiracy to support the law-breaking that was going on, what could we do? However, that is not now the point. I have suspected East. I have questioned him. He showed extraordinary levity, and was — to myself personally — what I can only call insolent. But he swore to me that he had not written the letters; and indeed I am convinced that he could not have written them. He is almost an illiterate — can barely read and write. I still suspect him. But if he is in it, it is only as a tool of some one else."

"And the son — Judith Sabin's son?"

"Naturally, I have turned my mind in that direction also. But John Broad is a very simple fellow — has no enmity against Meynell, quite the contrary. He vows that he never knew why his mother went abroad with Lady Fox-Wilton, or why she went to America; and though she talked a lot of what he calls 'queer stuff' in the few hours he had with her before my visit, he couldn't make head or tail of a good deal of it, and didn't trouble his head about it. And after my visit, he found her incoherent and delirious. Moreover, he declared to me solemnly that he knew nothing about the letters; and I certainly have no means of bringing it home to him."

The Bishop's blue eyes were sharply fixed upon the speaker. But on the whole Barron's manner in these remarks had favourably impressed his companion.

"We come then" — he said gravely — "to the further question which you will, of course, see will be asked — must be asked. Can you be certain that your own conversation — of course quite unconsciously on your part — has not given hints to some person, some unscrupulous third person, an enemy of Meynell's, who has been making use of information he may have got from you to write these letters? Forgive the inquiry — but you will realize how very important it is — for Church interests — that the suit against Meynell in the Church Courts should not be in any way mixed up with this wretched and discreditable business of the anonymous letters!"

Barron flushed a little.

"I have of course spoken of the matter in my own family," he said proudly. "I have already told you, my lord, that I confided the whole thing to my son Stephen very early in the day."

The Bishop smiled.

"We may dismiss Stephen I think — the soul of honour and devoted to Meynell. Can you remember no one else?"

Barron endeavoured to show no resentment at these inquiries. But it was clear that they galled.

"The only other members of my household are my daughter Theresa, and occasionally, for a week or two, my son Maurice. I answer for them both."

"Your son Maurice is at work in London."

"He is in business — the manager of an office," said Barron stiffly.

The Bishop's face was shrewdly thoughtful. After a pause he said:

"You have, of course, examined the handwriting? But I understand that recently all the letters have been typewritten?"

"All but two — the letter to Dawes, and a letter which I believe was received by Mrs. Elsmere. I gave the Dawes letter to Meynell at his request."

"Having failed to identify the handwriting?"

"Certainly."

Yet, even as he spoke, for the first time, a sudden misgiving, like the pinch of an insect, brushed Barron's consciousness. He had not, as a matter of fact, examined the Dawes letter very carefully, having been, as he now clearly remembered, in a state of considerable mental excitement during the whole time it was in his possession and thinking much more of the effect of the first crop of letters on the situation, than of the details of the Dawes letter itself. But he did remember, now that the Bishop pressed him, that when he first looked at the letter he had been conscious of a momentary sense of likeness to a handwriting he knew; to Maurice's handwriting, in fact. But he had repelled the suggestion as absurd in the first instance, and after a momentary start, he angrily repelled it now.

The Bishop emerged from a brown study.

"It is a most mysterious thing! Have you been able to verify the postmarks?"

"So far as I know, all the letters were posted at Mark-borough."

"No doubt by some accomplice," said the Bishop. He paused and sighed. Then he looked searchingly, though still hesitatingly, at his companion.

"Mr. Barron, I trust you will allow me — as your Bishop — one little reminder. As Christians, we must be slow to believe evil."

Barron flushed again.

"I have been slow to believe it, my lord. But in all things I have put the Church's interest first."

Something in the Bishop suddenly and sharply drew away from the man beside him. He held himself with a cold dignity.

"For myself, personally — I tell you frankly — I cannot bring myself to believe a word of this story, so far as it concerns Meynell. I believe there is a terrible mistake at the bottom of it, and I prefer to trust twenty years of noble living rather than the tale of a poor distraught creature like Judith Sabin. At the same time, of course, I recognize that you have a right to your opinions, as I have to mine. But, my dear sir" — and here the Bishop rose abruptly — "let me urge upon you one thing. Keep an open mind — not only for all that tells against Meynell, but all that tells for him! Don't — you will allow me this friendly word — don't land yourself in a great, perhaps a life-long self-reproach!"

There was a note of sternness in the speaker's voice; but the small parchment face and the eyes of china-blue shone, as though kindled from within by the pure and generous spirit of the man.

"My lord, I have said my say." Barron had also risen, and stood towering over the Bishop. "I leave it now in the hands of God."

The Bishop winced again, and was holding out a limp hand for good-bye, when Barron said suddenly:

"Perhaps you will allow me one question, my lord? Has Meynell been to see you? Has he written to you even? I may say that I urged him to do so."

The Bishop was taken aback and saw no way out.

"I have had no direct communication with him," he said, reluctantly; "no doubt because of our already strained relations."

On Barron's lips there dawned something which could hardly be called a smile — or triumphant; but the Bishop caught it. In another minute the door had closed upon his visitor.

Barron walked away through the Close, his mind seething with anger and resentment. He felt that he had been treated as an embarrassment rather than an ally; and he vowed to himself that the Bishop's whole attitude had been grudging and unfriendly.

As he passed on to the broad stone pavement that bordered the south transept he became aware of a man coming toward him. Raising his eyes he saw that it was Meynell.

There was no way of avoiding the encounter. As the

two men passed Barron made a mechanical sign of recognition. Meynell lifted his head and looked at him full. It was a strange look, intent and piercing, charged with the personality of the man behind it.

Barron passed on, quivering. He felt that he hated Meynell. The disguise of a public motive dropped away; and he knew that he hated him personally.

At the same time the sudden slight misgiving he had been conscious of in the Bishop's presence ran through him again. He feared he knew not what; and as he walked to the station the remembrance of Meynell's expression mingled with the vague uneasiness he tried in vain to put from him.

Meynell walked home by Forkéd Pond to Maudeley. He lingered a little in the leafless woods round the cottage, now shut up, and he chose the longer path that he might actually pass the very window near which Mary had stood when she spoke those softly broken words — words from a woman's soul — which his memory had by heart. And his pulse leapt at the scarcely admitted thought that perhaps — now — in a few weeks he might be walking the dale paths with Mary. But there were stern things to be done first.

At Maudeley he found Flaxman awaiting him, and the two passed into the library, where Rose, though bubbling over with question and conjecture, self-denyingly refrained from joining them. The consultation of the two men lasted about an hour, and when Flaxman rejoined his wife, he came alone.

"Gone?" said Rose, with a disappointed look.   "Oh! I did want to shake his hand!"

Flaxman's gesture was unsympathetic.

"It is not the time for that yet.   This business has gone deep with him.   I don't exactly know what he will do.   But he has made me promise various things."

"When does he see — Torquemada?" said Rose, after a pause.

"I think — to-morrow morning."

"H'm!   Good luck to him!   Please let me know also precisely when I may crush Lady St. Morice."

Lady St. Morice was the wife of the Lord Lieutenant, and had at a recent dinner party, in Rose's presence, hotly asserted her belief in the charges brought against the Rector of Upcote.   She possessed a private chapel adorned with pre-Raphaelite frescoes, and was the sister of one of the chief leaders of the High Orthodox party in convocation.

"She doesn't often speak to the likes of me," said Rose; "which of course is a great advantage for the likes of me.   But next time I shall speak to her — which will be so good for her.   My dear Hugh, don't let Meynell be too magnanimous — I can't stand it."

Flaxman laughed, but rather absently.   It was evident that he was still under the strong impression of the conversation he had just passed through.

Rose stole up to him, and put her lips to his ear.

"Who — was — Hester's father?"

Flaxman looked up.

"I haven't the least idea."

"But of course we must all know some time," said Rose discontentedly. "Catharine knows already."

Meynell passed that evening in his study, after some hours spent in the Christmas business of a large parish. His mind was full of agitation, and when midnight struck, ushering in Christmas Eve, he was still undecided as to his precise course.

Among the letters of the day lying scattered beside him on the floor there was yet further evidence of the power of Barron's campaign. There were warm expressions indeed of sympathy and indignation to be found among them, but on the whole Meynell realized that his own side's belief in him was showing some signs of distress, while the attack upon him was increasing in violence. His silence even to his most intimate friends, even to his Bishop; the disappearance from England of the other persons named in the scandal; the constant elaborations and embellishments of the story as it passed from mouth to mouth — these things were telling against him steadily and disastrously.

As he hung over the fire, he anxiously reconsidered his conduct toward the Bishop, while Catharine's phrase — "He, too, has his rights!" lingered in his memory. He more than suspected that his silence had given pain; and his affection for the Bishop made the thought a sore one.

But after all what good would have been done had he even put the Bishop in possession of the whole story?

The Bishop's bare denial would have been added to his; nothing more. There could have been no explanation, public or private; nothing to persuade those who did not wish to be persuaded.

His thought wandered hither and thither. From the dim regions of the past there emerged a letter. . . .

"My dear old Meynell, the thing is to be covered up. Ralph will acknowledge the child, and all precautions are to be taken.   I think what he does he will do thoroughly.   Alice wishes it — and what can I do, either for her or for the child?   Nothing.   And for me, I see but one way out — which will be the best for her too in the end, poor darling.   My wife's letter a week ago destroyed my last hope.   I am going out to-night — and I shall not come back.   Stand by her, Richard.   I think this kind of lie on which we are all embarked is wrong (not that you had anything to do with it!)   But it is society which is wrong and imposes it on us.   Anyway, the choice is made, and now you must support and protect her — and the child — for my sake.   For I know you love me, dear boy — little as I deserve it.   It is part of your general gift of loving, which has always seemed to me so strange.   However — whatever I was made for, you were made to help the unhappy.   So I have the less scruple in sending you this last word.   She will want your help.   The child's lot in that household will not be a happy one; and Alice will have to look on. But, help her! — help her above all to keep silence, for this thing, once done, must be irrevocable.   Only so can my poor Alice recover her youth — think, she is only twenty now! — and the child's future be saved.   Alice, I hope, will marry.   And when the child marries, you may — nay, I think you must — tell the husband. I have written this to Ralph. But for all the rest of the world, the truth is now wiped out. The child is no longer mine — Alice was never my love — and I am going to the last sleep. My sister Fanny Meryon knows something; enough to make her miserable; but no names or details. Well! — good-bye. In your company alone have I ever seemed to touch the life that might have been mine. But it is too late. The will in me — the mainspring — is diseased. This is a poor return — but forgive me! — my very dear Richard! Here comes the boat; and there is a splendid sea rising."

There, in a locked drawer, not far from him, lay this letter. Meynell's thought plunged back into the past; into its passionate feeling, its burning pity, its powerless affection. He recalled his young hero-worship for his brilliant kinsman; the hour when he had identified the battered form on the shore of the Donegal Lough; the sight of Alice's young anguish; and all the subsequent effort on his part, for Christ's sake, for Neville's sake, to help and shield a woman and child, effort from which his own soul had learnt so much.

Pure and sacred recollections! — mingled often with the moral or intellectual perplexities that enter into all things human.

Then — at a bound — his thoughts rushed on to the man who, without pity, without shame, had dragged all these sad things, these helpless, irreparable griefs, into the cruel light of a malicious publicity — in the name of Christ — in the name of the Church!

To-morrow! He rose, with a face set like iron, and went back to his table to finish a half-written review.

"Theresa — after eleven — I shall be engaged. See that I am not disturbed."

Theresa murmured assent, but when her father closed the door of her sitting-room, she did not go back immediately to her household accounts. Her good, plain face showed a disturbed mind.

Her father's growing excitability and irritation, and the bad accounts of Maurice, troubled her sorely. It was only that morning Mr. Barron had become aware that Maurice had lost his employment, and was again adrift in the world. Theresa had known it for a week or two, but had not been allowed to tell. And she tried not to remember how often of late her brother had applied to her for money.

Going back to her accounts with a sigh, she missed a necessary receipt and went into the dining-room to look for it. While she was there the front door bell rang and was answered, unheard by her. Thus it fell out that as she came back into the hall she found herself face to face with Richard Meynell.

She stood paralyzed with astonishment. He bowed to her gravely and passed on. Something in his look seemed to her to spell calamity. She went back to her room, and sat there dumb and trembling, dreading what she might see or hear.

Meanwhile Meynell had been ushered into Barron's

study by the old butler, who was no less astonished than his mistress.

Barron rose stiffly to meet his visitor. The two men stood opposite each other as the door closed.

Barron spoke first.

"You will, I trust, let me know, Mr. Meynell, without delay to what I owe this unexpected visit. I was of course quite ready to meet your desire for an interview, but your letter gave me no clue——"

"I thought it better not," said Meynell quietly. "May we sit down?"

Barron mechanically waved the speaker to a chair, and sat down himself. Meynell seemed to pause a moment, his eyes on the ground. Then suddenly he raised them.

"Mr. Barron, what I have come to say will be a shock to you. I have discovered the author of the anonymous letters which have now for nearly three months been defiling this parish and diocese."

Barron's sudden movement showed tne effect of the words. But he held himself well in hand.

"I congratulate you," he said coldly. "It is what we have all been trying to discover."

"But the discovery will be painful to you. For the author of these letters, Mr. Barron — is — your son Maurice."

At these words, spoken with an indescribable intensity and firmness, Barron sprang from his seat.

"It was not necessary, I think, sir, to come to my house

in order to insult my family and myself! It would have been better to write. And you may be very sure that if you cannot punish your slanderers we can — and will!"

His attitude expressed a quivering fury. Meynell took a packet from his breast-pocket and quietly laid it on the table beside him.

"In this envelope you will find a document — a confession of a piece of wrongdoing on Maurice's part of which I believe you have never been informed. His poor sister concealed it — and paid for it. Do you remember, three years ago, the letting loose of some valuable young horses from Farmer Grange's stables — the hue and cry after them — and the difficulty there was in recapturing them on the Chase?"

Barron stared at the speaker — speechless.

"You remember that a certain young fellow was accused — James Aston — one of my Sunday school teachers — who had proposed to Grange's daughter, and had been sent about his business by the father? Aston was in fact just about to be run in by the police, when a clue came to my hands. I followed it up. Then I found out that the ringleader in the whole affair had been your son Maurice. If you remember, he was then at home, hanging about the village, and he had had a quarrel with Grange — I forget about what. He wrote an anonymous post-card accusing Aston. However, I got on the track; and finally I made him give me a written confession — to protect Aston. Heavy compensation was paid to Grange — by your daughter —

and the thing was hushed up. I was always doubtful whether I ought not to have come to you. But it was not long after the death of your wife. I was very sorry for you all — and Maurice pleaded hard. I did not even tell Stephen; but I kept the confession. I came upon it a night or two ago, in the drawer where I had also placed the letter to Dawes which I got from you. Suddenly, the likeness in the handwritings struck me; and I made a very careful comparison."

He opened the packet, and took out the two papers, which he offered to Barron.

"I think, if you will compare the marked passages, you will see at least a striking resemblance."

With a shaking hand Barron refused the papers.

"I have no doubt, sir, you can manufacture any evidence you please! — but I do not intend to follow you through it. Handwriting, as we all know, can be made to prove anything. Reserve your documents for your solicitor. I shall at once instruct mine."

"But I am only at the beginning of my case," said Meynell with the same composure. "I think you had better listen . . . A passage in one of the recent letters gave me a hint — an idea. I went straight to East the publican, and taxed him with being the accomplice of the writer. I blustered a little — he thought I had more evidence than I had — and at last I got the whole thing out of him. The first letter was written" — the speaker raised his finger, articulating each word with slow precision, "by your son Maurice, and posted by

East, the day after the cage-accident at the Victoria pit;
and they have pursued the same division of labour ever
since.   East confesses he was induced to do it by the wish
to revenge himself on me for the attack on his license;
and Maurice occasionally gave him a little money.   I
have all the dates of the letters, and a statement of
where they were posted.   If necessary, East will give
evidence."

A silence.   Barron had resumed his seat, and was
automatically lifting a small book which lay on a table
near him and letting it fall, while Meynell was speaking.
When Meynell paused, he said thickly —

"A plausible tale no doubt — and a very convenient
one for you.   But allow me to point out, it rests entirely
on East's word.   Very likely he wrote the letters himself, and is attempting to make Maurice the scapegoat."

"Where do you suppose he could have got his information from?" said Meynell, looking up.   "There is no
suggestion that *he* saw Judith Sabin before her death."

Barron's face worked, while Meynell watched him
implacably.   At last he said:

"How should I know?   The same question applies
to Maurice."

"Not at all.   There the case is absolutely clear.
Maurice got his information from you."

"A gratuitous statement, sir! — which you cannot
prove."

"From you" — repeated Meynell.   "And from certain spying operations that he and East undertook

together. Do you deny that you told Maurice all that Judith Sabin told you — together with her identification of myself?"

The room seemed to wait for Barron's reply. He made none. He burst out instead —

"What possible motive could Maurice have had for such an action? The thing isn't even plausible!"

"Oh, Maurice had various old scores to settle with me," said Meynell, quietly. "I have come across him more than once in this parish —no need to say how. I tried to prevent him from publicly disgracing himself and you; and I did prevent him. He saw in this business an easy revenge on a sanctimonious parson who had interfered with his pleasures."

Barron had risen and was pacing the room with unsteady steps. Meynell still watched him, with the same glitter in the eye. Meynell's whole nature indeed, at the moment, had gathered itself into one avenging force; he was at once sword and smiter. The man before him seemed to him embodied cruelty and hypocrisy; he felt neither pity nor compunction. And presently he said abruptly —

"But I am afraid I have much more serious matter to lay before you than this business of the letters."

"What do you mean?"

Taking another letter from his pocket, Meynell glanced at it a moment, and then handed it to Barron. Barron was for an instant inclined to refuse it, as he had refused the others. But Meynell insisted.

"Believe me, you had better read it.   It is a letter from Mr. Flaxman to myself, and it concerns a grave charge against your son.   I bring you a chance of saving him from prosecution; but there is no time to be lost."

Barron took the letter, carried it to the window, and stood reading it.   Meynell sat on the other side of the room watching him, still in the same impassive "possessed" state.

Suddenly, Barron put his hand over his face, and a groan he could not repress broke from him.   He turned his back and stood bending over the letter.

At the same instant a shiver ran through Meynell, like the return to life of some arrested energy, some paralyzed power.   The shock of that sound of suffering had found him iron; it left him flesh.   The spiritual habit of a lifetime revived; for "what we do we are."

He rose slowly, and went over to the window.

"You can still save him — from the immediate consequences of this at least — if you will.   I have arranged that with Flaxman.   It was my seeing him enter the room alone where the coins were, the night of the party, that first led to the idea that he might have taken them.   Then, as you see, certain dealers' shops were watched by a private detective.   Maurice appeared — sold the Hermes coin — was traced to his lodgings and identified.   So far the thing has not gone beyond private inquiry; for the dealer will do what Flaxman wants him to do.   But Maurice still has the more famous of the two coins; and if he attempts to sell that, after the notices to the police, there may be an exposure any day. You must go up to London as soon as you can —— "

"I will go to-night," said Barron, in a tone scarcely to be heard. He stood with his hands on his sides, staring out upon the wintry garden outside, just as a gardener's boy laden with holly and ivy for the customary Christmas decorations of the house was passing across the lawn.

There was silence a little. Meynell walked slowly up and down the room. At last Barron turned toward him; the very incapacity of the plump and ruddy face for any tragic expression made it the more tragic.

"I propose to write to the Bishop at once. Do you desire a public statement?"

"There must be a public statement," said Meynell gravely. "The thing has gone too far. Flaxman and I have drawn one up. Will you look at it?"

Barron took it, and went to his writing-table.

"Wait a moment!" said Meynell, following him, and laying his hand on the open page. "I don't want you to sign that by *force majeure*. Dismiss — if you can — any thought of any hold I may have upon you, because of Maurice's misdoing. You and I, Barron, have known each other some years. We were once friends. I ask you — not under any threat — not under any compulsion — to accept my word as an honest man that I am absolutely innocent of the charge you have brought against me."

Barron, who was sitting before his writing-table, buried his face in his hands a moment, then raised it.

"I accept it," he said, almost inaudibly.

"You believe me?"

"I believe you."

Meynell drew a long breath. Then he added, with a first sign of emotion — "And I may also count upon your doing henceforth what you can to protect that poor lady, Miss Puttenham, and her kinsfolk, from the consequences of this long persecution?"

Barron made a sign of assent. Meynell left him to read and sign the public apology and retraction, which Flaxman had mainly drawn up; while the Rector himself took up a Bradshaw lying on the table, and walked to the window to consult it.

"You will catch the 1.40," he said, as Barron rose from the writing-table. "Let me advise you to get him out of the country for a time."

Barron said nothing. He came heavily toward the window, and the two men stood looking at each other, overtaken both of them by a mounting wave of consciousness. The events, passions, emotions of the preceding months pressed into memory, and beat against the silence. But it was Meynell who turned pale.

"What a pity — to spoil the fight!" he said in a low voice. "It would have been splendid — to fight it — fair."

"I shall of course withdraw my name from the Arches suit," said Barron, leaning over a chair, his eyes on the ground.

Meynell did not reply. He took up his hat; only saying as he went toward the door:

"Remember — Flaxman holds his hand entirely. The situation is with you." Then, after a moment's hesitation, he added simply, almost shyly — "God help you! Won't you consult your daughter?"

Barron made no answer. The door opened and shut.

BOOK IV

MEYNELL AND MARY

" . . . . but Life ere long
Came on me in the public ways and bent
Eyes deeper than of old ; Death met I too,
    And saw the dawn glow through."

CHAPTER XX

A MILD January day on the terrace of St. Germains. After a morning of hoar-frost the sun was shining brightly on the terrace, and on the panorama it commands. A pleasant light lay on the charming houses that front the skirts of the forest, on the blue-gray windings of the Seine, on the groves of leafless poplars interwoven with its course, on the plain with its thickly sown villages, on the height of Mont Valérien, behind which lay Paris. In spite of the sunshine, however, it was winter, and there was no movement in St. Germains. The terrace and the road leading from it to the town were deserted; and it was easy to see from the aspect of the famous hotel at the corner of the terrace that, although not closed, it despaired of visitors. Only a trio of French officers in the far distance of the terrace, and a white-capped *bonne* struggling against the light wind with a basket on her arm, offered any sign of life to the observant eyes of a young man who was briskly pacing up and down that section of the terrace which abuts on the hotel.

The young man was Philip Meryon. His dark tweed suit and fur waistcoat disclosed a figure once singularly agile and slender, on which self-indulgence was now beginning to tell. Nevertheless, as the *bonne* passed him

493

she duly noted and admired his pictorial good looks, opining at the same time that he was not French.   Why was he there?   She decided in her own mind that he was there for an assignation, by which she meant, of course, a meeting with a married woman; and she smiled the incorrigible French smile.

Assignation or no, she would have seen, had she looked closer, that the young man in question was in no merely beatific or expectant frame of mind.   Meryon's look was a look both of excitement — as of one under the influence of some news of a startling kind — and of anxiety.

Would she come?   And if she came would he be able to bring and hold her to any decision, without — without doing what even he shrank from doing?

For that ill chance in a thousand which Meynell had foreseen, and hoped, as mortals do, to baffle, had come to pass.   That morning, a careless letter enclosing the payment of a debt, and written by a young actor, who had formed part of one of the bohemian parties at the Abbey, during the summer, and had now been playing for a week in the Markborough theatre, had given Meryon the clue to the many vague conjectures or perplexities which had already crossed his mind with regard to Hester's origin and history.

"Your sanctified cousin, Richard Meynell" [wrote the young man] "seems after all to be made of the common clay.   There are strange stories going the round about him here; especially in a crop of anonymous letters of which the author can't be found. I send you a local newspaper which has dared to print one of them with dashes for the names. The landlord of the inn told me how to fill them up, and you will see I have done it. The beauteous maiden herself has vanished from the scene — as no doubt you know. Indeed you probably know all about it. However, as you are abroad, and not likely to see these local rags, and as no London paper will print these things, you may perhaps be interested in what I enclose. Alack, my dear Philip, for the saints! They seem not so very different from you and me."

The eagerness with which Philip had read the newspaper cutting enclosed in the letter was only equalled by the eagerness with which afterward he fell to meditating upon it; pursuing and ferreting out the truth, through a maze of personal recollection and inference.

Richard! — nonsense! He laughed, from a full throat. Not for one moment was Philip misled by Judith Sabin's mistake. He was a man of great natural shrewdness, blunted no doubt by riotous living; but there was enough of it left, aided by his recent forced contacts with his cousin Richard all turning on the subject of Hester, to keep him straight. So that without any demur at all he rejected the story as it stood.

But then, what was the fact behind it? Impossible that Judith Sabin's story should be all delusion! For whom did she mistake Richard?

Suddenly, as he sat brooding and smoking, a vision of Hester flashed upon him as she had stood laughing

and pouting, beneath the full length picture of Neville
Flood, which hung in the big hall of the Abbey. He had
pointed it out to her on their way through the house —
where she had peremptorily refused to linger — to the
old garden behind.

He could hear his own question: "There! — aren't
you exactly like him? Turn and look at yourself in the
glass opposite. Oh, you needn't be offended! He was
the handsome man of his day."

Of course! The truth jumped to the eyes, now that
one was put in the way of seeing it. And on this decisive
recollection there had followed a rush of others, no less
pertinent: things said by his dead mother about the
brother whom she had loved and bitterly regretted. So
the wronged lady whom he would have married but for his
wife's obstinacy was "Aunt Alice!" Philip remembered
to have once seen her from a distance in the Upcote woods.
Hester had pointed her out, finger on lip, as they stood
hiding in a thicket of fern; a pretty woman still. His
mother had never mentioned a name; probably she had
never known it; but to the love-affair she had always
attributed some share in her brother's death.

From point to point he tracked it, the poor secret,
till he had run it down. By degrees everything fitted in;
he was confident that he had guessed the truth.

Then, abruptly, he turned to look at its bearing on
his own designs and fortunes.

He supposed himself to be in love with Hester. At
any rate he was violently conscious of that hawk-like

instinct of pursuit which he was accustomed to call love. Hester's mad and childish imprudences, which the cooler self in Meryon was quite ready to recognize as such, had made the hawking a singularly easy task so far. Meynell, of course, had put up difficulties; with regard to this Scotch business it had been necessary to lie pretty hard, and to bribe some humble folk in order to get round him.   But Hester, by the double fact that she was at once so far removed from the mere *ingénue*, and so incredibly ready to risk herself, out of sheer ignorance of life, both challenged and tempted the man whom a disastrous fate had brought across her path, to such a point that he had long since lost control of himself, and parted with any scruples of conscience he might possess.

At the same time he was by no means sure of her.   He realized his increasing power over her; he also realized the wild, independent streak in her.   Some day — any day — the capricious, wilful nature might tire, might change. The prey might escape, and the hawk go empty home. No dallying too long!   Let him decide what to risk — and risk it.

Meantime that confounded cousin of his was hard at work, through some very capable lawyers, and unless the instructions he — Philip — had conveyed to the woman in Scotland, who, thank goodness, was no less anxious to be rid of him than he to be rid of her, were very shrewdly and exactly carried out, facts might in the end reach Hester which would give even her recklessness pause. He knew that so far Meynell had been baffled; he knew that he carried about with him evidence that, for the present, could be brought to bear on Hester with effect; but things were by no means safe.

For his own affairs, they were desperate. As he stood there, he was nothing more in fact than the common needy adventurer, possessed, however, of greater daring, and the *débris* of much greater pretensions, than most such persons. His financial resources were practically at an end, and he had come to look upon a clandestine marriage with Hester as the best means of replenishing them. The Fox-Wilton family passed for rich; and the notion that they must and would be ready to come forward with money, when once the thing was irrevocable, counted for much in the muddy plans of which his mind was full. His own idea was to go to South America — to Buenos Ayres, where money was to be made, and where he had some acquaintance. In that way he would shake off his creditors, and the Scotch woman together; and Meynell would know better than to interfere.

Suddenly a light figure came fluttering round the corner of the road leading to the château and the town. Philip turned and went to meet her. And as he approached her he was shaken afresh by the excitement of her presence, in addition to his more sordid preoccupation. Her wild, provocative beauty seemed to light up the whole wintry scene; and the few passers-by, each and all, stopped to stare at her. Hester laughed aloud when she saw

Meryon; and with her usual recklessness held up her umbrella for signal. It pleased her that two *rapins* in large black ties and steeple hats paid her an insolent attention as they passed her; and she stopped to pinch the cheek of a chubby child that had planted itself straight in her path.

"Am I late?" she said, as they met. "I only just caught the train. Oh! I am so hungry! Don't let's talk — let's *déjeuner*."

Philip laughed.

"Will you dare the hotel?"

And he pointed to the Pavillion Henri Quatre.

"Why not? Probably there won't be a soul."

"There are always Americans."

"Why' not, again? *Tant mieux!* Oh, my hair!"

And she put up her two ungloved hands to try and reduce it to something like order. The loveliness of the young curving form, of the pretty hands, of the golden brown hair, struck full on Meryon's turbid sense.

They turned toward the hotel, and were presently seated in a corner of its glazed gallery, with all the wide prospect of plain and river spread beneath them. Hester was in the highest spirits, and as she sat waiting for the first *plat*, chattering, and nibbling at her roll, her black felt hat with its plume of cock feathers falling back from the brilliance of her face, she once more attracted all the attention available; from the two savants who, after a morning in the Château, were lunching at a farther table; from an American family of all ages reduced to silence by sheer wonder and contemplation; from the waiters, and, not least, from the hotel dog, wagging his tail mutely at her knee.

Philip felt himself an envied person. He was, indeed, vain of his companion; but certain tyrannical instincts asserted themselves once or twice. When, or if, she became his possession, he would try and moderate some of this chatter and noise.

For the present he occupied himself with playing to her lead, glancing every now and then mentally, with a secret start, at the information he had possessed about her since the morning.

She described to him, with a number of new tricks of gesture caught from her French class-mates, how she had that morning outwitted all her guardians, who supposed that she had gone to Versailles with one of the senior members of the class she was attending at the Conservatoire, a young teacher, "*très sage*," with whom she had been allowed once or twice to go to museums and galleries. To accomplish it had required an elaborate series of deceptions, which Hester had carried through, apparently, without a qualm. Except that at the end of her story there was a passing reference to Aunt Alice — "poor darling!" — "who would have a fit if she knew."

Philip, coffee-cup in hand, half smiling, looked at her meantime through his partially closed lids. Richard, indeed! She was Neville all through, the Neville of the picture, except for the colour of the hair, and the soft femininity. And here she sat, prattling — foolish dear!

— about "mamma," and "Aunt Alice," and "my tire-some sisters!"

"Certainly you shall not pay for me! — not a *sou*," said Hester flushing. "I have plenty of money. Take it please, at once." And she pushed her share over the table, with a peremptory gesture.

Meryon took it with a smile and a shrug, and she, throwing away the cigarette she had been defiantly smok-ing, rose from the table.

"Now then, what shall we do? Oh! no museums! I am being educated to death! Let us go for a walk in the forest; and then I must catch my train, or the world will go mad."

So they walked briskly into the forest, and were soon sufficiently deep among its leaf-strewn paths, to be secure from all observation. Two hours remained of wintry sunlight before they must turn back toward the station.

Hester walked along swinging a small silk bag in which she carried her handkerchief and purse. Suddenly, in a narrow path girt by some tall hollies and withered oaks, she let it fall. Both stooped for it, their hands touched, and as Hester rose she found herself in Meryon's arms.

She made a violent effort to free herself, and when it failed, she stood still and submitted to be kissed, like one who accepts an experience, with a kind of proud patience.

"You think you love me," she said at last, pushing him away. "I wonder whether you do!"

And flushed and panting, she leant against a tree,

looking at him with a strange expression, in which melancholy mingled with resentment; passing slowly into something else — that soft and shaken look, that yearning of one longing and yet fearing to be loved, which had struck dismay into Meynell on the afternoon when he had pursued her to the Abbey.

Philip came close to her.

"You think I have no Roddy!" she said, with bitterness. "Don't kiss me again!"

He refrained. But catching her hand, and leaning against the trunk beside her, he poured into her ear protestations and flattery; the ordinary language of such a man at such a moment. Hester listened to it with a kind of eagerness. Sometimes, with a slight frown, as though ear and mind waited, intently, for something that did not come.

"I wonder how many people you have said the same things to before!" she said suddenly, looking searchingly into his face. "What have you got to tell me about that Scotch girl?"

"Richard's Scotch girl?" — he laughed, throwing his handsome head back against the tree — "whom Richard supposes me to have married? Well, I had a great flirtation with her, I admit, two years ago, and it is sometimes rather difficult in Scotland to know whether you are married or no. You know of course that all that's necessary is to declare yourselves man and wife before witnesses? However — perhaps you would like to see a letter from the lady herself on the subject?"

"You had it ready?" she said, doubtfully.

"Well, considering that Richard has been threatening me for months, not only with the loss of you, but with all sorts of pains and penalties besides, I have had to do something! Of course I have done a great deal. This is one of the documents in the case. It is an affidavit really, drawn up by my solicitor and signed by the lady whom Richard supposes to be my injured wife!"

He placed an envelope in her hands.

Hester opened it with a touch of scornful reluctance. It contained a categorical denial and repudiation of the supposed marriage.

"Has Uncle Richard seen it?" she asked coldly, as she gave it back to him.

"Certainly he has, by now." He took another envelope from his pocket. "I won't bother you with anything more — the thing is really too absurd! — but here, if you want it, is a letter from the girl's brother. Brothers are generally supposed to keep a sharp lookout on their sisters, aren't they? Well, this brother declares that Meynell's inquiries have come to nothing, absolutely nothing, in the neighbourhood — except that they have made people very angry. He has got no evidence — simply because there is none to get! I imagine, indeed, that by now he has dropped the whole business. And certainly it is high time he did; or I shall have to be taking action on my own account before long!"

He looked down upon her, as she stood beside him, trying to make out her expression.

"Hester!" he broke out, "don't let's talk about this any more — it's damned nonsense! Let's talk about ourselves. Hester! — darling! — I want to make you happy! — I want to carry you away. Hester, will you marry me at once? As far as the French law is concerned, I have arranged it all. You could come with me to a certain Mairie I know, to-morrow, and we could marry without anybody having a word to say to it; and then, Hester, I'd carry you to Italy! I know a villa on the Riviera — the Italian Riviera — in a little bay all orange and lemon and blue sea. We'd honeymoon there; and when we were tired of honeymooning — though how could any one tire of honeymooning, with you, you darling! — we'd go to South America. I have an opening at Buenos Ayres which promises to make me a rich man. Come with me! — it is the most wonderful country in the world. You would be adored there — you would have every luxury — we'd travel and ride and explore — we'd have a glorious life!"

He had caught her hands again, and stood towering over her, intoxicated with his own tinsel phrases; almost sincere; a splendid physical presence, save for the slight thickening of face and form, the looseness of the lips, the absence of all freshness in the eyes.

But Hester, after a first moment of dreamy excitement, drew herself decidedly away.

"No, no! — I can't be such a wretch — I can't! Mamma and Aunt Alice would break their hearts. I'm a selfish beast, but not quite so bad as that! No, Philip —

we can meet and amuse ourselves, can't we? — and get to
know each other? — and then if we want to, we can marry
— some time."

"That means you don't love me!" he said, fiercely.

"Yes, yes, I do! — or at least I — I like you. And
perhaps in time — if you let me alone — if you don't
tease me — I — I'll marry you. But let's do it openly.
It's amusing to get one's own way, even by lies, up to
a certain point. They wouldn't let me see you, or get
to know you, and I was determined to know you. So
I had to behave like a little cad, or give in. But marrying's different."

He argued with her hotly, pointing out the certainty
of Meynell's opposition, exaggerating the legal powers of
guardians, declaring vehemently that it was now or never.
Hester grew very white as they wandered on through
the forest, but she did not yield. Some last scruple of
conscience, perhaps — some fluttering fear, possessed
her.

So that in the end Philip was pushed to the villainy
that even he would have avoided.

Suddenly he turned upon her.

"Hester, you drive me to it! I don't want to — but
I can't help it. Hester, you poor little darling! — you
don't know what has happened — you don't know what
a position you're in. I want to save you from it. I
would have done it, God knows, without telling you the
truth if I could; but you drive me to it!"

"What on earth do you mean?"

She stopped beside him in a clearing of the forest. The pale afternoon sun, now dropping fast to westward, slipped through the slender oaks, on which the red leaves still danced, touched the girl's hair and shone into her beautiful eyes. She stood there so young, so unconscious; a victim, on the threshold of doom. Philip, who was no more a monster than other men who do monstrous things, felt a sharp stab of compunction; and then, rushed headlong at the crime he had practically resolved on before they met.

He told her in a few agitated words the whole—and the true — story of her birth. He described the return of Judith Sabin to Upcote Minor, and the narrative she had given to Henry Barron, without however a word of Meynell in the case, so far at least as the original events were concerned. For he was convinced that he knew better, and that there was no object in prolonging an absurd misunderstanding. His version of the affair was that Judith in a fit of excitement had revealed Hester's parentage to Henry Barron; that Barron out of enmity toward Meynell, Hester's guardian, and by way of getting a hold upon him, had not kept the matter to himself, but had either written or instigated anonymous letters which had spread such excitement in the neighbourhood that Lady Fox-Wilton had now let her house, and practically left Upcote for good. The story had become the common talk of the Markborough district; and all that Meynell, and "your poor mother," and the Fox-Wilton family could do, was to attempt, on the one hand, to meet the rush of scandal by absence and silence; and on the other to keep the facts from Hester herself as long as possible.

The girl had listened to him with wide, startled eyes. Occasionally a sound broke from her — a gasp — an exclamation — and when he paused, pursued by almost a murderer's sense of guilt, he saw her totter. In an instant he had his arm round her, and for once there was both real passion and real pity in the excited words he poured into her ears.

"Hester, dearest! — don't cry, don't be miserable, my own beautiful Hester! I am a beast to have told you, but it is because I am not only your lover, but your cousin — your own flesh and blood. Trust yourself to me! You'll see! Why should that preaching fellow Meynell interfere? I'll take care of you. You come to me, and we'll show these damned scandal-mongers that what they say is nothing to us — that we don't care a fig for their cant — that we are the masters of our own lives — not they!"

And so on, and so on. The emotion was as near sincerity as he could push it; but it did not fail to occur, at least once, to a mind steeped in third-rate drama, what a "strong" dramatic scene might be drawn from the whole situation.

Hester heard him for a few minutes, in evident stupefaction; then with a recovery of physical equilibrium she again vehemently repulsed him.

"You are mad — you are *mad!* It is abominable to

talk to me like this. What do you mean? 'My poor mother' — who is my mother?"

She faced him tragically, the certainty which was already dawning in her mind — prepared indeed, through years, by all the perplexities and rebellions of her girlhood — betraying itself in her quivering face, and lips. Suddenly, she dropped upon a fallen log beside the path, hiding her face in her hands, struggling again with the sheer faintness of the shock. And Philip, kneeling in the dry leaves beside her, completed his work, with the cruel mercy of the man who kills what he has wounded.

He asked her to look back into her childhood; he reminded her of the many complaints she had made to him of her sense of isolation within her supposed family; of the strange provisions of Sir Ralph's will; of the arrangement which had made her Meynell's ward in a special sense.

"Why, of course, that was so natural! You remember I suggested to you once that Richard probably judged Neville from the same Puritanical standpoint that he judged me? Well, I was a fool to talk like that. I remember now perfectly what my mother used to say. They were of different generations, but they were tremendous friends; and there was only a few years between them. I am certain it was by Neville's wish that Richard became your guardian." He laughed, in some embarrassment. "He couldn't exactly foresee that another member of the family would want to cut in. I love you — I adore you! Let's give all these people the slip.

Hester, my pretty, pretty darling — look at me! I'll
show you what life means — what love means!"

And doubly tempted by her abasement, her bewildered
pain, he tried again to take her in his arms.

But she held him at arm's length.

"If," she said, with pale lips — "if Sir Neville was my
father — and Aunt Alsie" — her voice failed her —
"were they — were they never married?"

He slowly and reluctantly shook his head.

"Then I'm — I'm — oh! but that's monstrous —
that's absurd! I don't believe it!"

She sprang to her feet. Then, as she stood confronting
his silence, the whole episode of that bygone September
afternoon — the miniature — Aunt Alice's silence and
tears — rushed back on memory. She trembled, and
the iron entered into her soul.

"Let's go back to the station," she said, resolutely.
"It's time."

They walked back through the forest paths, for some
time without speaking, she refusing his aid. And all
the time swiftly, inexorably, memory and inference were
at work, dragging to light the deposit — obscure, or
troubling, or contradictory — left in her by the facts and
feelings of her childhood and youth.

She had told him with emphasis at luncheon that he
was not to be allowed to accompany her home; that she
would go back to Paris by herself. But when, at the
St. Germains station, Meryon jumped into the empty
railway carriage beside her, she said nothing to prevent

him. She sat in the darkest corner of the carriage, her arms hanging beside her, her eyes fixed on objects of which she saw nothing. Her pride in herself, her ideal of herself, which is to every young creature like the protective sheath to the flower, was stricken to the core. She thought of Sarah and Lulu, whom she had all her life despised and ridiculed. But they had a right to their name and place in the world!—and she was their nameless inferior, the child taken in out of pity, accepted on sufferance. She thought of the gossip now rushing like a mud-laden stream through every Upcote or Markborough drawing-room. All the persons whom she had snubbed or flouted were concerning themselves maliciously with her and her affairs— were pitying "poor Hester Fox-Wilton."

Her heart seemed to dry and harden within her. The strange thought of her real mother — her suffering, patient, devoted mother — did not move her. It was bound up with all that trampled on and humiliated her.

And, moreover, strange and piteous fact, realized by them both! this sudden sense of fall and degradation had in some mysterious way altered her whole relation to the man who had brought it upon her. His evil power over her had increased. He felt instinctively that he need not in future be so much on his guard. His manner toward her became freer. She had never yet returned him the kisses which, as on this day, she had sometimes allowed him to snatch. But before they reached Paris she had kissed him; she had sought his hands with hers; and she had promised to meet him again.

While these lamentable influences and events were thus sweeping Hester's life toward the abyss, mocking all the sacrifices and the efforts that had been made to save her, the publication of Barron's apology had opened yet another stage in "the Meynell case."

As drafted by Flaxman, it was certainly comprehensive enough. For himself, Meynell would have been content with much less; but in dealing with Barron, he was the avenger of wrongs not his own, both public and private; and when his own first passion of requital had passed away, killed in him by the anguish of his enemy, he still let Flaxman decide for him. And Flaxman, the mildest and most placable of men, showed himself here inexorable, and would allow no softening of terms. So that Barron "unreservedly withdrew" and "publicly apologized" "for those false and calumnious charges, which to my great regret, and on erroneous information, I have been led to bring against the character and conduct of the Rev. Richard Meynell, at various dates, and in various ways, during the six months preceding the date of this apology."

With regard to the anonymous letters — "although they were not written, nor in any way authorized, by me, I now discover to my sorrow that they were written by a member of my family on information derived from me. I apologize for and repudiate the false and slanderous statements these letters contain, and those also included in letters I myself have written to various persons. I agree that a copy of this statement shall be sent to the Bishop of Markborough, and to each parish clergyman

in the diocese of Markborough; as also that it shall be
published in such newspapers as the solicitors of the Rev.
Richard Meynell may determine."

The document appeared first on a Saturday, in all the
local papers, and was greedily read and discussed by
the crowds that throng into Markborough on market
day, who again carried back the news to the villages of
the diocese.   It was also published on the same day in
the *Modernist* and in the leading religious papers.   Its
effect on opinion was rapid and profound.   The Bishop
telegraphed — "Thank God.   Come and see me."
France fidgeted a whole morning among his papers,
began two or three letters to Meynell, and finally decided
that he could write nothing adequate that would not also
be hypocritical.   Dornal wrote a little note that Meynell
put away among those records that are the milestones of
life.   From all the leading Modernists, during January,
came a rush of correspondence and congratulations, in all
possible notes and tones of indignant triumph; and many
leaders on the other side wrote with generous emotion and
relief.   Only in the extreme camp of the extreme Right
there was, of course, silence and chagrin.   Compared to
the eternal interests of the Church, what does one man's
character matter?

The old Bishop of Dunchester, a kind of English Döl-
linger, the learned leader of a learned party, and ready
in the last years of life to risk what would have tasked
the nerves and courage of a man in the prime of physical
and mental power, wrote:

"My Dear Richard Meynell: Against my better judgment, I was persuaded that you might have been imprudent. I now know that you have only been heroic. Forgive me — forgive us all. Nothing will induce me to preach the sermon of our opening day. And if you will not, who will, or can?"

Rose meanwhile descended upon the Rectory, and with Flaxman's help, though in the teeth of Anne's rather jealous opposition, she carried off Meynell to Maudeley, that she might "help him write his letters," and watch for a week or two over a man wearied and overtaxed. It was by her means also that the reaction in public opinion spread far beyond Meynell himself. It is true that even men and women of good will looked at each other in bewilderment, after the publication of the apology, and asked each other under their breaths — "Then is there no story! — and was Judith Sabin's whole narrative a delusion?" But with whatever might be true in that narrative no public interest was now bound up; and discussion grew first shamefaced, and then dropped. The tendency strengthened indeed to regard the whole matter as the invention of a half-crazy and dying woman, possessed of some grudge against the Fox-Wilton family. Many surmised that some tragic fact lay at the root of the tale, since those concerned had not chosen to bring the slanderer to account. But what had once been mere matter for malicious or idle curiosity was now handled with compunction and good feeling. People began to be very sorry for the Fox-Wiltons, very sorry for "poor

Miss Puttenham." Cards were left, and friendly inquiries were made; and amid the general wave of
scepticism and regret, the local society showed itself as
sentimental, and as futile as usual.

Meanwhile poor Theresa had been seen driving to the
station with red eyes; and her father, it was ascertained,
had been absent from home since the day before the
publication of the apology. It was very commonly
guessed that the "member of my family" responsible
for the letters was the unsatisfactory younger son; and
many persons, especially in Church circles, were secretly
sorry for Barron, while everybody possessed of any heart
at all was sorry for his elder son Stephen.

Stephen indeed was one of Meynell's chief anxieties
during these intermediate hours, when a strong man
took a few days' breathing space between the effort that
had been, and the effort that was to be. The young man
would come over, day by day, with the same crushed,
patient look, now bringing news to Meynell which they
talked over where none might overhear, and now craving news from Paris in return. As to Stephen's own
report, Barron, it seemed, had made all arrangements
to send Maurice to a firm of English merchants trading
at Riga. The head of the firm was under an old financial
obligation to Henry Barron, and Stephen had no doubt
that his father had made it heavily worth their while to
give his brother this fresh chance of an honest life. There
had been, Stephen believed, some terrible scenes between
the father and son, and Stephen neither felt nor professed

to feel any hope for the future.   Barron intended himself
to accompany Maurice to Riga and settle him there.
Afterward he talked of a journey to the Cape.   Meanwhile the White House was shut up, and poor Theresa
had come to join Stephen in the little vicarage whence
the course of events in the coming year would certainly
drive him out.

So much for the news he gave.   As to the news he
hungered for, Meynell had but crumbs to give him.   To
neither Stephen nor any one else could Alice Puttenham's
letters be disclosed.   Meynell's lips were sealed upon her
story now as they had ever been; and, however shrewdly
he might guess at Stephen's guesses, he said nothing,
and Stephen asked nothing on the subject.

As to Hester, he was told that she was well, though
often moody and excitable, that she seemed already to
have tired of the lessons and occupations she had taken
up with such prodigious energy at the beginning of her
stay, and that she had made violent friends with a young
teacher from the École Normale, a refined, intelligent
woman, in every way fit to be her companion, with whom
on holidays she sometimes made long excursions out of
Paris.

But to Meynell, poor Alice Puttenham poured out all
the bitterness of her heart:

"It seems to me that the little hold I had over her, and
the small affection she had for me when we arrived here,
are both now less than they were.   During the last week

especially (the letter was dated the fourteenth of January) I have been at my wits' end how to amuse or please her. She resents being watched and managed more than ever. One feels there is a tumult in her soul to which we have no access. Her teachers complain of her temper and her caprice. And yet she dazzles and fascinates as much as ever. I suspect she doesn't sleep — she has a worn look quite unnatural at her age — but it makes her furious to be asked. Sometimes, indeed, she seems to melt toward me; the sombre look passes away, and she is melancholy and soft, with tears in her eyes now and then, which I dare not notice.

"Oh, my dear friend, I am grateful for all you tell me of the changed situation at Markborough. But after all the thing is done — there can be no undoing it. The lies mingled with the truth have been put down. Perhaps people are ready now to let the truth itself slip back with the lies into the darkness. But how can we — Edith and I — and Hester — ever live the old life again? The old shelter, the old peace, are gone. We are wanderers and pilgrims henceforward!

"As far as I know, Hester is still in complete ignorance of all that has happened. I have told her that Edith finds Tours so economical that she prefers to stay abroad for a couple of years, and to let the Upcote house. And I have said also that when she herself is tired of Paris, I am ready to take her to Germany, and then to Italy. She laughed, as though I had said something ridiculous! One never knows her real mind. But at least I see no sign of any suspicion in her; and I am sure that she has seen no English newspaper that could have given her a clue. As to Philip Meryon, as I have told you before, I often feel a vague uneasiness; but watch as I will, I can find nothing to justify it. Oh! Richard, my heart

is broken for her. A little love from her, and the whole
world would change for me. But even what I once possessed these last few months seem to have taken from me!"

"The thing is done! — there can be no undoing it."
That was the sore burden of all Meynell's thoughts,
awakening in him, at times, the "bitter craving to
strike heavy blows" at he knew not what. What, indeed, could ever undo the indecency, the cruelty, the ugly
revelations of these three months? The grossness of
the common public, the weakness of friends, the solemn
follies to which men are driven by hate or bigotry: these
things might well have roused the angry laughter that
lives in all quick and honest souls. But the satiric mood,
when it appeared, soon vanished. He remembered the
saying of Meredith concerning the spectacle of Bossuet
over the dead body of Molière—"at which the dark
angels may, but men do not, laugh."

This bitterness might have festered within him, but for
the blessedness of Mary Elsmere's letters. She had seen
the apology; she knew nothing of its causes. But she
betrayed a joy that was almost too proud to know itself
as joy; since what doubt could there ever have been but
that right and nobleness would prevail? Catharine wrote
the warmest and kindest of letters. But Mary's every
word was balm, just because she knew nothing, and
wrote out of the fulness of her mere faith in him, ready
to let her trust take any shape he would. And though
she knew nothing, she seemed by some divine instinct to

understand also the pain that overshadowed the triumph; to be ready to sit silent with him before the irreparable. Day by day, as he read these letters, his heart burned within him; and Rose noted the growing restlessness. But he had heavy arrears of parish business upon him, of correspondence, of literary work. He struggled on, the powers of mind and body flagging, till one night, when he had been nearly a week at Maudeley, Rose came to him one evening, and said with a smile that had in it just a touch of sweet mockery —

"My dear friend, you are doing no good here at all! Go and see Mary!"

He turned upon her, amazed.

"She has not sent for me."

Rose laughed out.

"Did you expect her to be as modern as that?"

He murmured —

"I have been waiting for a word."

"What right had you to wait? Go and get it out of her! Where will you stay?"

He gasped.

"There is the farm at the head of the valley."

"Telegraph to-night."

He thought a little — the colour flooding into his face. And then he quietly went to Rose's writing-table, and wrote his telegram.

CHAPTER XXI

B UT before he took the midday train from Markborough to the North, on the following day, Meynell spent half an hour with his Bishop in the
episcopal library.

It was a strange meeting. When Bishop Craye first
caught sight of the entering figure, he hurried forward,
and as the door closed upon the footman, he seized
Meynell's hand in both his own.

"I see what you have gone through," he said, with
emotion; "and you would not let me help you!"

Meynell smiled faintly.

"I knew you wished to help me— but ——"

Then his voice dropped, and the Bishop would not
have pressed him for the world. They fell upon the
anonymous letters, a comparatively safe topic, and the
relation of Barron to them. Naturally Meynell gave the
Bishop no hint whatever of the graver matter which had
finally compelled Barron's surrender. He described his
comparison of the Dawes letters with "a document in the
young man's handwriting which I happened to have in
my possession," and the gradual but certain conviction
it had brought about.

"I was extraordinarily blind, however, not to find the
clue earlier."

519

"It is not only you, my dear Meynell, that need regret it!" cried the Bishop. "I hope you have sometimes given a thought to the men on our side compelled to see the fight waged ——"

"With such a weapon? I knew very well that no one under your influence, my lord, would touch it," said Meynell simply.

The Bishop observed him, and with an inner sympathy, one might almost say a profound and affectionate admiration, which contrasted curiously with the public position in which they stood to each other. It was now very generally recognized, and especially in Markborough and its diocese, that Meynell had borne himself with extraordinary dignity and patience under the ordeal through which he had passed. And the Bishop — whose guess had so nearly hit the truth, who had been persuaded that in the whole matter Meynell was but the victim of some trust, some duty, which honour and conscience would not let him betray in order to save himself — the Bishop was but the more poignantly of this opinion now that he had the man before him. The weeks of suffering, the long storm of detraction, had left their mark; and it was not a light one. The high-hearted little Bishop felt himself in some way guilty, obscurely and representatively, if not directly.

Yet, at the same time, when the personal matter dropped away, and they passed, as they soon did, to a perfectly calm discussion of the action in the Court of Arches which was to begin within a week, nothing could

be clearer or more irrevocable than the differences, ecclesiastical and intellectual, which divided these two
men, who in matters of personal feeling were so sensi-
tively responsive the one to the other.

Meynell dwelt on the points of law raised in the pleadings, on the bearing of previous cases — the *Essays and
Reviews* case above all — upon the suit. The antecedents of the counsel employed on both sides, the
idiosyncrasies of the judge, the probable length of the
trial; their talk ranged round these matters, without
ever striking deeper. It was assumed between them that
the expulsion of the Modernist clergy was only a question
of months — possibly weeks. Once indeed Meynell
referred slightly to the agitation in the country, to the
growing snowball of the petition to Parliament, to the
now certain introduction of a Bill "To promote an
amended constitution for the Church of England." The
Bishop's eyebrows went up, his lip twitched. It was the
scorn of a spiritual aristocracy threatened by the popu-
lace.

But in general they talked with extraordinary frankness and mutual good feeling; and they grasped hands
more than cordially at the end. They might have been
two generals, meeting before a battle, under the white
flag

Still the same mild January weather; with unseason-
able shoots putting forth, and forebodings on the part of
all garden-lovers, as fresh and resentful as though such

forebodings, with their fulfilments, were not the natural portion of all English gardeners.

In the Westmoreland dales, the month was rainier than elsewhere, but if possible, milder. Yellow buds were already foolishly breaking on the gorse, and weak primroses, as though afraid to venture, and yet venturing, were to be found in the depths of many woods.

Meynell had slept at Whindale. In the morning a trap conveyed him and his bag to the farmhouse at the head of the valley; and the winter sun had only just scattered the mists from the dale when, stick in hand, he found himself on the road to Mrs. Elsmere's little house, Burwood.

With every step his jaded spirits rose. He was a passionate lover of mountains, with that modern spirit which finds in them man's best refuge from modernness. The damp fragrance of the mossy banks and bare hedges; the racing freshness of the stream, and the little eddies of foam blown from it by the wind; the small gray sheep in the fields; the crags overhead dyed deep in withered heather; the stone farmhouses with their touch of cheerful white on door and window; all the exquisite detail of grass, and twig and stone; and overhead the slowly passing clouds in the wide sweep of the dale — these things to him were spiritual revival, they dressed and prepared him for that great hour to which dimly, yet through all his pulses, he felt he was going.

The little house sent up a straight column of blue smoke into the quiet air. Its upper windows were open; the sun was on its lichened porch, and on the silver stem of the birch tree which rose from the mossy grass beside it.

He did not need to knock. Mary was in the open doorway, her face all light and rose colour; and in the shadows of the passage behind her stood Catharine. When with the touch of Mary's hand still warm in his, Meynell turned to greet her mother, he was seized, even through the quiet emotion which held them all, by an impression of change. Some energy of physical life had faded from the worn nobility of Catharine's face, instead a "grave heavenliness" which disquieted the spectator, beautiful as it was.

But the momentary shock was lost in the quiet warmth of her greeting.

"You are going to take her for a walk?" she asked wistfully, as Mary left them alone in the little sitting-room.

"You allow it?" said Meynell, hardly knowing what he said, and still retaining her hand.

Catharine smiled.

"Mary is her own mistress." Then she added, with a deep, involuntary sigh: "Whatever she says to you, she knows she has her mother's blessing."

Meynell stooped and kissed her hand.

A few minutes later, he and Mary had taken the road along the dale.

Catharine stood under the little porch to look after them. Mingled sweetness and bitterness filled her mind.

She pictured to herself for an instant what it would have been if she had been giving Mary to a Christian pastor of the stamp of her own father, "sound in the faith," a "believer," entering upon what had always seemed to her from her childhood the ideal and exalted life of the Christian ministry. As things were, in a few weeks, Richard Meynell would be an exile and a wanderer, chief among a regiment of banished men, driven out by force from the National Church; without any of the dignity — that dignity which had been her husband's — of voluntary renunciation. And Mary would become his wife only to share in his rebellion, his defiance, and his exile.

She crossed her hands tightly upon her breast as though she were imprinting these sad facts upon her consciousness, learning to face them, to bear them with patience. And yet — in some surprising way — they did not hurt her as sharply as they would once have done. Trembling — almost in terror — she asked herself whether her own faith was weakening. And amid the intensity of aspiration and love with which her mind threw itself on the doubt, she turned back, tottering a little, to her chair by the fire. She was glad to be alone, passionately as she loved her Mary. And as she sat. now following Meynell and Mary in thought along the valley, and now listening vaguely to the murmur of the fire or the stream outside, there came upon her a first gentle premonition — as though a whisper, from far away — of the solitude of death.

Lines from the *Christian Year*, the book on which her girlhood had been nourished, stole into her mind:

> Why should we faint and fear to live alone,
> Since all alone, so Heaven has willed, we die?

Never had sunshine seemed to Meynell so life-giving as this pale wintry warmth. The soft sound of Mary's dress beside him; the eyes she turned upon him when she spoke, so frank and sweet, yet for her lover, so full of mystery; the lines of her young form, compact of health and grace; the sound of her voice, the turn of her head — everything about her filled him with a tumult of feeling not altogether blissful, though joy was uppermost. For now that the great moment was come, now that he trembled on the verge of a happiness he had every reason to think was his, he was a prey to many strange qualms and tremors. In the first place he was suddenly and sorely conscious of his age! Forty-four to her twenty-six! Was it fitting? — was it right? And more than that! Beside her freshness, her springing youth, he realized his own jaded spirit, almost with a sense of guilt. These six months of strenuous battle and leadership, these new responsibilities, and the fierce call which had been made on every gift and power, ending in the dumb, proud struggle, the growing humiliation of the preceding weeks, had left him ripened indeed, magnified indeed, as a personality; but it was as though down the shadowed vista of life he saw his youth, as "Another self," a Doppelgänger, disappearing forever.

While she! — before *her* were all the years of glamour, of happy instinctive action, when a man or woman is worth just what they dream, when dream and act flow together. Could he give her anything worth her having in exchange for this sheer youth of hers? He saw before him a long and dusty struggle; the dust of it choking, often, the purest sources of feeling. Cares about money; cares about health; the certain enmity of many good men; the bitterness that waits on all controversial success or failure: all these there must be — he could not shield her from them.

She, on her part, saw plainly that he was depressed, knew well that he had suffered. As the Bishop had perceived, it was written on his aspect. But her timidity as yet prevented her from taking the initiative with him, as later she would learn to do. She felt for him at this stage partly the woman's love, partly the deep and passionate loyalty of the disciple. And it was possibly this very loyalty in her from which Meynell shrank. He felt toward himself and his rôle, in the struggle to which he was committed, a half despairing, half impatient irony, which saved him from anything like a prophetic pose. Some other fellow would do it so much better! But meanwhile it had to be done.

So that, charged as was the atmosphere between them, it was some time before they found a real freedom of speech. The openings, the gambits, which were to lead them to the very heart of the game, were at first masked and hesitating. They talked a little — perfunctorily —

about the dale and its folk, and Mary fell without difficulty now and then into the broad Westmoreland speech,
which delighted Meynell's ear, and brought the laugh
back to his eyes.   Then, abruptly, he told her that the
campaign of slander was over, and that the battle,
instead of "infinite mess and dislocation," was now to be
a straight and clean one.   He said nothing of Barron;
but he spoke tenderly of the Bishop, and Mary's eyes
swam a little.

   She on her part dared to speak of Alice and Hester.
And very soon it was quietly recognized between these
two that Alice's story was known to Mary; and, for
the first time in his life, Meynell spoke with free emotion
and self-criticism of the task which Neville Flood had laid
upon him.   Had there been in Mary some natural dread
of the moment when she must first hear the full story of
his relation to Alice?   If so, it was soon dispelled.   He
could not have told the story more simply; but its beauty
shone out.   Only, she was startled, even terrified, by
certain glimpses which his talk gave her into his feeling
with regard to Hester.   She saw plainly that the possibility of a catastrophe, in spite of all he could do,
was ever present to him; and she saw also, or thought she
saw, that his conception of his own part in the great
religious campaign was strangely — morbidly — dependent upon the fate of Hester.   If he was able to save her
from herself and from the man who threatened her, well
and good; if not, as he had said to Mary once before,
he was not fit to be any man's leader, and should feel

himself the Jonah of any cause. There was a certain mystical passion in it, the strong superstition of a man in whom a great natural sensitiveness led often and readily to despondency; as though he "asked for a sign."

They passed the noisy little river by the stepping-stones and then climbed a shoulder of fell between Long Whindale and the next valley. Descending a sunny mountainside, they crossed some water meadows, and mounted the hill beyond, to a spot that Mary had marked in her walks. Beside a little tumbling stream and beneath a thicket of holly, lay a flat-topped rock commanding all the spectacle of flood and fell. Mary guided him there; and then stood silent and flushed, conscious that she herself had brought the supreme moment to its birth. The same perception rushed upon Meynell. He looked into her eyes, smiling and masterful, all his hesitations cleared away. . . .

"Sit there, my lady of the fells!"

He led her to the rocky throne, and, wrapped in his old Inverness cloak, he took a place on a lesser stone at her feet. Suddenly, he raised a hand and caught hers. She found herself trembling, and looking down into his upturned face.

"Mary! — Mary darling! — is it mine?"

The question was just whispered, and she whispered her reply. They were alone in a lovely wilderness of fell and stream. Only a shepherd walked with his flock in a field half a mile away, and across the valley a ploughman drove his horses.

At the murmur in his ear, Meynell, this time, put up both hands, and drew her down to him. The touch of her fresh lips was rapture. And yet —

"My rose!" he said, almost with a groan. "What can you make of such an old fellow? I love you — *love* you — but I am not worthy of you!"

"I am the judge of that," she said softly. And looking up he saw the colour in her cheeks fluttering, and two bright tears in her eyes. Timidly she took one hand away from him and began to stroke back the hair from his brow.

"You look so tired!" — she murmured — "as though you had been in trouble. And I wasn't there!"

"You were always there!"

And springing from his lowly seat, he came to the rock beside her, and drew her within the shelter of his cloak, looking down upon her with infinite tenderness.

"You don't know what you're undertaking," he said, his eyes moist, his lips smiling. "I am an old bachelor, and my ways are detestable! Can you ever put up with the pipes and the dogs? I am the untidiest man alive!"

"Will Anne ever let me touch your papers?"

"Goodness! what will Anne say to us! I forgot Anne," he said, laughing. Then, bending over her, "We shall be poor, darling! — and very uncomfortable. Can you really stand it — and me?"

"Shall we have a roof over our heads at all?" asked Mary, but so dizzily happy that she knew but vaguely what she said.

"I have already bespoken a cottage. They are going to make me Editor of the *Modernist*. We shall have bread and butter, dearest, but not much more."

"I have a little," said Mary, shyly.

Meynell looked rather scared.

"Not much, I hope!"

"Enough for gowns! — and — and a little more."

"I prefer to buy my wife's gowns — I will!" said Meynell with energy. "Promise me, darling, to put all your money into a drawer — or a money-box. Then when we want something really amusing — a cathedral — or a yacht — we'll take it out."

So they laughed together, he all the while holding her close crushed against him, and she deafened almost by the warm beating of a man's heart beneath her cheek.

And presently silence came, a silence in which one of the rare ecstasies of life came upon them and snatched them to the third heaven. From the fold of the hill in which they sat, sheltered both by the fell itself, and by the encircling hollies, they overlooked a branching dale, half veiled, and half revealed by sunny cloud. Above the western fells they had just crossed, hung towers and domes of white cumulus, beneath which a pearly sunshine slipped through upon the broad fell-side, making of it one wide sunlit pleasance, dyed in the red and orange of the withered fern, and dotted with black holly and juniper. Round the head of the dale the curtain of cloud hung thicker, save where one superb crag tore it asunder, falling sheer into the green gentleness of the fields. In the silence, all the voices of nature spoke; the rising wind, which flung itself against the hill-slopes at their feet; the insistent flow of the river, descending from the reservoirs far away; and the sharp chatter of the little beck leaping at their side from stone to stone. Passionately, in Meynell's heart the "buried life" awoke, which only love can free from the cavern where it lies, and bring into the full energy of day.

"One goes on talking — preaching — babbling — about love," he said to her; "what else is there to preach about? If love is not the key to life, then there is no key, and no man need preach any more. Only, my Amor has been till now a stern God! He has in his hands! — I know it! — all the noblest rewards and ecstasies of life; but so far, I have seen him wring them out of horror, or pain. The most heavenly things I have ever seen have been the things of suffering. I think of a poor fellow dying in the pit and trying to give me his last message to his wife; of a mother fading out of life, still clasping her babes, with hands twisted almost out of human shape by hard work; or a little lad —" his voice dropped —"only last week! — who saved his worthless brother's life by giving him warning of some escaping trucks, and was crushed himself. 'I couldn't help it, sir!' — *apologizing* to me and the foreman, as we knelt by him! — 'I knew Jim had the drink in him.' In all these visions, Love was divine — but awful! And here! — *here!* — I see his wings outspread upon that mountain-side; he comes clothed, not in agony, but in this golden peace — this beauty — this wild air; he lays your head upon my breast!"

Or again:

"There is a new philosophy which has possessed me for months; the thought of a great man, which seizes upon us dull lesser creatures, and seems to give us, for a time at least, new eyes and ears, as though, like Melampus, we had caught the hidden language of the world! It rests on the notion of the endless creativeness and freedom of life. It is the negation of all fate, all predestination. *Nothing* foreknown, nothing predestined! No *necessity* — no *anangké* — darling! — either in the world process, or the mind of God, that you and I should sit here to-day, heart to heart! It was left for our wills to do, our hearts to conceive, God lending us the world, so to speak, to work on! All our past cutting into — carving out— this present; all our past alive in the present; as all this present shall be alive in the future. There is no 'iron law' for life and 'will, beloved — they create, they are the masters, they are forever new. All the same!" — his tone changed — "I believe firmly that this rock knew from all eternity that you and I should sit here to-day!"

Presently, Mary disengaged herself. Her hat was not what it had been; her hair had escaped its bounds, and must be rigorously put to rights. She sat there flushed and bareheaded, her hands working; while Meynell's eyes devoured her.

"It is January, Richard, and the sun is sinking."

"In your world perhaps, dear, not in mine."

"We must go back to mother."   She laid a hand on his.

"We will go back to mother!" he said, joyously, with a tender emphasis on the word, without moving however. "Mary! — next to you I love your mother!"

Mary's sweet face darkened a little; she buried it in her hands.   Meynell drew them tenderly away.

"All that affection can do to soften the differences between us, shall be done," he said, with his whole heart. "I believe too that the sense of them will grow less and less."

Mary made no reply, except by the slight pressure of her fingers on his.   She sat in an absorbed sadness, thinking of her mother's life, and the conflict which had always haunted and scorched it, between love and religion; first in the case of her husband, and then in that of her daughter.   "But oh! how could I — how could I help it?" was the cry of Mary's own conscience and personality.

She turned with painful eagerness to Meynell.   "How did you think her? — how does she strike you?"

"Physically?"   He chose his words.   "She is so beautiful!   But — sometimes — I think she looks frail."

The tears sprang to Mary's eyes.   She quickly threw herself upon his misgiving, and tried to argue it away, both in herself and him.   She dwelt upon her mother's improvement in sleep and appetite, her cheerfulness, her increased power of walking; she was insistent, almost resentful, her white brow furrowed with pain, even while her hand lay warm in Meynell's. He must needs comfort her; must needs disavow his own impression. After all, what value had such an impression beside the judgment of her daily and hourly watchfulness? — the favourable opinion too, so she insisted, of their local doctor.

As they walked home, he startled her by saying that he should only have three days in the valley.

"Three days!" She looked her remonstrance.

"You know the trial begins next week?"

Yes, she knew, but had understood that the pleadings were all ready, and that a North-Western train would take him to London in six hours.

"I have to preach at St. Hilda's, Westminster," he said, with a shrug, and a look of distaste.

Mary asked questions, and discovered that the sermon would no doubt be made the opportunity for something like a demonstration; and that he shrank from the thought of it.

She perceived, indeed, a certain general flagging of the merely combative forces in him, not without dismay. Such moments of recoil are natural to such men — half saints, half organizers. The immediate effect of her perception of it was to call out something heroic and passionate in herself. She was very sweet, and very young; there were eighteen years between them; and yet in these very first hours of their engagement, he felt her to be not only rest, but inspiration; not only sympathy, but strength.

When they neared the little ivy-covered house, on their return home, Mary broke from him. Her step on the gravel was heard by Catharine. She came quickly to the door and stood awaiting them. Mary ran forward and threw herself into the tender arms that drew her into the shadows of the passage.

"Oh, mother! mother! — he does love you!" she said, with a rush of tears.

If Catharine's eyes also were dim, she only answered with a tender mockery.

"Don't pretend that was all he said to you in these two hours!"

And still holding Mary, she turned, smiling, to Meynell, and let him claim from her, for the first time, a son's greeting.

For three blissful days, did Meynell pitch his tent in Long Whindale. Though the weather broke, and the familiar rain shrouded the fells, he and Mary walked incessantly among them, exploring those first hours of love, when every tone and touch is charged, for lovers, with the whole meaning of the world. And in the evenings he sat between the two women in the little cottage room, reading aloud Catharine's favourite poets; or in the familiar talk, now gay now grave, of their new intimacy, disclosing himself ever more fully, and rooting himself ever more firmly in their hearts. His sudden alarm as to Catharine's health passed away, and Mary's new terror with it. Scarcely a word was said of the troubles ahead. But it was understood that

Mary would be in London to hear him preach at St. Hilda's.

On the last day of Meynell's visit, Catharine, greatly to her surprise, received a letter from Hester Fox-Wilton.

It contained a breathless account of an evening spent in seeing Œdipus Rex played by Mounet Sully at the Comédie Française. In this half-sophisticated girl, the famous performance, traditional now through two generations of playgoers, had clearly produced an emotion whereof the expression in her letter greatly disquieted Catharine Elsmere. She felt too — a little grimly — the humour of its address to herself.

"Tell me how to answer it, please," she said, handing it to Meynell with a twitching lip. "It is a language I don't understand! And why did they take her to such a play?"

Meynell shared her disquiet. For the Greek conception of a remorseless fate, as it is forever shaped and embodied in the tale of Œdipus, had led Hester apparently to a good deal of subsequent browsing in the literature—the magazine articles at any rate —of French determinism; and she rattled through some of her discoveries in this reckless letter:

"You talked to me so nicely, dear Mrs. Elsmere, that last evening at Upcote. I know you want me — you want everybody — 'to be good!'

"But 'being good' has nothing to do with us.

"How can it? — such creatures, such puppets as we are!

"Poor wretch, Œdipus! He never meant any one any harm — did he? — and yet — you see!

"'*Apollo, friends, Apollo it was, that brought all these my woes, my sore, sore woes! — to pass.*'

"Dear Mrs. Elsmere! — you can't think what a good doctrine it is after all — how it steadies one! What chance have we against these blundering gods?

"Nothing one can do makes any difference. It is, really very consoling if you come to think of it; and it's no sort of good being angry with Apollo!"

"Part nonsense, part bravado," said Catharine, raising clear eyes, with half a smile in them, to Meynell. "But it makes one anxious."

His puckered brow showed his assent.

"As soon as the trial is over — within a fortnight certainly — I shall run over to see them."

Meynell and Mary travelled to town together, and Mary was duly deposited for a few days with some Kensington cousins.

On the night of their arrival — a Saturday — Meynell, not without some hesitation, made an appearance at the Reformers' Club, which had been recently organized as a London centre for the Movement, in Albemarle Street.

It was no sooner known that he was in the building than a flutter ran through the well-filled rooms. That very morning an article in the *Modernist* signed R. M. had sounded a note of war, so free, lofty, and determined, that men were proud to be on Meynell's side in such a battle. On the following Tuesday the Arches Trial was to begin. Meynell was to defend himself; and the attention of the country would be fixed upon the duel between him and the great orthodox counsel, Sir Wilfrid Marsh.

Men gathered quickly round him. Most of the six clergy who, with him, had launched the first Modernist Manifesto, were present, in expectation of the sermon on the morrow, and the trial of the following week. Chesham and Darwen, his co-defendants in the Arches suit, with whom he had been in constant correspondence throughout the winter, came to discuss a few last points and understandings; Treherne, the dear old scholar in whose house they had met to draw up the Manifesto, under the shadow of the Cathedral, pressed his hand and launched a Latin quotation; Rollin, fat, untidy and talkative as ever, could not refrain from "interviewing" Meynell, for a weekly paper; while Derrick, the Socialist and poet, talked to him in a low voice and with eyes that blazed, of certain "brotherhoods" that had been spreading the Modernist faith, and Modernist Sacraments among the slums of a great midland town.

And in the voices that spoke to him, and the eyes that met his, Meynell could not but realize a wide and warm sympathy, an eagerness to make amends — sometimes a half confessed compunction for a passing doubt.

He stood among them, haggard and worn, but steeped in a content and gratitude that had more sources than

they knew. And under the kindling of their faith and
their affection, his own hesitations passed away; his will
steeled itself to the tasks before him.

The following day will be long remembered in the
annals of the Movement. The famous church, crowded
in every part with an audience representing science, literature, politics, the best of English thought and English
social endeavour, was but the outward and visible sign
of things inward and spiritual.

"*Can these dry bones live?*"

As Meynell gave out the text, there were many who
remembered the picture of Oxford hanging in Newman's
study at Edgbaston, and those same words written
below it.

"*Can these dry bones live?*" — So Newman had asked in
despair, of his beloved University, and of English religion,
in the early years after he had deserted Anglicanism for
Rome. And now, more than half a century afterward,
the leader of a later religious movement asked the same
question on the eve of another contest which would either
regenerate or destroy the English Church. The impulse
given by Newman and the Tractarians had spent itself,
though not without enormous and permanent results
within the life of the nation; and now it was the turn of
that Liberal reaction and recoil which had effaced Newman's work in Oxford, yet had been itself wandering for
years without a spiritual home. During those years
it had found its way through innumerable channels of

the national life as a fertilizing and redeeming force.   It had transformed education, law, science and history. Yet its own soul had hungered.   And now, thanks to that inner necessity which governs the spiritual progress of men, the great Liberal Movement, enriched with a thousand conquests, was sweeping back into the spiritual field; demanding its just share in the National Church; and laying its treasures at the feet of a Christ, unveiled, illuminated, by its own labour, by the concentrated and passionate effort of a century of human intelligence.

Starting from this conception — the full citizen-right within the Church of both Liberal and High Churchman — the first part of Meynell's sermon became a moving appeal for religious freedom; freedom of development and "variation," within organized Christianity itself. Simpler Creeds, modernized tests, alternative forms, a "unity of the spirit in the bond of peace," — with these ideas the Modernist preacher built up the vision of a Reformed Church, co-extensive with the nation, resting on a democratic government, yet tenderly jealous of its ancient ceremonies, so long as each man might inter-pret them "as he was able," and they were no longer made a source of tyranny and exclusion.

Then, from the orthodox opponent in whose eyes the Modernist faith was a mere beggarly remnant, Meynell turned to the sceptic for whom it was only a modified superstition.   An eloquent prelude, dealing with the pre-conceptions, the modern philosophy and psychology which lie at the root of religious thought to-day — and the rest of the sermon flowed on into what all Christian eloquence must ultimately be, the simple "preaching of Christ."

Amid the hush of the crowded church Meynell preached the Christ of our day — just as Paul of Tarsus preached the Christ of a Hellenized Judaism to the earliest converts; as St. Francis, in the Umbrian hills preached the Lord of Poverty and Love; as the Methodist preachers among the villages of the eighteenth century preached the democratic individualism of the New Testament to the English nascent democracy.

In each case the form of the preaching depended on the knowledge and the thought-world of the preacher. So with Meynell's Christ.

Not the phantom of a Hellenistic metaphysic; not the Redeemer and Judge of a misunderstood Judaism; not the mere ethical prophet of a German professorial theology; but the King of a spiritual kingdom, receiving allegiance, and asking love, from the free consciences of men; repeating forever in the ears of those in whom a Divine influence has prepared the way, the melting and constraining message: "This do in remembrance of me."

"'Of me — and of all the just, all the righteous, all the innocent, of all the ages, in me — pleading through me — symbolized in me! Are you for Man — or for the Beast that lurks in man? Are you for Chastity — or Lust? Are you for Cruelty — or Love? Are you for Foulness or Beauty? Choose! — choose this day.'

"The Christ who thus speaks to you and me, my

brethren, is no longer a man made God, a God made man.
Those categories of thought, for us, are past. But
neither is he merely the crucified Galilean, the Messianic
prophet of the first century. For by a mysterious and
unique destiny — unique at least in degree — that life
and death have become Spirit and Idea. The Power
behind the veil, the Spirit from whom issues the world,
has made of them a lyre, enchanted and immortal,
through which He breathes His music into men. The
setting of the melody varies with the generations, but
the melody remains. And as we listen to it to-day, expressed through the harmonies of that thought which is
ourselves — blood of our blood, life of our life — we are
listening now, listening always, as the disciples listened
in Nazareth, to the God within us, the very God who was
'in Christ reconciling the world unto Himself.'

"Of that God, all life is in some sense, the sacramental
expression. But in the course of ages some sacraments
and symbols of the divine are approved and verified
beyond others — immeasurably beyond others. This is
what has happened — and so far as we can see by the
special will and purpose of God — with the death-unto-
life — with the Cross of Christ. . . .

"The symbol of the Cross is concerned with our personal and profoundest being. But the symbol of the
Kingdom is social, collective — the power of every
reformer, every servant of men. . . .

"Many thinkers," said the preacher, in his concluding
passage, while all eyes were fixed on the head sprinkled

with gray, and the strong humanity of the face — "many
men, in all ages and civilizations have dreamed of a City
of God, a Kingdom of Righteousness, an Ideal State, and
a Divine Ruler. Jesus alone has made of that dream,
history; has forced it upon, and stamped it into history.
The Messianic dream of Judaism — though wrought
of nobler tissue — it's not unlike similar dreams in other
religions; but in this it is unique, that it gave Jesus of
Nazareth his opportunity, and that from it has sprung
the Christian Church. Jesus accepted it with the heart
of a child; he lived in it; he died for it; and by means of it,
his spiritual genius, his faithfulness unto death transformed a world. He died indeed, overwhelmed; with the
pathetic cry of utter defeat upon his lips. And the
leading races of mankind have knelt ever since to the
mighty spirit who dared not only to conceive and found
the Kingdom of God, but to think of himself as its Spiritual King — by sheer divine right of service, of suffering,
and of death! Only through tribulation and woe —
through the *peirasmos* or sore trial of the world — according to Messianic belief, could the Kingdom be
realized, and Messiah revealed. It was the marvellous
conception of Jesus, inspired by the ancient poetry and
prophecy of his nation, that he might, as the Suffering
Servant, concentrate in himself the suffering due from
his race, and from the world, and by his death bring
about — violently, "by force" — the outpouring of the
Spirit, the Resurrection, and the dawn of the heavenly
Kingdom. He went up to Jerusalem to die; he provoked

his death; he died.   And from the Resurrection visions which followed naturally on such a life and death, inspired by such conceptions, and breathing them with such power into the souls of other men, arose the Christian Church.

"The Parousia for which the Lord had looked, delayed. It delays still.   The scope and details of the Messianic dream itself mean nothing to us any more.

"But its spirit is immortal.   The vision of a kingdom of Heaven — a polity of the soul, within, or superseding the earthly polity — once interfused with man's thought and life, has proved to be imperishable, a thing that cannot die.

"Only it must be realized afresh from age to age; embodied afresh in the conceptions and the language of successive generations.

"And these developing embodiments and epiphanies of the kingdom can only be brought into being by the method of Christ — that is to say, by '*violence*.'

"Again and again has the kingdom 'suffered violence' — has been brought fragmentarily into the world '*by force*' — by the only irresistible force — that of suffering, of love, of self-renouncing faith.

"To that 'force' we, as religious Reformers, appeal.

"The parables of the mustard seed and the leaven do not express the whole thought of Christ.   When the work of preparation is over, still men must brace themselves, as their Master did, to the last stroke of 'violence' — to a final effort of resolute, and, if need be, revolutionary action — to the 'violence' that brings ideas to birth and shapes them into deeds.

"It was to 'violence' of this sacred sort that the Christian Church owed its beginning; and it is this same 'violence' that must, as the generations rise and fall, constantly maintain it among men. To cut away the old at need and graft in the new, requires the high courage and the resolute hand of faith. Only so can the Christian Life renew itself; only so can efficacy and movement return to powers exhausted or degenerate; only so 'can these dry bones live!'"

Amid the throng as it moved outward into the bustle of Westminster, Flaxman found himself rubbing shoulders with Edward Norham. Norham walked with his eyes on the ground, smiling to himself.

"A little persecution!" he said, rubbing his hands, as he looked up — "and how it would go!"

"Well — the persecution begins this week — in the Court of Arches."

"Persecution — nonsense! You mean 'propaganda.' I understand Meynell's defence will proceed on totally new lines. He means to argue each point on its merits?"

"Yes. The Voysey judgment gave him his cue. You will remember, Voysey was attacked by the Lord Chancellor of the day — old Lord Hatherley — as a 'private clergyman,' who 'of his own mere will, not founding himself upon any critical inquiry, but simply upon his own taste and judgment' maintained certain heresies.

Now Meynell, I imagine, will give his judges enough of 'critical inquiry' before they have done with him!"

Norham shrugged his shoulders.

"All very well! Why did he sign the Articles?"

"He signed them at four-and-twenty!" said Flaxman hotly. "Will you maintain that a system which insists upon a man's beliefs at forty-four being identical with his beliefs at twenty-four is not condemned *ipso facto!*"

"Oh I know what you say! — I know what you say!" cried Norham good-humouredly. "We shall all be saying it in Parliament presently — Good heavens! Well, I shall look into the court to-morrow, if I can possibly find an hour, and hear Meynell fire away."

"As Home Secretary, you may get in!" — laughed Flaxman — "on no other terms. There isn't a seat to be had — there hasn't been for weeks."

The trial came on. The three suits from the Markborough diocese took precedence, and were to be followed by half a dozen others — test cases — from different parts of England. But on the Markborough suits everything turned. The Modernist defendants everywhere had practically resolved on the same line of defence; on the same appeal from the mind of the sixteenth century to the mind of the twentieth; from creeds and formularies to history; from a dying to a living Church.

The chief counsel for the promoters, Sir Wilfrid Marsh, made a calm, almost a conciliatory opening. He was a man of middle height, with a large, clean-shaven face, a domed head and smooth straight hair, still jetty black.

He wore a look of quiet assurance and was clearly a man of all the virtues; possessing a portly wife and a tribe of daughters.

His speech was marked in all its earlier sections by a studied liberality and moderation. "I am not going to appeal, sir, for that judgment in the promoters' favour which I confidently claim, on any bigoted or obscurantist lines. The Church of England is a learned Church; she is also a Church of wide liberties."

No slavish submission to the letter of the Articles on the Liturgy was now demanded of any man. Subscription had been relaxed; the final judgment in the *Essays and Reviews* case had given a latitude in the interpretation of Scripture, of which, as many recent books showed, the clergy — "I refer now to men of unquestioned orthodoxy" — had taken reasonable advantage; prayer-book revision "within the limits of the faith," if constantly retarded by the divisions of the faithful, was still probable; both High Churchmen and Broad Churchmen — here an aside dropped out, "so far as Broad Churchmen still exist!" — are necessary to the Church.

But there are limits. "Critical inquiry, sir, if you will — reasonable liberty, within the limits of our formularies and a man's ordination vow — by all means!

"But certain things are *vital!* With certain fundamental beliefs let no one suppose that either the bishops, or convocation, or these Church courts, or Parliament, or what the defendants are pleased to call the nation " [one must imagine the fine gesture of a sweep-

ing hand] "can meddle." The *animus imponentis* is not
that of the Edwardian or Elizabethan legislation, it is
not that of the Bishops! it is that of the Christian
Church itself! — handing down the *depositum fidei* from
the earliest to the latest times.

" *The Creeds, sir, are vital!*   Put aside Homilies, Articles,
the judgments and precedents of the Church Courts — all
these are, in this struggle, beside the mark.   *Concentrate on the Creeds!*   Let us examine what the defendants
in these suits have made of the Creeds of Christendom."

The evidence was plain.   Regarded as historical statement, the defendants had dealt drastically and destruc-
tively with the Creeds of Christendom; no less than
with the authority of "Scripture," understanding "authority" in any technical sense.

It was indeed the chief Modernist contention, as the
orator showed, that formal creeds were mere "land-
marks in the Church's life," crystallizations of thought,
that were no sooner formed than they became subject
to the play, both dissolvent and regenerating, of the
Christian consciousness.

"And so you come to that inconceivable entity, a
Church without a creed — a mere chaos of private opinion,
where each man is a law unto himself."

On this theme, Sir Wilfrid — who was a man of singularly strong private opinions, of all kinds and on all
subjects — spoke for a whole day; from the rising almost
to the going down of the sun.

At the end of it Canon Dornal and a barrister friend, a

devout Churchman, walked back toward the Temple along the Embankment.

The walk was very silent, until midway the barrister said abruptly —

"Is it any plainer to you now, than when Sir Wilfrid began, what authority — if any — there is in the English Church; or what limits — if any — there are to private judgment within it?"

Dornal hesitated.

"My answer, of course, is Sir Wilfrid's. We have the Creeds."

They walked on in silence a moment. Then the first speaker said:

"A generation ago would you not have said — what also Sir Wilfrid carefully avoided saying — 'We have the Scriptures.'"

"Perhaps," said Dornal despondently.

"And as to the Creeds," the other resumed, after another pause — "Do you think that one per cent. of the Christians that you and I know believe in the Descent into Hell, or the Resurrection of the Body?"

Dornal made no reply.

Cyril Fenton also walked home with a young priest just ordained. Both were extremely dissatisfied with the later portions of Sir Wilfrid's speech, which had seemed to them tainted in several passages with Erastian complacency toward the State. Parliament especially, and a possible intervention of Parliament, ought never to have been so much as mentioned — even for denunciation — in an ecclesiastical court.

"*Parliament!*" cried Fenton, coming to a sudden stop beside the water in St. James' Park, his eyes afire, "What is Parliament but the lay synod of the Church of England!"

During the three days of Sir Wilfrid's speech, Meynell took many notes, and he became perforce very familiar with some of the nearer faces in the audience day after day; with the Bishop of S ——, lank and long-jawed, with reddish hair turning to gray, a deprecating manner in society, but in the pulpit a second Warburton for truculence and fire; the Bishop of D ——, beloved, ugly, short-sighted, the purest and humblest soul alive; learned, mystical, poetical, in much sympathy with the Modernists, yet deterred by the dread of civil war within the Church, a master of the Old Latin Versions, and too apt to address schoolgirls on the charms of textual criticism; the Bishop of F ——, courtly, peevish and distrusted; the Dean of Markborough, with the green shade over his eyes, and fretful complaint on his lips of the "infection" generated by every Modernist incumbent; and near him, Professor Vetch, with yet another divinity professor beside him, a young man, short and slight, with roving, grasshopper eyes.

The temperature of Sir Wilfrid's address rose day by day, and the case for the prosecution closed thunderously in a fierce onslaught on the ethics of the Modernist position, and on the personal honesty and veracity of

each and every Modernist holding office in the Anglican
Church, claiming sentences of immediate deprivation
against the defendants, of their vicarages and incum-
bencies, and of all profits and benefits derived therefrom
"unless within a week from this day they (the defendants)
should expressly and unreservedly retract the several
errors in which they have so offended."

The court broke up in a clamour of excitement and
discussion, with crowds of country parishioners standing
outside to greet the three incriminated priests as they
came out.

The following morning Meynell rose. And for one
brilliant week, his defence of the Modernist position held
the attention of England.

On the fourth or fifth day of his speech, the white-
haired Bishop of Dunchester, against whom proceedings
had just been taken in the Archbishop's Court, said to
his son:

"Herbert, just before I was born there were two
great religious leaders in England — Newman and
Arnold of Rugby. Arnold died prematurely, at the
height of bodily and spiritual vigour; Newman lived to
the age of eighty-nine, and to be a Cardinal of the Roman
Church. His Anglican influence, continued, modified, distributed by the High Church movement, has lasted till
now. To-day we have been listening again, as it were, to
the voice of Arnold, the great leader whom the Liberals
lost in '42. Arnold was a devoutly orthodox believer,
snatched from life in the very birth-hour of that New

Learning of which we claim to be the children. But a church of free men, coextensive with the nation, gathering into one fold every English man, woman and child, that was Arnold's dream, just as it is Meynell's. . . . And yet though the voice, the large heart, the fearless mind, and the broad sympathies were Arnold's, some of the governing ideas were Newman's. As I listened, I seemed" — the old man's look glowed suddenly — "to see the two great leaders, the two foes of a century ago, standing side by side, twin brethren in a new battle, growing out of the old, with a great mingled host behind them."

Each day the court was crowded, and though Meynell seemed to be addressing his judges, he was in truth speaking quite as consciously to a sweet woman's face in a far corner of the crowded hall. Mary went into the long wrestle with him, as it were, and lived through every moment of it at his side. Then in the evening there were half hours of utter silence, when he would sit with her hands in his, just gathering strength for the morrow.

Six days of Meynell's speech were over. On the seventh the Court opened amid the buzz of excitement and alarm. The chief defendant in the suit was not present, and had sent — so counsel whispered to each other — a hurried note to the judge to the effect that he should be absent through the whole remainder of the trial owing to "urgent private business."

In a few more hours it was known that Meynell had left England, and men on both sides looked at each other in dismay.

Meanwhile Mary had forwarded to her mother a note written late at night, in anguish of soul:

"Alice wires to me to-night that Hester has disappeared — without the smallest trace. But she believes she is with Meryon. I go to Paris to-night — Oh, my own, pray that I may find her! — R. M."

CHAPTER XXII

THE mildness of the winter had passed away.

A bleak February afternoon lay heavy on Long Whindale. A strong and bitter wind from the north blew down the valley with occasional spits and snatches of snow, not enough as yet to whiten the heights, but prophesying a wild night and a heavy fall. The blasts in the desolate upper reach of the dale were so fierce that a shepherd on the path leading over the pass to Marly Head could scarcely hold himself upright against them. Tempestuous sounds filled all the upper and the lower air. From the high ridges came deep reverberating notes, a roaring in the wind; while the trees along the stream sent forth a shriller voice, as they whistled and creaked and tossed in the eddying gusts. Cold gray clouds were beating from the north, hanging now over the cliffs on the western side, now over the bare screes and steep slopes of the northern and eastern walls. Gray or inky black, the sharp edges of the rocks cut into the gloomy sky; while on the floor of the valley, blanched grass and winding stream seemed alike to fly scourged before the persecuting wind.

A trap — Westmoreland calls it a car — a kind of box on wheels, was approaching the head of the dale from the

direction of Whinborough.   It stopped at the foot of the
steep and narrow lane leading to Burwood, and a young
lady got out.

"You're sure that's Burwood?" she said, pointing
to the house partially visible at the end of the lane.

The driver answered in the affirmative.

"Where Mrs. Elsmere lives?"

"Aye, for sure."   The man as he spoke looked curiously
at the lady he had brought from Whinborough station.
She was quite a young girl he guessed, and a handsome
one.   But there seemed to be something queer about her.
She looked so tumbled and tired.

Hester Fox-Wilton took out her purse, and paid him
with an uncertain hand, one or more of the shillings falling on the road, where the driver and she groped for them.
Then she raised the small bag she had brought with her
in the car, and turned away.

"Good day to yer, miss," said the man as he mounted
the box.   She made no reply.   After he had turned his
horse and started on the return journey to Whinborough,
he looked back once or twice.   But the high walls of
the lane hid the lady from him.

Hester, however, did not go very far up the lane.   She
sank down very soon on a jutting stone beneath the left-
hand wall, with her bag beside her, and sat there looking
at the little house.   It was a pleasant, home-like place,
even on this bitter afternoon.   In one of the windows
was a glow of firelight; white muslin curtains everywhere
gave it a dainty, refined look; and it stood picturesquely

within the shelter of its trees, and of the yew hedge which encircled the garden.

Yet Hester shivered as she looked at it. She was very imperfectly clothed for such an afternoon, in a serge jacket and skirt supplemented by a small fur collarette, which she drew closer round her neck from time to time, as though in a vain effort to get warm. But she was not conscious of doing so, nor of the cold as cold. All her bodily sensations were miserable and uncomfortable. But she was only actively aware of the thoughts racing through her mind.

There they were, within a stone's throw of her — Mary and Mrs. Elsmere — in the warm, cosy little house, without an idea that she, Hester, the wretched, disgraced Hester, was sitting in the lane so close to them. And yet they were perhaps thinking of her — they must have often thought about her in the last fortnight. Mrs. Elsmere must of course have been sorry. Good people were always sorry when such things happened. And Mary? — who was eight years older — *older!* than this girl of eighteen who sat there, sickened by life, conscious of a dead wall of catastrophe drawn between her and the future.

Should she go to them? Should she open their door and say — "Here I am! — Horrible things have happened. No decent person will ever know me or speak to me again. But you said — you'd help me — if I wanted it. Perhaps it was a lie — like all the rest?"

Then as the reddened eyelids fell with sheer fatigue,

there rose on the inward sight the vision of Catharine Elsmere's face — its purity, its calm, its motherliness. For a moment it drew, it touched, it gave courage. And then the terrrible sense of things irreparable, grim matters of fact not to be dreamed or thought away, rushed in and swept the clinging, shipwrecked creature from the foothold she had almost reached.

She rose hastily.

"I can't! They don't want to see me — they've done with me. Or perhaps they'll cry — they'll pray with me, and I can't stand that! Why did I ever come? Where on earth shall I go?"

And she looked round her in petulant despair, angry with herself for having done this foolish thing, angry with the loneliness and barrenness of the valley, where no inn opened doors of shelter for such as she, angry with the advancing gloom, and with the bitter wind that teased and stung her.

A little way up the lane she saw a small gate that led into the Elsmeres' garden. She took her bag, and opening the gate, she placed it inside. Then she ran down the lane, drawing her fur round her, and shivering with cold.

"I'll think a bit —" she said to herself — "I'll think what to say. Perhaps I'll come back soon."

When she reached the main road again, she looked uncertainly to right and left. Which way? The thought of the long dreary road back to Whinborough repelled her. She turned toward the head of the valley. Perhaps she might find a house which would take her in. The driver had said there was a farm which let lodgings in the summer. She had money — some pounds at any rate; that was all right. And she was not hungry. She had arrived at a junction station five miles from Whinborough by a night train. At six o'clock in the morning she had found herself turned out of the express, with no train to take her on to Whinborough. But there was a station hotel, and she had engaged a room and ordered a fire. There she had thrown herself down without undressing on the bed, and had slept heavily for four or five hours. Then she had had some breakfast, and had taken a midday train to Whinborough, and a trap to Long Whindale.

She had travelled straight from Nice without stopping. She would not let herself think now as she hurried along the lonely road what it was she had fled from, what it was that had befallen. The slightest glimpse into this past made her begin to sob; she put it away from her with all her strength. But she had had, of course, to decide where she should go, with whom she should take refuge.

Not with Uncle Richard, whom she had deceived and defied. Not with "Aunt Alice." No sooner did the vision of that delicate withered face, that slender form come before her, than it brought with it terrible fancies. Her conduct had probably killed "Aunt Alice." She did not want to think about her.

But Mrs. Elsmere knew all about bad men, and girls

who got into trouble. She, Hester, knew, from a few things she had heard people say — things that no one supposed she had heard — that Mrs. Elsmere had given years of her life, and sacrificed her health, to "rescue" work. The rescue of girls from such men as Philip? How could they be rescued? — when ——

All that was nonsense. But the face, the eyes — the shining, loving eyes, the motherly arms — yes, those, Hester confessed to herself, she had thirsted for. They had brought her all the way from Nice to this northern valley — this bleak, forbidding country. She shivered again from head to foot, as she made her way painfully against the wind.

Yet now she was flying even from Catharine Elsmere; even from those tender eyes that haunted her.

The road turned toward a bridge, and on the other side of the bridge degenerated into a rough and stony bridle path, giving access to two gray farms beneath the western fell. On the near side of the bridge the road became a cart-track leading to the far end of the dale.

Hester paused irresolute on the bridge, and looked back toward Burwood. A light appeared in what was no doubt the sitting-room window. A lamp perhaps that, in view of the premature darkening of the afternoon by the heavy storm-clouds from the north, a servant had just brought in. Hester watched it in a kind of panic, foreseeing the moment when the curtains would be drawn and the light shut out from her. She thought of the little room within, the warm firelight, Mary with her beautiful hair — and Mrs. Elsmere. They were perhaps working and reading — as though that were all there were to do and think about in the world! No, no! after all they couldn't be very peaceful — or very cheerful. Mary was engaged to Uncle Richard now; and Uncle Richard must be pretty miserable.

The exhausted girl nearly turned back toward that light. Then a hand came quietly and shut it out. The curtains were drawn. Nothing now to be seen of the little house but its dim outlines in the oncoming twilight, the smoke blown about its roof, and a faint gleam from a side-window, perhaps the kitchen.

Suddenly, a thought, a wild, attacking thought, leapt out upon her, and held her there motionless, in the winding, wintry lane.

When had she sent that telegram to Upcote? If she could only remember! The events of the preceding forty-eight hours seemed to be all confused in one mad flux of misery. Was it *possible* that they too could be here — Uncle Richard, and "Aunt Alice?" She had said something about Mrs. Elsmere in her telegram — she could not recollect what. That had been meant to comfort them, and yet to keep them away, to make them leave her to her own plans. But supposing, instead, its effect had been to bring them here at once, in pursuit of her?

She hurried forward, sobbing dry sobs of terror as though she already heard their steps behind her. What was she afraid of? Simply their love! — simply their sorrow! She had broken their hearts; and what could she say to them?

The recollection of all her cruelty to "Aunt Alice" in Paris — her neglect, her scorn, her secret, unjust anger with those who had kept from her the facts of her birth — seemed to rise up between her and all ideas of hope and help. Oh, of course they would be kind to her! — they would forgive her — but — but she couldn't bear it! Impatience with the very scene of wailing and forgiveness she foresaw, as of something utterly futile and vain, swept through the quivering nerves.

"And it can never be undone!" she said to herself roughly, as though she were throwing the words in some one's face. "It can never, *never* be undone! What's the good of talking?"

So the only alternative was to wander a while longer into these clouds and storms that were beginning to beat down from the pass through the darkness of the valley; to try and think things out; to find some shelter for the night; then to go away again — somewhere. She was conscious now of a first driving of sleet in her face; but it only lasted for a few minutes. Then it ceased; and a strange gleam swept over the valley — a livid storm-light from the west, which blanched all the withered grass beside her, and seemed to shoot along the course of the stream as she toiled up the rocky path beside it.

What a country, what a sky! Her young body was conscious of an angry revolt against it, against the north-

ern cold and dreariness; her body, which still kept as
it were the physical memory of sun, and blue sea, and
orange trees, of the shadow of olives on a thin grass, of
the scent of orange blossom on the broken twigs that
some one was putting into her hand.

Another fit of shuddering repulsion made her quicken
her pace, as though, again, she were escaping from pursuit. Suddenly, at a bend in the path, she came on a
shepherd and his flock. The shepherd, an old white-
haired man, was seated on a rock, staff in hand, watching
his dog collect the sheep from the rocky slope on which
they were scattered.

At sight of Hester, the old man started and stared.
Her fair hair escaping in many directions from the control
of combs and hairpins, and the pale lovely face in the
midst of it, shone in the stormy gleam that filled the basin
of the hills. Her fashionable hat and dress amazed him.
Who could she be?

She too stopped to look at him, and at his dog. The
mere neighbourhood of a living being brought a kind of
comfort.

"It's going to snow —" she said, as she stood beside
him, surprised by the sound of her own voice amid the
roar of the wind.

"Aye — it's onding o' snaw —" said the shepherd,
his shrewd blue eyes travelling over her face and form.
"An' it'll mappen be a rough night."

"Are you taking your sheep into shelter?"

He pointed to a half-ruined fold, with three sycamores

beside it, a stone's throw away.   The gate of it was open, and the dog was gradually chasing the sheep within it.

"I doan't like leavin' 'em on t' fells this bitter weather. I'm afraid for t' ewes.   It's too cauld for 'em.   They'll be for droppin' their lambs too soon if this wind goes on. It juist taks t' strength out on 'em, doos the wind."

"Do you think it's going to snow a great deal?"

The old man looked round at the clouds and the mountains; at the powdering of snow that had already whitened the heights.

"It'll be more'n a bit!" he said cautiously.   "I dessay we'll have to be gettin' men to open t' roads to-morrow."

"Does it often block the roads?"

"Aye, yance or twice i' t' winter.   An' ye can't let 'em bide.   What's ter happen ter foak as want the doctor?"

"Did you ever know people lost on these hills?" asked the girl, looking into the blackness ahead of them.   Her shrill, slight voice rang out in sharp contrast to the broad gutturals of his Westmoreland speech.

"Aye, missy — I've known two men losst on t' fells sin I wor a lad."

"Were they shepherds, like you?"

"Noa, missy — they wor tramps.   Theer's mony a fellow cooms by this way i' th' bad weather to Pen'rth, rather than face Shap fells.   They say it's betther walkin'. But when it's varra bad, we doan't let 'em go on — noa, it's not safe.   Theer was a mon lost on t' fells nine year ago coom February.   He wor an owd mon, and blind o' yan eye.   He'd lost the toother, dippin' sheep."

"How could he do that?" Hester asked indifferently, still staring ahead into the advancing storm, and trembling with cold from head to foot.

"Why, sum o' the dippin' stuff got into yan eye, and blinded him. It was my son, gooin afther th' lambs i' the snaw, as found him. He heard summat — a voice like a lile child cryin' — an he scratted aboot, an dragged th' owd man out. He worn't deed then, but he died next mornin'. An t' doctor said as he'd fair broken his heart i' th' storm — not in a figure o' speach yo unnerstan — but juist th' plain truth."

The old man rose. The sheep had all been folded. He called to his dog, and went to shut the gate. Then, still curiously eying Hester, he came back, followed by his dog, to the place where she stood, listlessly watching.

"Doan't yo go too far on t' fells, missy. It's coomin' on to snaw, an it'll snaw aw neet. Lor bless yer, it's wild here i' winter. An when t' clouds coom down like yon —" he pointed up the valley — "even them as knaws t' fells from a chilt may go wrang."

"Where does this path lead?" said Hester, absently.

"It goes oop to Marly Head, and joins on to th' owd road — t' Roman road, foak calls it — along top o' t' fells. An' if yo follers that far enoof you may coom to Ullswatter an' Pen'rth."

"Thank you. Good afternoon," said Hester, moving on.

The old shepherd looked after her doubtfully, then said to himself that what the lady did was none of his business, and turned back toward one of the farms across

"The old shepherd looked after her doubtfully"

the bridge. Who was she? She was a strange sort of body to be walking by herself up the head of Long Whindale. He supposed she came from Burwood — there was no other house where a lady like that could be staying. But it was a bit queer anyhow.

Hester walked on. She turned a craggy corner beyond which she was out of sight of any one on the lower stretches of the road. The struggle with the wind, the roar of water in her ears, had produced in her a kind of trance-like state. She walked mechanically, half deafened, half blinded, measuring her force against the wind, conscious every now and then of gusts of snow in her face, of the deepening gloom overhead climbing up and up the rocky path. But, as in that fatal moment when she had paused in the Burwood lane, her mind was not more than vaguely conscious of her immediate surroundings. It had become the prey of swarming recollections —captured by sudden agonies, unavailing, horror-stricken revolts.

At last, out of breath, and almost swooning, she sank down under the shelter of a rock, and became in a moment aware that white mists were swirling and hurrying all about her, and that only just behind her, and just above her, was the path clear. Without knowing it, she had climbed and climbed till she was very near the top of the pass. She looked down into a witch's cauldron of mist and vapour, already thickened with snow, and up into an impenetrable sky, as it seemed, close upon her head, from which the white flakes were beginning to fall, steadily and fast.

She was a little frightened, but not much. After all, she had only to rest and retrace her steps. The watch at her wrist told her it was not much past four; and it was February. It would be daylight till half-past five, unless the storm put out the daylight. A little rest — just a little rest! But she began to feel ill and faint, and so bitterly, bitterly cold. The sense of physical illness, conquering the vague overwhelming anguish of heart and mind, began to give her back some clearness of brain.

Who was she? — why was she there? She was Hester Fox-Wilton — no! Hester Meryon, who had escaped from a man who had called himself, for a few days at least, her husband; a man whom in scarcely more than a week she had come to loathe and fear; whose nature and character had revealed to her infamies of which she had never dreamed; who had claimed to be her master, and use her as he pleased, and from whom she had escaped by night, after a scene of which she still bore the marks.

"You little wild-cat! You think you can defy me — do you?"

And then her arms held — and her despairing eyes looking down into his mocking ones — and the helpless sense of indignity and wrong — and of her own utter and criminal folly.

And through her memory there ran in an ugly dance those things, those monstrous things, he had said to her about the Scotch woman. It was not at all absolutely

sure that she, Hester, was his wife. He had shown her
those letters at St. Germains, of course, to reassure her;
and the letters were perfectly genuine letters, written
by the people they professed to be written by. Still
Scotch marriage law was a damned business — one never
knew. He *hoped* it was all right; but if she did hate him
as poisonously as she said, if she did really want to get
rid of him, he might perhaps be able to assist her.

Had he after all tricked and ruined her? Yet as her
consciousness framed the question in the conventional
phrases familiar to her through newspapers and novels,
she hardly knew what they meant, this child of eighteen,
who in three short weeks had been thrust through the
fire of an experience on which she had never had time to
reflect. Flattered vanity, and excitement, leading up
almost from the first day to instinctive and fierce revolt
— intervals of acquiescence, of wild determination to be
happy, drowned in fresh rebellions of soul and sense —
through these alternations the hours had rushed on,
culminating in her furtive and sudden escape from the
man of whom she was now in mad fear — her blind
flight for "home."

The *commonness* of her case, the absence of any romantic or poetic element in it — it was that which
galled, which degraded her in her own eyes. Only three
weeks since she had felt that entire and arrogant belief
in herself, in her power over her own life and Philip's,
on which she now looked back as merely ludicrous! —
inexplicable in a girl of the most ordinary intelligence.

What power had girls over men? — such men as Philip Meryon?

Her vanity was bleeding to death — and her life with it. Since the revelation of her birth, she seemed to have been blindly struggling to regain her own footing in the world — the kind of footing she was determined to have. Power and excitement; *not* to be pitied, but to be followed, wooed, adored; not to be forced on the second and third bests of the world, but to have the "chief seat," the daintest morsel, the *beau rôle* always — had not this been her instinctive, unvarying demand on life? And now? If she were indeed married, she was tied to a man who neither loved her, nor could bring her any position in the world; who was penniless, and had only entrapped her that he might thereby get some money out of her relations; who, living or dead, would be a disgrace to her, standing irrevocably between her and any kind of honour or importance in society.

And if he had deceived her, and she were not his wife — she would be free indeed; but what would her freedom matter to her? What decent man would ever love her now — marry her — set her at his side? At eighteen — eighteen! all those chances were over for her. It was so strange that she could have laughed at her own thoughts; and yet at the same time it was so ghastly true! No need now to invent a half-sincere chatter about "Fate." She felt herself in miserable truth the mere feeble mouse wherewith the great cat Fate was playing.

And yet — after all — she herself had done it!— by

her own sheer madness. She seemed to see Aunt Alice's plaintive face, the eyes that followed her, the lip that trembled when she said an unkind or wanton thing; she heard again the phrases of Uncle Richard's weekly letters, humorous, tender phrases, with here and there an occasional note of austerity, or warning.

Oh yes — she had done it — she had ruined herself.

She felt the tears running over her cheeks, mingling with the snow as it pelted in her face. Suddenly she realized how cold she was, how soaked. She must — must go back to shelter — to human faces — to kind hands. She put out her own, groping helplessly — and rose to her feet.

But the darkness was now much advanced, and the great snowstorm of the night had begun. She could not see the path below her at all, and only some twenty yards of its course above her. In the whirling gloom and in the fury of the wind, although she turned to descend the path, her courage suddenly failed her. She remembered a stream she had crossed on a little footbridge with a rail; could she ever see to recross it again? — above the greedy tumult of the water? Peering upward it seemed to her that she saw something like walls in front of her — perhaps another sheepfold? That would give her shelter for a little, and perhaps the snow would stop — perhaps it was only a shower. She struggled on, and up, and found indeed some fragments of walls, beside the path, one of the many abandoned places among the Westmoreland fells that testify to the closer settlement of the dales in earlier centuries.

And just as she clambered within them, the clouds sweeping along the fell-side lifted and parted for the last time, and she caught a glimpse of a wide, featureless world, the desolate top of the fells, void of shelter or landmark, save that straight across it, from gloom to gloom, there ran a straight white thing — a ghostly and forsaken track. The Roman road, no doubt, of which the shepherd had spoken. And a vision sprang into her mind of Roman soldiers tramping along it, helmeted and speared, their heads bent against these northern storms — shivering like herself. She gazed and gazed, fascinated, till her bewildered eyes seemed to perceive shadows upon it, moving — moving — toward her.

A panic fear seized her.

"I must get home! — I must! ——"

And sobbing, with the sudden word "mother!" on her lips, she ran out of the shelter she had found, taking, as she supposed, the path toward the valley. But blinded with snow and mist, she lost it almost at once. She stumbled on over broken and rocky ground, wishing to descend, yet keeping instinctively upward, and hearing on her right from time to time, as though from depths of chaos, the wild voices of the valley, the wind tearing the cliffs, the rushing of the stream. Soon all was darkness; she knew that she had lost herself; and was alone with rock and storm. Still she moved; but nerve and strength ebbed; and at last there came a step into infinity — a sharp pain — and the flame of consciousness went out.

CHAPTER XXIII

THE February afternoon in Long Whindale, shortened by the first heavy snowstorm of the winter, passed quickly into darkness. Down through all the windings of the valley the snow showers swept from the north, becoming, as the wind dropped a little toward night, a steady continuous fall, which in four or five hours had already formed drifts of some depth in exposed places.

Toward six o'clock, the small farmer living across the lane from Burwood became anxious about some sheep which had been left in a high "intak" on the fell. He was a thriftless, procrastinating fellow, and when the storm came on about four o'clock had been taking his tea in a warm ingle-nook by his wife's fire. He was then convinced that the storm would "hod off," at least till morning, that the sheep would get shelter enough from the stone walls of the "intak," and that all was well. But a couple of hours later the persistence of the snowfall, together with his wife's reproaches, goaded him into action. He went out with his son and lanterns, intending to ask the old shepherd at the Bridge Farm to help them in their expedition to find and fold the sheep.

Meanwhile, in the little sitting-room at Burwood

Catherine Elsmere and Mary were sitting, the one with her book, the other with her needlework, while the snow and wind outside beat on the little house. But Catharine's needlework often dropped unheeded from her fingers; and the pages of Mary's book remained unturned. The postman who brought letters up the dale in the morning, and took letters back to Whinborough at night, had just passed by in his little cart, hooded and cloaked against the storm, and hoping to reach Whinborough before the drifts in the roads had made travelling too difficult. Mary had put into his hands a letter addressed to the Rev. Richard Meynell, Hotel Richelieu, Paris. And beside her on the table lay a couple of sheets of foreign notepaper, covered closely with Meynell's not very legible handwriting.

Catharine also had some open letters on her lap. Presently she turned to Mary.

"The Bishop thinks the trial will certainly end to-morrow."

"Yes," said Mary, without raising her eyes.

Catharine took her daughter's hand in a tender clasp.

"I am so sorry! — for you both."

"Dearest!" Mary laid her mother's hand against her cheek. "But I don't think Richard will be misunderstood again."

"No. The Bishop says that, mysterious as it all is, nobody blames him for being absent. They trust him. But this time, it seems, he *did* write to the Bishop — just a few words."

"Yes, I know. I am glad." But as she spoke, the pale severity of the girl's look belied the word she used. During the fortnight of Meynell's absence, while he and Alice Puttenham in the south of France had been following every possible clue in a vain search for Hester, and the Arches trial had been necessarily left entirely to the management of Meynell's counsel, and to the resources of his co-defendants, Darwen and Chesham, Mary had suffered much. To see his own brilliant vindication of himself and his followers, in the face of religious England, snuffed out and extinguished in a moment by the call of this private duty had been hard! — all the more seeing that the catastrophe had been brought about by misconduct so wanton, so flagrant, as Hester's. There had sprung up in Mary's mind, indeed, a *saeva indignatio,* not for herself, but for Richard, first and foremost, and next for his cause. Dark as she knew Meynell's forebodings and beliefs to be, anxiety for Hester must sometimes be forgotten in a natural resentment for high aims thwarted, and a great movement risked, by the wicked folly of a girl of eighteen, on whom every affection and every care had been lavished.

"The roads will be impassable to-morrow," said Catharine, drawing aside the curtain, only to see a window already blocked with drifted snow. "But — who can be ringing on such a night!"

For a peal of the front door bell went echoing through the little house.

Mary stepped into the hall, and herself opened the

door, only to be temporarily blinded by the rush of wind and snow through the opening.

"A telegram!" she exclaimed, in wonder. "Please come in and wait. Isn't it very bad?"

"I hope I'll be able to get back!" laughed the young man who had brought it. "The roads are drifting up fast. It was noa good bicycling. I got 'em to gie me a horse. I've just put him in your stable, miss."

But Mary heard nothing of what he was saying. She had rushed back into the sitting-room.

"Mother! — Richard and Miss Puttenham will be here to-night. They have heard of Hester."

In stupefaction they read the telegram, which had had been sent from Crewe:

"Received news of Hester on arrival Paris yesterday. She has left M. Says she has gone to find your mother. Keep her. We arrive to-night Whinborough 7.10."

"It is now seven," said Catharine, looking at her watch. "But where — where is she?"

Hurriedly they called their little parlour-maid into the room and questioned her with closed doors. No — she knew nothing of any visitor. Nobody had called; nobody, so far as she knew, had passed by, except the ordinary neighbours. Once in the afternoon, indeed, she had thought she heard a carriage pass the bottom of the lane, but on looking out from the kitchen she had seen nothing of it.

Out of this slender fact, the only further information

that could be extracted was a note of time.   It was, the girl thought, about four o'clock when she heard the carriage pass.

"But it couldn't have passed," Catharine objected, "or you would have seen it go up the valley."

The girl assented, for the kitchen window commanded the road up to the bridge.   Then the carriage, if she had really heard it, must have come to the foot of the lane, turned and gone back toward Whinborough again. There was no other road available.

The telegraph messenger was dismissed, after a cup of coffee; and thankful for something to do, Catharine and Mary, with minds full of conjecture and distress, set about preparing two rooms for their guests.

"Will they ever get here?" Mary murmured to herself, when at last the two rooms lay neat and ready, with a warm fire in each, and she could allow herself to open the front door again, an inch or two, and look out into the weather.   Nothing to be seen but the whirling snowflakes.   The horrid fancy seized her that Hester had really been in that carriage and had turned back at their very door.   So that again Richard, arriving weary and heart-stricken, would be disappointed.   Mary's bitterness grew.

But all that could be done was to listen to every sound without, in the hope of catching something else than the roaring of the wind, and to give the rein to speculation and dismay.

Catharine sat waiting, in her chair, the tears welling

silently. It touched her profoundly that Hester, in her sudden despair, should have thought of coming to her; though apparently it was a project she had not carried out. All her deep heart of compassion yearned over the lost, unhappy one. Oh, to bring her comfort! — to point her to the only help and hope in the arms of an all-pitying God. Catharine knew much more of Meryon's history and antecedents — from Meynell — than did Mary. She was convinced that the marriage, if there had been a marriage, had been a bogus one, and that the disgrace was irreparable. But in her stern, rich nature, now that the culprit had turned from her sin, there was not a thought of condemnation; only a yearning pity, an infinite tenderness.

At last toward nine o'clock there were steps on the garden path. Mary flew to the door. In the porch there stood the old shepherd from the Bridge Farm. His hat, beard, and shoulders were heavy with snow, and his face shone like a red wrinkled apple, in the light of the hall lamp.

"Beg your pardon, miss, but I've just coom from helpin' Tyson to get his sheep in. Varra careless of him to ha' left it so long! — aw mine wor safe i' t' fold by fower o'clock. An' I thowt, miss, as I'd mak bold, afore goin' back to t' farm, to coom an' ast yo, if t' yoong leddy got safe hoam this afternoon? I wor a bit worritted, for I thowt I saw her on t' Mardale Head path, juist afther I got hoam, from t' field abuve t' Bridge Farm, an' it wor noan weather for a stranger, miss, yo unnerstan', to be oot on t' fells, and it gettin' so black ——"

"What young lady?" cried Mary. "Oh, come in, please."

And she drew him hurriedly into the sitting-room, where Catharine had already sprung to her feet in terror. There they questioned him. Yes — they had been expecting a lady. When had he seen her? — the young lady he spoke of? What was she like? In what direction had she gone? He answered their questions as clearly as he could, his own honest face growing steadily longer and graver.

And all the time he carried, unconsciously, something heavy in his hand, on the top of which the snow had settled. Presently Mary perceived it.

"Sit down, please!" she pushed a chair toward him. "You must be tired out! And let me take that ——"

She held out her hand. The old man looked down — recollecting.

"That's noan o' mine, miss. I ——"

Catharine cried out —

"It's hers! It's Hester's!"

She took the bag from Mary, and shook the snow from it. It was a small dressing-bag of green leather and on it appeared the initials — "H. F.-W."

They looked at each other speechless. The old man hastened to explain that on opening the gate which led to the house from the lane his foot had stumbled against something on the path. By the light of his lantern he had seen it was a bag of some sort, had picked it up and brought it in.

"She *was* in the carriage!" said Mary, under her breath, "and must have just pushed this inside the gate before ——"

Before she went to her death? Was that what would have to be added? For there was horror in both their minds. The mountains at the head of Long Whindale run up to no great height, but there are plenty of crags on them with a sheer drop of anything from fifty to a hundred feet. Ten or twenty feet would be quite enough to disable an exhausted girl. Five hours since she was last seen! — and since the storm began; four hours, at least, since thick darkness had descended on the valley.

"We must do something at once." Catharine addressed the old man in quick, resolute tones. "We must get a party together."

But as she spoke there were further sounds outside — of trampling feet and voices — vying with the storm. Mary ran into the hall. Two figures appeared in the porch in the light of the lamp as she held it up, with a third behind them, carrying luggage. In front stood Meynell, and an apparently fainting woman, clinging to and supported by his arm.

"Help me with this lady, please!" said Meynell, peremptorily, not recognizing who it was holding the light. "This last little climb has been too much for her. Alice! — just a few steps more!"

And bending over his charge, he lifted the frail form

over the threshold, and saw, as he did so, that he was
placing her in Mary's arms.

"She is absolutely worn out," he said, drawing quick
breath, while all his face relaxed in a sudden, irrepressible
joy. "But she would come." Then, in a lower voice —
"Is Hester here?" Mary shook her head, and something in her eyes warned him of fresh calamity. He
stooped suddenly to look at Alice, and perceived that
she was quite unconscious. He and Mary, between
them, raised her and carried her into the sitting-room.
Then, while Mary ministered to her, Meynell grasped
Catharine's hand — with the brusque question —

"What has happened?"

Catharine beckoned to old David, the shepherd, and
she, with David and Meynell, went across, out of hearing,
into the tiny dining-room of the cottage. Meanwhile
the horses and man who had brought the travellers from
Whinborough had to be put up for the night, for the man
would not venture the return journey.

Meynell had soon heard what there was to tell. He
himself was gray with fatigue and sleeplessness; but there
was no time to think of that.

"What men can we get?" he asked of the shepherd.

Old David ruminated, and finally suggested the two
sons of the farmer across the lane, his own master, the
young tenant of the Bridge Farm, and the cowman from
the same farm.

"And the Lord knaws I'd goa wi you myself, sir" —
said the fine-featured old man, a touch of trouble in his

blue eyes — "for I feel soomhow as though there were a bit o' my fault in it. But we've had a heavy job on t' fells awready, an I should be noa good to you."

He went over to the neighbouring farm, to recruit some young men, and presently returned with them, the driver, also, from Whinborough, a stalwart Westmoreland lad, eager to help.

Meanwhile Meynell had snatched some food at Catharine's urgent entreaty, and had stood a moment in the sitting-room, his hand in Mary's, looking down upon the just reviving Alice.

"She's been a plucky woman," he said, with emotion; "but she's about at the end of her tether."   And in a few brief sentences he described the agitated pursuit of the last fortnight; the rapid journeys, prompted now by this clue, now by that; the alternate hopes and despairs; with no real information of any kind, till Hester's telegram, sent originally to Upcote and reforwarded, had reached Meynell in Paris, just as they had returned thither for a fresh consultation with the police at headquarters.

As the sound of men's feet in the kitchen broke in upon the hurried narrative, and Meynell was leaving the room, Alice opened her eyes.

"Hester?"   The pale lips just breathed the name.

"We've heard of her."   Meynell stooped to the questioner. "It's a real clue this time. She's not far away. But don't ask any more now. Let Mrs. Elsmere take you to bed—and there'll be more news in the morning."

She made a feeble sign of assent.

A quarter of an hour later all was ready, and Mary stood again in the porch, holding the lamp high for the departure of the rescuers. There were five men with lanterns, ropes, and poles, laden, besides, with blankets, and everything else that Catharine's practical sense could suggest. Old David would go with the rest as far as the Bridge Farm.

The snow was still coming down in a stealthy and abundant fall, but the wind showed some signs of abating.

"They'll find it easier goin', past t' bridge, than it would ha' been an hour since," said old David to Mary, pitying the white anxiety of her face. She thanked him with a smile, and then while he marched ahead, she put down the lamp and leant her head a moment against Meynell's shoulder, and he kissed her hair.

Down went the little procession to the main road. Through the lane the lights wavered, and presently, standing at the kitchen window, Catharine and Mary could watch them dancing up the dale, now visible, now vanishing. It must be at least, and at best, two or three hours before the party reappeared; it might be much more. They turned from useless speculation to give all their thoughts to Alice Puttenham.

Too exhausted to speak or think, she was passive in their hands. She was soon in bed, in a deep sleep, and

Mary, having induced her mother to lie down in the sitting-room, and having made up fires throughout the house, sent the servants to bed, and herself began her watch in Alice Puttenham's room.

Dreary and long, the night passed away. Once or twice through the waning storm Mary heard the deep bell of the little church, tolling the hours; once or twice she went hurriedly downstairs thinking there were steps in the garden, only to meet her mother in the hall, on the same bootless errand. At last, worn with thinking and praying, she fell fitfully asleep, and woke to find moonlight shining through the white blind in Alice Puttenham's room. She drew aside the blind and saw with a shock of surprise that the storm was over; the valley lay pure white under a waning moon just dipping to the western fells; the clouds were upfurling; and only the last echoes of the gale were dying through the bare, snow-laden trees that fringed the stream. It was four o'clock. Six hours, since the rescue party had started. Alack! — they must have had far to seek.

Suddenly — out of the dark bosom of the valley, lights emerged. Mary sprang to her feet. Yes! it was they — it was Richard returning.

One look at the bed, where the delicate pinched face still lay high on the pillows, drenched in a sleep which was almost a swoon, and Mary stole out of the room.

There was time to complete their preparations and renew the fires. When Catharine softly unlatched the front door, everything was ready — warm blankets, hot milk, hot water bottles. But now they hardly dared speak to each other; dread kept them dumb. Nearer and nearer came the sound of feet and lowered voices. Soon they could hear the swing of the gate leading into the garden. Four men entered, carrying something. Meynell walked in front with the lantern.

As he saw the open door, he hurried forward. They read what he had to say in his haggard look before he spoke.

"We found her a long way up the pass. She has had a bad fall — but she is alive. That's all one can say. The exposure alone might have killed her. She hasn't spoken — not a word. That good fellow" — he nodded toward the Whinborough lad who had brought them from the station — "will take one of his horses and go for the doctor. We shall get him here in a couple of hours."

Silently they brought her in, the stalwart, kindly men, they mounted the cottage stairs, and on Mary' bed they laid her down.

O crushed and wounded youth! The face, drawn and fixed in pain, was marble-cold and marble-white; the delicate mire-stained hands hung helpless. Masses of drenched hair fell about the neck and bosom; and there was a wound on the temple which had been bandaged, but was now bleeding afresh. Catharine bent over her in an anguish, feeling for pulse and heart. Meynell, whispering, pointed out that the right leg was broken below the knee. He himself had put it in some rough splints, made out of the poles the shepherds were carrying.

Both Catharine and Mary had ambulance training, and, helped by their two maids, they did all they could. They cut away the soaked clothes. They applied warmth in every possible form; they got down some spoonfuls of warm milk and brandy, dreading always to hear the first sounds of consciousness and pain.

They came at last — the low moans of one coming terribly back to life. Meynell returned to the room, and knelt by her.

"Hester — dear child! — you are quite safe — we are all here — the doctor will be coming directly."

His tone was tender as a woman's. His ghostly face, disfigured by exhaustion, showed him absorbed in pity. Mary, standing near, longed to kneel down by him, and weep; but there was an austere sense that not even she must interrupt the moment of recognition.

At last it came. Hester opened her eyes —

"Uncle Richard? — Is that Uncle Richard?"

A long silence, broken by moaning, while Meynell knelt there, watching her, sometimes whispering to her.

At last she said, "I couldn't face you all. I'm dying." She moved her right hand restlessly. "Give me something for this pain — I — I can't stand it."

"Dear Hester — can you bear it a little longer? We will do all we can. We have sent for the doctor. He has a motor. He will be here very soon."

"I don't want to live. I want to stop the pain. Uncle Richard!"

"Yes, dear Hester."

"I hate Philip — now."

"It's best not to talk of him, dear. You want all your strength."

"No — I must. There's not much time. I suppose — I've — I've made you very unhappy?"

"Yes — but now we have you again — our dear, dear Hester."

"You can't care. And I — can't say — I'm sorry. Don't you remember?"

His face quivered. He understood her reference to the long fits of naughtiness of her childhood, when neither nurse, nor governess, nor "Aunt Alice" could ever get out of her the stereotyped words "I'm sorry." But he could not trust himself to speak. And it seemed as though she understood his silence, for she feebly moved her uninjured hand toward him; and he raised it to his lips.

"Did I fall — a long way? I don't recollect — anything."

"You had a bad fall, my poor child. Be brave! — the doctor will help you."

He longed to speak to her of her mother, to tell her the truth. It was borne in upon him that he *must* tell her — if she was to die; that in the last strait, Alice's arms must be about her. But the doctor must decide.

Presently, she was a little easier. The warm stimulant dulled the consciousness which came in gusts.

Once or twice, as she recognized the faces near her, there was a touch of life, even of mockery. There was a moment when she smiled at Catharine —

"You're sweet. You won't say — 'I told you so'!"

In one of the intervals when she seemed to have lapsed again into unconsciousness Meynell reported something of the search. They had found her a long distance from the path, at the foot of a steep and rocky scree, some twenty or thirty feet high, down which she must have slipped headlong. There she had lain for some eight hours in the storm before they found her. She neither moved nor spoke when they discovered her, nor had there been any sign of life, beyond the faint beating of the pulse, on the journey down.

The pale dawn was breaking when the doctor arrived. His verdict was at first not without hope. She *might* live; if there were no internal injuries of importance. The next few hours would show. He sent his motor back to Whinborough Cottage Hospital for a couple of nurses, and prepared, himself, to stay the greater part of the day. He had just gone downstairs to speak to Meynell, and Catharine was sitting by the bed, when Hester once more roused herself.

"How that man hurt me!— don't let him come in again."

Then, in a perfectly hard, clear voice, she added imperiously — "I want to see my mother."

Catharine stooped toward her, in an agitation she found it difficult to conceal.

"Dear Hester! — we are sending a telegram as soon as the post-office is open to Lady Fox-Wilton."

Hester moved her hand impatiently.

"She's not my mother, and I'm glad. Where is — *my mother?*" She laid a strange, deep emphasis on the word, opening her eyes wide and threateningly. Catharine understood at once that, in some undiscovered way, she knew what they had all been striving to keep from her. It was no time for questioning. Catharine rose quietly.

"She is here, Hester,   I will go and tell her."

Leaving one of the maids in charge, Catharine ran down to the doctor, who gave a reluctant consent, lest more harm should come of refusing the interview than of granting it. And as Catharine ran up again to Mary's room she had time to reflect, with self-reproach, on the strange completeness with which she at any rate had forgotten that frail ineffectual woman asleep in Mary's room from the moment of Hester's arrival till now.

But Mary had not forgotten her. When Catharine opened the door, it was to see a thin, phantom-like figure, standing fully dressed, and leaning on Mary's arm. Catharine went up to her with tears, and kissed her, holding her hands close.

"Hester asks for you — for her mother — her real mother. She knows."

"*She knows?*" Alice stood paralyzed a moment, gazing at Catharine. Then the colour rushed back into her face. "I am coming — I am coming — at once," she said impetuously. "I am quite strong. Don't help me, please. And — let me go in alone. I won't do her harm. If you — and Mary — would stand by the door — I would call in a moment — if ——"

They agreed. She went with tottering steps across the landing. On the threshold, Catharine paused; Mary remained a little behind. Alice went in and shut the door.

The blinds in Hester's room were up, and the snow-covered fells rising steeply above the house filled it with a wintry, reflected light; a dreary light, that a large fire could not dispel. On the white bed lay Hester, breathing quickly and shallowly; bright colour now in each sunken cheek. The doctor himself had cut off a great part of her hair — her glorious hair. The rest fell now in damp golden curls about her slender neck, beneath the cap-like bandage which hid the forehead and temples and gave her the look of a young nun. At first sight of her, Alice knew that she was doomed. Do what she would, she could not restrain the low cry which the sight tore from the depths of life.

Hester feebly beckoned. Alice came near, and took the right hand in hers, while Hester smiled, her eyelids fluttering. "Mother!" — she said, so as scarcely to be heard — and then again — "*Mother!*"

Alice sank down beside her with a sob, and without a word they gazed into each other's eyes. Slowly Hester's filled with tears. But Alice's were dry. In her face there was as much ecstasy as anguish. It was the first look that Hester's *soul* had ever given her. All the past was in it; and that strange sense, on both sides, that there was no future.

At last Alice murmured:

"How did you know?"

"Philip told me."

The girl stopped abruptly.   It had been on her tongue to say — "It was that made me go with him."

But she did not say it.   And while Alice's mind, rushing miserably over the past, was trying to piece together some image of what had happened, Hester began to talk intermittently about the preceding weeks.   Alice tried to stop her; but to thwart her only produced a restless excitement, and she had her way.

She spoke of Philip with horror, yet with a perfectly clear sense of her own responsiblity.

"I needn't have gone — but I would go.   There was a devil in me — that wanted to know.   Now I know — too much.   I'm glad it's over.   This life isn't worth while — not for me."

So, from these lips of eighteen, came the voice of the world's old despairs!

Presently she asked peremptorily for Meynell, and he came to her.

"Uncle Richard, I want to be sure" — she spoke strongly and in her natural voice — "am I Philip's wife — or — or not?   We were married on January 25th, at the Mairie of the 10th Arrondissement, by a man in a red scarf.   We signed registers and things.   Then — when we quarrelled — Philip said — he wasn't certain

about that woman — in Scotland. You might be right.
Tell me the truth, please. Am I — his wife?"

And as the words dropped faintly, the anxiety in her
beautiful death-stricken eyes was strange and startling
to see. Through all her recklessness, her defiance of
authority and custom, could be seen at last the strength
of inherited, implanted things; the instinct of a race, a
family, overleaping deviation.

Meynell bent over her steadily, and took her hand in
both his own.

"Certainly, you are his wife. Have no anxiety at all
about that. My inquiries all broke down. There was
no Scotch marriage."

Hester said nothing for a little; but the look of relief
was clear. Alice on the farther side of the bed dropped
her face in her hands. Was it not only forty-eight hours
since, in Paris, Meynell had told her that he had received
conclusive evidence of the Scotch marriage, and that
Hester was merely Philip's victim, not his wife? Passionately her heart thanked him for the falsehood. She saw
clearly that Hester's mortal wounds were not all bodily.
She was dying partly of self-contempt, self-judgment.
Meynell's strong words — his "noble lie" — had lifted,
as it were, a fraction of the moral weight that was de-
stroying her; had made a space — a freedom, in which
the spirit could move.

So much Alice saw; blind meanwhile to the tragic
irony of this piteous stress laid at such a moment, by one
so lawless, on the social law!

Thenceforward the poor sufferer was touchingly gentle and amenable. Morphia had been given her liberally, and the relief was great. When the nurses came at mid-day, however, the pulse had already begun to fail. They could do nothing; and though within call, they left her mainly to those who loved her.

In the early afternoon she asked suddenly for the Communion, and Meynell administered it. The three women who were watching her received it with her. In Catharine's mind, as Meynell's hands brought her the sacred bread and wine, all thought of religious difference between herself and him had vanished, burnt away by sheer heat of feeling. There was no difference! Words became mere transparencies, through which shone the ineffable.

When it was over, Hester opened her eyes — 'Uncle Richard!" The voice was only a whisper now. "You loved my father?"

"I loved him dearly — and you — and your mother — for his sake."

He stooped to kiss her cheek.

"I wonder what it'll be like" — she said, after a moment, with more strength — "beyond? How strange that — I shall know before you! Uncle Richard — I'm — I'm sorry!"

At that the difficult tears blinded him, and he could not reply. But she was beyond tears, concentrating all the last effort of the mind on the sheer maintenance of life. Presently she added:

"I don't hate — even Philip now. I — I forget him. Mother!" And again she clung to her mother's hand, feebly turning her face to be kissed.

Once she opened her eyes when Mary was beside her, and smiled brightly.

"I've been such a trouble, Mary — I've spoilt Uncle Richard's life. But now you'll have him all the time — and he'll have you. You dear! — Kiss me. You've got a golden mother. Take care of mine — won't you? — my poor mother!"

So the hours wore on. Science was clever and merciful and eased her pain. Love encompassed her, and when the wintry light failed, her faintly beating heart failed with it, and all was still. . . .

"Richard! — Richard! — Come with me."

So, with low, tender words, Mary tried to lead him away, after that trance of silence in which they had all been standing round the dead. He yielded to her; he was ready to see the doctor and to submit to the absolute rest enjoined. But already there was something in his aspect which terrified Mary. Through the night that followed, as she lay awake, a true instinct told her that the first great wrestle of her life and her love was close upon her.

CHAPTER XXIV

ON THE day following Hester's death an inquest was held in the dining-room at Burwood. Meynell and old David, the shepherd, stood out chief among the witnesses.

"This poor lady's name, I understand, sir," said the gray-haired Coroner, addressing Meynell, when the first preliminaries were over, "was Miss Hester Fox-Wilton; she was the daughter of the late Sir Ralph Fox-Wilton; she was under age; and you and Lady Fox-Wilton — who is not here, I am told, owing to illness — were her guardians?"

Meynell assented. He stood to the right of the Coroner, leaning heavily on the chair before him. The doctor who had been called in to Hester sat beside him, and wondered professionally whether the witness would get through.

"I understand also," the Coroner resumed, "that Miss Fox-Wilton had left the family in Paris with whom you and Lady Fox-Wilton had placed her, some three weeks ago, and that you have since been in search of her, in company I believe with Miss Fox-Wilton's aunt, Miss Alice Puttenham. Miss Puttenham, I hope, will appear?"

The doctor rose —

"I am strongly of opinion, sir, that, unless for most urgent reasons, Miss Puttenham should not be called upon. She is in a very precarious state, in consequence of grief and shock, and I should greatly fear the results were she to make the effort."

Meynell intervened.

"I shall be able, sir, I think, to give you sufficient information, without its being necessary to call upon Miss Puttenham."

He went on to give an account, as guarded as he could make it, of Hester's disappearance from the family with whom she was boarding, of the anxiety of her relations, and the search that he and Miss Puttenham had made.

His conscience was often troubled. Vaguely, his mind was pronouncing itself all the while — "It is time now the truth were known. It is better it should be known." Hester's death had changed the whole situation. But he could himself take no step whatever toward disclosure. And he knew that it was doubtful whether he should or could have advised Alice to take any.

The inquiry went on, the Coroner avoiding tne subject of Hester's French escapade as much as possible. After all there need be — there was — no question of suicide; only some explanation had to be suggested of the dressing-bag left within the garden gate, and of the girl's reckless climb into the fells, against old David's advice, on such an afternoon.

Presently, in the midst of David's evidence, describing his meeting with Hester by the bridge, the handle of the dining-room door turned. The door opened a little way, and then shut again. Another minute or two passed, and then the door opened again timidly as though some one were hesitating outside. The Coroner annoyed, beckoned to a constable standing behind the witnesses. But before he could reach it, a lady had slowly pushed it open, and entered the room.

It was Alice Puttenham.

The Coroner looked up, and the doctor rose in astonishment. Alice advanced to the table, and stood at the farther end from the Coroner, looking first at him and then at the jury. Her face — emaciated now beyond all touch of beauty — and the childish overhanging lip. quivered as she tried to speak; but no words came.

"Miss Puttenham, I presume?" said the Coroner. "We were told, madam, that you were not well enough to give evidence."

Meynell was at her side.

"What do you wish?" he said, in a low voice, as he took her hand.

"I wish to give evidence," she said aloud.

The doctor turned toward the Coroner.

"I think you will agree with me, sir, that as Miss Puttenham has made the effort, she should give her evidence as soon as possible, and should give it sitting."

A murmur of assent ran round the table. Over the weather-beaten Westmoreland faces had passed a sudden wave of animation.

Alice took her seat, and the oath. Meynell sitting

opposite to her covered his face with his hands. He foresaw what she was about to do, and his heart went out to her.

Everybody at the table bent forward to listen. The two shorthand writers lifted eager faces.

"May I make a statement?" The thin voice trembled through the room.

The Coroner assured the speaker that the Court was willing and anxious to hear anything she might have to say.

Alice fixed her eyes on the old man, as though she would thereby shut out all his surroundings.

"You are inquiring, sir — into the death — of my daughter."

The Coroner made a sudden movement.

"Your daughter, madam? I understood that this poor young lady was the daughter of the late Sir Ralph and Lady Fox-Wilton?"

"She was their adopted daughter. Her father was Mr. Neville Flood, and I — am her mother. Mr. Flood, of Sandford Abbey, died nearly twenty years ago. He and I were never married. My sister and brother-in-law adopted the child. She passed always as theirs, and when Sir Ralph died, he appointed — Mr. Meynell — and my sister her guardians. Mr. Meynell has always watched over her — and me. Mr. Flood was much attached to him. He wrote to Mr. Meynell, asking him to help us — just before his death."

She paused a moment, steadying herself by the table.

There was not a sound, not a movement in the room. Only Meynell uncovered his eyes and tried to meet hers, so as to give her encouragement.

She resumed —

"Last August the nurse who attended me — in my confinement — came home to Upcote. She made a statement to a gentleman there — a false statement — and then she died. I wished then to make the truth public — but Mr. Meynell — as Hester's guardian — and for her sake, as well as mine — did not wish it. She knew nothing — then; and he was afraid of its effect upon her. I followed his advice, and took her abroad, in order to protect her from a bad man who was pursuing her. We did all we could — but we were not able to protect her. They were married without my knowing — and she went away with him. Then he — this man — told her — or perhaps he had done it before, I don't know — who she was. I can only guess how he knew; but he is Mr. Flood's nephew. My poor child soon found out what kind of man he was. She tried to escape from him. And because Mrs. Elsmere had been always very kind to her, she came here. She knew how ——"

The voice paused, and then with difficulty shaped its words again.

"She knew that we should grieve so terribly. She shrank from seeing us. She thought we might be here — and that — partly — made her wander away again — in despair — when she actually got here. But her

death was a pure accident — that I am sure of.   At
the last, she tried to get home — to me.   That was the
only thing she was conscious of — before she fell.   When
she was dying — she told me she knew — I was her
mother.   And now — that she is dead ——"

The voice changed and broke — a sudden cry forced
its way through —

"Now that she is dead — no one else shall claim her
— but me.   She's mine now — my child — forever —
only mine!"

She broke off incoherently, bowing her head upon
her hands, her slight shoulders shaken by her sobs.

The room was silent, save for a rather general clearing
of throats.   Meynell signalled to the doctor.   They both
rose and went to her.   Meynell whispered to her.

The Coroner spoke, drawing his handkerchief hastily
across his eyes.

"The Court is very grateful to you, Miss Puttenham,
for this frank and brave statement.   We tender you our
best thanks.   There is no need for us to detain you
longer."

She rose, and Meynell led her from the room.   Outside
was a nurse to whom he resigned her.

"My dear, dear friend!"   Trembling, her eyes met the
deep emotion in his.   "That was right — that will bring
you help.   Aye! you have her now — all, all your own."

On the day of Hester's burying Long Whindale lay
glittering white under a fitful and frosty sunshine.   The

rocks and screes with their steep beds of withered heather made dark scrawls and scratches on the white; the smoke from the farmhouses rose bluish against the snowy wall of fell; and the river, amid the silence of the muffled roads and paths, seemed the only audible thing in the valley.

In the tiny churchyard the new-made grave had been filled in with frozen earth, and on the sods lay flowers piled there by Rose Flaxman's kind and busy hands. She and Hugh had arrived from the south that morning.

Another visitor had come from the south, also to lay flowers on that wintry grave. Stephen Barron's dumb pain was bitter to see. The silence of spiritual and physical exhaustion in which Meynell had been wrapped since the morning of the inquest was first penetrated and broken up by the sight of Stephen's anguish. And in the attempt to comfort the younger, the elder man laid hold on some returning power for himself.

But he had been hardly hit; and the depth of the wound showed itself strangely — in a kind of fear of love itself, a fear of Mary! Meynell's attitude toward her during these days was almost one of shrinking. The atmosphere between them was electrical; charged with things unspoken, and a conflict that must be faced.

The day after Hester's funeral the newspapers were full of the sentence delivered on the preceding day, in the Arches Court, on Meynell and his co-defendants. A telegram from Darwen the evening before had conveyed the news to Meynell himself.

The sentence of deprivation *ab officio et beneficio* in the Church of England, on the ground of heretical opinion and unauthorized services, had been expressed by the Dean of Arches in a tone and phraseology of considerable vehemence. According to him the proceedings of the Modernists were "as contrary to morality as to law," and he marvelled how "honest men" could consent to occupy the position of Meynell and his friends.

Notice of appeal to the Privy Council was at once given by the Modernist counsel, and a flame of discussion arose throughout England.

Meanwhile, on the morning following the publication of the judgment, Meynell finished a letter, and took it into the dining-room, where Rose and Mary were sitting. Rose, reading his face, disappeared, and he put the letter into Mary's hands.

It was addressed to the Bishop of Dunchester. The great gathering in Dunchester Cathedral, after several postponements to match the delays in the Court of Arches, was to take place within a fortnight from this date, and Meynell had been everywhere announced as the preacher of the sermon, which was to be the battle-cry of the Movement, in the second period of its history; the period of open revolt, of hot and ardent conflict.

The letter which Mary was invited to read was short. It simply asked that the writer should be relieved from a task he felt he could not adequately carry out. He desired to lay it down, not for his own sake, but for the sake of the cause. "I am not the man, and this is not my job. This conviction has been borne in upon me during the last few weeks with an amazing clearness. I will only say that it seems to represent a command — a prohibition — laid upon me, which I cannot ignore. There are of course tragic happenings and circumstances connected with it, my dear lord, on which I will not dwell. The effect of them at present on my mind is that I wish to retire from a public and prominent part in our great Movement; at any rate for a time. I shall carry through the Privy Council appeal; but except for that intend to refuse all public appearance. When the sentence is confirmed, as of course it will be, it will be best for me to confine myself to thinking and writing in solitude and behind the scenes. 'Those also serve who only stand and wait.' The quotation is hackneyed, but it must serve. Through thought and self-proving, I believe that in the end I shall help you best. I am not the fighter I thought I was; the fighter that I ought to be to keep the position that has been so generously given me. Forgive me for a while if I go into the wilderness — a rather absurd phrase, however, as you will agree, when I tell you that I am soon to marry a woman whom I love with my whole heart. But it applies to my connection with the Modernist Movement, and to my position as a leader. My old friends and colleagues — many of them at least — will, I fear, blame the step I am taking. It will seem to them a mere piece of flinching and cowardice. But each man's soul is in his own keeping; and he alone can judge his own powers."

The letter then became a quiet discussion of the best man to be chosen in the writer's stead, and passed on into a review of the general situation created by the sentence of the Court of Arches.

But of these later pages of the letter Mary realized nothing. She sat with it in her hands, after she had read the passage which has been quoted, looking down, her mouth trembling.

Meynell watched her uneasily — then came to sit by her, and took her hand.

"Dearest! — you understand?" he said, entreatingly.

"It is — because of Hester?" She spoke with difficulty.

He assented, and then added —

"But that letter — shall only go with your permission."

She took courage. "Richard, you know so much better than I, but — Richard! — did you ever neglect Hester?"

He tried to answer her question truly.

"Not knowingly."

"Did you ever fail to love her, and try to help her?"

He drew a long breath.

"But there she lies!" He raised his head. Through the window, on a rocky slope, half a mile away, could be seen the tiny church of Long Whindale, and the little graveyard round it.

"It is very possible that I see the thing morbidly" — he turned to her again with a note of humility, of sad appeal, that struck most poignantly on the woman's heart — "but I cannot resist it. What use can I be to any human being as guide, or prophet, or counsellor — if I was so little use to her? Is there not a kind of hypocrisy — a dismal hypocrisy — in my claim to teach — or inspire — great multitudes of people — when this one child — who was given into my care ——"

He wrung her hands in his, unable to finish his sentence.

Bright tears stood in her eyes; but she persevered. She struck boldly for the public, the impersonal note. She set against the tragic appeal of the dead the equally tragic appeal of the living. She had in her mind the memory of that London church, with the strained upturned faces, the "hungry sheep" — girls among them, perhaps, in peril like Hester, men assailed by the same vile impulses that had made a brute of Philip Meryon. During the preceding months Mary's whole personality had developed with great rapidity, after a somewhat taciturn and slowly ripening youth. The need, enforced upon her by love itself, of asserting herself even against the mother she adored; the shadow of Meynell's cloud upon her, and her suffering under it, during the weeks of slander; and now this rending tragedy at her doors—had tempered anew the naturally high heart, and firm will. At this critical moment, she saved Meynell from a fatal step by the capacity she showed of loving his cause, only next to himself. And, indeed, Meynell was made wholesomely doubtful once or twice whether it were not in truth his cause she loved in him. For the sweet breakdowns of love which were always at her lips she banished by a mighty effort, till she should have won or lost. Thus throughout she showed herself her mother's daughter — with her father's thoughts.

It was long, however, before she succeeded in making any real impression upon him. All she could obtain at first was delay, and that Catharine should be informed.

As soon as that had been done, the position became once more curiously complex. Here was a woman to whom the whole Modernist Movement was anathema, driven finally into argument for the purpose of compelling the Modernist leader, the contriver and general of Modernist victory, to remain at his post!

For it was part of Catharine's robust character to look upon any pledge, any accepted responsibility, as something not to be undone by any mere feeling, however sharp, however legitimate. You had undertaken the thing, and it must, at all costs, be carried through. That was the dominant habit of her mind; and there were persons connected with her on whom the rigidity of it had at times worked harshly.

On this occasion it was no doubt interfered with — (the Spirit of Comedy would have found a certain high satisfaction in the dilemma) — by the fact that Meynell's persistence in the course he had entered upon must be, in her eyes, and *sub specie religionis*, a persistence in heresy and unbelief. What decided it ultimately, however, was that she was not only an orthodox believer, but a person of great common sense — and Mary's mother.

Her natural argument was that after the tragic events which had occurred, and the public reports of them which had appeared, Meynell's abrupt withdrawal from public life would once more unsettle and confuse the public mind. If there had been any change in his opinions —

"Oh! do not imagine" — she turned a suddenly glowing face upon him — "I should be trying to dissuade you, if that were your reason. No! — it is for personal and private reasons you shrink from the responsibility of leadership. And that being so, what must the world say — the ignorant world that loves to think evil?"

He looked at her a little reproachfully.

"Those are not arguments that come very naturally from you!"

"They are the right ones! — and I am not ashamed of them. My dear friend — I am not thinking of you at all. I leave you out of count; I am thinking of Alice — and — Mary!"

Catharine unconsciously straightened herself, a touch of something resentful — nay, stern — in the gesture. Meynell stared in stupefaction.

"Alice! — *Mary!*" he said.

"Up to this last proposed action of yours, has not everything that has happened gone to soften people's hearts? to make them repent doubly of their scandal, and their false witness? Every one knows the truth now — every one who cares; and every one understands. But now — after the effort poor Alice has made — after all that she and you have suffered — you insist on turning fresh doubt and suspicion on yourself, your motives, your past history. Can't you see how people may gossip about it — how they may interpret it? You have no right to do it, my dear Richard! — no right whatever. Your 'good report' belongs not only to yourself — but — to Mary!"

Catharine's breath had quickened; her hand shook upon her knee. Meynell rose from his seat, paced the room and came back to her.

"I have tried to explain to Mary" — he said, desperately — "that I should feel myself a hypocrite and pretender in playing the part of a spiritual leader — when this great — failure — lay upon my conscience."

At that Catharine's tension gave way. Perplexity returned upon her.

"Oh! if it meant — if it meant" — she looked at him with a sudden, sweet timidity — "that you felt you had tried to do for Hester what only grace — what only a living Redeemer — could do for her ——"

She broke off. But at last, as Meynell, her junior by fifteen years — her son almost — looked down into her face — her frail, aging, illumined face — there was something in the passion of her faith which challenged and roused his own; which for the moment, at any rate, and for the first time since the crisis had arisen revived in him the "fighter" he had tried to shed.

"The fault was not in the thing preached," he said, with a groan; "or so it seems to me — but in the preacher. The preacher — was unequal to the message."

Catharine was silent.   And after a little more pacing he said in a more ordinary tone — and a humble one —

"Does Mary share this view of yours?"

At this Catharine was almost angry.

"As if I should say a word to her about it!   Does she know — has she ever known — what you and I knew?"

His eyes, full of trouble, propitiated her.   He took her hand and kissed it.

"Bear with me, dear mother!   I don't see my way, but Mary — is to me — my life.   At any rate, I won't do in a hurry what you disapprove."

Thus a little further delay was gained.   The struggle lasted indeed another couple of days, and the aspect of both Meynell and Mary showed deep marks of it by the end.   Throughout it Mary made little or no appeal to the mere womanly arts.   And perhaps it was the repression of them that cost her most.

On the third day of discussion, while the letter still lay unposted in Meynell's writing-case, he went wandering by himself up the valley.   The weather was soft again, and breathing spring.   The streams ran free; the buds were swelling on the sycamores; and except on the topmost crags the snow had disappeared from the fells. Harsh and austere the valley was still; the winter's grip would be slow to yield; but the turn of the year had come.

That morning a rush of correspondence forwarded from Upcote had brought matters to a crisis.   On the days immediately following the publication of the evidence given at the inquest on Hester the outside world had made no sign.   All England knew now why Richard Meynell had disappeared from the Arches Trial, only to become again the prey of an enormous publicity, as one of the witnesses to the finding and the perishing of his young ward.   And after Alice Puttenham's statement in the Coroner's Court, for a few days the England interested in Richard Meynell simply held its breath and let him be.

But he belonged to the public; and after just the brief respite that decency and sympathy imposed, the public fell upon him.   The Arches verdict had been given; the appeal to the Privy Council had been lodged.   With every month of the struggle indeed, as the Modernist attack had grown more determined, and its support more widespread, so the orthodox defence had gathered force and vehemence.   Yet through the length and breadth of the country the Modernist petition to Parliament was now kindling such a fire as no resistance could put out.   Debate in the House of Commons on the Modernist proposals for Church Reform would begin after Easter.   Already every member of the House was being bombarded from both sides by his constituents.   Such a heat of religious feeling, such a passion of religious hope and fear, had not been seen in England for generations.

And meanwhile Meynell, whose action had first released the great forces now at work, who as a leader was now doubly revered, doubly honoured by those who clamoured to be led by him, still felt himself utterly unable to face the struggle. Heart and brain were the prey of a deadly discouragement; the will could make no effort; his confidence in himself was lamed and helpless. Not even the growing strength and intensity of his love for Mary could set him, it seemed, spiritually, on his feet.

He left the old bridge on his left, and climbed the pass. And as he walked, some words of Newman possessed him; breathed into his ear through all the wind and water voices of the valley:

> *Thou* to wax fierce
>   In the cause of the Lord
> To threat and to pierce
>   With the heavenly sword!
> Anger and Zeal
>   And the Joy of the brave
> Who bade *thee* to feel —

Dejectedly, he made his way along the fatal path; he found the ruin where Hester had sheltered; he gradually identified the route which the rescue party had taken along the side of the fell; and the precipitous scree where they had found her. The freshly disturbed earth and stones still showed plainly where she had fallen, and where he and the shepherds had stood, trampling the ground round her. He sat down beside the spot, haunted by the grim memory of that helpless, bleeding form amid

the snow. Not yet nineteen! — disgraced — ruined —
the young body broken in its prime. Had he been able
to do no better for Neville's child than that? The load
of responsibility crushed him; and he could not resign
himself to such a fate for such a human being. Before
him, on the chill background of the fells, he beheld,
perpetually, the two Hesters: here, the radiant, unman-
ageable child, clad in the magic of her teasing, provocative
beauty; there, the haggard and dying girl, violently
wrenched from life. Religious faith was paralyzed
within him. How could he — a man so disowned of
God — prophesy to his brethren? . . .

Thus there descended upon him the darkest hour of
his history. It was simply a struggle for existence
on the part of all those powers of the soul that make
for action, against the forces that make for death and
inertia.

It lasted long; and it ended in the slow and difficult
triumph, the final ascendency of the "Yeas" of Life
over the "Nays," which in truth his character secured.
He won the difficult fight not as a philosopher, but as a
Christian; impelled, chastened, brought into line again,
by purely Christian memories and Christian ideas.
The thought of Christ healed him — gradually gave him
courage to bear an agony of self-criticism, self-reproach,
that was none the less overwhelming because his calmer
mind, looking on, knew it to be irrational. There was no
prayer to Christ, no "Christe eleison" on his lips. But
there was a solemn kneeling by the Cross; a solemn open-

ing of the mind to the cleansing and strengthening forces that flow from that life and death which are Christendom's central possession; the symbol through which, now understood in this way, now in that, the Eternal speaks to the Christian soul.

So, amid "the cheerful silence of the fells," a good man, heavily, took back his task. From this wreck of affection, this ruin of hope, he must go forth to preach love and hope to other men; from the depths of his grief and his defeat he must summon others to struggle and victory.

He submitted.

Then — not till then — naked and stripped as he was of all personal complacency; smarting under the conviction of personal weakness and defeat; tormented still, as he would ever be, by all the "might have beens" of Hester's story, he was conscious of the "supersensual moment," the inrush of Divine strength, which at some time or other rewards the life of faith.

On his way back to Burwood through the gleams and shadows of the valley, he turned aside to lay a handful of green moss on the new-made grave. There was a figure beside it. It was Mary, who had been planting snowdrops. He helped her, and then they descended to the main road together. Looking at his face, she hardly dared, close as his hand clung to hers, to break the silence.

It was dusk, and there was no one in sight. In the shelter of a group of trees, he drew her to him.

"You have your way," he said, sadly.

She trembled a little, her delicate cheek close against his.

"Have I persecuted you?"

He smiled.

"You have taught me what the strength of my wife's will is going to be."

She winced visibly, and the tears came into her eyes.

"Dearest! — " he protested. "Must you not be strong? But for you — I should have gone under."

The primitive instinct of the woman, in this hour of painful victory, would have dearly liked to disavow her own power. The thought of ruling her beloved was odious. Yet as they walked on hand in hand, the modern in Mary prevailed, and she must needs accept the equal rights of a love which is also life's supreme friendship.

A few more days Meynell spent in the quiet of the valley, recovering, as best he could, and through a struggle constantly renewed, some normal steadiness of mood and nerve; dealing with an immense correspondence; and writing the Dunchester sermon; while Stephen Barron, who had already resigned his own living, was looking after the Upcote Church and parish. Meanwhile Alice Puttenham lay upstairs in one of the little white rooms of Burwood, so ill that the doctors would not hear of her being moved. Edith Fox-Wilton had proposed to come and nurse her, in spite of "this shocking business which had disgraced us all." But Catharine at Alice's entreaty had merely appealed to the indisputable fact that the tiny house was already more than full. There was no danger, and they had a good trained nurse.

Once or twice it was, in these days, that again a few passing terrors ran through Mary's mind, on the subject of her mother. The fragility which had struck Meynell's unaccustomed eye when he first arrived in the valley forced itself now at times, though only at times, on her reluctant sense. There were nights when, without any definite reason, she could not sleep for anxiety. And then again the shadow entirely passed away. Catharine laughed at her; and when the moment came for Mary to follow Meynell to the Dunchester meeting, it was impossible even for her anxious love to persuade itself that there was good reason for her to stay away.

Before Meynell departed southward there was a long conversation between him and Alice; and it was at her wish, to which he now finally yielded, that he went straight to Markborough, to an interview with Bishop Craye.

In that interview the Bishop learnt at last the whole story of Hester's birth and of her tragic death. The beauty of Meynell's relation to the mother and child was plainly to be seen through a very reticent narrative; and to the tale of those hours in Long Whindale no man of heart like the little Bishop could have listened unmoved. At the end, the two men clasped hands in silence; and the Bishop looked wistfully at the priest that he and the diocese were so soon to lose.

For the rest, as before, they met as equals, curiously congenial to each other, in spite of the battle in front. The Bishop's certainty of victory was once more emphatically shown by the friendly ease with which he still received his rebellious incumbent. Any agreeable outsider of whatever creed — Renan or Loisy or Tyrrell — might have been thus welcomed at the Palace. It was true that till the appeal was decided Meynell remained formally Rector of Upcote Minor. The church and the parish were still in his hands; and the Bishop pointedly made no reference to either. But a very few weeks now would see Meynell's successor installed, and the parish reduced to order.

Such at least was the Bishop's confidence, and in the position in which he found himself — with seven Modernist evictions pending in his diocese, and many more than seven recalcitrant parishes to deal with, he was not the man to make needless friction.

In Meynell's view, indeed, the Bishop's confidence was excessive; and the triumph of the orthodox majority in the Church, if indeed it were to triumph, was neither so near, nor likely to be so complete, as the Bishop believed. He had not yet been able to resume all the threads of leadership, but he was clear that there had been no ebbing whatever of the Modernist tide. On the contrary, it seemed to him that the function at Dunchester might yet ring through England, and startle even such an optimist as Bishop Craye.

The next few days he spent among his own people,

and with the Flaxmans. The old red sandstone church of Upcote Minor was closely packed on Sunday; and the loyalty of the parish to their Rector, their answer to the Arches judgment, was shown in the passion, the loving intelligence with which every portion of the beautiful Modernist service was followed by an audience of working men and women gathered both from Upcote itself and from the villages round, who knew very well — and gloried in the fact — that from their midst had started the flame now running through the country. Many of them had been trained by Methodism, and were now returning to the Church that Wesley had been so loath to leave. "The Rector's changed summat," said men to each other, puzzled by that aspect — that unconscious aspect — of spiritual dignity that falls like a robe of honour, as life goes on, about the Knights of the Spirit. But they knew, at least, from their newspapers, how and when that beautiful girl who had grown up from a child in their midst had perished; they remembered the winter months of calumny and persecution; and their rough, kind hearts went out to the man who was so soon, against their will and their protest, to be driven out from the church where for twenty years he had preached to his people a Christ they could follow, and a God they could adore.

The week passed, and the Dunchester meeting was at hand. Meynell was to spend the night before the great service with the old Bishop, against whom — together with the whole of his Chapter — Privy Council action was now pending. Mary was to be the guest of one of the Canons in the famous Close.

Meynell arrived to find the beautiful old town in commotion. As a protest against the Modernist demonstration, all the students from a famous Theological College in a neighbouring diocese under a High Church bishop had come over to attend a rival service in the second church of the town, where the congregation was to be addressed "on this outrage to our Lord" by one of the ablest and most saintly of the orthodox leaders — the Rev. Cyril Fenton, of the Markborough diocese — soon, it was rumoured, to be appointed to a Canonry of St. Paul's. The streets were full of rival crowds, jostling each other. Three hundred Modernist clergy were staying in or near the town; the old Cathedral city stared at them amazed; and from all parts had come, besides, the lay followers of the new Movement thronging to a day which represented for them the first fruits of a harvest, whereof not they perhaps but their children would see the full reaping.

On the evening before the function Meynell went into the Cathedral with Mary just as the lengthening March afternoon was beginning to wane. They stepped through the western doors set open to the breeze and the sunshine into a building all opal and ebony, faintly flooded with rose from the sky without; a building of infinite height and majesty, where clustered columns of black marble, incredibly light, upheld the richness of the bossed roof, where every wall was broidered history, where every step was on "the ruined sides of Kings," and the gathered fragments of ancient glass, jewels themselves, let through a jewelled light upon the creamy stone.

For the first time, since Hester's death, Meynell's sad face broke into joy. The glorious church appeared to him as the visible attestation of the Divine creative life in men, flowing on endlessly, from the Past, through the Present, to the unknown Future.

From the distance came a sound of chanting. They walked slowly up the nave, conscious of a strange tumult in the pulse, as though the great building with its immemorial history were half lending itself to, half resisting, the emotion that filled them. In the choir a practice was going on. Some thirty young clergy were going through the responses and canticles of the new service-book, with an elder man, also in clerical dress, directing them. At the entrance of the southern choir aisle stood the senior verger of the Cathedral in his black gown — openmouthed and motionless, listening to the strange sounds.

Meynell and Mary knelt for a moment of impassioned prayer, and then sat down to listen. Through the fast darkening church, chanted by half the choir, there stole those words of noblest poetry:

"*A new commandment — a new commandment — I give unto you . . .*" To be answered by the voices on the other side — "*That ye love — ye love one another!*"

And again:

"I have called you friends.   Ye are my friends" ——
With the reply:
"If ye do the things which I command you."
And yet again:
" The words that I speak unto you :" ——
" They — they are spirit; and they are life!"

A moment's silence, before all the voices, gathering
into one harmony, sent the last versicle ringing through
the arches of the choir, and the springing tracery of
the feretory, and of the Lady Chapel beyond.

*" Lord to whom shall we go? — Thou — thou hast the
words of eternal life!"*

"Only a few days or weeks," murmured Meynell,
as they passed out into the evening light, "and we two
— and those men singing there — shall be outcasts and
wanderers, perhaps for a time, perhaps while we live.
But to-day — and to-morrow — we are still children in
the house of our fathers — sons, not slaves! — speaking
the free speech of our own day in these walls, as the men
who built them did in theirs.   That joy, at least, no one
shall take from us!''

At that "sad word Joy" Mary slipped her hand into
his, and so they walked silently through the Close,
toward the Palace, pursued by the rise and fall of the
music from within.

The great service was over, with its bold adaptation
of the religious language of the past, the language which

is wrought into the being of Christendom, to the needs
and the knowledge of the present.   And now Meynell
had risen, and was speaking to that thronged nave,
crowded by men and women of many types and many
distinctions, with that mingling of passion and simplicity
which underlies success in all the poetic arts, and, first
and foremost, the art of religious oratory.   The sermon
was to be known in after years by the name of "The
Two Christianities"—and became one of the chief land-
marks, or, rather, rallying cries of the Modernist cause.
Only some fragments of it can be suggested here; one
passage, above all, that Mary's brooding memory will
keep close and warm to her life's end:

"... Why are we here, my friends?   For what
purpose is this great demonstration, this moving rite in
which we have joined this day?   One-sixth at least of
this congregation stands here under a sentence of ecclesiastical death.   A few weeks perhaps, and this mighty
church will know its white-haired Bishop no more.
Bishop and Chapter will have been driven out; and we,
the rank and file, whose only desire is to cling to the
Church in which we were baptized and bred, will find
ourselves exiles and homeless.

"What is our crime?   This only — that God has spoken
in our consciences, and we have not been able to resist
Him.   Nor dare we desert our posts in the National
Church, till force drive us out.   Why?   Because there is
something infinitely greater at stake than any reproach

that can be hurled at us on the ground of broken pledges — pledges made too early, given in ignorance and good faith, and broken now, solemnly, in the face of God and this people — for a greater good. What does our personal consistency — which, mind you, is a very different thing from personal honesty! — matter? We are as sensitive as any man who attacks us on the point of personal honour. But we are constrained of God; we bear in our hands the cause of our brethren, the cause of half the nation; and we can no other. Ask yourselves what we have to gain by it. Nay! With expulsion and exile in sight — with years perhaps of the wilderness before us — we stand here for the liberties of Christ's Church! — its liberties of growth and life. . . .

"My friends, what is the life either of intellect or spirit but the response of man to the communication of God? Age by age, man's consciousness cuts deeper into the vast mystery that surrounds us; absorbs, transmutes, translates ever more of truth, into conceptions he can use, and language he can understand.

"From this endless process arise science — and history — and philosophy. But just as science, and history, and philosophy change with this ever-living and growing advance, so religion — man's ideas of God and his own soul.

"Within the last hundred years man's knowledge of the physical world has broadened beyond the utmost dreams of our fathers. But of far greater importance to man is his knowledge of himself. There, too, the century

of which we are now the heirs has lifted the veil — for
us first among living men — from secrets hitherto unknown. HISTORY has come into being.

"What is history? Simply the power — depending
upon a thousand laborious processes — of constructing a
magic lens within the mind which allows us to look
deep into the past, to see its life and colour and movement again, as no generation but our own has yet been
able to see it. We hold our breath sometimes, as for a
brief moment perhaps we catch its very gesture, its very
habit as it lived, the very tone of its voices. It has been
a new and marvellous gift of our God to us; and it has
transformed or is transforming Christianity.

"Like science, this new discipline of the human mind
is divine and authoritative. It lessens the distance
between our human thought and the thought of God,
because, in the familiar phrase, it enables us to "think, in
some sort, His thoughts after Him." Like science it
marches slowly on its way; through many mistakes;
through hypothesis and rectification; through daring
vision and laborious proof; to an ever-broadening certainty. History has taken hold of the Christian tradition. History has worked upon it with an amazing
tenderness, and patience, and reverence. And at the
end of a hundred years what do we see? — that half
of Christendom, at least, which we in this church represent?

"We see a Christ stripped of Jewish legend, and Greek
speculation, and medieval scholasticism; moving simply

and divinely among the ways of His Jewish world, a man among men. We can watch, dimly indeed by comparison with our living scrutiny of living men, but still more clearly than any generation of Christendom since the disappearance of the first has been able to watch, the rise of His thoughts, the nature of His environment, the sequence of His acts, the original significance, the immediate interpretation, the subsequent influence of His death. We know much more of Jesus of Nazareth than the fathers of Nicæa knew; probably than St. Paul knew; certainly than Irenæus or Clement knew.

"But that is only half the truth; only half of what history has to tell. On the one side we have to do with the recovered fact: on the other with its working through two thousand years upon the world.

"*There,* for the Modernist, lies revelation! - - in the unfolding of the Christian idea, through the successive stages of human thought and imagination, it has traversed, down to the burst of revelation in the present day. Yet we are only now at the beginning of an immense development. The content of the Christian idea of love — love, self-renouncing, self-fulfilling — is infinite, inexhaustible, like that of beauty, or of truth. Why? At this moment, I am only concerned to give you the Christian answer, which is the answer of a reasonable faith. Because, like the streams springing forever from 'the pure founts of Cephisus,' to nourish the swelling plains below, these governing ideas of our life — tested by life, confirmed by life — have their source in the very being of God, sharers in His Eternity, His Ever-Fruitfulness. . . .

᠅ "But even so, you have not exhausted the wealth of Christianity. ᠅ For to the potency of the Christian idea is added the magic of an incomparable embodiment in human life. The story of Jesus bears the idea which it enshrines eternally through the world. It is to the idea as the vessel of the Grail.

". . . Do these conceptions make us love our Master less? Ask your own hearts? There must be many in this crowded church that have known sorrow — intolerable anguish and disappointment — gnawing self-reproach — during the past year, or months, or weeks; many that have watched sufferings which no philosophic optimism can explain, and catastrophes that leave men dumb. Some among them will have been driven back upon their faith — driven to the foot of the Cross. Through all intellectual difference, has not the natural language of their fathers been also their language? Is there anything in their changed opinions which has cut them off from that sacrifice

> "Renewed in every pulse,
> That on the tedious Cross
> Told the long hours of death, as, one by one,
> The life-strings of that tender heart gave way?

"Is there anything in this new compelling knowledge that need — that does — divide *us* — whose consciences dare not refuse it — from the immortal triumph of that death? In our sharpest straits, are we not comforted and cleansed and sustained by the same thoughts, the same visions that have always sustained and comforted the Christian? No!—the sons of tradition and dogma have no monopoly in the exaltation, the living passion of the Cross! We, too, watching that steadfastness grow steadfast; bowed before that innocent suffering, grow patient; drinking in the wonder of that faith, amid utter defeat, learn to submit and go forward. In us too, as we behold—Hope 'masters Agony!'—and we follow, for a space at least, with our Master, into the heavenly house, and still our sore hearts before our God."

Quietly and low, in tones that shook here and there, the words had fallen upon the spell-bound church.

Mary covered her eyes. But they saw only the more intently the vision of Hester maimed and dying; and the face of Meynell bending over her.

Then from this intimity, this sacredness of feeling, the speaker passed gradually and finally into the challenge, the ringing yet brotherly challenge, it was in truth his mission to deliver. The note of battle — honourable, inevitable battle — pealed through the church, and when it ceased the immense congregation rose, possessed by one heat of emotion, and choir and multitude broke into the magnificent Modernist hymn, "Christus Rex" — written by the Bishop of the See, and already familiar throughout England.

The service was over. Out streamed the great congre-gation. The Close was crowded to see them come. Lines of theological students were drawn up there, fresh-faced boys in round collars and long black coats, who, as the main body of the Modernist clergy ap-proached, began defiantly to chant the Creed. Meynell, with the old yet stately Bishop leaning on his arm, passed them with a friendly, quiet look. He caught sight for a moment of the tall form of Fenton, standing at their rear — the long face ascetically white, and sternly fixed.

He left the Bishop at the gates of the Palace, and went back quickly for Mary. Suddenly he ran into an ad-vancing figure and found his hand grasped by Dornal.

The two men gazed at each other.

"You were not there?" said Meynell, wondering.

"I was." Dornal hesitated a moment, and then his blue eyes melted and clouded.

"And there was one man there — not a Modernist — who grieved, like a Modernist, over the future!"

"Ah, the future!" said Meynell, throwing his head back. "That is not for you or me — not for the bishops, nor for that body which we call the Church — that is for *England* to settle."

But another meeting remained.

At the parting with Dornal, Meynell turned a corner and saw in front of him, walking alone, a portly gentle-man, with a broad and substantial back. A start ran through him. After a moment's hesitation, he began to quicken his steps, and soon overtook the man in question.

Barron — for it was he — stopped in some astonishment, some confusion even, which he endeavoured to hide. Meynell held out his hand — rather timidly; and Barron just touched it.

"I have been attending the service at St. Mathias," he said, stiffly.

"I imagined so," said Meynell, walking on beside him, and quite unconscious of the fact that a passing group of clergy opposite were staring across the street in amazement at the juxtaposition of the two men, both well known to them. "Did it satisfy you?"

"Certainly. Fenton surpassed himself."

"He has a great gift," said Meynell, heartily. They moved on in silence, till at last Meynell said, with renewed hesitation — "Will you allow me to inquire after Maurice? I hope your mind is more at ease about him."

"He is doing well — for the moment." Another pause — broken by Barron, who said hurriedly in a different voice — "I got from him the whole story of the letters. There was nothing deliberate in it. It was a sudden, monkeyish impulse. He didn't mean as much harm by it as another man would have meant."

"No doubt," said Meynell, struck with pity, as he looked at the sunken face of the speaker. "And anyway — bygones are bygones. I hope your daughter is well?"

"Quite well, I thank you. We are just going abroad."

There was no more to be said. Meynell knew very

well that the orthodox party had no room in its ranks, at that moment, for Henry Barron; and it was not hard to imagine what exclusion and ostracism must mean to such a temper. But the generous compunctions in his own mind could find no practical expression; and after a few more words they parted.

Next morning, while every newspaper in the country was eagerly discussing the events at Dunchester, Catharine, in the solitude of Long Whindale, and with a full two hours yet to wait for the carrier who brought the papers from Whinborough, was pondering letters from Rose and Mary written from Dunchester on the preceding afternoon. Her prayer-book lay beside her. Before the post arrived she had been reading by herself the Psalms and Lessons, according to the old-fashioned custom of her youth.

The sweetness of Mary's attempt to bring out everything in the Modernist demonstration that might be bearable or even consoling to Catharine, and to leave untold what must pain her, was not lost upon her mother. Catharine sat considering it, in a reverie half sorrow, half tenderness, her thin hands clasped upon the letter:

"Mother, beloved! — Richard and I talked of you all the way back to the Palace; and though there were many people waiting to see him, he is writing to you now; and so am I. Through it all, he feels so near to you — and to my father; so truly your son, your most loving son. . . .

"Dearest — I am troubled to hear from Alice this

628 THE CASE OF RICHARD MEYNELI

morning that yesterday you were tired and even went to lie down. I know my too Spartan mother doesn't do that without ten times as much reason as other people. Oh! do take care of yourself, my precious one. To-morrow, I fly back to you with all my news. And you will meet me with that love of yours which has never failed me, as it never failed my father. It will take Richard and me a life time to repay it. But we'll try! . . . Dear love to my poor Alice. I have written separately to her."

Rose's letter was in another vein.

"Dearest Catharine, it is all over — a splendid show, and Richard has come out of it finely, though I must say he looks at times more like a ghost than a man. From the Church point of view, dear, you were wise not to come, for your feelings must have been sadly mixed, and you might have been compelled to take Privy Council proceedings against yourself. I need not say that Hugh and I felt an ungodly delight in it — in the crowd and the excitement — in Richard's sermon — in the dear, long-nosed old Bishop (rather like a camel, between you and me, but a very saintly one) and in the throng of foolish youths from the Theological College who seemed to think they settled everything by singing the Creed at us. (What a pity you can't enjoy the latest description of the Athanasian Creed! It is by a Quaker. He compares it to 'the guesses of a ten-year old child at the contents of his father's library.' Hugh thinks it good — but I don't expect you to.)"

Then followed a vivacious account of the day and its happenings.

"And now comes the real tug of war. In a few weeks the poor Modernists will be all camping in tents, it seems, by the wayside. Very touching and very exciting. But I am getting too sleepy to think about it. Dear Cathie — I run on — but I love you. Please keep well. Good-bye."

Catharine laid the letter down, still smiling against her will over some of its chatter, and unconsciously made happy by the affection that breathed from its pages no less than from Mary's.

Yet certainly she was very tired. She became sharply conscious of her physical weakness as she sat on by the fire, now thinking of her Mary, and now listening for Alice's step upon the stairs. Alice had grown very dear to Catharine, partly for her own sake, and partly because to be in bitter need and helplessness was to be sure of Catharine's tenderness. Very possibly they two, when Mary married, might make their home together. And Catharine promised herself to bring calm at least and loving help to one who had suffered so much.

The window was half open to the first mild day of March; beside it stood a bowl of growing daffodils, and a pot of freesias that scented the room. Outside a robin was singing, the murmur of the river came up through the black buds of the ash-trees, and in the distance a sheep-dog could be heard barking on the fells. So quiet it was — the spring sunshine — and so sweet. Back into Catharine's mind there flowed the memory of her own love-story in the valley; her hand trembled again in the hand of her lover.

Then with a sudden onset her mortal hour came upon her. She tried to move, to call, and could not. There was no time for any pain of parting. For one remaining moment of consciousness there ran through the brain the images, affections, adorations of her life. Swift, incredibly swift, the vision of an opening glory — a heavenly throng! . . . Then the tired eyelids fell, the head lay heavily on the cushion behind it, and in the little room the song of the robin and the murmur of the stream flowed on — unheard.

THE END

www.ingramcontent.com/pod-product-compliance
Lightning Source LLC
Chambersburg PA
CBHW032250020726
47495CB00001B/42

* 9 7 8 1 4 3 4 4 1 6 0 5 6 *